'The concept is so o
get it out of my head
reader to explore que
family and belonging
adventure. The world c ... is both similar
and different enough to our own that the story feels
disorientingly real and supremely relevant.'

– Sarah Hagger-Holt, author of *Nothing Ever Happens Here* and *The Fights That Make Us*

'At *Joe with an E*'s core is a clever, convincing concept of reversal with echoes of *Noughts and Crosses* but in terms of gender identity instead of race. This disturbing dystopia offers so much more as well. Through his eponymous protagonist, Joe, his parents, new friends Nats and Cain, and many more absorbing allies and villains, Paul Rand immerses you fully and skilfully into Joe's unnervingly plausible world.'

– Jennifer Burkinshaw, author of *Happiness Seeker* and *Igloo*

'A group of young people are trapped in a future where acceptance comes at the price of life-changing surgery. Paul Rand's dystopian thriller is thought-provoking and gripping by turns, with the science of genetics and fertility cleverly woven into an adrenaline-fuelled quest for survival.'

– K E Salisbury, author of *The Face That Pins You*

This novel includes scenes and themes which may be upsetting to some readers. A list of content warnings can be found at the back of the book (p. 391).

JOE WITH AN E

BY PAUL RAND

To Jules

Diffeent is Good

Paul Rand

Beaten Track

www.beatentrackpublishing.com

Joe with an E

First published 2024 by Beaten Track Publishing

Paperback: 978 1 78645 642 7
eBook: 978 1 78645 643 4

Beaten Track Publishing,
Burscough, Lancashire.
www.beatentrackpublishing.com

Author's Notes

My wife, Joanna, was told by her mum that had she been born a boy, she would have been named Joseph because either way, my mother-in-law wanted to call her baby Jo (or Joe). The convention is that the female names Joanna, Joanne, or Josephine are shortened to Jo (without an 'e'), whereas Joseph and other male names starting with the same letters are shortened to Joe (with an 'e'). However, maybe this isn't a widely known convention because others often write my wife's name as Joe and meanwhile some don't follow the rules, such as Jo Johnson, brother of the infamous rule-breaking former UK prime minister.

In this book, the main character is called Joe because he's a boy, but the name he was given at birth is Joh (intended to sound exactly the same as Joe or Jo) because he is born into a *neut* society in which names are genderless, and in which his differences must remain hidden. So in some chapters, the main character is referred to as Joe and in others he's called Joh, depending on whose head we are in. However, later in the book, these conventions are intentionally blurred as Georgy, Joe's parent, recognises that it's time for their son to no longer hide as Joh but to become Joe, with an 'e'.

The typeface used in this book breaks with conventions for fiction publishing. Most fiction is published using a serif typeface, e.g. Georgia. However, it is increasingly recognised that such typefaces are difficult to read for people who are dyslexic, neurodivergent, or visually impaired. Therefore, in line with the 'Different is Good' themes of this book, I have opted to use Atkinson Hyperlegible – a typeface designed to be accessible. Also for accessibility reasons, I have gone for the less attractive but easier to read left alignment (with a ragged right-hand side) rather than the conventional and neat, justified text.

For my wife, Jo, whose name is often misspelt.

You told me this book probably wasn't possible,
but then supported me all the way.

Part 1

Chapter 1

THE CONSTANT THRUM of the trawler's engine dropped to a *put-put-put*. The island, which had been so close, began to drift away as waves hurled them back towards the mainland.

'Why have we stopped?' Joe shouted. 'Look! I can see the jetty!'

'Sorry, kiddo, but I cannae put in there.' The skipper left the wheelhouse and strode towards him. 'I daren't risk it wi' this wind. There's rocks just under those there waves. One wee gust in the wrong direction and we'll be smashed agin them.'

Another huge wave slapped at the boat and spat its spray over them.

'Don't worry, I'll get you back to the mainland. Mebbe someone else can bring you out in the morning. If you still wannae go.'

The skipper's weathered face creased with new worries – nothing to do with the waves or rocks. Here was another pair of eyes refusing to look directly at Joe. So far, the roll and pitch of the deck hadn't troubled him, but now his hot chocolate from Carlisle station threatened to resurface. Was that really only this morning? Turning back wasn't an option. He scanned the deck. The tarpaulin flapped against the upturned rowing boat under which he'd hidden as they left the mainland.

'I'll take that.' He threw off the tarpaulin. 'Just help me get it into the water and you needn't worry about me anymore.'

'You must be joking, pal! If I return to the harbour without ma lifeboat, I'll have questions tae answer.'

'But you don't want me coming back with you, do you?' Joe shouted through the wind. 'Someone might see me, and then you'd be in trouble. And what about the money? I gave you more than what's fair.'

In fact, he'd handed over everything he had, so certain this was the end of his journey. What if the skipper took him back but refused to return the money? He gulped a mouthful of briny air, urging the chocolatey reflux to stay down. That jetty was smaller each time it rocked into view.

The skipper shrugged and turned back towards the wheelhouse.

'No, wait!' Joe cried, but his words blew back in his face. 'So I can have your lifeboat then?' he muttered, confident he wouldn't be heard.

Ignoring the splinters driving into his soft hands, he gave the lifeboat a tug. Too slow. He hoisted the bow upwards and ducked underneath. His ragged breaths echoed around the hull. The stench of stale fish wrestled his stomach for its bile. Forcing himself up, he lurched his wooden shell towards the trawler's edge.

'Oi, whadaya think you're doing?'

One more step and he'd reach the railings. As if hearing his thoughts, the deck tipped him forward. Hoisting the boat as high as he could, he dropped its front end onto the railings with a thud.

Heavy boots stomped towards him. Joe scuttled further under. If he could lift this back end higher than the front, gravity should do the rest. Hands flat against the floor of the lifeboat, he thrust it upwards. *Crunch!* The back of the hull glanced off something solid. *Crack!* Was that his skull or the wood of the boat? His head throbbed, but he was still on his feet. Meanwhile, his opponent staggered backwards, hand on bleeding chin.

Joe's muscles protested, begged him to let the boat drop. The sea taunted, tipping him back towards the centre of the deck. The wind joined the game, barged its way through his arms, ripped the boat out of his hands, and threw it overboard.

He should have thrown himself straight in after it. Instead, he took a small, steadying step backwards, into the skipper. Strong, tattoo-covered arms coiled around him. An intricately inked dragon leered at him, teeth bared, egging him on. He sank his teeth into the dragon's hide. The skipper cursed. The constriction relaxed. Kicking back, Joe broke free, took a flying leap, and plunged into the sea.

He gasped and choked as icy water flooded his clothes, dragging him below the waves. Jeering gulls circled overhead. *Stupid fool, you're done for now.* The water churned as the trawler's engine kicked back into action. The skipper was leaving him to drown.

'Wait!' he tried to cry out through a mouthful of sea. He coughed, gasped in a quick breath, and shut his mouth tight before the wake of the trawler engulfed him.

By the time he'd resurfaced, the retreating boat was already halfway back to the mainland, but however small it looked, Joe was a speck in comparison – a speck that would soon be swallowed forever by the infinite ocean. *Wait! Where's the lifeboat?* He should have swum to it as soon as he hit the water, instead of fretting about the trawler. He thrashed around, turning surely more than a full three-sixty before spotting it, bobbing up into view, not too many strokes away. He could still manage that, probably, just about.

His numb fingers could barely feel the lifeboat's rough edges when they finally made contact. He tried to hoist himself up enough to clamber in, but whenever his muscles offered some grudging effort, the boat threatened to capsize. He thrashed in panic, spotting the approach of an enormous wave, but forced himself to stop. *If I just float here, maybe it'll lift me in.* But no, the cruel wave raised the boat at least as much as it did him.

The gulls could jeer all they liked. He'd worked it out. Easing back down into the water, he edged around the boat to put it between himself and the approaching waves. He experimented with the next few waves, until he spied the big one racing towards them. Holding the boat at arm's length, he lifted his legs as high as they would go. The wave tried its hardest to rip the boat from his hands. Gritting his teeth, he dug his nails deeper into the splintery wood. *It's working!* The boat was sledging down the back of the wave and he was gliding on top of it. He let go with his right hand, pulled with his stronger left, kicked his legs, and tumbled into the boat.

As if conceding defeat, the wind and waves settled into a calmer rhythm. The island beckoned. *Was that a shout carrying across the breeze?* Joe fumbled with frozen fingers to unfasten the oars. He'd had a go at rowing once, on the little lake at Shibden, but there'd been no waves to contend with there. The scariest thing had been the shuffling around to take control of the oars from Georgy. It wasn't the right technique – he knew that – but with arms like lead, he grasped just one of the oars with both hands and started to paddle.

JOE PRETENDED FOR a while that he was making progress, that each feeble paddle wasn't weaker than the last. He couldn't blame the wind now. If anything, the steady breeze was wafting him towards the shore. Maybe he could stop paddling. No, he had to stay alert, keep driving forward. A short rest first though.

Letting the oar drop from his aching fingers, he pulled his knees tight to his chest, striving in vain to squeeze the shivers into submission. Curled up into a damp quivering ball, he tried to draw fresh energy into his lungs and then, through chattering teeth, to blow heat back into his core. Water lapped against his wooden cradle.

'Come on, you can do it!' a distant voice might have called. Or was it just gulls, cheering on their fledgling chicks?

THE SCRAPE OF the hull on sand awoke him with a start. He eased his stiff body up onto his elbows and blinked the crusty salt from his eyes. Feet splashed towards him.

'Hello! Are you OK?' a youthful voice asked.

The face belonging to the voice stared down at him in a disorientating, upside-down sort of way. Wild hair, longer than he'd ever seen, draped down around him, tickling his cheeks. Excited breath warmed his nose and lips.

'I thought you were never going to make it, but the tide washed you in and now you're here. What's your name?'

'I'm Joe,' he rasped. 'Joe with an "e", cos I'm a boy.'

Chapter 2

I'LL ALWAYS REMEMBER every detail of the day we found out we were having a boy.

We'd both taken the whole day off work to go for our twenty-week scan. I'm not sure why they call it a 'scan'. Aren't the babies all under constant surveillance? Everyone knows the 'scans' are only for the parents' benefit.

We arrived for our nine-thirty appointment at eleven minutes past nine. As soon as we'd parked the car, Cris was complaining that there would have been time for a cooked breakfast after all, but I'd rather be twenty minutes early than one minute late. By five to ten, Cris was bristling beside me, as we'd witnessed two others jump the queue.

At nine fifty-eight, the nurse approached us and led us through, not into the scan observation room, but a small consulting room just off the waiting area. The consultant stood up and walked around the desk to shake hands before signalling for us to sit on a squeaky, wipe-clean sofa.

'Cris, Georgy, I'm Dr Khan. Thank you for your patience. I'm sorry that you've had a bit of a wait.'

Cris had no patience for false pleasantries. 'Dr Khan, we've both taken the day off work to come and see our baby. Can we see it now, or is there some sort of problem?'

I put my hand on Cris's arm and drew breath, ready to intervene and let the doctor proceed. Cris took the hint, sat back and gave a nod to Dr Khan.

The consultant continued with a grunt of thanks. 'You will recall that, when we began this process, we advised you that dual-parent procreation carries a higher risk than the single-parent alternative?'

My breath held itself as we waited for Dr Khan's next sentence. 'I regret to have to inform you that we have detected a serious abnormality in the foetus. So, regrettably –'

'What do you mean *abnormality*?' demanded Cris. 'What sort of abnormality has our baby got?'

'Which means, regrettably, that we have no option but to terminate the pregnancy.'

'Terminate the pregnancy?' Cris exclaimed. 'I'm sorry, Doctor, but until we have more information on this so-called abnormality, we'll agree to nothing of the sort. This is our *baby* you're talking about. The baby you sent us pictures of at ten weeks and fifteen weeks.'

With a calm, if not cold manner, a subtle smile passed across Dr Khan's face. 'I'm sure that you read the fertilisation agreement before signing it. So you will be familiar with clause seventeen-B that states, and I quote, "all genetic material provided by the parent, slash parents, for the purposes of creating a foetus remains the property of the clinic until the parent, slash parents, take delivery of the fully gestated baby on or around the two hundred and eighty-seventh day of the pregnancy".'

The silence jangled my brain.

'It is therefore the responsibility of this clinic, and myself as its lead consultant, to act in the best interests of the foetuses under my care and to terminate those for which a healthy and fulfilling life will not be possible.'

Dr Khan sat back and waited.

An eternity passed. I couldn't think, let alone speak.

Cris again spoke for us both, managing somehow to be composed and quiet. 'So have you done it already – the termination?'

The consultant edged forward again. 'As a courtesy, we always inform the parents before any action is taken. But I'm afraid the protocols allow for no alternative.'

At last, I found my voice. 'Can we see it, before you –'

'I'm afraid that won't be possible,' Dr Khan replied, attempting sympathy. 'This is also covered in the fertilisation agreement.'

Our hearts sank through the floor. The fight had gone out of Cris and, if I'm honest, had never found its way into me.

Seeing our utter defeat, Dr Khan offered some final words. 'You are welcome to stay in this room for as long as you need, and when you are ready, Nurse Taylor will sign you out. I hope that, in time, we will see you here again in happier circumstances. I would strongly recommend our single-parent option. Most of our clients do find this works very well for them, even when there is a strong two-parent relationship into which a child can be brought.'

With no further words, the consultant stood, bowed briefly in our direction, and left.

Cris swivelled towards me and took my hands. Neither of us could find any words. We just sat, processing, stroking each other's hands. How had this happened? How had the last twenty weeks passed by without a hint of anything amiss? What about the pictures we'd been sent of our developing baby? Why us?

There was a quiet knock on the door before it was eased open, allowing Nurse Taylor to peek in. The hubbub of expectant parents also wafted in, stirring up the smell of disinfectant off the wipe-clean sofa. 'Can I get you anything? A tea or a coffee perhaps?'

In sync with each other, we both shook our heads. I looked up and made a decision.

'I think we'd like to go now,' I stammered, looking to Cris for affirmation. With an almost imperceptible nod to each other, we stood up.

Nurse Taylor patiently held the door open for us and led us towards the reception desk. Having filled in our departure time of ten-seventeen, the nurse handed us the pen to add our signatures. As I signed my own name, a small, folded piece of paper was slipped under my left hand. Without thinking, I started to unfold the note, but with a subtle shake of the head, the nurse gave us all the warning we needed and ushered us out of the building.

We sat in the car, engine off. I took a practised long breath in through my nose, let the air hover there for a moment, then pushed it steadily back through my lips. I unfolded the now-crumpled piece of paper, which I'd held so tightly in my fist all the way across the car park. Written in a hasty scrawl were just nine words and a time.

Your baby is safe. Meet me at Square Peg, 17:30.

THE SQUARE PEG was bustling with office workers as, at twenty-eight minutes past five, we pushed our way in through the door. We felt conspicuous, scanning the crowded pub. Actually, nobody showed us the slightest bit of interest, except for the youthful nurse, waving at us from a small table in the darkest corner of the room. Out of uniform, Nurse Taylor looked almost too young to be in a pub alone.

It had been a long and stressful wait from ten-seventeen in the morning until now. Neither of us had eaten, and we'd become increasingly short with each other as the day wore on. Too tense to consider driving into town, we'd opted to take public transport. My stomach had churned as the overcrowded bus lurched from stop to stop.

Nurse Taylor was already seated, with a full glass of lemonade, so as we weaved our way across the busy room, Cris peeled off to the bar. The nurse stood and introduced themself as Jay, reaching out a slender hand to assertively squeeze mine.

I sat on my hands, willing Cris to hurry so we could find out the meaning of Jay Taylor's note. Two long minutes later, having handed me my glass of wine, Cris joined us and launched straight in.

'So what's this all about? Is our baby OK or not?'

Jay paused for a moment and then began. 'You appear to have a perfectly healthy baby. It's just that it's what once would have been called a boy.'

The old clock above our table ticked as we tried to decipher what the nurse had said. Everything made sense, except for that last word, *boy*.

'Sorry, what do you mean, *boy*? What's a *boy*?' Cris asked.

The clock did some more ticking. 'OK, so you know how with most animals there are two types – cows and bulls, ewes and rams, hens and cockerels? Well, we think humans must have been like that once too. When we could reproduce naturally, like the animals do.'

'So you're saying that we've made an animal…a monster?' Cris cut in. 'Doesn't sound perfectly healthy to me.'

'No, Cris, that's not what Jay said.' I turned back to Jay, my mind still trying to formulate the question I needed to ask. 'Our baby. Which is it? A cow or a bull?' I slapped Cris hard on the thigh, halting what I knew would have been another unhelpful interruption. Cris glared at me with narrow eyes. I looked squarely at the youthful nurse. From their surprised expression, I judged they were not in a relationship.

'Ah, yes, sorry…a bull. Well…not a bull, actually, because no, your baby isn't a monster or any sort of animal, other than human, that is. Your baby is simply a male human.'

Cris leaned forward, ready to launch another volley. I gave the slapped thigh a gentle squeeze and sucked in air through my nose, reminding Cris to think for a moment before speaking.

'So if a…what you call *male* human is natural, what does that make us? Are we unnatural? Cos I don't know about you, but I don't think I know any male humans.' Cris's ears started to redden again. I thought about intervening, but I had to admit, I was thinking the same thing. 'It sounds to me as if our baby is abnormal, like the doctor told us.'

'No, not abnormal, just unusual.' Jay had clearly used these words before. 'For too long, the fertility units have been terminating foetuses as soon as they spot what looks like an abnormality. People don't want their children to be different from themselves. People are scared that a different child might not do so well in life. Understandably, people want things to be perfect for their children. But different doesn't have to be bad. We believe that different is good.'

Different is good. Those words ran so contrary to my professional training but fizzed pleasantly around the back of my skull.

'Are you saying that our baby doesn't have to be terminated?' I asked, dreading a repeat of Dr Khan's regretful words, in spite of all that Jay had told us.

'No. I mean, yes, I am saying that your baby doesn't have to be terminated. If you are willing to accept him, just as he is. We will save him and keep him for you to full term.'

'But I don't understand,' Cris interjected. 'The doctor clearly said this morning that termination was the only option. What's changed?'

Jay looked directly at both of us, the fierceness in those eyes showing twice their maturity. 'Nothing has changed. If your baby stays in that fertility unit, it will be terminated tomorrow morning. But with your consent, I can get him out of there...'

With our consent, our baby would be moved that very night to a secret, off-grid fertility unit, run by a group calling themselves simply DiG, standing for Different is Good. When it, I mean *he*, was born, arrangements would be made for us to collect *him* and take *him* home. We could then live a 'normal' life together as parents and child. There were people in place who could arrange the necessary paperwork so that our baby would have a birth certificate and would legally exist.

'But I have to warn you,' Jay concluded, 'it won't be easy for either you or him. He will be different, and although, as we say, different is good, there are things you will have to keep hidden.'

Jay looked at the two of us expectantly. Did we have to decide right now? Couldn't we go away and talk it through, just the two of us – sleep on it, weigh up the risks?

But could we really let our baby be terminated, given a choice?

My brain wouldn't stop tingling. *Different is good.* Cris and I looked at each other. Under the table, Cris squeezed my hand and I squeezed back.

'We'll do it, whatever it takes,' Cris announced. 'Just show us where to sign.'

Jay smiled and, though visibly relaxing, also betrayed nervousness as they leaned in towards us. 'There can be no signatures, no paperwork that connects us. We leave no trail. You will need to trust me. I will rescue your baby tonight and you will be contacted again – but not by me – when he is ready to be handed over to you.'

'But can't we see it, I mean *him*. After the move?' I asked, hope pumping my heart. If I couldn't see our baby, how would I know that this was all real – that there was still hope? Surely, they could sneak us into this secret fertility unit. *Please say yes*, I begged silently as the bubbles in my brain threatened to blur my vision.

Jay's eyes wouldn't meet mine, choosing instead to study a scratch on the table. 'I would love to say yes, but I'm afraid it's not possible. We have to do everything we can to protect our operation. I'm sorry, you have a long wait ahead of you. But I promise, we will do everything we can to protect your child and deliver him safely to you at full term.'

And that was that. The young nurse, who we were only just getting to know, stood up, took the empty lemonade glass back to the bar, and disappeared out of the door.

Chapter 3

DRIFTING INTO CONSCIOUSNESS to the raised voices of his parents was nothing unusual, but these voices were not Georgy and Cris, and Joe was not snuggled up under his own duvet. The scratchy blanket smelled musty, like ancient Adey's flat.

One of the voices was deeper than any he'd heard before. 'But we haven't got time to wait. We need to send him as soon as he's fit to go. Otherwise, it will be next year before anything happens.'

The other voice was a more normal pitch but was full and rounded, like the low notes from his clarinet; nothing like the coarse, nasal tones he'd grown up with. 'We can't! The poor boy's only just made it to safety, and you're wanting to send him back? Let him settle in for a bit and get to know us. Then maybe we can explain your mission and let him decide.'

Joe sucked in a breath and strained his ears. Was this argument about him already?

The deep voice again. 'You know that won't work. It'll just be harder for him to leave. And more risky. He won't pass as a neut for long. If we miss this chance, how long'll it be before we get another boy?'

'Which is another reason to keep him here for a while. You can't father every new child on this island.'

Joe was still holding his breath. He relaxed his jaw and tried to let the air seep slowly out before taking another long, full breath, like Georgy had shown him when he felt worried about something. What was Deep Voice wanting to send him away for? And what did Clarinet mean by 'fathering new children'? Surely, that would mean leaving the island too – to get new children here.

'But if we keep him here long enough to follow your rules for mating, he definitely will be too old to go.'

'Well, let's just give him a chance to wake up and meet everyone first, shall we? And don't you dare go filling his head with talk of your mission.'

Joe opened his eyes a crack to explore his new surroundings. Like in his own room, there was a discoloured damp patch in one corner of the ceiling, but this brown-edged stain must have been there a hundred years more, and whatever paper had peeled off the wall below it had long since been torn away. Across the ceiling, an empty light socket hung from a cracked yellow-white cable. Dust danced in the beams of sunlight that pierced their way through moth-eaten curtains. Joe blinked and opened his eyes wider.

'Ah, so you are awake! I knew you were.'

He sat up with a start and then, aware of his bare torso, tugged the sheet and blanket around himself. He shivered, but not from cold. Under the bedclothes, he was completely naked, and there was someone here in the room with him.

Perched in a chair beside his bed, grinning at him, was the same wild-haired face that had greeted him last night, though they'd pulled a brush through their hair and tied it back into a loose, frizzy ponytail.

'They told me to leave you alone today, but I knew you'd want some company. Come on, put these on and I'll show you round.'

The wild kid threw some linen shorts and a T-shirt onto Joe's bed and stood up expectantly, as if they thought he'd leap out from under the covers to join them straight away. Heat flooded into his cheeks, which the kid seemed to find funny.

'What're you blushing for? Don't you think I've seen a boy's tonker before?'

Nobody had seen his 'tonker' before, except Georgy and Cris, of course, and whoever had stripped his wet clothes off him last night. Maybe it was this kid who'd done that, in which case, they'd seen all of him already. He was never naked, except behind the locked bathroom door in their flat.

Joe pulled up a knee under the covers to mask the stiffening he could do nothing to stop. Why did it have to do that? How many other times had it delayed his getting up in the morning while Georgy stood at the door, threatening to come in and pull off his duvet if he didn't get moving in the next two minutes? At least that wasn't being threatened...yet.

'Are you a girl?' Joe asked, not daring to look at them in case they took it the wrong way, even if they didn't seem to mind staring at him.

'Might be. Does it matter if I am?' The kid gave an exaggerated sigh and turned towards the low door in the corner of the room. 'Oh, OK. If it'll make it quicker, I'll wait outside. But don't be too long. We've wasted half the day already!'

As the door opened and shut again, strains of the debate that was still going on wafted in from somewhere beyond, but the voices were quieter now and it was impossible to hear what was being said. Maybe the girl would explain. She must have heard the arguing voices too, at least as much as he had. She was a girl, wasn't she? *She* – it felt strange using that word for a fellow human being, even though Joe's parents had always made a point of calling him 'he' when they were alone with him and had told him there were others he'd meet one day who were 'she'. He edged around and sat up on the edge of the bed, careful to keep himself covered, despite now being alone.

It took a while to ease the new T-shirt over his aching arms and shoulders. Where were his underpants? None of his own clothes were anywhere to be seen. Had someone taken them to be washed and dried, or had they been thrown away? For now, there was nothing but the shorts the 'she' had given him. How would it feel, going around without underpants that tucked everything neatly into place? Of course, he didn't need to hide what he was anymore, but did that mean he should just let everything swing about?

'Come on, Joe, I'm not going to wait much longer,' sang out the voice from the other side of the door.

The blood rose to his face again. He grabbed the shorts and pulled them on. However naked he still felt, he couldn't stay hidden in here all day. He'd just have to be careful how he positioned himself and hope his 'tonker' behaved. At least the shorts were long and baggy. He slipped his feet into some old but clean trainers, which had been left at the foot of the bed, and ventured out of the room.

A bright-red apple was thrust at his chest. 'Well, come on then, we'd better get away while we still can.'

A warm hand grabbed his and pulled him through another door. Joe tugged his hand free to shield his eyes from the bright sunlight. A gust of sea air ruffled his clothes. They were standing amongst a small cluster of ramshackle cottages that couldn't have been far from the shore, judging by the clear sound of waves crashing on a pebbly beach. Could he hear the shrieks of little kids playing? Surely not. As he searched for where the sound was coming from, his eyes widened, seeing someone stoop to lift a crying baby out of its cradle.

Perplexed, Joe turned towards his guide. 'How come they're here? I didn't think anyone came here until they were, you know, our sort of age.'

'Oh, they didn't come here. They were born here! The two little kids are Peter and Katie. They were the first two. Then that's Eva and her baby daughter, Grace. She was born just three weeks ago.'

'You mean you've got a fertility unit on the island?' Joe asked, astounded.

'Don't be silly. Babies are born naturally here.'

What did she mean? How else were babies born except in fertility units?

A shout from inside the cottage interrupted them. 'Natasha, is that you? Is Joe with you?'

Joe looked at the kid, whom he guessed probably was a girl, like Eva, but younger and wilder. He turned to go back into the cottage, but the girl tugged on his arm.

'They'll catch up with us soon enough, but let's have some fun first. Anyway, you need some things explaining to you, and there's no-one better at explaining things than me!' She led him to the corner of the cottage and pointed towards a grassy hilltop. 'See that hill there?' Her eyes sparkled. 'Race you to the top!' Without checking for agreement, she was off up the stony lane and away from the cluster of cottages.

Joe glanced back towards the open door once more. No-one called for him to return. So, with every muscle protesting, he set off at a slow, stiff jog after the girl. His unsecured bits flapped about inside his shorts.

He slowed to a more comfortable walk – she'd just have to wait.

A few others waved to him as he passed other cottages. Like Eva, several of them had babies, either in their arms or strapped to their backs. 'Hi, Joe!' they each called out. One girl hailed him from the top of a ladder and then turned back to fixing the slates on the roof of her cottage. Another, who was out digging in a vegetable patch, paused to watch him as he passed. As she waved and shouted her greeting, her stomach bulged ominously under her T-shirt.

Joe thought he only saw one other boy. In the doorway of the last cottage, a figure, a little bigger than himself, sat in the shadows, rocking on his chair, head down studying fidgeting hands. No shout of greeting came as Joe ran past. He wasn't even sure if the other boy had seen him.

HEART THUMPING, JOE gradually managed to slow his panting with deep breaths of the fresh, clear air. Gulls glided and dipped over the sparkling sea. There were other islands in almost all directions – some larger and craggier than this one, others tiny pimples that sometimes disappeared beneath the waves. Some were a distant dot on the horizon, one or two almost close enough to swim to, but there were no other signs of habitation. For a moment, Joe was back in the rowing boat, the night before, floating all alone in an infinite sea.

'Well, you took your time!' Her chirpy voice snapped Joe back to the present and the fact that he was now far from alone. She sat, leaning back against a jumble of rocks, taking large bites from a juicy apple. 'Come and sit down then, and we'll introduce ourselves properly.'

Joe eased himself down, tucking the loose bits of his shorts tightly under his legs to keep the breeze out and his bits in. The girl lunged for the apple she'd given him earlier as it rolled out of his pocket and threatened to tumble off back down the hill. She presented it to him again and settled beside him, so close that their sleeves brushed against each other.

'You eat that while I talk. You must be famished!'

Her name was Natasha, or Nats, or Nat, or sometimes Tasha. Stef, the only parent she could remember, had always called her Nat, but people here wanted to call her Natasha, insisting that she adopt a more feminine name now she was on the island. Some then shortened this to Tasha, which she hated. She didn't see why she couldn't just be Nat or Nats, like she'd always been. Joe should call her Nats and nothing else, please.

'So, what about you Joe? Have you always been Joe with an "e"? Is that the name your parents gave you?'

On his birth certificate, his name was written as Joh. Georgy had explained to him that they'd wanted to call him Joe with an 'e' at the end, like people used to in the old days, but Joh was better because it was more normal. Not that the two spellings sounded any different, but they knew it *was* different, and that somehow also made it sound different.

'They'll probably try to call you Joseph here. They like us all to use names that sound definitely male or female. Here, *different is good*, we say.'

Joe wasn't sure he could ever imagine being Joseph. He'd always had such a simple name. Joseph sounded unnecessarily complicated. Anyway, how would he spell it? Josef or Joseff? Or maybe it was spelt Joseph with a 'p-h' at the end. Who knew?

'I think I'd rather stick with Joe,' he said, staring out once more across the sea. 'I feel different enough here as it is. Everyone else I've seen so far seems to be a girl, except for that boy outside the last house.'

'That's Cain. He was the last to arrive before you. Came months ago, right at the start of spring, before any of this year's lambs were born, and I've still not heard him speak. I'm not sure anyone has much. Apart from Cain, there are two other boys – Anthony, who's co-leader with Sandra – and Tom, who lives in a little run-down hovel on the far side of the island and keeps himself to himself. That's why we're all so excited about you arriving Joe,' she said with a wide smile. 'Soon as I found you, I could tell you weren't going to be silent like Cain or a recluse like Tom. You're not like Anthony either, and that's a good thing.'

'But if you're all so excited about me arriving, what was that I heard about sending me away again? You must have heard it too – how long were you sitting there by my bed?'

'Oh, don't take any notice of what Anthony says.' Nats waved her hand as if swatting at a fly. 'Yes, I heard that too, and Sandra's right. There's no way we can send you away. We need you too much here.'

Joe was intrigued and confused at the same time. He'd never felt 'needed' before. He knew his parents loved him, but he also knew life would have been much easier for them without him, and he'd never had friends who'd needed him. 'Need me for what?' he asked.

'To help make the babies, of course,' Nats said with an excited squeal. 'Anthony's been helping to make almost all the babies here so far, but Sandra says we need other boys to help as well – that Anthony can't do it all on his own. Although she also says nobody should do it until they're ready. So Sandra will have to decide when you're ready.'

'But you said you didn't have a fertility unit. How do you make the babies here without a fertility unit?'

'They grow inside the girls. Baby Grace – she grew inside Eva. And did you see Sally in her garden on the way up here? She's got a baby inside her at the moment. It'll be coming out any day, they reckon.'

Joe wondered, but wasn't sure he wanted to know, how they got the baby out. No doubt Nats would explain that to him at some point.

'What about you? Is there a baby inside you too?' he dared to ask.

'No, of course there isn't. It can't happen for me yet, cos I'm not old enough and my bleeding hasn't started yet either. A girl's bleeding needs to have started before she can have a baby, and even then, Sandra says it's better to wait.'

Joe's mind whirred, contemplating how he might ask what part he'd be expected to play in helping to make babies and how Sandra decided when someone was ready, but Nats was on her feet again, apparently ready to dash off somewhere else.

'Come on, I need to show you the rest of the island.'

Joe eased himself up. Nats spun him around to look out over the harbour and the small cluster of cottages they'd come from. 'That's the village. We'll go back there later, but for now, we're going this way.' She grabbed his hand and yanked him back around, launching them both down the other side of the hill.

They startled some sheep, scattering them in different directions away from their peaceful grazing. The cows at the bottom of the hill looked up as they passed but soon returned to their ruminations.

Through a gate and onto an old, weedy and crumbling tarmac road, they stopped to catch their breath. As Nats pulled the gate closed behind them, Joe let out a surprised shriek. Charging towards him where he stood, came a flock of about thirty chickens. He stood on tiptoes, surrounded by the feathery clucking beasts. Nats laughed raucously.

'Hello, ladies,' she sang out. 'I've forgotten to feed you this morning, haven't I?' Taking Joe's hand again, she led him through the churning sea of feathers to a small metal dustbin. 'Here, grab a handful of this,' she said, lifting the lid with the flourish of a magician.

Before Joe had a chance to react, Nats grabbed a large handful of grain for herself, and as if she was magnetic, the sea of chickens moved as one around her, leaping and squawking as stray kernels fell from her hand.

Joe dug into the bin, and instantly he was surrounded. In haste, he hurled the handful into the swarm of feathers and watched as it eddied away, centring itself on the spot where the largest portion had landed.

Nats strode around, filling troughs with more seed and transferring water from a water butt to a can, to other troughs. Lid back on the dustbin and watering can back next to the water butt, she turned again to Joe. 'Ready to go again?' she half asked him, already setting off down the road.

Joe lurched after her, determined not to be left behind again. A few chickens seemed keen to join them but soon lost interest and fell back to scratching around for grubs or investigating the feeding troughs.

They ambled on, now at a more manageable pace, past a couple of cosy-looking cottages with smoke curling up from their chimneys. Beside these cottages were fields of vegetables in neat rows. Joe recognised cauliflowers and cabbages, carrot tops peeking out of the soil and beanstalks climbing tepees of long, straight sticks.

As they walked, Nats pointed things out. Where they milked the cows; where the reservoir was that supplied them with clean drinking water; who lived in which house and what each person did to support the community. They were going to have to start a school soon, and Nats had volunteered to be the teacher, but Sandra and Anthony had turned her down, claiming they needed someone a bit older; someone who was perhaps mother to one of the children herself. Nats looked forward to a time when she was no longer the youngest, not counting the kids and babies.

They left the road over an old rickety stile in the wall and squelched their way across boggy fields towards the place that Nats said was the absolutely best place on the island. Joe almost didn't notice the low, grass-roofed bungalow perched all alone on a slight rise in the landscape, a makeshift fence carefully marking out the boundary of the property.

'That's Tom's place,' Nats whispered. 'He's all right when you get to know him, but I wouldn't go knocking on his door without an invitation.' Nats went on to explain that before he'd moved out here, Tom had lived in the room Joe had been given. Joe imagined Tom's new place must be mustier than that old blanket and ancient Adey's flat put together.

Just past Tom's hovel, they dropped down onto a tiny, sparkling beach. As his feet crunched onto the beach, Joe looked down and gasped. What he'd assumed was shingle was actually thousands of tiny seashells.

'Told you it was the best place,' Nats said with a smile, holding a handful of shells under his nose. 'Look, each one is unique. No two are the same.'

In quiet companionship, they crouched amongst the shells, foraging for the best specimens. For a while, they were innocent children, playing on the beach. Neither of them noticed the tall, stocky figure stalking towards them, and both jumped when he spoke.

'All right, you two?'

Joe's eyes grew wider as they moved from the thick hairy legs standing beside him, up to the face, which seemed to be sprouting clumps of dark curls on its cheeks and chin.

'Oh, hi, Tom. Nice of you to come and meet Joe,' said Nats, grinning up at the bushy face.

Tom nodded and grunted at Joe. 'Everyone's looking for you both. I thought I might find you here, in Nats' favourite place.'

Nats threw down her handful of shells and stood up. 'I s'pose we should go see what they want.'

'Community meeting apparently,' said Tom. 'Thought I might come along myself.'

Joe's ribcage squeezed on his lungs. He gasped in a quick breath and fought to control the outflow. Was this it? Were Tom and Anthony going to wrestle him back out into the sea? Or perhaps this was the time when Sandra would decide in front of everyone that he was ready to help make babies, and then all the girls would scowl at him and hand him over to Anthony and Tom to throw him off the island when he confessed that he didn't know how.

Chapter 4

JOE FOLLOWED IN Nats' wake as she pushed her way into the already crowded café. Apparently, it was the biggest room in the village's largest cottage and about the only indoor space where the whole community could meet. The hubbub of chatter dimmed as they made their way to the last empty table. Joe counted twenty-three girls, including all of those he'd seen earlier in the day. A few might've been around the same age as him, but most, he thought, were probably older. Six babies were being passed around like pass-the-parcels, and then there were Peter and Katie, chasing each other under tables and squeezing between chairs. Cain perched on a stool in a dark corner, acknowledging no-one as he muttered to himself. Standing by a long counter, a tall, fair-haired boy conferred with a red-haired girl, who was, if anything, a centimetre or two taller. By a process of elimination, the boy must be Anthony. Like Tom, Anthony had hair on his face, though it was softer and fluffier than Tom's dark curls.

Joe's view of the tall, earnest pair at the bar was interrupted by an apron-enwrapped tank of a girl pushing her way directly towards him. A plate was balanced expertly on the fingertips of her left hand whilst, with her right, she shoved other patrons out of her path.

'Hiya, Joe, my name's Victoria, but you'll call me Vicki.' Leaning across Nats, she set the plate down in front of Joe.

Joe's stomach rumbled as he eyed the thick doorstep sandwich, made with the densest bread he'd ever seen. A mound of steaming, chunky chips competed for space on the plate.

'Thought you might be hungry,' Vicki said with a wide grin. 'It's on the house.'

As Joe mumbled his thanks, Nats reached across to help herself to some of the plentiful chips, but before her hand could reached the plate, Vicki slapped it away. 'Oi, they're not for you, young lady! If you want something to eat, you can pay for it like everybody else, thank you very much.' Then, turning to Joe, 'You make sure you eat it all yourself. You look like you could use it.'

Whilst Joe tucked into the food and allowed Nats to steal a few chips, the café filled up with even more girls until there were no more seats and a few were left standing in the space around the door.

Joe was shoving the last piece of sandwich into his mouth when the tall redhead hammered a table with a spoon.

'Thank you, everyone, if we can bring this meeting to order.'

The room was now fully attentive, save for the quiet chattering of Peter and Katie and the tittering of a few younger teenagers, amused at Sandra's formality.

'Thank you,' Sandra repeated. 'It looks like we're all here, so can I begin by...'

A commotion in the crowd around the door drowned the end of Sandra's sentence. The room gasped as Tom ducked in and pushed the door closed again with his back. So he had decided to come after all. When they'd got halfway back along the road, Tom had told the two of them to go on ahead, that he'd catch them up, even though his long strides had so far shown no sign of struggling to keep up. 'He's bottled it. He won't come now,' Nats had said before they were even out of Tom's earshot.

'Don't mind me,' Tom grunted as several of the girls jostled to make space for his large frame.

A flustered Sandra shuffled some papers before continuing. 'So, as I was saying, let's begin by welcoming our new arrival, Joe, in the er, customary way.'

The ground shook as the assembled crowd all stamped their feet in unison. Then the thundering stamps were overlaid with a crescendo of whoops and cheers. It was several minutes before Sandra succeeded in bringing the gathering back to order, and even then, she had to pause several times as stray whoops ricocheted around the room.

'Now, it won't have escaped your notice that Joe is a boy.' She was forced to wait again as a few more whoops echoed back and forth. 'And I know that we've all been waiting for more boys to arrive for some time.' Joe had been staring self-consciously at his empty plate but now looked over at Sandra, expecting to see a mischievous grin. But there was no trace of humour in her face.

Having once again waited for the attention of her audience, Sandra impressed on them the importance of giving the new member of their community adequate time to settle in before expecting too much of him. 'And may I remind you,' she added, 'in case any of you are entertaining any um...fantasies, that Joe is off limits in that regard until I say otherwise.'

'Reckon they like the look of you.' Nats chuckled and dug her elbow into Joe's ribs as, on hearing Sandra's edict, disgruntled muttering erupted around one crowded table.

Sandra raised her hand and battled on with her speech, despite the ongoing murmurs. 'I know some of you think it's all just a bit of fun, and yes, we do want to grow our community with more babies. But that's all the more reason to take it seriously, and to recognise the consequences of our actions.' No-one could miss her pointed glance towards the door. Following the path of her eyes, Joe caught Tom raising his eyebrows before fixing his gaze firmly on his feet.

Sandra moved the meeting on, going through various aspects of routine island business. Rotas were handed out, detailing who was responsible over the next few weeks for things like collecting and disposing of waste, chopping firewood, and keeping watch for new arrivals. There were updates from various people about current milk yields, which vegetable crops were due to be harvested, and plans for mating the ewes and rams. Joe tried to follow it all as exhaustion pushed its way in through the soles of his feet and flooded up his body until it submerged him completely.

The room fell silent. Was everyone now watching him falling asleep? He forced his eyes open again and shuffled himself back into an alert-looking position. No, Sandra had taken a seat on a high stool and everyone's eyes were now on Anthony, who stood in Sandra's place, holding a tatty book aloft in his left hand.

The deep resonance of Anthony's voice was hypnotic. 'Five months ago, this book came into our possession.' He raised it even higher. 'It was brought to us by our good friend Cain.'

Everyone looked over towards Cain, who didn't look back at anyone.

'This book is a sort of diary, which the author called a logbook, from a time long before even our parents' parents were born, when people like us, males and females, were considered normal. A time when neuts were almost non-existent. A time when all babies were nurtured not inside pregnancy pods, but in the wombs of their mothers, as they are here.'

Anthony had the complete attention of every soul in the room. Even the babies and toddlers had fallen under his spell. Unnecessary as it was, Anthony's voice rose to a climax. 'This book confirms what we have always known in our hearts. We are not anomalies. We are not abnormal. We belong in this world.'

The room erupted in a spontaneous cheer and more foot stamping. But silence soon returned, as Anthony had not finished.

'This diary also tells the wretched story of how and why the world changed. How, by the actions of a few selfish people, our kind were driven to extinction. That story will be told here another day, and may it be a lesson to us all.' Anthony took a moment to look at each member of his audience.

'But this book also holds the promise of a much greater truth. I have read all the words carefully, and it is clear to me that there is a world beyond the one in which we all grew up. A world beyond the realm of the neuts. A world that the neut authorities must surely know about but have cut us off from. A world that remained untouched by the plague that neutered our own ancestors.'

Anthony's voice dropped to almost a whisper. 'We need to find that world. We *can* find that world.' Again, he paused to make eye contact with everyone in the room. His gaze lingered a long time on Joe. Joe shuffled in his seat. And then Anthony was talking again, now at a faster tempo. 'We plan to send out an expedition from our community here, to make contact with that world. To find the place beyond this small, remote island where I am convinced there are people like us. Not a few dozen, but millions.'

The spell was broken, and all around the room, people started talking amongst themselves.

'When will you be going?' someone shouted.

Anthony raised his voice above the din. 'I would love to lead this expedition myself, but sadly, I could never pass as a neut.' He stroked a fluffy cheek. 'No, this mission must fall to some of our younger friends here. At least one girl and one boy, to show our friends in the world beyond that we are just like them.' Again, Anthony's gaze burrowed into Joe. 'I'm not looking for volunteers tonight, but I will be setting up a planning group for those who would like to help in whatever way they can.'

The meeting dissolved. Futile though it was, Sandra stood up again to thank everyone for coming. A gust of air told Joe that the door had been opened, and looking over, he saw that Tom had gone. A few others followed soon after, but most stayed in the café. There was plenty to talk about, and animated chatter filled the room. Drinks were soon being passed out from the bar, and from somewhere, a battered violin was produced. To Joe's surprise, the violin was passed to Cain, who struck up a jaunty tune. Joe yearned for his precious clarinet, abandoned amongst his meagre pack of belongings on that dratted trawler.

Entranced by Cain's music, Joe barely noticed Nats say something about going to get some drinks and wasn't aware of Anthony taking her place at the table until his deep voice cut through the music. Startled, Joe shuffled back in his chair.

'Don't worry Joe,' Anthony said with a smile. 'Like I said, I'm not asking for volunteers tonight. All I'm asking is that you read this.'

And there it was, the wrinkly old book – apparently far older than the grandparents Joe had never met – being pushed across the table towards him.

Chapter 5

25/03/2031

Observations recorded by Dr M. Harvey

Wrexford Fertility Centre

07:50

Serious anomalies observed in all 36 hr+ embryos during routine checks at 07:30 this morning. ALL embryos have failed, disintegrated into culture.

I have started this new logbook to record all further observations and developments related to this incident.

08:35

Technician S. Robbins has also checked all 36 hr+ embryos and concurs with my findings. No viable embryos remain in any of the batches.

We agreed to bring forward the first checks on newly fertilised embryos from yesterday. Whilst there is less evidence of the existence of any previously viable embryos, these appear to have suffered the same fate. We have no viable active embryos in this clinic.

08:50

Reviewed data logs of oxygen, CO_2 and nutrient feeds for the last 24 hours. Levels all within tolerance throughout. Routine top-up of nutrient feed recorded at 14:30 yesterday, carried out by FertiChem in accordance with normal maintenance contract. Environment logs also show stable temperature and humidity throughout.

Protocol says this needs to be immediately reported to HFEA.

09:20

Doesn't normally take this long to get through to HFEA. Beginning to wonder whether whatever's happened might extend beyond our clinic.

09:30

Suspicions confirmed via email from Telford clinic, seeking second opinion. Attached pictures almost identical to ours.

09:55

Just finished call with HFEA. Instructions are as follows:

Cancel all appointments for the rest of the week (our licence has been temporarily revoked, pending an inspection).

Send all staff home, except receptionist and myself (HFEA emailing through standard wording for receptionist to use when answering any calls).

Don't touch anything. Inspectors will be in contact in due course, but don't expect anyone today.

13:20

According to the news, we are one of 38 IVF clinics so far to have shut their doors today, cancelling all appointments. One news site is reporting that in one unnamed clinic, all unfrozen embryos have been destroyed. HFEA has released a statement, saying that all appointments at fertility clinics are being postponed as a precaution, pending further investigation.

13:30

Decided not to wait for HFEA inspectors before doing own research. Taking a closer look using our electron microscope won't be disturbing anything more than we have already in this morning's routine checks.

15:05

Took a selection of embryo culture samples through to the research lab to examine through our electron microscope. Sample included cross-section of 36 hr+ batches, which had been in various stages of development, and also a few from yesterday's batches.

All samples show the same: amongst the disintegrated embryo cells, thousands of tiny virus particles, like nothing I've seen before in all my years in training, research, and practice. This virus also reproduces faster than any I've seen before.

Spent about 45 minutes searching through online libraries of known viruses but found nothing remotely matching the profile or behaviour of the little beasts in our embryo cultures.

How has this virus been introduced? First theory is via nutrient feed, last topped up at 14:30 yesterday.

16:30

Took three empty, sterilised culturing containers, dosed them each with 1.5 ml sterilised water and checked for presence of virus. No virus present. Plugged them into spare slots in the incubator for one hour.

Result: all three samples from the incubator filled with same virus particles as seen in embryo cultures.

Conclusion: virus is resident in incubator unit, probably introduced through nutrient feed.

I've got to share this with HFEA, even if they did tell me not to touch anything.

17:45

Either someone else has made the same discovery as me or my email and photos were seen pretty quickly and passed on up the chain. Urgent bulletin released by DHSC reads as follows:

To prevent propagation of an as yet unknown virus, all IVF clinics and labs are to be locked down with immediate effect.

Please ensure that mains power and water are both shut off before leaving and securing the building.

Engineers from all the utility companies are being urgently assigned to isolate the clinics from the wastewater system.

22:55

Brought this logbook home, in case I can't get back into the lab tomorrow.

Spent evening scrolling through news and on WhatsApp comparing notes with colleagues from other clinics. Everyone who'd checked confirmed that their nutrient feed had been topped up some time yesterday. Most clinics don't have in-house research labs equipped with an electron microscope, so only I and one other have seen the virus itself.

Breaking news now on most news sites: a group calling themselves ANF – Alliance for Natural Families – has claimed responsibility for what is now being referred to as a biological terrorist attack on over 40 IVF clinics. ANF campaign against IVF treatment for same sex couples, arguing that the state should not be promoting what they call 'unnatural families', i.e. those not consisting of a father and a mother. ANF has been a blight on our industry for years, but they've always seemed fairly innocuous. Their literature is brutal and full of vitriol, but other than that, their action's been limited to 'peaceful protests' outside clinics.

26/03/2031

06:25

Woken ten minutes ago by call from Craig Walker, a friend who works in A&E at the infirmary, giving me the heads-up before I heard it from anyone else. Two women treated at our clinic yesterday have suffered miscarriages overnight. Both brought into A&E with severe haemorrhaging and are now stable, but links are already being drawn to ANF virus.

07:15

Morning news is reporting that A&E departments up and down the country are being swamped with haemorrhaging IVF patients. Some are predicting an imminent 2020-style national lockdown.

Don't like it, but everyone's calling this the ANF virus, or just ANFV. Shouldn't be giving ANF any publicity, good or bad. Some claim this is a new strain of the Zika virus because that also causes serious complications with pregnancy – babies born with microcephaly or dying in utero. Zika was tame compared with this, and there have been no reported cases for ten years, even in South America. The virus I saw yesterday looked nothing like the pictures I've seen of Zika.

10:30

Spent last few hours researching different types of virus, having heard them talking about Zika on the radio. If we can find what this one might have mutated from, we can start to work out how to fight it. Problem is, nothing else looks anything like it to me. But I'm an embryologist, not a virologist. By now, the DHSC will have virologists on the case.

10:50

Had a call from Dr Iqbal asking if I can come to the infirmary as soon as possible. He's the consultant gynaecologist for our two women who miscarried last night. He's seen the pictures from the email I sent to HFEA but wants me to come and look at samples taken from the women to confirm the presence of the same virus.

13:45

It is the same virus. I've just got back home from meeting with Dr Iqbal. Although the medium the virus was in was somewhat different from the clean embryo culture from our lab, the virus was unmistakably the same and very much active, which means it's not contained in our IVF clinics.

The government has now announced a complete international travel ban: no-one to leave or enter Britain until the virus is contained.

17:10

Can hardly believe it. Just come off the phone to the Health Secretary. Thought it was a hoax at first when a well-spoken gentleman called and, after confirming my identity, announced that he was putting me through to the Secretary of State for Health. But it was definitely her. Having been shown the work I did yesterday afternoon, she's asked me to attend a SAGE meeting down in London. They're sending a car to pick me up at 7:00 tomorrow morning.

27/03/2031

Not sure how much I should report about the events of today, given that I was on official government business. Shall stick to the facts that are public knowledge.

There have been more miscarriages across the country, taking the total to over 200. Of those, three women have died of severe blood loss and five more are in intensive care. All the women have one thing in common – they all had embryos implanted at IVF clinics on Wednesday. All of them are also being kept in quarantine, but given that the haemorrhaging started before they arrived at hospital, the value of the quarantine is being questioned.

An appeal has gone out for all women who've had IVF treatment in the past week to report to their local hospital for tests and monitoring, although in reality, it's only monitoring because we don't have a test for this virus in place yet.

There has been chaos at both British and foreign airports with foreign nationals and British citizens who had holidays planned insisting they have the right to leave the country. Meanwhile, British holidaymakers abroad have been turning up at airports clamouring to be repatriated despite the virus threat. The travel ban has remained firmly in place, though. It is our duty to ensure that this doesn't spread beyond our shores.

I guess I can also say that I'm currently in a hotel room in London because they want me back at DHSC headquarters tomorrow.

28/03/2031

A shorter day of meetings today, as things have calmed down somewhat. No new IVF/virus-related miscarriages reported in the last 24 hours. We think that all the women who received implants at affected clinics on Wednesday have been accounted for and all have miscarried. It's hoped that next week, we can begin a process of 'decontamination' of our clinics, though it's not yet clear how long the virus can survive outside a living organism. It will be some weeks, possibly months before things are back to normal.

The international travel ban will remain in place until we're certain that we are free of the virus.

I think it's OK to report that they want me back in the lab next week, running tests on some of the frozen embryos with carefully controlled samples of the virus. First thing is to get consent from the couples whose embryos we want to use.

22:25

It seems we might have been premature with our collective sigh of relief.

Had a call from another member of the SAGE. The Royal Victoria in Newcastle has reported a new case of a virus-like miscarriage, with the characteristic severe haemorrhaging. But this woman conceived naturally and has never been near an IVF clinic. They're flying me up to Newcastle tomorrow morning to verify whether this is a case of ANFV. We need a more appropriate name for this thing, but no time for that now.

29/03/2031

05:25

Waiting for the car to pick me up and take me to the airbase. Newcastle now has three suspected cases of the virus in non-IVF women. There are a further two in Bournemouth, but I can't be at two ends of the country at the same time!

As yet, none of this has been made public, but before today's out, the DHSC is going to have to release a statement and guidance for pregnant women and anyone trying to conceive.

11:45

It is, without doubt, the same virus, which means the virus has made the leap to the general population. The poor women have been interrogated thoroughly over all their movements and the contact they've had with other people over the last week. There is no identifiable link between any of them and any IVF clinic or any of the previous women affected by the virus. None of them had visited the Royal Victoria or any other hospital in the last two weeks. They do all live within two miles of the hospital, though, and the Royal Victoria did experience some of the earliest cases of IVF-related ANFV miscarriages in the country.

The worried staff at the hospital were questioning me as if I was the world's no. 1 authority on ANFV. I couldn't really answer any of their questions, except to confirm that this was a positive case of it. I'm only a humble embryologist who happens to have been one of the first to identify the virus.

Someone else has been sent to Bournemouth. Still waiting to hear news from them.

15:10

Back at hotel in London. Reports have now come in of new outbreaks at 22 hospitals across the country, including one which hadn't dealt with any cases of the original IVF-related miscarriages. This is now officially an epidemic.

Official advice from DHSC is as follows:

Any women trying to conceive should put their plans on hold and return to using contraception.

Women who are already pregnant or suspect that they might be pregnant, should continue as normal unless they experience bleeding. They should keep away from hospital, except in the case of a medical emergency.

Women who experience unexpected or excessive bleeding should call 111 but should remain at home and not take themselves to hospital. They will be assessed at home and transferred to hospital if necessary.

Although it's too early to tell, it looks like this is only affecting pregnancies in the very early stages. Maternity wards are continuing to report normal healthy births.

30/03/2031

14:30

Back in my own lab after some early morning meetings in London.

The current theory is that the virus entered the closed-loop water recycling plants, which process wastewater and provide 75% of drinking water in most cities and large towns. As soon as a woman who was bleeding flushed the toilet or medical staff cleaned down after treating one of the ANFV cases, the virus was in that system, and the water-treatment processes are powerless against it.

Given that 92% of the British population live in cities, current estimates are that at least 85% could already be carriers of the virus, including babies born in the last few days.

16:30

Others have already contacted a number of my IVF patients, seeking consent to use some of their frozen embryos to learn more about this virus. Three couples have so far consented, so I have identified and labelled two embryos from each patient, ready to start trials tomorrow.

A special sealed container of the virus-infected nutrient feed has been delivered and is ready to be plugged in.

17:00

Decided to test my own blood. I am a carrier.

Chapter 6

JOE REACHES FOR the handle and pushes open the classroom door. The heads of his classmates all turn to look at him. For a split second, everyone is silent. One child screams and then starts crying. Others point and laugh. They're all staring at his crotch. Joe looks down at himself in horror. He is completely naked. He tries to cover his penis with his hands, but as he does so, it just gets bigger, and he can't hide it.

Joe wakes up, his face hot and dripping from the blush in his dream. His crotch is still throbbing and engorged. Under the covers, he is not actually naked, he has his shorts on, but there's a hand in his shorts, and it is not his hand.

He snaps his eyes open. Lying beside him, reaching across to him, almost on top of him, breathing all over him, is the girl from the café – Vicki or Victoria.

'What are you doing? Get off me!'

Joe throws himself backwards out of the bed, pulling the covers off and around himself to cover all nakedness. But in covering his own nakedness, he uncovers hers. Because there she is, lying across the sheet, stark naked and making no attempt to cover herself. Joe has never seen such curvy flesh, and his face flushes even redder. He averts his eyes, staring down, concentrating on the wriggling of his toes under his bedsheet wrappings.

'I'm sorry, Joe. I...I was outside your window and heard you cry out.' What was she doing outside at this time of night? 'Were you having a bad dream? I thought you might want comforting.' How can she think that touching him there will comfort him? A place no-one else has touched him since he was a little boy, and then only to clean him. 'Come back to bed. I promise I won't touch you again. Unless you'd like me to.'

Joe blinks twice, three times. If he is still dreaming, it isn't going away.

'Come on, I'm getting cold now.'

He throws the bedding towards her and turns his back, wrapping his arms around his naked torso and shivering as the beads of perspiration rapidly cool him. Sucking the chill night air through his nose, he holds it in for as long as he can before expelling it back through his chattering teeth.

'Get out of my room.'

She doesn't move. She simply lies there, eyes burrowing into his back.

'Get out of my room!'

The seconds tick by with no sound of movement. A stifled sob draws his head around, daring to look as she wraps herself in the covers, grabs a discarded nightdress from the floor, and stumbles out of the room.

Pulling on his T-shirt, Joe lies back down on the edge of his naked bed, cowering away from the warmth where her body had been. His heart beats quick and fast. If he shuts his eyes, all he sees is the laughing, pointing classmates, every other one bearing Victoria's face. If he opens them, the ancient damp stains on the ceiling leer at his cold, exposed body. He pulls on the under-sheet, untucking it from the edges of the bed and covering his body as best he can. And he lies there, willing himself back to sleep, but his mind is racing around a thousand worries. Is this what they do here? Is it normal to touch each other in those places they've had to keep hidden all their lives? It doesn't feel right, but is it wrong?

Chapter 7

NATS BURST INTO the room without knocking. 'Wakey, wakey, sleepy head! It's time to get up. The sun's shining, and I've got loads more to show you today.'

Joe lay as still as possible. Fought to slow his breathing.

'Heck, Joe, what have you done with your bed? Have you been having nightmares?'

The voice came closer. He thought she was going to reach out and touch him and almost flinched but managed to maintain the pretence of sleep. What if she decided to lie beside him on the bed, take off her clothes, do what Victoria had done?

Still standing over him, her sigh brushed his cheek. 'Oh, well, s'pose we'll catch up later. Reckon you could sleep for England.'

Her footsteps retreated across the room, and a moment later, Joe dared to open his eyes a little to watch the door shutting behind her. He felt bad now. Nats was all right. Yes, she talked a lot, but she'd spent the whole day with him yesterday showing him round, and in all that time, she'd shown no interest in touching anything other than his hand. But then she had wanted to sit there and watch him get dressed yesterday morning and talked about having seen a tonker before as if it was all perfectly normal to see each other's naked bodies. Dust danced in the beams of sunlight that forced their way into his room. He pulled the bedsheet up over his head.

THE SKY OUTSIDE had dulled when Joe woke again, not realising he'd dropped off in the first place. He needed to get up, find the boat. What if they'd taken it away, hidden it, like they had his clothes? No, he didn't know they'd hidden his clothes. They'd probably taken them to be washed. But he couldn't go back to the mainland, go back home in the loose and baggy things he'd worn yesterday. He needed to find his own clothes as well as the boat, somehow.

Or he could stay. He could just not speak to anyone, like Cain; find a hovel to live in away from everyone else, like Tom. He could volunteer for Anthony's mission and say he was quite happy to go alone, no need for anyone else to come. He gulped. He'd never been alone before. Well, only when Georgy and Cris had left him on his own in the flat or had persuaded themselves and him that it would be good for him to go out on his bike or to the shops without them, although they'd all been more nervous about that recently. He could go back home to them and stay in the flat all the time. At least then he'd be with people he could trust. But what if there was a fire or some other emergency and he had to leave the flat? Then all the neighbours would see the freak he was becoming, with his huge feet and hairy face. The wind outside rattled the window. He'd miss the fresh air too; Georgy always made sure they got plenty of fresh air.

Whatever he decided, he couldn't stay lying on this bed. He squinted at the door – still firmly shut, as Nats had left it. He swivelled off the bed and pulled on the T-shirt. He was still achy and bruised from his wrestling with the skipper and the boat. Could he manage to row all the way back to the mainland? If he did, how would he get back to Leeds? He had no phone to call Georgy and Cris, and no money for train tickets. Anthony must have ideas about how his expedition volunteers would travel.

On a little table near the door, someone had left a glass of what looked like, and proved to be, apple juice and a bundle of cloth, which when unwrapped, turned out to be a still-warm fried-egg sandwich made with more of that dark, heavy bread he'd first tasted last night in the café. Joe glugged the juice and wolfed down the sandwich without tasting it.

HE COULDN'T SAY what he'd expected when he stepped out onto the street, but there were no gaggles of curious girls, eager to make his acquaintance. Nor was Nats 'on guard' outside the door, waiting for him to appear. In fact, as far as he could tell, there was nobody around in the village at all. He turned in the opposite direction to the way Nats had led him yesterday, towards the shore he felt certain he'd arrived at. It would be good to make sure the boat was still there. Children's squeals and shrieks blew towards him, mixed with the smell of seaweed. If they were down there, someone older would be with them. He could check later; another day even. He'd ruled out leaving today, hadn't he?

He should get to know this island a bit better. Maybe find somewhere he could hide out, if necessary. He followed the road up out of the village, in the same direction that he'd chased after Nats yesterday. He dared to pause, to look more carefully at the various buildings he'd rushed past the day before. Peering through windows, he half yearned and half feared being spotted by another living soul. Whether because they were all busy going about their daily routines or because they were following Sandra's instructions to give him some space to get acclimatised to his new surroundings, or maybe because they'd all heard how he'd rejected Vicki, no-one showed themselves and Joe had soon left the village behind, following the overgrown tarmac track that passed for the island's main road.

He should climb back up to the top of that hill, have another look at the whole island, but he'd already passed the route that he and Nats had taken yesterday. There had to be other ways up there, though. He left the road and stumbled through long grass that kept trying to trip him up and then squelched right into a bog that soaked his trainers. Every time he tried to climb to higher ground, he met more bogs. Surely, the higher you went, the less boggy it should be, but the island didn't seem to agree.

Finally, he spotted a firmer path winding up the hill and struck out towards it, but no sooner was he on it than his way was blocked by a huge cow.

'Oi, go on, get outta the way!' he shouted, waving his arms at the same time, as Georgy had shown him to do on occasions when they'd met cows on walks in the countryside around Leeds. The beast didn't move. He clapped his hands. She turned her head towards him and stared back with her huge, wet eyes, her mouth munching at the coarse grass she'd pulled up. His mind filled up again with visions of Victoria, sprawled naked across his bed. He turned and ran back down the hill, no longer caring about how many bogs he splashed through.

Joe barely saw the wall in time to stop before he ran into it. He put his hand out to steady himself on one of the rough stones and panted. Smoke tickled his nostrils, and he looked up to see a wisp of it rising from the chimney of what he now recognised to be Tom's hovel. Maybe Tom could tell him what he should do. But that would mean telling Tom about what had happened, and anyway, hadn't Nats told him not to go knocking on Tom's door without an invitation? He skirted around Tom's perimeter wall until he was standing where they had yesterday, gazing down towards the sea and the shell beach, which started to sparkle as the sun pushed a heavy cloud aside. Longing for the carefree spirit of yesterday, he turned his back on the hill and the hovel and trudged on down to the beach.

By the time he got there, the sun was tucked once more behind its shroud and a chill breeze was coming in off the sea. The myriad shells, so thrilling yesterday, were dull and indistinguishable from one another. Joe squatted down and trawled his fingers absent-mindedly through the shingly shells, occasionally grabbing handfuls to throw at the sea.

The chattering of his teeth was joined by the crunch of approaching feet. Before he had time to look up, large feet on muscled, hairy legs were standing beside him and then bending as Tom sat down.

Joe gratefully accepted the windbreak Tom's bulk offered, and for a while, neither spoke.

'You hoped you'd fit right in here, didn't you?'

A gust straight off the sea found its way right into Joe's heart.

'Expected to finally find somewhere you belonged, where you weren't different from everyone else.'

The wind direction changed, attempting to push him out to sea.

He didn't need to reply to Tom's statements, and it seemed that Tom didn't expect him to. There was another long but comfortable pause before Tom spoke again. 'Sorry, mate, don't let me pass my misery off on to you. Where's Nats today? You and her look like you've formed a bit of a friendship already. I'm glad. She needs a friend like you – someone who doesn't see her as the little girl she used to be.'

Perhaps that was all Nats was after. Simple friendship.

'She's a good lass. I've got more time for her than most of the others here. She doesn't take herself too seriously. I'd stick close to her if I were you. If you ask me, as long as you've found one soul in common on this island, you'll be fine.'

'What about you?' Joe ventured. 'Do you have a someone you can call a friend?'

'Oh, I used to think so, but let's say we didn't have all that much in common after all.' Tom inhaled slowly. 'But that's all in the past, and I'm quite happy out here on my own, in my little "hovel" as I know some call it.' He turned his face from gazing out to sea and towards Joe. 'Not sure that'd suit you, though, would it? You're not so happy in your own company.' Tom stood up as if to go. 'So I suggest you go find Nats. I think she's looking after the kids today.' He offered Joe a hand to pull him up. 'If you find them, which shouldn't be too difficult, you'll find her.'

'But what if Nats only wants the same as what Victoria wanted?' Joe blurted out, instantly regretting it as the blood rose to his face.

'Wha's Vicki been up to?'

Joe could feel Tom's eyes interrogating him. He couldn't think what to say. Could he tell Tom that he'd woken up to find her hand on his tonker? What if there really was nothing wrong with touching each other's secret parts here and it was what you were expected to do? His head throbbed, and the lump in his throat threatened to choke him.

'Has she tried it on with you? She has, hasn't she? What exactly did she do? You should tell Sandra. In fact, no, I'll deal with it. I'll go pay a visit to Victoria. I'll walk back there with you now.'

'What? No!' Joe hadn't even told Tom what Vicki had done. What if when he confronted her and the truth came out, it turned out that she'd done nothing wrong? 'It doesn't matter. I told her to go away, and she did.'

'Well, that's something, I suppose. But you should still tell Sandra what she did, and someone should still have words with Vicki. Sandra told them all you were off limits, and Vicki can't pretend she didn't know that. I don't agree with Sandra about much, but she's right about that.' Tom put a hand on Joe's shoulder. Joe tried not to flinch at the touch and ended up shrugging instead. 'All right. I'll keep what you've told me to myself for now. But if Vicki or any of the others try anything like that again, you come straight to me. Yeah?'

Joe nodded and studied the handful of shells he'd picked up without thinking. Nats was right: each one was different, even in this dull light, but there was one in particular that sparkled at him right now.

'And what if it's Nats who tries something like that? I don't want to lose her as a friend or get her into trouble with Sandra.'

'Nats? Nah, I can already imagine you two making something more of your friendship in the future, but only when you're both ready. Right now, she'll be more interested in whether she can beat you at football than whether you'll mate with her.' Tom stood up. 'Go on, you go find her. She'll be wondering where you've got to.'

Chapter 8

FROM THAT EVENING when we met Jay Taylor in the Square Peg, it was one hundred and twenty-three long days before we heard anything further about our son. Imagine that. Knowing, or at least trusting that you had a baby on the way, growing steadily bigger in its pregnancy pod, but never being able to go and watch the 3D images of its tiny face and feet and hands. Never being able to listen to the whirr of its persistent heartbeat. Not even knowing where it was, or who was tending to its daily needs. Sometimes I wished I could forget about him and then have a nice surprise when suddenly the day arrived. It was like those nights before your birthday or Exmas, when you'd be willing yourself to go to sleep so the morning would arrive quicker. But sleep refused to come.

Then on day one hundred and twenty-three, we got a call, out of the blue, from someone calling themself Leslee, from DiG. 'Can I come and see you?' they said. 'We need to make some preparations.' It was as unspecific as that. We agreed to a time the next day; sleep refused to come to either of us that night.

I opened the door before they had the chance to ring the bell. We suggested sitting in the comfort of front room, but Leslee declined and said we'd be more discreet in the kitchen, at the back of the house. It occurred to me then that Leslee had arrived at the house on foot – no car parked on our drive or even on the street.

As soon as we were all sitting at the kitchen table, Leslee assured us that everything was OK. Our son was growing well and would be ready for birthing at the usual time, exactly two weeks from today.

'Can we be there, at the birthing?' Cris asked before I could get the same question out myself.

The sympathetic look in Leslee's eyes told us the answer, but it didn't make it any easier when it was put into words. 'We would love to have you there, but I'm afraid it's too risky for both of you, for us, and of course, most of all, for your son.'

As Leslee explained the inevitable consequences if the authorities discovered what we were doing, I had to concede that it wasn't worth the risk. DiG's operation would be shut down for a start, ending the life and hope for all the other foetuses they were protecting. We would probably be imprisoned as accomplices, and our baby would undoubtedly be put through 'corrective surgery' before being fostered by a stranger willing to care for a disfigured child in exchange for meagre government maintenance payments.

So, instead of meeting our son for the first time as he emerged from the waters of his pregnancy pod and took his first breath, he would be handed over to us in a remote layby like contraband goods. Then, if we followed Leslee's advice, we would whisk him away to some holiday let that wasn't going to be his home.

'It will give you the chance to get to know your son and get used to...' Leslee hesitated, 'his, er, unusual features, away from the cooing of friends and family.' We obviously looked in need of reassurance. 'Don't worry. Lots of folk choose to begin their new life as parents with a little holiday these days.'

Leslee could offer us no leaflets or self-help guides on how to look after baby boys. Producing and distributing literature that illustrated the male anatomy was another thing that was judged to be too risky. We were treated to a quick, rough sketch, but as soon as we'd both had a look, the paper was ripped from our hands, run under the tap, torn into shreds, and scattered into the food waste bin.

'Have you had any thoughts about names?' Leslee enquired, trying to lighten the atmosphere.

I looked at Cris. Of course, we'd talked about names many times while trying to pretend we weren't doing so, unwilling to put too much hope in that brief conversation we'd had with Jay Taylor all those months ago. Cris consented to my unspoken query with the slightest of nods.

'We like the name Joh,' I answered.

'Oh, yes, a very good choice. Simple but with pedigree. Not too common, but nor is it overly unusual. I believe it used to be a very popular name for both boys and girls in the past. J-O-E for a boy, usually short for Joseph and just J-O for a girl, which could be short for Josephine but more often for Joanne or Joanna.' Leslee clearly considered themself to be something of an authority on historical names. 'Of course, I would have to advise that you adopt the more conventional J-O-H spelling, at least in public, and it's probably best not to confuse the poor boy with different spellings at home.'

Leslee had a few other recommendations and instructions for us before leaving, but if I'm honest, neither of us took any of it in. We knew now where and when we would meet our son, and the rest, we would work out as it happened.

For the next two weeks, I kept preparing myself for the worst. That we might sit in that layby for hours before eventually driving home in the early hours of the morning with no baby and no-one there to tell us why. Because that's how it would happen if things went wrong, I'm sure of it. We would just hear nothing; it would be 'too risky' to tell us anything more.

It felt like it would never come, but then, without warning, the twenty-fourth of January was upon us. The schedule for the day was etched in my mind. The birthing sequence would be initiated at 9:30 a.m. precisely. By ten past ten, our son was expected to take his first breath. For the rest of that hour, and the whole of the next, he would be put through an elaborate series of tests to assess the strength of his lungs, heart, reactions and senses. These were the only professional postnatal checks he would get. Once he was with us, he was completely off radar. He would also receive small doses of all the essential infant vaccinations, all in one toxic-sounding cocktail.

He would be kept under observation for the rest of that day and overnight. Someone would give him his first feed, and his second and third. They expected to change his nappy at least three times too and to give him his first bath. We would hear nothing of any of this.

Through the night, he would be hooked up to machines closely monitoring his heart, his breathing, his waking and sleeping. An experienced paediatric nurse would be on duty throughout the hours of darkness, volunteering and risking a night at the secret fertility unit in between their more regular nursing shifts, all for our baby.

Nobody would call us. They would just meet us at the rendezvous point, as long as all had gone to plan.

'We're going to be late. What if they don't wait for us?' We'd spent ten minutes longer than planned wrestling with the pristine baby seat, which was now secured to the back seat. My blood pressure rose as one traffic light after another changed from green to red in front of us. But as we eventually pulled into the designated layby, we came to rest behind a small silver hatchback, and though my heart beat ever faster, I breathed a sigh of relief. For beside the other car stood a young couple, one holding the back door open as the other gently lifted their sleeping newborn out into the fresh air. Except this wasn't their baby, he was ours.

I don't remember their faces. I'm not sure whether either told us their names. I confess that I can't recall to this day if I thanked them. The one holding our son smiled and held him out for me to clumsily take into my arms. An involuntary tear trickled down my cheek as I witnessed the almost imperceptible rise and fall of his sleeping chest and felt his warmth seeping through both our layers of clothing. I was completely lost in the moment, until I noticed the silver hatchback slowly moving away.

Shocked at how suddenly we were being left alone, I pushed the sleeping bundle at Cris and stepped forward towards the retreating car, my hand raised in... what? A grateful wave goodbye? A panicked request to stop and wait a while? I couldn't actually tell you which, but it made no difference because within seconds, we were alone. I turned away in time to see a large, brown envelope slip from Cris's hand and drop into a puddle.

As Cris secured a hold on the son that had been thrust into their arms, I dithered over whether to rescue the baby or the envelope. Concluding quickly that the baby was safe, I bent down to retrieve the envelope. 'What's this?' I enquired.

'I think it's a birth certificate,' Cris replied.

I eased the slightly damp contents out of the envelope, and there it was in clear print.

NAME: JOH TURNER
PARENT(S): CRIS TURNER, GEORGY TURNER

'Well, I guess we'd better call him Joh then,' said Cris, reading over my shoulder.

As if he already knew his name, Joh stirred and let out a whimper, which morphed before our eyes into an unrelenting, rasping wail. Cris and I looked at each other in terrified apprehension, *'What do we do?'* and *'What have we done?'* the coupled unspoken questions between us.

'Let's put him in his seat,' Cris suggested, passing the screaming bundle to me.

'Shouldn't we try to work out what's wrong?' I protested as I tried without success to joggle the cries into submission.

'This is hardly the best place to change our first nappy or attempt the first feed,' Cris shouted over the din.

Feeling like the cruellest parent on the planet, I lowered our protesting son into his seat and eased the straps around his outstretched arms and legs. I then dashed around the other side of the car to sit on the back seat beside him, hoping that holding his hand might be received as some form of consolation. It didn't work, but by what felt at the time like divine intervention, Joh calmed as we pulled back onto the road, and within minutes, I was again mesmerised by the steady rise and fall of his tiny chest.

Fourteen years and seven months later, I would find myself again holding the hand of our sleeping son in the back of our car, driving towards another rendezvous with DiG. But this time, we would be handing him back.

Chapter 9

JOE WANDERED DOWN the pebble beach towards a roaring Nats, hair looking wilder than ever as she bounded after the two kids, who both squealed with excitement. Nats gave up the chase and turned to meet him, feet firmly planted on the beach, hands on hips.

'Where have you been all morning? Everyone's been looking for you! Sandra wanted to see you and came asking me where you were, but I couldn't tell her because I've been here with the kids, and when I left you, you were asleep, except I know you weren't really, you were just pretending. What did you do that for? I thought we were friends. Did you find the egg sandwich I left for you? Well, Victoria asked me to give it to you actually, but she didn't want to come and give it to you herself. Hey, has something happened between you and Victoria?' She must've noticed his blushing. 'It has, hasn't it! Well, Sandra won't be happy about that. I want all the details later. What did it feel like? Do you think she'll be having your baby now?' Nats stopped, unable to ignore the kids tugging on her legs anymore, and besides, she had to take a breath at some point!

Nats turned back to him, having kicked a ball for the kids to chase after. 'You'll have to tell me later. Sandra's desperate to see you. Don't tell her about the Victoria thing for the moment. We'll work out how much you should own up to later. You'll find her in the second cottage up there on the left. It's what we call the Head House.'

Joe stood, staring at her, speechless.

'Well, don't just stand there gawping at me.' Nats wafted him away. 'You're already late for Sandra, and she's not someone who likes to be kept waiting. I'll catch you later.' With that, she raced after the ball, which was floating away on a wave. Was that what Joe should do try to do too? Just float away from here?

Nobody answered when Joe knocked on the door of the Head House, so after two spells of knocking, he nudged his way in. As the door clicked shut behind him, Sandra's voice summoned him from behind another door that stood slightly ajar.

'Come on in Joe, I'm in the front room.'

How she knew it was him, he couldn't fathom, until he ventured on through and saw the large bay window overlooking the pebble beach and the road up into the village.

Sitting behind a desk, Sandra looked up and studied Joe through a tatty pair of glasses that looked like they might be more detrimental than beneficial to her eyesight. 'Welcome, Joe. I'm sorry it's taken this long to get to meet you properly. Natasha rather monopolised you yesterday, and I presume you've had a bit of an explore on your own this morning.'

Joe nodded. For a moment, he was thrust back into his old headteacher's office, long ago. How old was Sandra? Georgy had said that no-one on the island would be more than a few years older than him. That was said to reassure him, but he'd been able to see that it worried Georgy and Cris.

'I'm s-sorry,' Joe stuttered, 'I didn't realise you wanted to see me.'

Sandra waved his apology away. 'No matter, you're not to blame. It's good that you're here now because there are things we need to talk through.'

Should he tell her now about Vicki? Tom had thought he should, but Nats had said not to say anything to Sandra until he'd told her about it. What if what Vicki had done wasn't anything Sandra would be bothered about? He hadn't actually given Tom any details of what had happened. Maybe he could talk about it with Nats first, at a time when she was ready to listen.

Joe sucked in a lungful of air through his nose and slowly let it out. Did Sandra expect him to stand here quietly, in front of her desk, like a naughty school kid? He should probably try to be more assertive, like Georgy had told him.

'Er, do you mind if I sit down?' he asked, pointing at an empty chair.

'No, I mean yes, of course, please do. Sorry. Rude of me to keep you standing all this time. Most of the others come straight in and take a seat, you know.' Clearly trying to control her blustering, Sandra looked back down at her notes and added a few superfluous dots to the page. Her nervousness knocked a year or two off her age. 'OK, so what I wanted to talk with you about is what you can do. I mean, what part you might play in our little community here.'

Sandra went on to explain with great fluency how each member of the community took on different jobs or responsibilities – duties vital to their survival and self-sufficiency and also roles that helped to improve and develop the island facilities and community life. Some things people were expected to do without anything in return, 'a form of tax of people's time, if you like.' Other services that they provided to one another, folk could ask to be paid for. Few people had arrived on the island with any real cash, so the community had found their own currency – old plastic bottle tops. Quite a stash had been found on a beach soon after the first members had arrived on the island. The bottle tops weren't made anymore on the mainland, and Sandra was pretty sure they'd found all that were left to find, but anyone was welcome to do a bit of prospecting if they wanted to, and good luck to them.

Sandra pushed a drawstring bag, made from a bit of old curtain, across the desk towards Joe. It rattled as he picked it up.

'Those are a gift from the community for you to have something to spend until you've worked out how to earn some for yourself,' she explained. 'We've kept it simple. They're all worth the same, and you can't be charged more than three at a time for anything you want to buy. If something's worth more than three tops, it should be offered for free, for the good of the community.'

Sandra looked back down at her notes. 'So, we need to work out what your role's going to be. What do you think? What are you good at?'

Joe thought for a moment and remembered Cain and his violin. 'Well, I can play the clarinet, only I left it with all the rest of my things when I jumped off the trawler that was supposed to bring me here.'

'Hmm, I agree that music's good to raise people's spirits, but it's hardly vital for our survival or even something you're likely to earn tops from, particularly when you don't actually have a clarinet. I'm afraid we don't have a spare one for you to borrow. What about school? What were your best subjects at school?'

'I wasn't at school for long.' Joe thought about the great education he had received from Georgy.

'I'm good with computers, though,' he said. 'Georgy – one of my parents – taught me to code when I was really young, and then I taught myself lots more in my spare time, so then Georgy said I'd need to start teaching them.' He hesitated. 'But I don't suppose you've got any computers here either.' He scanned the room, feeling useless.

'Well, no, we don't,' Sandra began, trying to sound positive, 'but it sounds like you're a good problem solver.' She sat for a while, deep in thought, forefingers pressed together against her lips.

Joe tried to think too but didn't know where to start. His mind meandered back and forth over the events of the last few days.

'Got it!' said Sandra, snapping him back into the room. 'What do you think about teaching yourself to fish?'

Surprisingly, considering they were surrounded by sea, no-one had yet tried to make use of the rich source of food that swam all around them. One or two had tried catching fish off the jetty with a makeshift line, but only as a bit of fun rather than to provide food. One of the problems was that, until Joe had arrived, they'd not had any seaworthy boats on the island. Some had been lucky enough to be brought by pilots all the way to the jetty; others had leapt off boats and swum ashore, perhaps grabbing and clinging to some sort of floatation aid. Joe was the first to actually commandeer a rowing boat. Any boats left behind by the former inhabitants of the island had long ago evolved into leaky sieves.

'We did find some nets in the cottage next door to this one, which might be useable. You'll need to do a few repairs on them, I think.' Sandra was animated and excited, her glasses in her hands rather than on her face, so Joe could see now her teenage-looking eyes sparking with thoughts.

So it was settled. Assuming Joe decided to stay, not that he'd let on to Sandra that perhaps he wouldn't, he would become the island's first fisherman. He'd have to take his turn on the watch list as well, of course – perhaps he could even do some shifts from the boat – and there were various other chores that everyone had to take their turn at doing, but Sandra was satisfied that they'd found Joe's vocation.

Emerging from the Head House a few minutes later clutching his bag of tops, Joe heard his name called from somewhere up the street. He scanned around until he spotted the owner of the voice, sitting at a table outside the café. Anthony beckoned him over. There was no sign of Vicki. Even if she did emerge, she wouldn't try anything out in the open, would she?

Two plates of food sat on the table. One, well on the way to being empty, sat in front of Anthony. The other appeared untouched – heaped high with mashed potatoes, vegetables, and some sort of gravy.

'Have a seat,' Anthony directed, then pushed the full plate of food towards Joe. 'I got this for you. Sorry, might not be all that hot anymore. I'd hoped Sandra would release you a bit sooner.'

Joe sat down and gratefully dug in.

'I gather things didn't go too well with Vicki last night,' Anthony said. Joe spluttered, spraying the table with mash. A slight smirk played across Anthony's furry face. 'Oh, don't worry. I'm the only one she's told, and it'd be best if we kept it between us for now, if that's OK with you. I look out for Vicki. I think she sees me as her older brother and she's the little sister I never had. Anyway, she knows she shouldn't have come and bothered you like that, and she won't try it on again, unless, of course, you'd like to give it a go. If so, if you're too shy to go to her yourself, have a quiet word in my ear, and Sandra needn't hear anything about it. Like I say, Vick's like a sister to me. It wouldn't feel right mating with her myself, and Tom's only interested in the one girl he can't have, so when you're ready, let me know.'

The mash felt like whole, uncooked potatoes as Joe did his best to swallow it down.

'Of course, you're welcome to get a few tips from the expert before you have your next go with a lady.'

Joe knew a bit about how animals mated to produce offspring from a brief exploration of the topic with Georgy. Had they realised that on the island, humans might also mate? Was that what he'd be expected to do with some of the girls? Was that what Anthony was doing? He fixed his eyes firmly back on the plateful of food he now only felt like picking at.

'On the other hand, if you're not sure that being a prize breeding stud is really your calling in life...' Anthony paused briefly, 'you could volunteer for the expedition. It'd give you some time to have a few adventures before settling down and starting some families. I'd value your involvement in my little planning group anyway.'

Before Joe had a chance to reply, not that he knew how to respond to any of Anthony's offers, Nats appeared beside them at the table.

'Hi, Anthony, hi, Joe.' She sat down beside him, grabbed Joe's discarded fork, and helped herself to a large and precariously balanced mountain of vegetables and mash. 'You know, you really should stop expecting other people to feed you,' she said through a mouthful, a glint of mischief in her eyes.

Having shovelled in a couple more mouthfuls, Nats leapt up, almost toppling her chair backwards. 'Come on, I'll show you where the food store is. There are lots of things you can help yourself to for free – and a few extras you can spend your tops on, if you want to.' She pointed at the bag still clutched in Joe's left hand.

Joe looked towards Anthony, automatically seeking permission to leave the table. Anthony shrugged and nodded, which served as a starting pistol for Nats to race off up the road. Joe pushed his chair back and followed.

Chapter 10

THEY SAY THAT being a parent is the best thing you'll ever do with your life. But if they really mean it, why was I the only one left in the world to actually do it full time?

Some overflowed with praise at what a wonderful parent I was being, to sacrifice my career and dedicate all my time to caring for Joh, but I could tell that the majority disapproved.

'Do you really think it's wise to put your career on hold for so long? Wouldn't it be better to keep your hand in, even if you were just part time?'

'You know, it's been scientifically proven that babies who spend time in a nursery with other babies do better once they're at school.'

'So you're like, totally financially dependent on Cris? How does that work?'

'You've got to start trusting other people to help you out. We wouldn't mind babysitting from time to time. You only need to ask.'

'Isn't there anyone we could leave him with, just for one evening out as the two of us?'

'Why has that couple brought their baby with them to the restaurant? Poor thing would have been much happier left at home with a babysitter.'

If I could be taken back to that meeting with Jay Taylor, knowing all that I know now, would I still agree to be parent to a baby boy? Yes, of course I would. He's our child and always will be, but it's not easy. I'd love to let other people look after him from time to time, and it would be wonderful to be able to put him into a nursery part time. I feel awful about not giving him those social experiences with other little ones. Thing is, we don't even really spend time with other parents with babies. I tried to once or twice, but – and I know they were trying to be friendly – I ended up feeling interrogated on all the details about the pregnancy and birth. So from then on, I stuck to spending time with our childless friends. They didn't show the slightest bit of interest in comparing notes on experiences of the various scans, the tension of the birthing process, how it felt to see him emerge from the pregnancy pod, how much he weighed at birth, or when he had his first feed. They also didn't have snotty-nosed babies who might pass something onto Joh; we can't take him to the doctor if he gets sick.

So will it ever be safe to leave him with other adults and other kids? Well, we need to get through potty training for a start. When does that happen? Two? Three? Is it the same for boys as it is for us neutrals? Even if it is, will he be able to understand at that age that he mustn't let anyone else see it? He won't understand that at three, will he? What about at four or five, when he starts school? Of course, strange and alien as it looks to us, it's as natural a protrusion for him as a nose is to the rest of us. Well, OK, when we leave him for a few minutes with nothing on his bottom – in the privacy of our home, it goes without saying – he does seem to play with it rather more than he does his nose the rest of the time, but he doesn't know it makes him so different from everyone else in his world.

It's an odd little thing really. Like an untameable hosepipe. From what I've heard, even normal babies can produce an impressive jet sometimes, but at least it goes in a predictable direction! At first, getting one nappy off and the next one on was done faster than a tyre change in a Formula 1 pit! We soon realised that it needed to be done with the precision of a Formula 1 tyre change as well as the speed – get that little snake pointing in the wrong direction and you could easily get through five sets of clothes in a day!

So no, those first few months weren't easy, but then came the day when we had to leave behind any part of our life that still felt familiar and find somewhere else to call home.

Thanks to government budget cuts, it almost didn't happen – the house call from the health visitor. Of course, we weren't on anyone's system, so there were no reminders to go and have Joh weighed. Not even surveys to complete about our child's development. When we got past three months, we felt certain we were outside the danger zone. But then, one afternoon, as I'd got Joh settled for his afternoon nap, the doorbell rang and there they were – Nurse Temple, in crisp, navy uniform, free from any sign of a crease except for those around their eyes as they did their best to wear a disarming smile.

'Good afternoon. I hope I'm not disturbing you.' The nurse made a weak attempt at empathy as Joh began to wail from within the house. 'One of your friends, Larch's parent, happened to mention at baby clinic yesterday that they'd not seen you and your child – Joh, is it? – in quite a while, and they were concerned about you. We seem to have misplaced your records. May I come in?' They pushed their way into the hall.

We'd planned exactly what to say and do in this situation, but it didn't stop me from stammering as I searched for my well-rehearsed words.

'It-it's very good of you to have come round, but Joh's not well. Some sort of rash. I've looked it up and I think it could be Cornish measles. Perhaps you could come and have a look to see what you think.'

Surely, Nurse Temple could hear my racing heart without the stethoscope in that bag. Surely, they would see through the deception. But no, it worked! That bag was hoisted back up as if our carpet were crawling with cockroaches.

'Cornish measles? Are you sure about that?'

Hearing an edge of unease in the nurse's tone, I risked pushing a bit further. 'Well, that's what it looks like, going off the pictures I've seen on the hub, but if you wouldn't mind having a look, it would set our minds at rest.'

It was the nurse's turn to appear flustered, whilst backing towards the front door. 'No, no, I'm sure you'll be correct in your diagnosis. Just make sure you keep the child well hydrated - you've done the right thing to keep them at home, away from others. I shall pop back in about three weeks to find out how things are. We can leave the routine checks until then. Goodbye now.'

I breathed a sigh of relief as the door was pulled firmly shut. Despite the comprehensive inoculation programmes, medical professionals remained surprisingly nervous of certain viruses - Cornish measles being one of them. I'm pleased to say I've never had it myself, and I don't think I know of anyone who ever has. I'm not even sure what it does to you exactly - probably should have looked it up, really, before afflicting Joh with it. But simply naming the virus had clearly given us the desired effect of sending Nurse Temple fleeing back down the path.

This was no time for celebrating, though. We'd told each other repeatedly over the last few months that it would probably never happen, that we were formulating a 'just in case' plan. Now that plan had to be put into action. In the next couple of days, we would pack up as much as we could fit in the car and leave the place that Cris and I had called home for the last six years. So, when Nurse Temple rang the doorbell again in three weeks' time, as I am certain would happen, its chime would reverberate around a deserted house.

We'd chosen Manchester as our new hometown – a city in which we could be anonymous. After five nights in a grotty budget hotel, we found a tiny one-bedroom flat, which we could afford to rent for six months on the savings we'd left untouched for this eventuality.

For four and a half months, Cris applied for every graphic design job going. After the few that bothered to interview, the follow-up phone call was agonisingly repetitive. 'You interviewed really well and we adored your portfolio work, but without any references, I'm afraid we can't offer you the position.'

Twenty weeks after our move, Cris came back from an evening of delivering pizzas wearing a weary but optimistic smile. 'I've got a job. I start tomorrow.'

At last! I pulled my partner into a relieved hug. 'Which one is it?' I couldn't recall any we were still waiting to hear back from.

'One of the other delivery drivers has put in a good word for me with their boss. It's just packing orders in a warehouse, but it sounds like they can give me loads of hours if I can be flexible.'

'But what about the design jobs?' I protested, stepping away and heading for the computer, still open on the latest jobs hubsite I'd been scouring. 'Look, I'll show you three more that have come up today. If you keep applying, I'm sure you'll land a fantastic job soon. Everyone who's seen it loves your work.'

'No, Georgy, all we can be sure of is that even with the delivery work, we've got another two months, tops, before the money runs out. I need to go to bed, and tomorrow, I'm going to that warehouse.'

That was probably the longest conversation I had with Cris in the seven months between then and the night before we had to leave Manchester. It wasn't that we'd fallen out. We just barely saw each other. Cris would leave the flat whilst I caught up on the sleep I'd missed from feeding Joh and keeping him quiet through the night so that Cris could have an undisturbed night. From the warehouse, Cris would go straight to the pizza takeaway and run deliveries until they closed. Some nights, we would sit for a few minutes in silent, exhausted companionship, sipping mugs of cocoa; more often, I would be feeding or changing Joh when Cris walked through the door and then Joh and I would both get a gentle kiss before Cris collapsed into bed and slept.

Starved of adult company, I eventually plucked up the courage to visit a toddler group, and it was there that Joh and I met Kae and Jorden. From the weary but warm smile that Kae gave me when I walked into the shabby community hall, I got the immediate sense that here was someone who would understand me. It turned out that Kae too was a full-time parent, and like Joh, Jorden apparently preferred a nocturnal existence, catching up on sleep in inconveniently short bursts throughout the day. Kae also had a partner, Samo, who worked all the hours of daylight and beyond in some high-powered city job which also required frequent nights away from home.

I began to wonder whether we had even more in common. Had we stumbled across another two-parent family with a boy, or perhaps a girl? But then, on our third visit to the toddler group, my hopes were quashed as Kae cheerfully changed Jorden's nappy on the floor between our chairs. Even so, over the next few weeks, Kae and I became firm friends. Joh and Jorden seemed to hit it off as well, crawling around after each other across the worn wooden floor of the community hall.

At around the time that both children discovered that walking was more fun than crawling and as the weather took us out of the dingy hall into parks and playgrounds, Kae started inviting me back to their house for lunch after mornings at toddler group. Life at last felt good again as we chatted and sunned ourselves in Kae and Samo's expansive but well-tended back garden with one eye each on our children as they toddled around exploring the boundaries.

It was all going brilliantly until, on our thirteenth afternoon together, I noticed the paddling pool that had appeared in the garden, and by then it was too late. Jorden was already standing naked in the middle of the pool, gleefully stamping one foot in the splashy water. Joh was watching, giggling and rapidly pulling off his clothes.

'Oh my goodness! What's that between Joh's legs?' Kae exclaimed as, to my horror, Joh's naked body waddled across the lawn, his appendage flopping around freely. Launching myself off the garden lounger, I ran towards Joh and scooped him up. As he wriggled in protest, I somehow managed to grab his discarded clothes with a spare hand and retreat into Kae's house.

By the time Kae had retrieved a dripping Jorden from the pool and pulled shut the patio doors, Joh was fully dressed again and strapped securely into his pushchair. 'What's going on, Georgy?' Kae probed with a mix of concern and alarm.

'I'm really sorry, I've got to leave now. It's been great knowing you.' I reversed the pushchair out of the front door.

'Let me give you a lift home?' Kae called after me as I freed the pushchair from its fight with the gate and accelerated down the pavement.

'How could you be so stupid?' Cris screamed at me, kicking off the longest exchange of words we'd had in seven months. I stared, motionless and silent, at the scratches in the kitchen table as Cris vociferated over how hard it had been to keep us in this flat and put food on the table. How long it had taken to build up trust with employers. How their imminent hopes of a better paid, more satisfying job requiring fewer hours was now dashed because I'd got too relaxed with someone and taken my eye off the ball.

'I think you'll find it's two balls I took my eyes off,' I retorted, desperate to lighten the mood. It was too late for humour, though. 'Look, maybe we don't need to move. I think I can trust Kae. We've become friends. I could call them and explain. Jorden and Joh get on so well together. I'm sure Kae won't want to do anything to jeopardise that.'

'But we don't know, do we? And what about the partner? Your friend Kae is bound to blab to them about what they've seen. Can we trust the partner too, and whoever they might be friends with?' Cris had already retrieved one of the cardboard boxes from on top of the kitchen cupboards and was violently throwing in the contents of the same cupboards. I had to admit that I'd never met Samo.

By midday tomorrow, our flat would be empty and we would be on our way to a fresh start in Leeds. At least, that was the 'just in case' plan we'd agreed a few months before.

I LAY AWAKE and alone in bed. Cris was on nights, and today had been Joh's first day at school. He'd been so brave as he'd let go of my hand in the playground and walked towards his smiling teacher, not daring to glance back at me. We had weighed him down with a lot more than the enormous backpack he carried on his tiny shoulders. For weeks, we'd drilled him on the ways in which he was different, how he must never take his clothes off in front of anyone at school, how to get changed discreetly into his PE kit, what to do in the unlikely event of him wetting himself. Too much to pile onto a not quite five-year-old.

His face had broken into a huge grin as he'd spotted me standing apart from the clusters of other parents and childminders this afternoon. But was it a sign that he'd had a good day and couldn't wait to tell me about it, or that he'd had an awful day and was relieved it was over?

He'd not been all that talkative as we walked home, but then by nature, he'd never been a talkative child.

When we got home, I'd allowed him to immerse himself in his familiar toys.

As I watched him eat his tea, I'd been careful not to interrogate him with too many questions about his day.

Yes, he said his teacher was nice. No, nobody had been unkind to him. Yes, he was looking forward to going back tomorrow.

Light seeped in from the hallway as the bedroom door was eased open. Small, bare feet padded across to the bed and a little boy in pyjamas clambered into the bed beside me, wrapped his arm around my middle and burrowed his warm face into my neck.

After a minute or two, I could feel the dampness of tears trickling into the hollow above my chest bone. I carefully untangled myself in order to study his face. 'What's the matter, love?' I asked tenderly.

'Had a bad dream,' he volunteered through soundless sobs.

Tears leaked unbidden out of the corners of my own eyes as Joh recounted the simple but harrowing dream of standing in the doorway of his classroom and discovering that he was naked as other children laughed and pointed.

'Can I stay here with you tomorrow?'

I dearly wanted to say yes, but could I? I pulled him towards me, and without waiting for my answer, he settled into me and drifted off to sleep.

I did persuade him to give school another try the next day, and the day after that. By the time Saturday came around, he was disappointed that school wasn't happening for two days. Joh and I never spoke about the dream again, but I suspect it was a recurring one. I know as a parent, you should encourage your kids to sleep in their own beds, but it became quite a habit, when Cris was on nights, for my little boy to come and snuggle in next to me, and when he woke up with his little heart racing in the middle of the night, he didn't need to tell me why. He'd just bury his face into me and a few tears would wet my neck.

It was Wednesday morning during our first school holiday. The mid-morning sun penetrated the thin bedroom curtains. Joh sprawled diagonally across three-quarters of the bed, snoring softly. I'd been dozing since I'd heard Cris come through the front door a couple of hours earlier. I'd kept on telling myself I ought to move, but at the same time, I knew Cris would be quite content in the kitchen with no competition for our one armchair, cup of strong coffee in hand, radio on, stomach filled with a perfectly cooked breakfast.

It was my phone ringing that finally got me moving. It didn't make sense for my phone to be ringing. Cris was in the kitchen – I could still hear the radio. School was closed for the week. Nobody else had my number.

'Hello?' I mumbled into the phone, my sleepy head still searching for full consciousness.

'Georgy, hi, it's Jay Taylor, from the fertility unit. Can I come and see you? There are some...new developments I need to talk through with you and Cris.'

'How do you have my number?' That was the first question that had fought its way to the surface of my confused brain.

'Don't worry about that. Can I come this Saturday? You're in Leeds, aren't you.'

Chapter 11

THE NETS WERE buried under heaps of other junk in a room that should have had a label on the door reading 'stuff we might find a use for one day but probably won't'. There were ancient plastic crates; antiquated steel bicycle wheels, the rubber tyres all cracked and perished; a wheelbarrow without a wheel; an old electric sewing machine that had been scavenged to the bone for parts that might prove useful on the hand-operated machines that several of the islanders had become experts in using and maintaining. Joe even found an old computer keyboard but no CPU or monitor to go with it, and even if there were, there was no electricity with which to power a computer.

'Nats, stop!' Joe had to shout as he heard the inevitable ripping sound.

'Oops, sorry,' Nats said, dropping a fistful of net and toppling herself off the rusty old garden chair she'd been kneeling on to reach the nets.

On his own, Joe would have probably spent all day reorganising, cataloguing and stacking all the items into appropriate neat piles. With Nats' help, this wasn't feasible. As a result, less than an hour later, Joe stood in the corner furthest from the door, almost submerged in heavy bundles of net, surveying the precarious pile of artefacts that surrounded him.

'If you pass them to me here,' suggested Nats confidently, standing and wobbling back and forth on a rickety stool, 'then you can shift over there near the door and I'll throw them across.'

'I don't think throwing them anywhere will be very productive,' Joe said, brooding over more sensible alternatives. It took a while to coax Nats into clearing a wide enough pathway along which he could tread, careful not to snag on anything as he went. It was a relief to drop the heavy nets onto the clear floor just over the threshold. Who knew that a load of holes tied up with rope could be so heavy?

'Your nets are full of holes, and I'm not talking about the ones they're supposed to have!' Nats mocked as they spread the nets out on the beach. She pulled the edges this way and that to accentuate the numerous large sections where the fibres had frayed and disintegrated. 'Even my chickens could escape through these holes! They'll never hold any fish.'

'Well, they might have been in better shape if someone hadn't tried to tug them out from under several tonnes of junk!'

Nats harrumphed and trudged off back across the pebbles to the road. 'Got my own jobs to do now,' she hollered over her shoulder.

JOE SAT BACK to admire his handiwork, squinting into the failing light, the sun no longer visible behind the hill. That was why his eyes were aching and why the last few weights had taken so long to thread. He would have to inspect the finished net more closely in the morning. It would be somewhat smaller and less perfectly round than the original, but it followed the same broad design, and all his knots and the strands of nylon between them were sound.

He'd started with three nets, chosen the one that appeared most intact, and carefully folded the second best to save as a spare. The third, he'd butchered to make grafts for patching the first, later also relieving it of half its weights. The weights on his reconstruction weren't perfectly spaced, but to do that, he'd have had to start by removing all the ones that were already tied in. He wasn't that much of a perfectionist.

Joe got stiffly to his feet and made sure everything was folded and anchored under large pebbles. His stomach grumbled at him. He'd not even thought about what he might eat tonight, or how to cook it. So far, food had just appeared in front of him, but today was the day to start fending for himself. Clambering off the beach, he made his way towards the food store, exhausted but satisfied and with a new sense of self-confidence.

Joe had learnt that morning that he shared the cottage he'd been sleeping in with Anthony. He'd already got the impression, though, that Anthony didn't spend much time at home and wasn't one for idle chit-chat or housemate bonding.

When he got back from the food store, he was relieved to find the front door standing ajar as he juggled the carrots, mushrooms, and three eggs that he'd picked out, along with the potatoes and an onion that he'd stuffed into his pockets. He must remember to take a box or a bag to put stuff in next time. Joe pushed his way through the door. He didn't call out any greeting, unsure how the relationship between him and Anthony was supposed to be, or even whether he wanted to be friends with Anthony.

'You took your time!' exclaimed the intruder's cheery voice out of the darkness, from the corner where Joe knew an old armchair resided. Nats' face glowed out of the gloom as she lit the stub of a candle. 'Hmm, that's an interesting selection. I suppose it would make an omelette of sorts.' Nats began to relieve Joe of his armful of provisions. 'Shall I make it for you? I'm very good at omelettes.'

Deducing that 'no' would be the wrong answer, Joe stood by as Nats threw pans around and chopped, beat, and flipped the various ingredients into submission, all the while nattering at random about all the things she'd done since leaving him on the beach. At one point, she disappeared outside, leaving Joe worried that whatever was on the stove might burn to cinders in her absence, but she returned after a couple of minutes with a sprig of something green and leafy, which she shredded and tossed into the pan with the flourish of a TV chef demonstrating their art.

Soon, Nats' creation was divided between two mismatched plates. 'I made a bit much for one person to eat on their own. You don't mind, do you?' she declared as she slid the plates onto the table and sat beside him.

Joe stared at the more-than-generous helping she'd allocated to herself. Without speaking, he swapped the plates, Nats' cutlery already hovering for the kill, and started digging in.

'All right,' she conceded. 'I suppose you have been working hard.'

It wasn't a bad omelette, albeit made with a slightly odd combination of ingredients, and it was good to share food and company with a friend. Nats abandoned her knife and fork on her empty plate and broke the silence. 'Come on then, Joe, spill the beans on what happened between you and Vicki.'

Joe almost choked on his penultimate mouthful, gulped it past the growing lump in his throat, and resolved to give himself time to formulate his reply whilst scraping together his final forkful and chewing the last morsels.

'I woke up to find her in my bed, with her hand in my shorts.'

The look of horror on Nats' face lifted the weight off Joe's chest, which had been pressing down on him even as he'd relished the challenge of repairing the nets.

'So she shouldn't have done that, should she?'

'No, she bleedin' shouldn't have!' Nats replied with a snap but then paused, mouth open in thought. 'Although, I suppose this is all sort of new for us – you know, having another boy around. Our choice has been a bit limited. Anyway, what did you do?'

Was Nats now changing her mind – thinking it was natural to expect the island's girls to want to come and fiddle with his private parts while he slept? Remnants of his omelette crept back up his throat. He swallowed, sipped his water, but they clung on.

'You didn't let her do it did you?'

'Do what?'

'Mate with you.'

Joe felt his face flushing red, right down to his neck. Could Nats see that too, in the candlelight? He was glad not to be having this conversation in daylight. Did human males and females mate in the same way mammals did? Joe wished he'd asked Georgy more questions about how different animals reproduced. The textbooks they'd studied only ever covered the mechanics of it in the briefest of details, as if it wasn't right for humans to concern themselves with such primitive things. Livestock farmers must need to know more about how it works, but...

'You do know what mating is, don't you?' Nats interrupted his thoughts. 'You know, like how sheep make lambs or cows make calves, without needing a fertility unit? Well, it works the same with us too.'

Joe no longer felt like talking about the intimate details of what Victoria had done to him and whether or not it amounted to mating. He was pretty certain they'd not got anywhere near mating, but did that make it less wrong?

'No. As soon as I woke up, I shouted at her to get out of my bed, and she ran away.' He decided to leave out the bits about her lying there naked, pleading with him to come back onto the bed.

'Well, you did right, and I shouldn't think Vicki will try again after that. But maybe you should tell Sandra what happened, just in case she does or in case anyone else does.'

Joe didn't feel up to the interrogation Sandra might put him through. No girl had tried to visit him in his bed last night, so maybe none of the others were desperate to mate with him. Maybe neuts were more civilised than these people on the island who called themselves natural humans. Georgy had explained how they and Cris had been a couple for years before deciding to have a baby together, and that although people could have babies on their own, it was very special when two people decided to do it together, each giving a part of themselves to make the new baby. That reminded Joe of something Tom had said yesterday.

'Tom told me he had a friend once. A special one, I mean.'

'You've been talking to Tom?'

'Yes.' Joe waited, hoping Nats would tell him more, but she seemed to be lost in thought. 'So,' he prompted, 'who was Tom's friend and what happened?'

'Oh, yes, sorry, it was Sandra.' Nats' attention was brought back to the moment. 'She and Tom were best buddies, really close. They made a brilliant team too. We all looked on them as like parents. They always had the answer for what to do in any situation.'

'What about Anthony? I thought he was the leader,' Joe said. 'Alongside Sandra, of course.' At that moment, they heard the front door, and a few seconds later, Anthony himself poked his head around the kitchen door. Joe and Nats sat in guilty silence, like he'd caught them deviously plotting, but no suspicion showed up on his face. He just nodded to them both and disappeared as quickly as he'd appeared.

Nats continued their conversation in a whisper, though it was hardly necessary. They'd both heard his bedroom door shut. 'Anthony might be one of our leaders now, but back then, he only thought he should be. He's not as old as Tom and Sandra, and when they were in charge, he was just an annoying kid.'

Nats unfolded the story. When they'd got everything running smoothly on the island, Tom and Sandra had decided to have a baby together. Nobody knew that they'd been trying, until about five months into the pregnancy. Then they called a meeting and Sandra stood in front of them and showed them how she wasn't just getting fat, except she was, but it was because there was a baby inside her. There had been a baby once before, but it hadn't lived, and Nats wasn't going to go into all that at the moment. Perhaps another time, although she didn't like thinking about that story.

Shortly after the announcement, someone had asked Tom for his opinion about when to start harvesting the oats, and he'd snapped back at them and told them they'd best ask Sandra. Sandra, meanwhile, had told them they ought to be able to work things like that out for themselves and not rely on her and Tom to make the decisions all the time.

Before the end of that day, Tom had walked out of the village carrying a huge backpack. That was when he'd moved to his hovel, and ever since, he'd rarely been seen in the village. He'd not even shown up when baby Katie was born, though Nats had caught him watching his daughter at times when she looked after the children. Sometimes she even took them over to the shell beach especially so Tom could see Katie.

'Does anyone know what caused them to split up?' Joe interrupted when Nats briefly paused for a breath.

'Well, that's the thing.' Nats put on her fount-of-all-knowledge voice. 'They never were an item. Well, not according to Sandra. Tom loved Sandra and wanted them to be, but Sandra just wanted them to carry on being best friends. They probably shouldn't have even thought of having a baby together, but Sandra was desperate to see if it was possible to have a baby successfully, and Tom was the only boy she was willing to have as the father. She certainly wouldn't have asked Anthony! Thing is, Sandra's not into boys at all. It's her and Eva that are an item.'

Joe sat dumbfounded at all this new information. What Sandra had done sounded wrong and a long way from the careful decisions that neut couples made to have babies. Should he say so to Nats? But Nats was ready to move on to a new topic. 'So what's in this diary that Anthony gave you? Have you read any of it yet?'

Chapter 12

31/03/2031

Consent from five couples, giving total of 15 embryos for trials. Ideal would be at least double that. One embryo from each donor couple (A to E) dosed with the virus, one embryo at a time.

Samples A & B:	Virus particles behave like sperm around an ovum. Each virus particle attacking its nearest embryo cell. First penetration to cell nucleus achieved in under five minutes. When penetrating particle reaches cell nucleus, other nearby particles cluster around penetrated cell, further breaking it down.
Sample C:	Penetration of one cell did not attract other virus particles. Each virus particle continued to operate independently, bombarding its own cell. Thus, each cell took longer to break down, but more cells broken down in parallel with each other. Closer inspection of cell nuclei from an uninfected cell revealed that this was a 46XY (male) embryo.

Looked back at samples A & B to check allosome pairing.

Sample A: All cell nuclei destroyed. No identifiable allosomes.

Sample B: Some healthy cells remained. Confirmed as 46XX (female).

> Note – must check and record allosome pairing of each embryo before introducing virus.

Sample D: 46XY. Like sample C, virus particles ignored the actions of their neighbours and dissolved the embryo gradually from the outside in.

Sample E: 46XX. Like samples A and B. Also observed that the virus was more active in sample E than in sample D, initial penetration taking place more quickly.

Concluding hypothesis

Virus attack differs depending on sex of embryo (although four is statistically too small a sample size to be confident of this).

01/04/2031

New hypothesis: all or most females in Britain are now probably infertile (wish this was an April fool but it's not).

Test 1: Thawed and tested all ten remaining embryo samples from couples A–E. Four 46XY and six 46XX.

Findings:

Samples appear to confirm hypothesis that the virus operates differently depending on the sex of the embryo. 46XX embryos are broken down using a burrowing technique where successful frontline virus particles are supported by neighbouring particles to break down a few key cells at a time. In 46XY embryos, the virus particles show no evidence of cooperation except that between them they successfully break down all cells around the outer perimeter of the embryo and then move into the next layer.

Cell penetration appears to take longer in the male embryo cells. Mean penetration time for the six 46XX: 308 seconds. Mean penetration time for the four 46XY: 532 seconds.

Closer observation of the allosome pairs may hint at reason for these differences. When a virus particle reaches the cell nucleus, X chromosomes emit a cloudy ejaculate. Y chromosomes show no such emission. Thus in 46XX cells, these emissions are twice as vigorous as in a 46XY cells. Some sort of a pheromone to the virus? Concentration of this pheromone may only be high enough to attract other virus particles when there are two emitting chromosomes, i.e. two X chromosomes.

Test 2: Investigated X and Y chromosomes in isolation by observing any effect of virus on gametes.

Findings:

1. **Tests on female gametes**

   Used frozen ova from couple D. (Consent obtained covered all genetic material, not just fertilised embryos.) Thawed one batch of two ova and dosed both with virus.

   In both samples, within 240 seconds of introducing virus, the single cell gamete had been penetrated. The one X chromosome then started pumping out the 'pheromone'. Gamete utterly destroyed within further 180 seconds.

2. **Test on male gametes**

   No consented frozen sperm currently in lab. Solution: used own sample.

   No need to add virus. Sample already swarming with virus particles amongst the remains of massacred sperm cell. (Had almost forgotten I was already a carrier.) After initial shock, realised that not all sperm had been destroyed. Many appeared scarred but still actively swimming around, behaving like normal healthy sperm. Zoomed in on small cluster of sperm, slowing as sample cooled. All observed surviving gametes were Y chromosome cells. In 45 minutes of searching, failed to find one sperm with an X chromosome.

Concluding hypotheses

Based on very limited samples, ANFV positive females are likely to be infertile – all ova destroyed by virus. ANFV positive males at least partially infertile – unable to father female offspring. Unidentified but non-lethal effect also observed on Y chromosome sperm.

Based on official estimates on the spread of the infection, this makes us an infertile island and makes it all the more important that this virus is contained within our shores.

Next steps

Have put in request for more frozen embryo and ovum samples from a wider cohort and as many batches of frozen sperm as can be released from donations made before the virus attack.

Subject to availability of test samples, plans are as follows:

a) Observe virus activity when introduced to batches of uninfected sperm.
b) Repeat tests performed on ova using samples from wider cohort.
c) Attempt to fertilise healthy ovum with active but ANFV-positive Y chromosome sperm.

02/04/2031

No further tests to report on today, as I was called to attend meeting in London. The following goals have been established:

1. find a way to eradicate the virus;
2. develop a retroviral treatment for those infected with the virus;
3. produce viable, virus-resistant embryos.

The purpose of objectives 1 and 2 is to get us out of quarantine with the rest of the world. If, as we suspect, the virus has already rendered almost all our female population infertile, these objectives do little to help those already infected. It's early days, but the virus appears to cause no adverse symptoms in postnatal humans, unless they happen to be in the early stages of pregnancy (an increasingly unlikely situation).

Objective 3 (which I've been asked to work on, together with geneticists Prof Frances O'Leary and Dr David Carmichael) is probably the only hope for the future fertility of the millions already infected. Even if we can achieve it, it will mean no natural conceptions for a generation. All British children will have to be conceived via IVF, probably using some sort of genetically engineered ova.

For the moment, my hypotheses have been classed as official secrets.

Glued in opposite is a copy of the official press release.

As our meeting ended, news came through that cases of the virus have now been confirmed in Ireland, both north and south of the border. The Prime Minister and her retinue left to call the Irish Prime Minister and Northern Irish First Minister.

Can we contain this?

DEPARTMENT OF HEALTH & SOCIAL CARE

PRESS RELEASE: 2ND APRIL 2031

On 25th March 2031, a terrorist group calling themselves the Alliance for Natural Families (ANF), having infiltrated contract companies responsible for maintaining IVF incubation systems, introduced an unknown virus into the nutrient feed systems at 43 IVF clinics across Britain. The virus has led to the destruction of thousands of developing embryos at IVF laboratories and miscarriages for women who had infected embryos implanted and also some women in the early stages of pregnancy who conceived naturally but subsequently came into contact with the virus.

The contractors and IVF clinics are cooperating fully with the National Crime Agency in identifying and apprehending those responsible for this biological attack.

The government has reconstituted SAGE (the Scientific Advisory Group for Emergencies) to include top researchers and practitioners in the fields of embryology, virology, and genetics. Good progress is already being made in identifying the virus and its effect on humans and human embryos.

Initial research suggests that the virus poses no immediate threat to the health of adults, children, babies, or foetuses beyond three months gestation.

Until more is understood, the following controls and advice remain in place:

- An international travel ban remains in force until the virus can be controlled.
- British citizens and residents abroad will not be repatriated until the travel ban is lifted. They should not seek to return home but should remain in whichever country they are currently staying and seek further advice and help from the British embassy in that country.
- Women in Britain should not attempt to conceive and should either abstain from sexual intercourse or use medically approved contraceptive methods.
- All IVF treatment programs have been suspended for an initial period of three months. Patients enrolled in IVF programs will be contacted within the next 14 days to discuss their cases. Please do not try to contact your IVF clinic.
- Women who experience excessive or unexpected vaginal bleeding should call 111.
- Anyone who suspects they have the virus should call 111 and not visit either their doctor or hospital.
- There is no need to stockpile food or medicines. People should continue to go about their normal day-to-day business. Parents should continue to send their children to school and there is no need to avoid public spaces and gatherings or observe any form of social distancing.

Chapter 13

OVER THE NEXT few weeks, Joe and Nats fell into the routine of sharing all their meals. Who did Nats do things with before? Joe never raised this with her because he liked things as they were. Nats did most of the cooking because, according to her, she was the better cook. On the occasions when Joe cooked, he apparently used weird combinations of ingredients or one element was overcooked or undercooked or, mysteriously, both at the same time. There was that rather good cheesy potato bake he'd made with layered slices of potato and onion, all topped with the wet clumpy stuff that passed for cheese here. After Nats had taken her first few mouthfuls, she'd pronounced that it wasn't bad, but the onions were a bit raw still and it was a waste of a good bit of cheese that had cost him a whole one top. Even so, she managed to polish off her plateful and help herself to seconds.

Anthony kept his distance whenever Nats was around, grabbing a few things from the chill cupboard and taking them back to his room. Did Anthony begrudge sharing his house with someone else? He was friendly enough when it was just the two of them and was always asking questions.

'Where did you live before coming here?'

'Did you live with both your parents or just one of them?'

'When did you find out about the island?'

'How did you find out about the island?'

Was it your decision to come here or did your parents send you?'

Joe wondered who actually knew him better – Anthony or Nats. Nats was more of a friend, but he'd barely told her one tenth of what Anthony knew about him.

'How are you getting on with the diary?' was Anthony's other repeated question.

Was Joe missing something? So far, he'd not spotted the glorious message of hope that seemed to have so stirred Anthony's imagination.

'Wouldn't it be awesome to discover that there was a whole world of men and women, people like us, out there somewhere, living their lives, going out to work, loving and mating openly, without having to hide who they are? Not being stuck with a load of immature and bossy girls on a poxy little island.'

Joe was growing to like this *poxy little island*, now that he no longer feared visitations from strange girls in the night, and he'd become quite attached to the bossy girl who'd attached herself to him. It was hard to imagine a whole world of people like them. Would he feel any more normal or welcomed in that world than in the world of the neuts he'd left behind? How would they find or make contact with this other world filled with men and women living normal lives? Joe wasn't convinced Anthony had the first clue even which direction they'd need to travel to get there from here.

Nobody else had volunteered to be on Anthony's expedition planning group. For that matter, Joe couldn't recall having volunteered himself. Had he inadvertently led Anthony to believe he had a disciple for his mission?

How could they be sure that the virus hadn't spread all around the world? And if it hadn't, would they be accepted and welcomed in the virus-free world? What if the virus had survived in the bodies of successive generations of neuts undetected and without harming them?

'If that was the case, how were we born?' was Anthony's confident rhetorical question when Joe asked him, and he had a point. The logbook seemed clear that the virus destroyed all male and female babies before had a chance to grow inside their mothers, so surely, the same would have been the case in the pregnancy pods. Even if it hadn't, would they have been able to have male and female babies here on the island if they had the virus?

None of that stopped Joe from worrying about it. Didn't the author of the diary write about being a 'carrier' of the virus, which seemed to mean that it didn't hurt him but could still harm others if he passed it on to them? What if they were still carriers, somehow? They were OK, keeping themselves to themselves here on the island, weren't they?

Chapter 14

'WON'T CATCH FISHIES on the beach!' Katie and Peter giggled, dancing around Joe with the taunt that Nats had evidently rehearsed with them. That did it. He'd had enough. Keeping his face firmly turned away from Nats and avoiding tripping over the kids whilst not looking at them, Joe bundled up his net and stomped away across the pebbles in search of a more secluded place to practise. It had been foolish to think he could perfect his casting technique with spectators around.

He'd worked out the theory of what to do pretty quickly. The round net needed to be thrown out to land as flat as possible on the surface of the water. The weights would then pull the edges of the net down to the sea floor, making the net into a dome-shaped cage for all those fish teeming underneath it. All Joe then had to do was use the rope, which he'd tied to his wrist, to pull the net back in towards the boat with the fish tangled up inside it. That was the theory.

But how did you actually get the net to land flat on the water? Throwing it from a safe sitting position in the boat was hopeless. It became clear on the first day that, before anything else, he needed to teach himself how to stand in the boat without falling in. Nats and the kids howled with laughter from the beach as he stood in the boat, feet apart to stabilise himself, throwing his imaginary net out from either side of the boat. They laughed even harder when after one vigorous throw, the boat rocked so much that it cast him overboard, arms and legs flailing as he went.

'Won't catch fishies on beach!'

Having mastered the art of standing and pretend casting in the boat, he needed to work out how to cast the net without worrying about being out on the water. That was why he'd been practising on the beach.

'Won't catch fishies on beach!'

The taunt still echoed around his head as, after two full days of spectator-free practice in a flat grassy field, he decided that tomorrow was the day to get back out onto the water.

Getting up early, he made himself a sandwich, dolloping into it the rest of that good bit of cheese he'd bought, wrapped it in some cloth, and bundled that and a couple of apples into the old leather bag he'd claimed from the junk store.

There was nobody else about, but wary of attracting an audience later, Joe rowed the boat to a quiet cove surrounded by cliffs. The air held a gentle breeze and the water was calm and clear. He fastened the end of the rope around his left wrist and bundled the rest of it into loose hoops, ready to unravel as the net was cast. Methodically gathering up the net itself, Joe slowly stood up, knees bent a little, feet planted either side of the boat's centre line. Rocking under control, he crouched slightly, at the same time twisting his body around to the left. Deep breath in, and swing...

Yes!

The net landed perfectly flat on the surface of the rippling water.

Breath stuttering with excitement, Joe counted to twenty as the weights sank out of sight, then added another ten for good measure, drawing in a lungful of nostril-tingling sea air as he did so.

Readjusting his feet, he gave the rope an experimental tug and then, feeling steady enough to keep going, started to haul it in, dropping coils of wet rope between his feet as he went. There was a promising sense of resistance, surely, a school of plump fish straining against their inevitable fate.

No such luck. Slimy water trickled down his calves as he untangled two large pebbles and multiple vacant seashells from the waterlogged, lifeless net. It was frustrating and time-consuming to unpick all the seaweed and depressing when the cleaned net still felt three times its previous weight. The sun mocked from the heights of the sky as the tide drove him into the kelp-littered shallows. The past few days of practice on dry land with a clean, dry net had all been for nothing.

On each of the next fourteen attempts, the net flopped into the water like a crumpled handkerchief before his weary arms hauled it back in as fast as they could manage, willing it not to entrap anymore seaweed. For his sixteenth throw, his complaining muscles somehow managed to pull off an almost satisfactory landing. The nineteenth was finally good enough to allow the weights to sink all the way to the seafloor.

The rope offered little resistance as he spooled it in, and sure enough, having lifted the last bit of net out of the water, all he could see was a small bundle of greeny-brown slime. At least it wouldn't take so long to clean this time.

One more attempt and he'd have to take a break. The tide was drawing him further from the island, and he had to reserve some strength for the row back to shore. He hoisted the sodden coils of rope over his aching left shoulder and reached across to liberate the ball of slime. The slime wriggled. His hands hovered, shaking with weary strain, inches from the now animated slime. He sucked in a quick breath and lunged at the writhing bundle of seaweed. His feet slipped underneath him. Elbows and knees scrabbled across lumpy nylon knots. The floor rocked. He tightened his grip on his trophy and pushed himself up off his elbows. The slippery contents of his hand spasmed. He squeezed harder and cursed as the silvery streak of life ejected itself and plopped into the sea like a bar of soap in the bath.

Joe rolled onto his back and wiped his free hand down his leg before attending to the muck that the escapee had flicked into his eye. He lay there squinting at the bright, clear sky. A shadow darted across the sun, which now tickled the cliffs. Joe blinked and was just in time to catch a human silhouette ducking out of sight. *Oh, great!* Someone had been watching his humiliating efforts and was probably even now rolling around with laughter on the grassy clifftops.

His tummy rumbled and he coughed past his salt-dried throat. If people wanted to watch, they could watch him eat his lunch on the beach. Maybe after that, he'd give it another go.

'URGHH, STINKS IN here!' was the first thing Nats had to say as she walked into the kitchen that evening whilst Joe proudly fried a small fish on the stove, its skin turning from silver to brown. She glanced at the tiny morsel in the pan and lifted the lid to inspect a simmering pan of potatoes beside it. 'I'd say you need four or five of those little things to go with the number of potatoes you've done there. Where have you put the rest of your catch? I'll fetch a few more.'

'This *is* my catch,' Joe muttered, his pride draining away.

'Oh, well, at least you caught something,' Nats said sympathetically, having detected the disappointment in Joe's voice. 'How about we fry a couple of my eggs to go with it instead then?'

OVER THE TEN days that followed, Joe succeeded in netting a total of eight fish in a range of sizes but all of them small, two crabs, and what must have amounted to at least a tonne of seaweed. He suggested they might try cooking some of the seaweed, but Nats wrinkled her nose and said they'd tried that when they first arrived on the island, and it tasted rank. They did try to salvage something edible from the crabs, but it was fiddly and wasn't worth the effort for the tiny, shell-free fragments that ended up in their soup.

'I could have caught more in a day fishing with a kiddie's net off the jetty,' teased both Nats and Anthony on separate occasions.

'But I've not actually had that much time out on the water yet,' Joe protested. A lot of the time, the sea had been too rough. He'd tried a few times to stand up in the boat and prepare his net whilst the boat bounced up and down on the waves, and on one occasion, he'd even managed to successfully cast the net out onto the churning water, but the energy it took soon led him to conclude that he was better off waiting for the calmer moments. Some days, he spent almost the whole day crouching on the gusty beach checking the integrity of the net, urging the wind to die down.

He'd also had to take his turn on the watch, and although Sandra had suggested he might do this from the boat, he determined that, at least at first, he'd post himself at the normal designated watch station on a high clifftop facing the mainland. He didn't want other people thinking he wasn't doing his duty properly.

The purpose of the watch was to look out for any boats coming near to the island so that they could be prepared for any visitors, welcome or otherwise. Nats told of several occasions when a boatful of adventurous neuts had landed on the island and started to explore or simply set up a picnic on the beach. A few spooky-sounding howls soon sent the visitors hurrying back to their boat, gathering up their picnic paraphernalia as they went. There had been fewer of these sorts of visits as time went on, and they didn't think anyone had visited more than once, thanks to the scare tactics.

More importantly, they were watching for the arrival of any new residents. Nats had been on watch the night Joe arrived, which was why it had been her face peering down at him as he was washed ashore.

Joe was still the latest arrival and was only the third new arrival since last winter. Nobody had ever arrived in the winter months, although the watch was maintained throughout the year and whatever the weather. The watcher was always issued with a flask of hot soup from Victoria's café, a poncho made from a thick, woollen blanket, and an ancient heavy pair of binoculars, which Anthony claimed credit for finding when they first scoured the island's deserted cottages for anything of practical value. That was also when the junk room had started to evolve.

So, with the reducing numbers of unwelcome visitors and rarity of any new residents arriving, the six hours that each islander had to spend on watch were not really the highlight of anyone's week. Although there were occasions when the sun was shining and there was a pleasant breeze, everyone concurred that most of the time, the watch station was the wildest, wettest, and at night, darkest spot on the island.

When he was out on the water attempting to fish, particularly when he was out at twilight, Joe was aware that he had a watcher – not from the watch station clifftop but from the cliffs around his fishing cove. Despite his lack of success in this quiet sheltered spot, he'd returned there each day, sure that with its clear water at what he judged to be the right depth, it was the ideal place to be casting his net. On the few occasions when he caught a glimpse of his watcher, whoever it was ducked out of sight before he could identify them.

Joe had been going to the cove for two weeks. The water today was crystal clear, and the boat only rocked when Joe repositioned himself. He got to his feet like an expert, and after a few seconds, the water was free of ripples and he could see the bottom. As he bent down to start coiling the rope tied to his wrist, he cast a long shadow across the water. Strange, his shadow was lengthening. Then it morphed and part of it broke away. That wasn't shadow; that was a shoal of fish, darting away into deeper water.

Dropping back onto his bottom, Joe grabbed the oars and propelled the boat as calmly as possible out in pursuit. Every three or four rows, he stopped and waited for the water to settle before staring through it, searching for movement below the surface. On the second occasion, there they were again – the murmuration of hundreds of fish swimming as one. Brushing the water with the oars, he eased the boat on towards the shifting underwater cloud, letting himself drift as soon as he thought he was within a net's reach of his target.

Keeping low in the boat, ready to pounce, he coiled the rope and gathered up the net in his hands. He eased himself to his feet, not daring to breathe. As soon as he was up, he twisted and flung the net out over his prey. *Now wait; patience; count to twenty, slower; best make it thirty.*

He gave the rope a tug. No resistance. He'd failed once again. Resigned to hauling in another empty net, he fed the rope quickly through his hands. But then there it was, a definite tug against him. He watched, open-mouthed, as the rope slipped back through his hands. It burned as he forced on the brakes, clamping his hands again around the rope. He strained and started again to heave.

Surely, a tug of war against both Tom and Anthony would be easier than this! Every arm-length of rope pulled in was soon conceded back to his underwater opponents. If he didn't up his game, the contest would be lost. He braced himself and reached out his free hand as far as he dared and a little bit further. Giving an almighty heave, he dragged the other team up towards the boat, but there was no time to reposition his feet before the opposition regrouped and heaved back. He wobbled. The boat wobbled more, resigned from the team, and tossed him into the water.

The rope knotted around his wrist kept on tugging. Thrashing wildly, he got his head out into the air but could only splutter before being towed back under. Now the rope had his legs too, and kicking only made the lasso tighter. Waving his arms and kicking his feet together in what felt like the world's worst attempt at butterfly stroke, he pushed his head back out of the water once more, lungs burning. *Shout something, quick. No time to shout. Only time to choke. Too late. Sinking.*

Chapter 15

A HAND REACHED THROUGH the water and grabbed his wrist. In panic, he pulled away and kicked out, his feet making jarring contact with another body. He opened his eyes in time to see the cold, silver-blue glint of a blade coming towards him. At the same time, there was a renewed tug on the rope tied to his wrist. Thrashing with his feet to fend off his attacker, he fumbled with the numb fingers of his right hand at the knot that was pulling ever tighter against his left wrist.

There was another sudden jerk on the rope, this time from a force much closer than the writhing mass of net several metres below. The hand that had been on his wrist now clamped around the rope, inches way, and in another hand, the blade was again reaching towards him. He twisted away and the blade just missed him, catching the rope instead. With all his remaining strength, he wrenched his wrist away from the hacking knife and punched himself in the face as the final thread snapped.

The last remnants of the rope slithered off his legs as he gave a kick and emerged, gasping, into the air. Stinging salty water mingled with the tang of blood trickling from his throbbing nose. As the oxygen flooded through the myriad channels in his lungs and he felt the sudden lightness and freedom of his limbs, a new energy gave him the strength he needed to tread water and scan for his boat, which bobbed up and down nonchalantly a few feet away.

An arm wrapped around him from behind. He wriggled and thrashed, but the clamping grip around his chest only got tighter. The fight gone out of him, he allowed himself to be dragged backwards through the water and rolled unceremoniously into the hard bottom of the boat.

He lay there, shivering and exhausted, unable to even contemplate moving. Suddenly, the boat rolled, and he rolled with it. Joe reached out blindly for the sides, for something firm to hold on to, desperate not to be tipped back out into the sea. Another body rolled in over him, almost capsizing the boat. Joe scrambled backwards into the bow, all the time holding tight to the sides and trying to steady the rocking boat.

Cain propped himself up onto his elbows and frowned directly at Joe. 'You didn't make that easy, did you? But you'd have drowned if I hadn't saved you.'

Joe stared down at the severed end of the rope that was stilled knotted around his wrist and then looked back at Cain, his rescuer.

Cain held up the already frayed end that had been attached to the bit left on Joe's wrist. 'I rescued your net as well, what's left of it. Got snagged on a few rocks, I'm afraid.' With that, he started pulling on the rope, winding the slack around his forearm as he went, until the bedraggled and shredded remains of half a net emerged from the water, dripping and adorned with strands of slimy seaweed.

Seeing the pitiful remains of his net was the last straw for Joe's fragile emotions. All he could do was curl up like a baby in the bottom of the boat and sob. Unspeaking, Cain took hold of the oars and rowed them around the edge of the cove and back to the beach.

Chapter 16

JAY TAYLOR WAS quite different from the memory I'd constructed from our brief meeting five and a half years ago. Taller and thinner. An angular face with a sharply defined jawbone and worried eyes rather than soft, friendly, and optimistic. As far as I could remember, the face hadn't worn the glasses that the eyes now seemed to find their security behind.

From the way Jay looked at Cris and me, and the concerned questions about how we were doing, I wondered whether we also looked like we'd aged ten years in half that time.

'So, on the phone, you told Georgy there's been some sort of worrying development,' prompted Cris, keen to move the conversation on from the small talk.

'Oh, it's nothing to worry about really,' said Jay. 'Just some, how shall I say this, interesting changes with some of our older children, which we weren't one hundred per cent prepared for. Well, not prepared for at all, if I'm honest.' With this last statement, Jay smiled at us nervously.

What was happening to the girls sounded most worrying. They had started to change shape. Most noticeably, their nipples had got bigger and their chests had started to swell. Some had also developed hips that were wider than their waists so that normal trousers no longer fitted them – either too tight around the hips or too baggy around the waist or both at the same time.

The most alarming thing with the girls, though, was the bleeding. Over the past twelve months, one frightened parent after another had turned up at the fertility unit lookihg for Jay, all with similar stories. It started with complaints of stomach pains for a day or two, and then to everyone's horror, blood would be discovered in their daughter's underwear. This was the point at which they'd come in search of Jay, panicking for their daughter's life but unable to take her to see a doctor or go to a hospital.

'Fortunately, I've been able to allay their fears. I didn't mention this before, but I've got a sister,' Jay explained. 'See, a few years after my parent had me, we moved in with my step-parent. It wasn't long before they decided to have a baby together, and my little sister, Alex, was born. This was before the fertility units got good at spotting female foetuses early enough for termination, so it wasn't picked up until she was born. They had a sympathetic doctor who didn't push for Alex to have corrective surgery, and they let my parents keep her and didn't log anything about it on her medical records. That doctor was one of the founders of DiG, and it's thanks to them, and the experience of growing up with Alex, that got me into the job I do now.'

So Jay had seen their own sister go through the changes and experience the bleeding for the first time. Apart from the stomach cramps, Alex had suffered no ill effects, and after a couple of worrying days at home in bed, the bleeding had petered out and stopped and she was right as rain. But then, about a month later, it all happened again and the bleeding seemed to be heavier than before. They'd consulted with other medically trained members of DiG, including the doctor who had been there at Alex's birthing, but none could shed light on what was happening.

Whilst in all other ways, Alex seemed perfectly well, they were reluctant to put her through any invasive and potentially risky examinations in an area of the anatomy with which they were totally unfamiliar. Again, the bleeding reduced and then stopped after a few days. Ever since then, at an increasingly regular interval of approximately one month, the bleeding happened. The closest they'd got to an explanation was from the partner of one of the other nurses, who was a vet. They explained how if female dogs were left unneutered, they would bleed for a few days when they were in their fertile period, which was like a signal to the male dogs that they were ready to mate. But in dogs, this only happened every six months or so, and the bleeding was much lighter.

Alex was lucky that she'd been at home on the first few occasions her bleeding had started, and as she started to recognise the pattern, she always made sure she was prepared. One of the other girls had not been so fortunate. Her first bleed had started very publicly at school. The school had rushed her to hospital, and it was only thanks to the casualties of a major accident being brought in at the same time that her parents were able to whisk her away before she was seen. That night, they escaped to another town.

Cris and I glanced at each other, in those brief moments reliving the trauma of our own hasty relocations. I felt cautiously thankful that Joh was a boy and not a girl. All the worrying changes that Jay had so far explained happened to the girls. But perhaps they had less experience with boys. What was waiting around the corner to freak us out and give us more parental stress?

'And what about the boys?' I ventured.

'Yes, well, there aren't so many boys, and we've not heard yet about anything quite so alarming as the bleeding for them.' I breathed a wary sigh of relief, aware that there was a 'but' coming in Jay's commentary. 'But one or two do seem to be growing unnaturally tall and getting quite hairy. Their feet might also cause a problem.'

'What's the problem with their feet?' Cris interjected.

'Oh, only that Tommie's parents are struggling to find shoes that will fit him. The poor boy's feet are totally out of proportion to the rest of his body. He's not even grown that tall yet, but if his feet carry on growing at the same pace as the rest of him, he'll end up looking like he's walking around in diver's flippers.' Jay laughed at this admittedly comical image.

I wasn't sure I liked the more light-hearted direction the conversation seemed to be going in. This was Joh we were talking about here, and Jay hadn't set my mind at rest and hadn't yet explained everything.

I brought the conversation back on track. 'You said the boys were getting quite hairy. What do you mean?'

'Ah, yes, well, both boys and girls are starting to grow hair around their secret areas, which is a bit disconcerting but not too much of a problem. After all, we're keeping those bits covered anyway. But particularly for some of the darker-haired children, it seems to be sprouting in all sorts of more noticeable places – on their legs, on their arms, and even more under their arms. Of course, with carefully selected clothing, none of this should cause any great problem, but you can't do much to cover up the hair that grows on the boys' faces.'

'Hair on their faces?' I exclaimed, rather too loudly, because at that point Joh came running through with a worried look on his soft, hair-free face. We'd set him up in front of the TV in our bedroom, not wanting to disturb him for the moment with whatever Jay had come to tell us in this hurriedly arranged visit.

'Hi, Joh, how are you?' Jay's tone with Joh was friendly and unpatronising as they turned for a moment to give him their full attention.

'Hello, Jay. What are you doing here?' Joh asked in the blunt, uncomplicated way that children manage much more easily than us adults. It was so blunt that it made us all laugh, until Cris turned aggressively back towards Jay.

'Hang on. How does our son know your name? He's never met you, and we've never talked about you or anyone else from DiG for that matter. What the hell's going on?'

Jay looked flustered for a moment but regained composure through talking. 'Yes, well, you've done the right thing to keep things low key. That's the way we like to keep it, but we like to see how our kids are getting on once they start school, so I've popped into Joh's school a couple of times to visit him. All undercover, you understand. We have a friend in the education ministry. We go in as government researchers, studying gifted children.'

I could see that Cris was fuming. 'Undercover or not, you had no right to befriend our son without our consent. Gifted children? We don't want anyone doing anything that might single him out as being different. Isn't that the point?'

Getting up from the kitchen table, I ushered Joh back towards our bedroom, and we found another of his favourite programmes to watch – one that he'd watched a thousand times and never tired of. We sat there together for a moment that stretched into minutes, my pulse gradually slowing, me stroking his smooth cheek whilst he patted my knee. Soon, he was giggling away to the banal antics of the colourful characters on the screen, and I reluctantly left him to it and returned to the turgid tension in our kitchen.

It looked as if barely a word had passed between Cris and Jay during my absence. I sat back down and reached for Cris's hand under the table before attempting to reboot the conversation.

'There's one thing I'm a bit confused about,' I said, leaving a brief pause before continuing. 'All these changes you've talked about didn't start until the children were what, eleven at the very earliest? Am I right?' Jay affirmed my question with a nod and I carried on quickly, to prevent any interruption. 'Joh's only just started school and won't have to face any of this for another six or seven years. Longer, in fact, based on what you've said about the boys starting to change later. So why are you really here?' From the little contact we'd had with DiG, one thing was clear: they were invisible and mute unless they thought something had to happen now.

With measured words, Jay got to the point. 'OK, so as an organisation, we've done up a big old farmhouse, up in the Scottish wildlands. Have you ever been up to the wildlands?' Jay left no gap for us to reply. 'It's a bit spooky. You can go for miles and miles with no sign of human life, and then you come across a cluster of houses, except they're all derelict ruins. Us neuts are such city dwellers, aren't we?'

What did they mean, *neuts*?

'Anyway, our farmhouse isn't derelict, not anymore. We're setting it up as a...how shall I put it? As a residential home for all the children we have saved from termination. No, that sounds too formal.' There was finally a pause whilst Jay thought. 'I think I'd rather call it a safe place where these remarkable children can grow up without needing to hide who they are, far from the interference of any neuts who might do them harm. And where we can monitor them as they grow up.'

'You mean, experiment on them?' interrupted Cris.

'Not at all,' Jay answered with calm defensiveness. 'Our aim is simply to help them as they and we discover together what it means to be them. And to protect them, of course. They wouldn't be on their own. Hani, one of my close friends in DiG, has volunteered to live with them and act like a parent to them all, and others of us would visit them regularly.'

On the face of it, it sounded wonderful to think that, at some point in the future, Joh might be able to be Joe, living in safety with his own kind. But there was still a big niggle inhabiting the back half of my brain.

'Why come to us now? Surely, you're not suggesting that Joh should move with you to this farmhouse. He's not even five yet, and he belongs here with us.'

'Of course he does,' Jay reassured, 'but we recognise the pressure and stress of bringing up a child like Joh, of keeping his true nature hidden from the world, of living day-by-day knowing that you might need to up sticks and move at a moment's notice. The last thing we want to do is take little Joh away from you, but he would be very welcome, either now or in the future.'

Cris squeezed my hand and was about to speak as I pulled my hand away. I knew what they were thinking. Cris loved Joh very much, but although we'd never been explicit about it, if we could go back to the only other meeting we'd had with Jay Taylor knowing what it would cost us, I sensed that Cris would have walked away from it all with barely a moment's hesitation. That wasn't an argument I wanted to have in front of anyone else.

Discerning the potential conflict inside and between each of us, Jay stood up and prepared to leave. 'There will never be an ideal time to make this sort of decision, and it's not one that we're trying to make for you. I will come back at the same time a fortnight today. With your consent, I will take Joh with me then, and he can join the others at the farmhouse. You just need to have his bag packed for when I arrive. I won't hang about long enough for last-minute changes of heart.'

I didn't know what to say and Cris remained obediently silent beside me. Jay smiled and pushed back their chair. 'Now, if you don't mind, I'll go and say goodbye to Joh and then I'll get out of your hair.'

Before we could protest, Jay had gone through to our room where they spent a couple of moments with Joh before coming back through the kitchen and deserting us without another word.

It was the cold draught from the front door that broke the ceasefire between us.

'I thought you were going to talk to the owner about that,' Cris shot at me. 'How can we keep Joh safe in this dump of a flat when the front door doesn't even shut properly?'

'And I told you, I have done,' I fired back. 'I'm sure they'll fix it eventually. But don't worry, I always check it's shut properly whenever I come through it.'

Cris was closer to it but made no move. I got up, shuffled around the table, pushed in Jay's abandoned chair to get past it, and leant my back against the door until I heard the latch click. 'There, safe now, so no need to send Joh away to that farmhouse in the wildlands.'

'But don't you think it would be a better home for him than this place?'

'This place is his home because this is where we are. And we're his parents, in case you've forgotten.'

''Course I haven't. But from what Jay says, we'll have to send him there eventually, unless we want to keep him locked up in this flat all day every day. So we should consider it as an option now before it comes to that, or before we have to run away to some other hole.'

'I can't believe you're even contemplating it – giving away our child and never ever seeing him again.'

Chapter 17

THE RUDE SOUND of repeated knocking cut through the engulfing water of Joe's dream. He wasn't sure how long he'd slept for, but the room had definitely darkened. He looked down at the sodden heap of clothes he'd left on the floor and pulled the bedclothes up around his neck, shivering from his still-damp hair. The knocking had stopped; perhaps it had been part of the dream.

The brief pause was interrupted by more determined knocking that wasn't going to stop. Joe pulled the covers off the bed with him and waddled across the room to peer out of the window. He couldn't make out who it was waiting out there in the gloom. It wouldn't be Nats. She would have barged straight in. Nor could it be Anthony because he lived here. Whoever it was, they showed no sign of giving up, so Joe pulled on some dry clothes and hobbled to the door.

'Can I come fishing with you?' asked Cain, matter of factly, as if this morning hadn't happened.

'Can't,' replied Joe. 'The net's wrecked, remember?'

'That's all right. I found where you'd put your other bits of net, and I've made this.' Cain held up a repaired version of the second of the three old nets Joe and Nats had found. He'd done a good job on it. It could even be claimed that it was better than the first one.

'Thanks, that looks great, but isn't it a bit late in the day to go fishing? Anyway, I've decided I'm no good at it.' Feeling a bit rude, but also reluctant to stand for much longer in the way of a chilly autumnal breeze, Joe started to shut the door.

'You *are* a good fisherman, though.' Cain moved forward slightly, putting his hand against the door. 'I've been watching, and you can cast that net really well. You just need some of these.' He pulled a rusty old tin out of his pocket and opened it up for Joe to peer in. Inside was a writhing mixture of worms and maggots, supplemented with a bit of oatmeal. ''Course, you also need a bit of help pulling the net in when it's full of fish...if you don't want to be pulled in again,' Cain added to complete his argument.

'OK, I'll give it one more try first thing tomorrow, and thanks. You can come with me,' Joe conceded and again attempted to shut the door.

'Now's the best time, though,' Cain persisted. 'Fish are out most when the light's going.'

'How do you know so much about fishing?' Joe questioned a little belligerently, following quickly with, 'Sorry, that sounded rude.'

'Been watching,' Cain said confidently, then, shrinking a little into himself, 'and parents were fishers. Watched them too.'

Somehow, Cain was now inside, leaning his heavier frame against the closed front door. 'Shall I go ahead and get the boat ready then?' he offered, ignoring or misreading Joe's disinclination to head back out.

Joe sighed and returned to his room for some warmer layers. 'No. I won't be long.'

Rowing them back out into the cove, Cain pointed to a spot a little to the left of where Joe had almost caught his netful of fish that morning. Pointing then at the clifftop and back at the same spot on the water, he explained, 'From up there, I've seen lots of fish are often swimming around over there.'

As they drifted closer to the place that he had picked out, Cain pulled the oars into the boat and retrieved his tin of bait. 'You start getting your net ready while I tempt them with some of this.' Cain expertly scattered handfuls out onto the water's surface.

'You can throw the net as well if you like,' offered Joe. 'Show me how your parents did it.'

'Nah, I could never get the hang of that.' Cain shrank into himself again. 'But you're good,' he added, more confident again.

Joe shuffled onto his feet and started coiling the rope, hands clumsier than before, brain crunching its way into gear. All around where Cain had scattered the bait, little circular ripples popped the water's surface. Why hadn't he thought of using bait? Gathering up the net, he bent, twisted, and threw. Whether because he was nervous, or because he was being watched, or because of the slight differences in this new net, the net flumped into the water in an untidy heap and was pulled downwards straight away by the clustered weights.

'Never mind,' said Cain without any hint of the frustration that Joe himself felt. 'We'll give it a few minutes for them to get back their confidence, and then you can have another go.'

With Cain's help, hauling the net back in was done in seconds, and there was even one fish caught in its grasp, which Cain quickly untangled and dropped into the bottom of the boat.

A few minutes later, after Cain had once more scattered the bait, Joe had another go, and this time, the net landed almost perfectly on the bubbling water. This catch would be even bigger than the one he'd almost had this morning. He shivered and gasped at the memory and nearly tumbled into the water again as Cain reached over for a handful of the rope tethered to Joe's wrist.

They laughed as they worked together to draw the net slowly but surely up towards the edge of the boat, between them never allowing it to slip even an inch further away. Then magically, hundreds of slippery fish were flapping against each other in the bottom of the boat as they shook the last few free from the net.

'Told you it was the best time to fish.' Cain grinned as he took to the oars again and manoeuvred the boat around to head back the way they'd come.

THERE WERE PLENTY of pats on the back and words of congratulations for Cain and Joe as they sat at their table in the café with Nats, each with a generous helping of Victoria's special fish pie. Nats had tried to argue that hers should be on the house, like the boys', because she'd helped to dig the nets out of the junk room and given Joe lots of moral support over the last couple of weeks. In fact, she'd done almost as much to help as Cain had, she claimed. As far as Victoria was concerned however, the issue was non-negotiable. It was only Joe and Cain who had actually caught the fish, so only Joe and Cain got the complimentary meal. Joe tried to ignore the wink Victoria gave him as she put the plate down in front of him. What had Anthony said to her about their conversation outside the café? Had that really been on only his second full day here? He'd managed to push all that stuff to the back of his mind while he concentrated on the fishing.

Nats was soon distracted from arguments over entitlement to free meals when Sally and three-week-old baby Mikey came through the door. Nats never missed an opportunity to seize control of the baby from his mother.

Joe had been polite and looked at the little creature on the occasions when Nats had brought it over to show to him but had so far shied away from any physical contact. Not having had any siblings, he'd never really seen a baby this small before and still couldn't get his head around where this one had come from or how it had got from inside Sally to the outside world, leaving Sally looking like she was still on one piece. It had all happened one day during the week when Joe had been practising casting his net on a secluded beach. Nats wouldn't believe him when he insisted that he hadn't heard all the shouting and screaming that Sally had done. She said he must have been on a completely different island all day. Joe decided he'd rather not know why the birthing of a baby had caused so much noise, and Nats was mercifully sketchy on the details.

Once the café had filled up, Sandra and Anthony called for quiet in order to start the community meeting. There were no new arrivals to welcome this time, and the meeting was a lot more subdued. People knew that winter was on its way, when fresh food would be limited, daily work would be colder and wetter, and coping with illness would be harder.

The mood of the meeting got blacker when Sandra announced that wood for burning would be rationed this year because if they carried on felling trees at the same rate as they had over the last two winters, they would be out of mature trees within five years,and the new saplings would take a lot longer than that to be ready.

'But we'll have been rescued by then, won't we?' asked Victoria.

'Only if we send someone on a dangerous and uncertain mission to make contact with people like us in the world beyond,' replied Sandra. 'And if there are people in the world beyond who are willing to help us, assuming whoever we sent managed to make contact in the first place.' She looked towards Anthony, who was standing beside her. 'Are you telling them, or shall I?'

Anthony sighed and stepped up, ready to address the gathering. 'The idea of sending people out to find men and women in the world beyond is still on the table, but not for this year. Sandra and I have agreed that we can't risk sending anyone now, at least not until the spring. And with so few new arrivals this year, even in the spring we might not be able to spare people to send until more arrive.'

'And we need to consider that those of us here now may be too old to safely pass as neuts,' added Sandra.

'Quite,' continued Anthony, annoyed she had interrupted his flow. It was evidently Sandra who had vetoed any plans for a rescue mission. 'So we keep on trying to grow and strengthen our community here, at the same time continuing to study the books and maps we have found on the island to make the best preparations we can for any future mission.'

There was a general hubbub of consent - some enthusiastic about continuing on the path of self-sufficiency, others sharing Anthony's indisposition towards the status quo.

After further discussion of how the wood rationing would work in practice and what sounded like perennial debates over whether the watch really needed to continue twenty-four hours a day through the winter, the meeting broke up. Many drifted off, but a few called on Cain to get out his violin, and it wasn't long before he acquiesced to their request. As he struck up with a folky tune in a minor key that caught but also lifted the prevailing mood, Joe felt the yearning for his clarinet again, dreaming of him and Cain becoming a celebrated musical duo as well as a fantastic fishing team.

Chapter 18

THANKFULLY, THE HAMMERING on the door had stopped. Joe was about to turn over and go back to sleep when his bedroom door was flung open by a hysterical Victoria, watch binoculars swinging like a pendulum around her neck, closely followed by a still drowsy Anthony. Joe sat up, careful to pull his blanket up with him to fully cover himself, even though he was wearing his usual nighttime T-shirt and shorts.

'There's a boatful of people being smashed to pieces on the rocks!' said Victoria breathlessly. 'You need to go and rescue them in your boat.'

Having been the one to answer the door, Anthony was a few seconds ahead of Joe in terms of wakefulness. 'You mean a boatful of neuts? What would they be doing out on the sea at this time in the morning?'

'No, not neuts. Kids. Joe needs to come now.'

'But that doesn't make any sense, Vicki,' Anthony objected. 'It's November, and the weather's terrible. They never send kids in November, and they wouldn't *dream* of sending anyone in the storms we've been having this week. On top of all that, you said a boatful. That's crazy. It can't be more than two. They've never sent more than two at a time.'

'I'm telling you, it's true. Come and see for yourselves,' insisted Victoria.

Anthony was pulling on his shoes and a coat, ready to follow Victoria, who was already heading out of the door when Joe cut in. Although he was still sleepy, his brain had slowly whirred into gear.

'Wait!' he shouted with as much force as he muster, still shaking off the sleep. 'If Victoria's right, we've no time to waste proving her wrong.'

Anthony and Victoria stared, opened mouthed, as Joe took control of the situation. 'Victoria, go and wake Sandra and take her up to the watch point to have another look. We'll need you to somehow direct us to the wreckage. Anthony, find Cain and bring him down to the boat. I'll go get it ready.'

JOE DIDN'T DARE push the boat out onto the churning water before Anthony and Cain were there to help, though it felt like precious minutes were lost as he waited, helpless on the beach. When, at last, they arrived, it took the three of them quite a few more minutes to get the little rowing boat afloat without it being pushed back against the pebbles. Joe and Cain leapt aboard, and Anthony would have followed had Cain not shoved him away.

'No!' he shouted through the crashing waves. 'Don't want no passengers till we get out to the wreck.'

'But I could help!' Anthony waded back towards them through the water.

'Cain's right,' Joe shouted as Cain started working the oars. 'If we take you, there'll be less space for others, and you've not got the experience for weather like this.'

To be fair, Joe didn't feel he had the experience to be out on the boat in a storm like this either. He and Cain had become a bit more adventurous recently over the sort of weather they were willing to go out fishing in, and because they worked so well together, they'd found they could catch almost as many fish on a blustery day as on a calm one. But this storm was something else.

As Cain continued to wrestle with the oars, Joe scoured the bouncing clifftops for a sight of Victoria and hopefully Sandra. The sounds of shouting eventually enabled him to locate them, only to lose them again twice before managing to mark their position repeatably. Even then, he was unable to decipher any sense from their shouts over the howling of the wind and the continual crashing of the waves against, and over, their little vessel.

Thankfully, whilst Victoria sought to project her shouts further by cupping her hands around her mouth, Sandra soon saw the futility of this and resorted to signalling directions with her arms, and so, following her signals, Joe was able to direct Cain slowly towards the wreck.

They knew they were getting close when they spotted the first splintered chunks of wood littering the water. Whatever boat these people had set out on was now in hundreds of scattered pieces. Joe stared through the squall at one of the larger fragments of debris. There was something different about it. He shouted to Cain and pointed. It was a person draped over a sodden chunk of timber.

Cain pushed on the oars to bring them to a sort of standstill, thrown up and down by the waves but no longer making the painstaking progress they had been towards the centre of the wreck. 'Why have we stopped?' hollered Joe in confusion.

Cain passed the oars to Joe and started pulling off his heavy windproof jacket. 'Can't risk going closer to the rocks. You do your best to keep the boat steady here. I'll bring bodies to you.'

Before Joe could challenge the plan, Cain had thrown himself into the water and all Joe could see of him was his arms pummelling through the foamy spray. Joe then looked down at the oars in his hands and remembered Cain's instructions at the same time feeling the boat being dragged ever closer to the rocks. He battled to get the weightless little rowing boat under control against the raging sea and infuriated wind.

Just as all his muscles were about to give out, the boat seemed to crash against something more solid. Certain he was about to be smashed against the rocks, Joe thrashed at the water with the oars. 'Keep still for the moment!' came the fraught reply as Cain surfaced, wrapped around a waterlogged bundle. Joe hastily stowed the oars and reached out to grab at what was slipping from Cain's grasp. Like a bulging net of fish, the body rolled and dropped into the boat. But then, unlike the net, it lay still in the bottom. In an instant, Cain was away again and Joe was left alone with his new, lifeless-looking passenger.

Joe was soon morbidly grateful for the extra weight in the boat, as it made it easier to keep under control. Cain made two more trips, each time returning with human salvage, dropping it at Joe's feet like a dog returning with a stick. Hauling himself back into the boat, Cain gave the command to row back to shore.

Their poor little boat sat so low in the water that with each minute surge forward, the sea washed in and enveloped them more and Cain had to turn his ebbing energy to scooping the sea back out of the boat as Joe continued to propel them slowly forward.

About to leave the ever-spreading field of debris behind them, Joe thought he heard a quiet but desperate yell. He turned his ear to where he thought the cry had come from and sure enough, he heard it again, a distant-sounding 'Help me!'

'There's someone else out there still,' he called to Cain as he fought to manoeuvre the boat around to face the source of the appeal.

''Course there is,' was Cain's reply. 'I saw at least four others, but this is all we can carry.' He waved his arms desperately at the three lifeless heaps in the bottom of the boat.

'But there's someone calling out to us,' Joe persisted. 'We can't leave them behind.'

'We'll come back for them.'

Joe ignored Cain's instructions and paddled closer to the repeated but diminishing cries as if their owner was losing hope.

Heedless of the danger, Joe ploughed them closer to the rocks, all the time searching the waves for signs of life. He almost missed the tiny hand reaching out to them from virtually underneath the boat. As soon as he saw it, some unconscious reflex kicked itself to life and he leaned out further than he ever thought he'd dare and grabbed the hand.

This smallest of the bodies they'd yet salvaged came quickly and willingly to them and soon lay choking and gasping on top of the others.

Having regained some of his strength, Cain took command of the oars and resolutely drove them ashore as Joe turned to cradling their new passenger in his own ebbing warmth.

By the time they reached the beach, there was quite a welcoming committee wading out to meet them.

Multitudinous hands reached out to relieve them of their cargo as Sandra gently prised the shallow-breathing, curled-up form out from Joe's stiff arms.

Before Joe had a chance to disembark himself, Cain was already dragging the boat back out into the storm. They made another four exhausting return trips out to the site of the wreck, each one more physically and mentally draining than the last. They carried back another three bodies on each of the first three trips. On the fourth, with a mixture of reluctance and relief, they agreed to call off the search and returned to shore empty in every way.

On each of the last three returns, there had been a melee of frenzied activity on the shore, and Joe had noticed Sandra and a couple of the other girls pumping the chests of some of those they'd already rescued. Now, as they drew close to shore, the beach looked subdued and almost deserted.

As others dragged the boat onto the pebbles, Joe stood on his jelly legs and surveyed the scene. He counted twelve lifeless bodies laid out in neat rows on the beach. On each one, an item of clothing, torn from their body in an effort to save them, now lay draped over an unseeing face. Desperately, Joe looked for number thirteen, the smallest of them all.

At first, he thought it was a heap of discarded blankets piled on Nats' lap. But Nats was talking quietly but incessantly to the heap of blankets, and as Joe stumbled closer, he spotted the tiny face peeking out from amongst them. Nats turned and smiled through uncontrolled tears as he collapsed onto the ground beside her.

'Joe, this is Charlie, and he's a boy.'

'Are you Alex?' whispered the child through chattering teeth.

'No, I'm Joe.' Joe frowned in confusion. 'I don't think we have an Alex here.'

That same small hand that had reached out to Joe from under the waves now reached out again from under the blankets. This time, it held a crumpled but surprisingly dry envelope. As Joe accepted the envelope, he turned it over to find it addressed with a single name: *Alexandra.*

'That will be for me.' A weary Sandra appeared behind him. He turned and surrendered the mysterious letter to her.

To my dear sister, Alexandra,

I hope that you will be handed fourteen copies of this letter. I have written it out so many times in case some are lost.

I am sorry to have to send you so many new children all at once, but I am sure that you will discern from the timing of their arrival that things are desperate.

Our fertility unit has been discovered and all the pregnancy pods have been destroyed, together with their current occupants. Someone must have blabbed because within forty-eight hours, all the other members of DiG had been arrested. I was tipped off by Leslee minutes before the police came for them. I could hear the shouts at their door in the background as we ended our call.

Fortunately, I am the only one who knew all the current locations of the children. So I have spent the past three weeks travelling the country, frightening parents with the truth and urging them to let me take their children to safety. I have gathered these fourteen children, as many as I could fit in my van, and am sending them to you on a stolen boat. Charlie, the youngest, is four.

There are a few more that I need to rescue, but then I hope to bring them to you myself. I might not make it, though, and this may be the last you hear from me. Everywhere I turn, I see my face staring back at me from news screens.

Take care of these that have made it to you.

Your loving sibling,

Jay.

LOOKING UP FROM the letter, Sandra counted the twelve bodies and added on the small heap of blankets. She studied the almost-dead figures of Joe and Cain slumped over the lumpy pebbles. She glanced out at the sea, certain that it had got ten times wilder in the time it had taken to read the letter.

Folding the letter, she pushed it deep into her pocket, emptied her lungs and then took a deep breath before speaking.

'Come on. Let's get every living soul off this beach and up to the café.'

Part 2

Chapter 19

'I WON'T HANG ABOUT long enough for last-minute changes of heart.'

I often wonder how long Jay Taylor did actually wait. How many times the buzzer was pushed at the foot of our block of flats.

I know how many times I pushed Joh, giggling and whooping on the swing in the park around the corner. One thousand, two hundred and fifty-three times. Added to the five hundred and thirty-eight rocks back and forth on the seesaw with me on one end and Cris and Joh together on the other, and the ninety-seven times we let Joh clamber up and whoosh down the slide, we calculated that we'd been out long enough.

There was no car waiting out on the road, nor any note in our letterbox when we arrived back.

I also often wonder how much Joh understood of the decision that was made that day, or how much he'd heard of the arguments Cris and I had tried not to have. We never spoke of it, but as Cris bent over to kiss him on the forehead whilst he ate his lunch, Joh shuffled off his chair and wrapped his arms tightly around Cris's waist, forcing them to beg for release in order to go out to work. Then, when Cris had gone, he insisted on sitting on my lap to finish his sandwich, ignoring my mock protests that he was much too big a boy for that.

Chapter 20

JOE SAT ALONE in the gusty graveyard, knees pulled tight to his chest, watching the thirteen mounds of freshly turned soil. Watching them served no practical purpose. It wasn't going to help any of their unnamed occupants, but to Joe, they deserved more than the perfunctory committal they'd received earlier that afternoon.

It wasn't that his fellow islanders hadn't been respectful or unmoved by the tragedy. Each of them had laid a pebble, carried from the beach, at the head of each of the graves such that thirteen small cairns now stood as memorials to the dead. The daffodil bulbs pushed into the earth at each foot, which would lie dormant and hidden until spring, had been watered by more than a few tears. It had all been finished and done with, and people had started traipsing back down the hill, before Joe had even begun to take in his surroundings. How had he lived here for three whole months and not known about this place for the dead?

Besides that, how could you do justice to all the life a person had lived in the few short minutes it had taken to put them in the ground, shovel back the soil, and perform a couple of simple rituals? It shouldn't make a difference that they knew little of these people's stories, nor that those stories had only lasted a small number of years. They still deserved to be remembered, watched for a while. So, as he'd watched the last of his neighbours go and get on with whatever daily life demanded, Joe had stayed, turned back, and sat down to keep watching.

The thirteenth body had been spotted after the rain had stopped and the sun had made a brief appearance before setting on a day that might as well have been a continuation of the night. It felt like an alien sea that they paddled out on, rocking almost imperceptibly over the lethargic waves. They were able to navigate their way easily, without danger, between the rocks that had earlier been so unforgiving and deadly. As Cain manipulated the oars, Joe squinted in the sparkling wet brightness, searching each protrusion for what Sandra had declared with certainty was the final victim of the wreck. The dullness of the dark, sodden clothing against the otherwise glittery rock made it easy to spot in the end, and soon Cain was drawing the boat alongside what was now unmistakably the small, lifeless body of another boy.

Although the clothes were saturated, the body felt light and fragile as they reached across and dragged it as sensitively as they could from the rock. Any hope that life might have lingered in this body was extinguished as soon as they saw the pale, empty eyes staring unseeing back at them. Joe and Cain shivered in unison before Cain leaned over the side and retched into the water. Joe struggled to hold back the bile rising in his own throat.

So thirteen graves had been dug, looking like two rows of seven except for the fact that one, little Charlie, had cheated death. So the place where his grave could have been was churned up only by the feet of the gravediggers as they'd laboured at their final hole.

NATS PLONKED HERSELF down next to him and said something like, 'What are you still doing up here?'

Joe couldn't think of an answer, and didn't think it would have made any difference to offer one, so instead nodded and pointed with his eyes towards the older rows of grass-covered mounds. 'Tell me about those people,' he said.

Nats leapt to her feet, grateful for the opportunity to move around and do what she did best – imparting information. Standing by each of the old graves in turn, she told the story of that person.

'This is Abbie, or Abbs. I think she preferred Abbs. Sandra insisted on calling her Abigail. She was gonna to have a baby, but then something went wrong. They said the baby had been inside her for about six months, but you couldn't really see it from the outside, unless you looked at her really carefully. Then one day last spring, she got sick all of a sudden, and nobody was allowed to see her except Sandra and Eva, and then one day, they came out of her house and told us that Abbs was dead and so was her baby. I never saw the baby. Just a tiny weeny bundle that they put in there with her the next day when we buried her. So I guess this is actually Abbs and her baby, but the baby was never given a name. I don't even know if it was a boy or a girl.'

Next to Abbs was a girl whom Nats thought was called Hope, who'd almost drowned as she'd swum ashore having leapt into the sea from a passing luxury yacht. Sally, who'd been on watch, had been keeping a close eye on the yacht in case it came too close to the island, and she witnessed the moment when Hope had appeared from below a hatch on the deck, shocking the pair of neuts who'd been sunning themselves on deckchairs. Then, just as suddenly, Hope had thrown herself onto the water. Thankfully, the neuts looked like they'd been so spooked by what had happened that they hoisted their sail and raced back towards the mainland without even a second glance to see what had become of Hope.

They weren't sure that Hope was her name, but that was what she seemed to be saying to them as she lay gasping on the beach. Despite it having been a hot week in the middle of summer, Hope had shivered under multiple blankets for two days, only occasionally half-surfacing from sleep to utter some delirious exclamations. On her third morning on the island, they found her dead, and that same evening, they laid her to rest in the ground.

There were two others beside Hope. A boy, who had come in the spring of the same year, and a girl, who had arrived towards the end of the previous summer as the weather had started to turn. Neither had made it to land alive.

The rest of the graves belonged to people who had been part of the first group that settled the island. To tell their story, Nats had to begin at the beginning.

Joe couldn't believe Nats had been just four, the same as little Charlie, when she joined the others at the farmhouse. Charlie had been wrenched from his home out of necessity, in an emergency. Nats, on the other hand, as far as he could tell, had just been sent off by her parents to live with a load of other kids like them on a farm in the middle of nowhere, looked after by some neut called Hani.

Nats claimed she hadn't been that bothered by it. It was fun living with lots of other kids, she said, although she was the youngest by a couple of years, so it did sometimes feel like she had eighteen different parents.

Hani tried to give the kids some sort of lessons each day, but most of the time, they could do what they liked as long as they stayed within sight of the farmhouse. There were chores to do as well. It was at the farmhouse that Nats first learnt to look after chickens and Eva had mastered extracting milk from their two resident cows. Meanwhile, some of the other kids tended the vegetable patches that Hani had helped them to mark out and dig next to the house. Once a week, Hani would leave Sandra and one or two of the older kids in charge and would drive off into the nearest town, which couldn't have been that near. It would normally be after dark before Hani returned. When they heard the car coming back, the younger ones would all dash out and help unload provisions, eager to see what treats had been bought.

Other neuts would occasionally come to visit and chat with them all at the dinner table as if they were the kids' best friends. Sandra's older sibling, Jay, came the most. Nats didn't mind Jay. Sandra was nicer too when her sibling was there. Joe's mind wandered back over the visits that Jay had made to him over the years, both at school and at home, and also that time when they were expecting a visit from Jay but his parents decided to go out to the playground so that they weren't at home.

Returning to the present, Joe realised Nats was pointing out two of the graves. 'This is Kitty. Well, actually, Kitty and her baby.' Then she took a step to the side. 'And next to Kitty is Matt. Matt and Kitty were lovers.'

Kitty and Matt had started sneaking off together, Nats didn't know where, but she was pretty sure they weren't following the rule of staying within sight of the house. Anyway, this went on for a few months and then one day, they came back looking as white as two sheets. They told Sandra what had happened, and she decided it was best not to tell Hani but said she'd let Jay know about it on their next visit. Soon, everyone was whispering about how the two of them had been kissing and cuddling with no clothes on in the woods on the edge of the farm, and a group of neut kids who'd been playing in the woods had found them and then run off shouting and screaming. Nobody knew where the neut kids had come from; the whole point of the farm was that it was far away from where any neuts chose to live.

'Maybe they were camping nearby,' suggested Joe, remembering his own camping trips out in the countryside with Georgy and Cris.

As far as Nats knew, Hani never got to hear about what Kitty and Matt had been up to, and nor did Jay. 'We only saw Hani one more time anyway, at breakfast the next morning. It was shopping day, so we were left on our own and then the house was on fire, and we all had to run away.'

After dark, but before Hani had returned, they were all sitting in the big living room. Sandra had insisted that everyone had to stay inside all day, even though it was one of those warm early autumn days where you want to make the most of the sunshine before the winter comes. Tom was telling spooky ghost stories, which Sandra didn't like him doing, but at least it had stopped them running around and annoying each other. Nats loved the ghost stories and would sneak back downstairs to listen at the door if she'd been forced to go to bed before the others.

So it was that Nats heard the smashing glass from her corner, leaning on the doorframe with one ear pressed against the door. Scared that the others might open the door to see what the noise was and find her out of bed – but not as scared as she should have been of the crash she'd heard – she'd tiptoed towards the kitchen.

She remembered the cold draught coming through the hole in the kitchen window and the smell of smoke blowing past her. It was only when she stepped into the kitchen, though, that she noticed the fire engulfing the old oak table. By the time she'd pushed her way into the living room, frightening them half to death in the middle of the scariest bit of Tom's story, persuaded them that the house was on fire, and dragged one of them out to come and see, it was no longer possible to go anywhere near the kitchen and smoke filled the hallway.

Coughing and spluttering, they clambered, one by one, out through the living room window.

Some wanted to stay as near as they could to the burning house to wait for Hani to return, but Tom and Sandra both agreed they needed to get as far away as they could before the fire brigade and police turned up.

'So we ran away, and that's when we came here.'

'But how did you all get here?' Joe wasn't satisfied with this sudden conclusion.

'Well, I guess the farm must have been quite near the sea because before it got light, we were on a beach, all hiding in a little cave.'

The next morning, Tom and Matt had gone out to explore and found a boat. Matt had heard that there were some deserted islands. One of the places he'd lived when he was growing up, before he moved to the farmhouse, was right on the coast and, he thought, not that far from here.

'Tom and Matt set out in the boat to find an island for us to live on while we all huddled in the cave. They didn't come back all day, and when it started to get dark, Kitty wouldn't stop crying. She was sure that they must have drowned or been caught or something. We waited all night with nobody sleeping because of Kitty's crying, and they still hadn't come back in the morning.'

Tom and Matt reappeared that afternoon, just after Sandra had finally agreed that someone needed to venture out to try to find something to eat. No-one was ever sent, though, because as soon as Tom and Matt got back, the older ones seemed to have forgotten about food. Or at least the sort of food that might be eaten straight away.

They raved about how they'd found an island that people had lived on before but they were sure nobody lived there anymore. Well, no humans anyway. They'd seen cows and sheep roaming rampant across the island's scrubland and chickens running wild. They'd also spotted plants that looked very like the plants in the vegetable garden at the farmhouse but way bigger and overgrown. There were also quite a few houses that looked like they could be lived in.

So from then until well after dark, they'd ferried a few at a time across to the island. Nats was in the second boat load, and they'd had to wait for so long that it felt like the boat was never going to come back from dropping the first lot off. But she was glad when she got there that she'd not been first because by the time she did arrive, a fire had been lit and some massive potatoes had been dug up and were boiling away in a pot that had been found in one of the houses. The potatoes were very salty because someone had the bright idea of boiling them in sea water. So then others had to be sent in search of fresh water from a pond or something to take away the salty taste and quench their thirst. But that water hadn't tasted too good either.

There was a third boatful, but then the fourth and final boatful never made it to land. 'I think they made it a bit too full because they wanted to get everyone who was left. It was getting too dark and windy as well.'

The overloaded boat had sunk a few hundred metres off the island. Matt, Tom, and three of the others had managed to swim and drag each other to shore, but five others drowned.

'So these ones are Jamie, Beth, Katie, Peter, and Matilda. Well, the last one's not actually Matilda because her body was never found, but we made a grave for her anyway.'

Nats moved over to the final three graves that hadn't been mentioned. 'These three are Christina, Lucy, and Steven. They all got really sick during our first winter here, and there was nothing anyone could do to make them better.'

Nats sat back down next to Joe.

'What happened to Kitty and Matt? How did they die?' Joe asked, exhausted from vividly told tales of fires, drowning, and sickness but determined to hear everyone's story.

'Kitty got sick too, but her sickness was different from the other three. They went downhill really quickly and never recovered. Kitty vomited almost every day for months and often didn't want to eat her food but at other times she was bright and cheery. She was also worried that her bleeding wasn't happening anymore. From what I've heard about it, that shouldn't be something to complain about, but Kitty seemed really worried.

'Nobody realised she was having a baby because nobody else had had a baby inside them before. Even after her tummy got massive, and even when we'd all seen cows and sheep giving birth, we didn't realise that was what was happening to Kitty.

'I can't tell you what happened exactly on the day she died because Sandra and Eva kept the rest of us away – even Matt. We could all hear the screaming, and at one point, Eva came out and told us not to worry because Kitty was just having a baby, like the cows and sheep had. It sounded a lot more complicated and painful than that, though.'

Joe hadn't yet seen any cows or sheep giving birth. It happened mostly in the spring, apparently. Why were girls still choosing to have babies if it was so painful?

'Eventually,' continued Nats, 'the screaming stopped, and then after quite a lot longer, Sandra and Eva came out and told us that the baby was dead when it came out and also that Kitty was very, very weak. They let Matt go in to see her, but the rest of us had to go away.'

Kitty had died later that evening. Nats said she thought it was because she had bled too much while the baby was being born. 'There's a lot of blood when a baby's born,' she explained.

The next day, they buried Kitty and her baby, and the day after that, they found Matt's body at the bottom of the cliff near the watch station. Everybody said that he did it because he blamed himself for all the people who had died, and that Kitty and the baby dying was the final straw. He'd confided in Tom that if he and Kitty hadn't done what they'd done in the woods by the farmhouse, the farmhouse wouldn't have been set on fire and they wouldn't have had to run away to the island.

'Everyone was sad when Matt died because he didn't need to,' concluded Nats. 'The other deaths were sad too, but they were accidents that we weren't strong enough or clever enough to stop from happening. But if we'd known what Matt was going to do, someone could have stopped him.'

Nats looked across to Cain, who had joined them at some point during her long narrative. 'Hi, Cain, how's Charlie? Did they let you see him? Why didn't they let him come up for the funerals?'

It had been decided without discussion that, given his age, Charlie should live with Sandra, Eva, and the little kids. Nobody else had been allowed to see him during the rest of that first day or this morning. Then, when the rest of the community had processed solemnly up the hill to bury the thirteen victims of the wreck, Eva had remained back at the village with the kids and Charlie.

'Why do you always have to ask three questions at the same time?' retorted Cain.

'Oh, sorry. Forgot you could only cope with one thing at a time,' replied Nats. 'So, question one. Has Charlie remembered the names of the others who were with him?'

'That wasn't the first question you asked. In fact, it wasn't any of them, and you don't even know that I saw him yet.'

Joe hadn't quite worked out whether Cain and Nats really didn't like each other or just enjoyed winding each other up. He'd wondered at first whether Nats had felt put out by his developing friendship with Cain. If it had upset her, she'd at least resigned herself to the three of them sharing their meals most of the time, and Joe spent a portion of most evenings watching the two of them playing chess. Nats seemed determined to keep on challenging Cain to rematches, even though he won every game with unflustered ease.

Nats tried again to get some news of Charlie out of Cain. 'So did you see him, and is he OK?'

'That's still two questions,' Cain muttered. 'But yes, I did see him. As to whether he's OK... Physically, he seems fine in my opinion, but...' Cain stopped abruptly and looked down at his fidgeting hands. Nats moved over to sit beside him and reached out to still them.

Joe had never seen them touch before. Cain wasn't one for unnecessary physical contact but seemed to accept this uncharacteristically thoughtful gesture from Nats.

'It's not right, it's not right,' Cain started to mutter over and over again.

'What's not right, Cain?' Nats probed, but for a while, Cain just kept on repeating himself.

Just as Joe thought he might never stop, Cain pulled his hands away from Nats' grasp and clasped them together around the back of his head. At the same time, he stopped talking, took a deep breath, and held it. When he finally exhaled, he looked at each of them in turn.

'There's almost as many dead people on this island as living. That's what's not right.' He paused and held his breath again. 'Thirty-seven living and twenty-nine dead, counting all the babies born here.' Another pause, another breath held. 'Fifty-five have tried to come here, and only twenty-eight of us have survived. That's only just over half. I tell you, it's not right.'

'But what can we do about it?' said Nats. 'All we can do is survive as best we can.'

'No, surviving's not enough anymore.' Cain was calmer and less fragile now.

'So what's your plan?' Nats enquired a little less forgivingly.

'We've got to go find France.'

'What do you mean, find France? Who's France?'

'It's not who's France, it's where's France,' Cain corrected. 'France is a place. France is the beginning of Anthony's world beyond.' Cain stood up. 'C'mon, I'll show you.'

Chapter 21

CAIN'S HOME WAS covered in books. He must have swept the whole island of anything that could be read and brought it all here to this one room. Books were stacked like rock formations of various heights on every flat surface, including the floor. There was no apparent sense of order, no careful cataloguing system, yet despite Cain not having spent more than five waking minutes in his own house recently, he knew exactly where to locate the large, coloured atlas.

Lifting a pile of books almost as tall as Joe, Cain toppled them into Joe's arms, grabbed the atlas from the top of what remained of the pile on the desk, and cast it aside in time to relieve Joe of his load before it tumbled onto the floor. Somehow, he cleared a space on his cluttered table, big enough to open up the atlas to one of the pages already marked by a slip of paper poking out of the top, and then emptied two more chairs of their books so that Joe and Nats could sit down.

Joe gaped at the map in front of him. Familiar to him from maps that he'd studied with Georgy was the wiggly outline of Britain, but the maps he'd seen before had all implied that around Britain and its smaller satellite islands there was only endless sea. This map, however, showed a large island not far away to the west, confusingly called Ireland, and then a mass of connected lands to the south and east of Britain, some parts looking barely further away than Ireland at its closest. This extra land was colour coded into different sections, each with wiggly outlines like Britain but not all joining to the sea. Some sections had no contact with the sea at all. It didn't take long for Joe to spot the section labelled 'France', the nearest of all to Britain, except for Ireland.

'Well, it's very colourful, but what are we looking at?' asked Nats, a novice to the whole concept of maps.

Excited by this new knowledge, Joe jumped in to explain before Cain had the chance. 'This is Britain, the island where we live – not this little island that we live on now but the bigger island that our island's a part of, or next to.'

'You mean there's sea all the way round it, like there is for our island?'

'Yes. I thought everyone knew that,' Joe replied. 'But what's more important is that there are more lands as well, and they're actually quite close to us. Other places where people like us might still live.'

Getting the hang of it, Nats pulled her chair closer. A nearby stalagmite of books wobbled at the sudden disturbance. 'So can we see our little island on this?' she asked, already scanning the coastlines for what might look right.

Joe looked towards Cain, who was hovering behind them.

'Well, our island's tiny on this map and I'm not completely sure, but I think it's one of these little dots up here.' Cain waved his finger around the northwest coast of Britain.

'So it'd be easy get across to this one here in your boat,' suggested Nats, pointing. 'What's it called? I-re-land?'

'We could, but that wouldn't help us much. According to the logbook, Ireland got the virus just after Britain.'

'So you've read the diary too?' asked Joe, somewhat surprised and put out that he wasn't in quite so exclusive a club as he'd thought.

'Of course I have. It's actually a logbook, not a diary as Anthony calls it, but I brought it here in the first place, remember? Did you think I just delivered it without reading it?'

'But where did you get it from?' queried Joe.

'My parents gave it to me when I left to come here. They've always had it, and they said that I should have it. We think M. Harvey was a sibling of one of our ancestors, though we can't be sure because all the old birth records were destroyed sometime around the beginning of last century.'

'What for?' Joe asked, but Nats interrupted before Cain could start to hypothesise on what, in truth, he didn't really know.

'This is all very interesting,' Nats deliberately yawned, 'but if Ireland's no better than Britain, what can we do?'

'We head for France,' declared Cain, pointing at the big section due south of Britain.

'But that's miles!' cried Nats in disbelief. 'It would take years to get there in the boat cos you'd have to go all the way round here.' She traced her finger from where Cain had said their island was all the way to the north and around the top and back down the other side until she got to the northeast tip of France. 'It might even be quicker to go here instead,' she suggested in a way that Joe wasn't sure whether or not to take seriously, pointing at a really wobbly coasted bit labelled Norway.

Cain waited impatiently in the background while Nats continued with her ideas.

'I suppose you could go the other way instead, round here.' She put her finger back on the northwest coast but traced it anticlockwise this time, past all of Ireland, around the long, pointy bits and along the south coast. 'But that's miles too.'

'Shall we let Cain tell us what he's thinking?' Joe finally managed to suggest.

'We'd need to go across, not round,' Cain began. 'You're right. Taking a little rowing boat all that way would take too long, and it would be dangerous. We'd have to stay quite a long way out from land so the neuts didn't spot us and get suspicious of who we were and what we were up to. I know it sounds crazy, but I think the safest as well as the quickest way is to go back to the mainland and straight across.' Cain dragged his finger right across Britain in a straight line from northwest to southeast.

'Then how would you get across that other bit of sea to France? It wouldn't work to carry your boat all that way. *That* would look suspicious!'

Joe sighed. 'We'd have to somehow find another boat when we got down to here.' He pointed at the bottom right-hand corner of Britain then turned in his chair to face Cain. 'But is it safe? Sandra said that all of DiG had been rounded up and arrested, so we couldn't count on any help from them. Coming here was risky enough, even with their help. Could we really get safely all the way across the country?'

'At least we're young enough still to pass as neuts,' said Cain. 'Tom and Anthony would have no hope. Nor most of the girls.'

'So you're saying it's us or nobody?' Joe questioned. Surely, he wasn't really on the brink of agreeing to this madcap scheme!

'Yup, unless you're thinking of sending Charlie back the way he came?'

'This is all very well,' said Nats, 'but Sandra will never buy it. How are you going to get her and the others to agree?'

'We don't tell them,' Cain concluded. 'We tell no-one.'

'Not even Anthony?' Joe asked, surprised at where this was going.

'Especially not Anthony!' said Cain.

Chapter 22

07/04/2031

Finally got authorisation late Friday evening to proceed with larger-scale trials on pre-virus gametes. Delivery of diverse sample set of frozen ova and sperm arrived at 09:00. No authorisation at present for use of further pre-fertilised embryos.

Would ideally have sample sizes at least five times as big as what we've got, but there's no appetite for decimating our nation's supply of frozen gametes before the virus has been brought under control.

Test 1.1

Dosed sperm samples (90 batches from a total of 30 subjects) with virus to observe effect on X sperm and Y sperm.

Results:

In all samples observed, virus attacked both X and Y chromosome gametes, but there was a distinct increase in virus activity around X gametes and evidence of 'pheromone' emission. X gametes subsequently disintegrated. Y gametes show signs of damage and deformation but as active as normal healthy sperm.

All infected samples refrozen for use in test 2.3.

Test 1.2

Dosed further ovum samples with virus to confirm conclusions reached based on tests on ova from couple D. (1 ovum from each of 30 subjects)

Results:

Common pattern observed, analogous to couple D sample from last Tuesday. Gamete penetration occurs between approx. 190 and 300 seconds after virus introduction. Complete disintegration within 10 minutes.

08/04/2031

Test 2.1

Fertilised non-infected ovum samples with non-infected sperm samples under virus-free conditions, introducing virus immediately once zygote is formed. (1 ovum from each of 10 subjects with 1 sperm batch from each of 10 subjects.)

Results:

All fertilisations successful in virus-free environment, producing normal-looking zygotes. All zygotes penetrated and destroyed within 20 minutes of virus introduction. 7 samples were 46XX, typically destroyed in under 10 minutes. 3 samples were 46XY which survived longer, 15–20 minutes.

Test 2.2

Attempted to fertilise non-infected ovum samples with virus-mutated Y chromosome sperm to assess chances of successful fertilisation and subsequent development. (1 ovum from each of 10 subjects with 1 sperm batch from each of 10 subjects.)

Results:

Impossible to introduce infected sperm to ova without also introducing virus. Therefore ova were destroyed well before fertilisation could occur. Aborted test after two samples, as it was clear, given results from test 1.2 that all ova would be destroyed on introduction of infected sperm sample.

Test 2.3

After thorough clean down and donning of fresh PPE, fertilised non-infected ovum samples with non-infected sperm samples under virus-free conditions. (1 ovum from each of 10 subjects with 1 sperm batch from each of 10 subjects.)

Plan to introduce virus after seven days' culturing in virus-free conditions.

Conclusions so far:

Hypotheses from last week are holding with regards to effect of the virus on both embryos and gametes.

Natural conception appears impossible if either party carries the virus.

Ongoing successful live births suggests that a more developed foetus would not be destroyed by the virus. If embryos could be cultured in vitro for longer, e.g. 8–10 weeks, in a virus-free environment, it may be possible to implant in a uterus at a later stage, after the risk from the virus has passed.

Problems with this:

a) Technology for in vitro culturing of more mature embryos is still in its infancy.

b) Do we have sufficient quantities of virus-free water and can we succeed in keeping it virus free?

c) Probability of success in implanting more mature embryos/foetuses would be significantly lower, fusing developing placenta with uterus wall.

d) Infected couples would only be able to have babies that were biologically theirs if they have pre-virus frozen gametes or embryos (i.e. only couples already part of IVF programmes) and stocks are limited! The progeny would also probably be virus carriers.

e) It's almost certain that the entire UK and Irish female populations are now infertile (with perhaps a handful of lucky remote exceptions), meaning that any solution involving existing stocks of frozen gametes or embryos would be exhausted in a few years at most.

Therefore, our future as a nation rests in the hands of our geneticists O'Leary & Carmichael. Can they develop and engineer virus-resistant gametes?

15/04/2031

Results of Test 2.3

We were meticulously careful with all the equipment and culturing solutions to ensure they were sterile and virus free.

Contrary to normal procedures, we left the samples untouched and unchecked for the whole seven days in order to eliminate all risk of contamination throughout the trial.

In spite of all our efforts, when we removed the samples from the incubator, all ten were infected and all ten embryos utterly destroyed by the virus. It is my best guess that they have been like this for several days.

Very depressing.

Chapter 23

IT HAD BEEN seven months since Jay had offered to take Joh off to live in a farmhouse with other children like him, and seven months minus three days since Cris and I had last argued about it. But then came the day when Joh threw his bag at me and dashed to the toilet as soon as we got in through the door after school.

'Joh? Is everything all right?' I dropped his bag on the floor, gave the front door my practised shove to make sure the latch clicked into position, and then hurried after him.

I knocked on the bathroom door. 'Joh, can I come in?' Even in the flat, I insisted he shut the bathroom or bedroom door behind him before taking any clothes off. He hadn't locked the door, though, so I eased it open.

'Oh dear, never mind, love.' My little boy sat on the toilet, rubbing his eyes to push back the tears, wet trousers dangling around his ankles. I admit, we'd probably kept Joh in nappies for longer than most, but from the day he gave them up, he'd never once been wet. He'd always been a good judge of when he needed to go. 'Let's put you straight in the bath, shall we?'

As the hot water pummelled the bottom of the old plastic tub, I turned my attention back to Joh, kneeling to untie his shoes and ease off the urine-soaked trousers and pants. 'Don't worry, my love,' I said again as tears plopped onto the bit of toilet seat between his bare knees. 'These things happen. It's not the end of the world.' I raised his arms and pulled jumper and T-shirt together over his head before lifting him off the toilet and into the bath. 'We'll give you a good wash, get you into your pyjamas, then you can snuggle up in our bed and watch some TV while I cook us some tea. How's that sound?'

'What do you expect us to do? We can't move again just because he won't go to the toilet at school anymore,' snapped Cris in frustration when I explained later that night what Joh had told me.

It had taken a while, but as we snuggled up together on the bed after tea, Joh described how, earlier that week, a couple of the other children at school had ended up stuck in the toilet cubicles. It had caused quite a panic, and then, it seems, parents had complained to the school that their children had been endangered even though they'd just been stuck in a toilet. So how had the school responded? Had they tried to fix the locks on the cubicle doors? No, they'd decided in their wisdom to take the doors off altogether. The headteacher had apparently explained to the whole school that it was safer for everyone that way and nobody should be worried about it because going to the toilet is a perfectly natural thing, which everyone does, so there's no need to hide behind little doors whilst we're doing it.

'That's not fair, Cris,' I snapped back. 'It's not that he won't go to the toilet at school anymore, it's that he can't. How can he risk using the toilets when he'll be sitting there with his bits dangling between his legs for all to see?'

Cris thought for a moment. 'Can't we just help him to be more discreet about it? I'm sure the other children and teachers won't be actively trying to watch him while he's on the loo. As long as he's careful –'

'But he shouldn't have to be being careful all the time! He has to be careful about enough other stuff already, and you know what kids can be like.'

'So what're you planning to say to the school? "Please can you put the doors back on the toilets because my child is actually a boy with something called a penis that they urinate out of and they need to be able to do it in private"?'

'Don't be absurd, Cris! Of course I'm not going to do that.'

Honestly, I had no idea what we could do about it. However easy it might feel to suggest just moving somewhere else and leaving this particular problem behind us, I wasn't sure we'd survive another move with our little family intact.

I sighed and moved towards Cris for a hug. 'I don't know what to do, except that I'm keeping him off school tomorrow.'

One day off school extended to the rest of that week. Then, because by the end of the weekend we had no solution other than Cris's ludicrous suggestion that Joh could just be discreet, I called school again on the Monday morning to say he was still not well and might need a few more days at home.

It was quite fun being back at home together all day. We painted, we baked cakes, we made a den out of sheets, I lost count of how many games of snap I let him win. I probably let him watch a bit too much TV whilst I tidied and cleaned the tiny flat that we'd made such a mess of. I knew it couldn't carry on, though. Even as early as the Tuesday afternoon, we were both feeling starved of fresh air and open space.

On the Wednesday morning, I almost suggested he could try going to school again, but then I thought of him desperately trying to hold it in all day or, worse, not managing to hold it in.

It was just after end of school time on the Thursday that the sound of the buzzer interrupted our mid-afternoon slouch in front of the telly. I panicked. What if it was someone from the school coming to check up on Joh?

What if they'd contacted the child welfare office?

I tugged the duvet, which we'd moulded it into a sort of sofa, out from under my bewildered child, threw it over him, and pulled the edge right up to his chin. The buzzer buzzed again.

I flew to the bathroom, seized a flannel, held it under the tap and then wrung it out before rushing back to drape it across Joh's forehead. The buzz was longer and more insistent this time.

Shoving the garishly iced buns out of sight in the still-warm oven, I waved a tea towel over the mixing bowl I'd just washed up. Three long and loud buzzes sounded as I thrust the bowl into Joh's hands. I didn't need to tell him to pretend to be ill. He already looked sick with worry at the strange things his parent was doing to him.

I reached the intercom just as our ears were assaulted by the buzzer for the fourth time. I stood still for a moment, trying to catch my breath and calm my racing heart. My blood pulsed in the end of my finger as I held down the button to speak. Before I'd uttered anything more than a questioning hello, a familiar voice crackled up through the wires.

'Hi, Georgy, it's Jay. Jay Taylor. Can I come up?'

Relieved that it was nobody worse, I hesitated for less than a second before pushing the other button, which would unlock the door down below.

'Ah, so the poor boy really is sick,' cried Jay a little too dramatically, having walked straight through the kitchen and searched the flat, finding Joe in our bedroom before I'd even had the chance to shut the front door. Whipping the flannel of his forehead, Jay replaced it with a hand for a few seconds and frowned. 'He does feel a bit on the warm side, but he's probably overheating under this duvet, and it is a bit stuffy in here. Do you mind if I open a window?'

My mouth goldfished for a few seconds before I could formulate my question. The same question I remembered Joh asking little more than half a year before.

'Hello, Jay. What are you doing here?'

'Oh, yes. Sorry. I went to the school this afternoon to pay Joh a visit, and they told me he was off sick and they'd not seen him for over a week. They're getting worried, you know. They said they'd not heard from you since Monday and were talking about needing to make a home visit.'

Jay spotted the panicked look in my eyes and soon judged the truth of the situation. 'Oh, don't worry, they snapped up my offer to come in their stead. I've promised to report back in the morning, so we'd better get our story straight. What would you like me to tell them?' They perched on the edge of the bed and looked up at me expectantly.

It took me a while to process the question. Too many of my own questions were whizzing around my head. Had Jay carried on visiting Joh at school even after our decision to not send him to the farm? Or was it just a coincidence that Jay had visited today? If so, it was a damn lucky coincidence if the school was on the brink of sending someone round to check up on us. Unless it wasn't a coincidence at all because we were somehow constantly under DiG's surveillance.

Still staring at me, Jay repeated the question. 'What shall we tell them, Georgy?'

'He's not going back to that school. He can't,' I blurted out.

'OK, WELL THERE are a number of possible options which we could explore.' Jay seemed a little too optimistic for how I was feeling about the situation as we sat facing one another across the kitchen table a short while later. 'Dare I say that Cris could well be right? Joh understands how he's different from the rest of us, including all the other kids at school. I know he's still quite small, but he probably could manage to be discreet when he uses the toilets, and the chances are that nobody will notice his differences. I'd be happy to have a chat with him about that myself if you think it would help.'

Jay paused, reading the doubtful expression on my face. 'Of course, none of us believe that Joh should be put under that sort of pressure at school – or anywhere else for that matter.'

'You said there were a number of possibilities?' I prompted.

'Of course, yes. Well, for a start, there'll always be a place for Joh at the farmhouse. It really is lovely there. In fact, I've got some photos I can show you if you'd like.' Jay glanced in my direction and paused again. 'But I can see that you're not yet ready for that possibility.'

There was no sign of any attempt to persuade me otherwise...yet.

'That leaves us with a choice between two other options,' Jay continued. 'We move Joh to another school, where they have doors on the toilets, or we go for home ed.'

'Home ed?' I queried.

'Home education,' Jay clarified, realising I hadn't picked up the abbreviation. 'If you think you could do it, that's probably easier than transferring him to a different school. There'd be lots of questions about why he needed to move, and then there are no guarantees you won't meet other problems like the toilet doors in a few months' time.

'With home ed, on the other hand, you just need to apply for a home ed permit, and then they'll want to come and inspect your home and the resources you're planning to use. As long as you show that you're following the approved curriculum, you'll get it signed off and then Joh will never have to go to school again.'

'Won't that make him even more isolated than he is already?' I wondered out loud. 'I do want him to grow up with friends his own age, even if he does have to hide who he really is.'

'That's no problem,' Jay replied, again with great optimism. 'People who home educate make sure their children get involved in lots of other groups with others their own age. He could learn to play a musical instrument and then join an orchestra. I could help you find a music teacher he could go to if you like.'

My mind flooded with ideas about spending every day with Joh, as we had done this week, but not confined to the flat all day, getting under each other's feet. We could spend our days doing all sorts of things outside, visiting interesting places, exploring nature, discovering the world. And we'd be doing it all above board. Jay offered to speak to the school and get hold of the necessary forms. I was also promised a pack of 'approved teaching resources' to get us started. I wanted to start right away.

Before leaving, Jay urged me to look at the farmhouse photos, even though we'd agreed that Joh was staying here. It was true, it did look lovely, so much more space than our poky little city flat, and a garden with space for growing vegetables as well as running around. There was even woodland visible in the background. Then there were the pictures of children feeding chickens and a couple of docile-looking cows. The children in the photos all looked so happy and free, but my eyes welled up as Jay showed me the picture of little Natasha, even younger and smaller than Joh. Sure, she looked happy, but was it really best for her to grow up away from her parents? The lump in my throat grew bigger as I saw pictures of two older boys with that dark, fluffy hair growing on their faces. How long would it be before Joh needed more than a cubicle door to keep what he was from the world?

Chapter 24

15/07/2031

Breakthrough!

Frances O'Leary just confirmed by phone that the latest batch of gene-edited pseudo-ova appear to have survived first exposure to the virus. They've successfully identified and inhibited some of the genes on the X chromosome responsible for emitting the protein stream that acts as a pheromone to the virus. They're still detecting low levels of the pheromone, but whatever they've done seems enough to protect the gamete from attack. They're calling them λ-ova because all the gene suppression has been on the 'top-right' arm of the X chromosome.

O'Leary & Carmichael coming down tomorrow with three batches of the λ-ova.

Test plan is as follows:

Test Ref.	Method
7.1	Attempt to fertilise batch 1 with non-infected sperm to see if we can create λX and λY zygotes.
7.2	Attempt to fertilise batch 2 with the Y-only virus-infected sperm to see if we can create λY zygotes with sperm of the sort we expect to be the only sort now available from British men.
7.3	Use batch 3 to attempt to create λλ zygotes from a pair of λ-ova.

These tests cover all permutations of zygote using the new λ chromosome. We then see whether any remain viable and thrive over the following few days.

16/07/2031

Initial observations from λ-ova trials:

Test 7.1

λ-ova are inherently ANFV-positive, having been created out of stem cells harvested after the virus attack. Therefore, λX pairings are not viable. X gamete is rapidly destroyed by virus particles resident in λ-ova.

Sperm with a Y chromosome were attacked by the virus, as in Test 1.1, but remained broadly intact and continued to be active. Four λ-ova were successfully fertilised by Y gametes producing apparently viable λY zygotes.

Test 7.2

As with Y gametes in Test 7.1, virus-damaged sperm successfully fertilised the λ-ova producing apparently viable λY zygotes.

Test 7.3

Stimulation of two λ-ova to fuse them into λλ zygotes was extremely challenging. We succeeded in fusion stage on 5/16 pairs. On all five, however, the previously dormant virus particles then appeared to go hyperactive and rapidly destroyed the newly formed zygote.

Theory: the low level of pheromone still emitted by the λ chromosome reaches a high enough concentration to stimulate the virus when two λ chromosomes are combined in the same immature cell.

Conclusions

Out of the three chromosome permutations, λX, λY and λλ, only λY produces zygotes that appear viable and virus resistant. These zygotes will now be incubated and cultured for 72 hours, being checked and photographed at 12-hour intervals to assess ongoing viability and vitality.

18/07/2031

Thirteen healthy-looking eight-cell embryos after 72 hours' incubation.

65% survival rate very respectable.

Sadly, had to destroy all 20 samples. Photos and report filed, including request for permission on longer term trials.

23/07/2031

O'Leary & Carmichael brought two new batches of λ-ova with lower pheromone emission.

Fertilisations with Y-gametes all successful.

Successful fusing of two λ-ova to form λλ zygotes. 7 samples in total. Appear virus resistant.

26/07/2031

None of the new samples progressed past zygote stage.

Still awaiting permission for longer trial with original λY configuration.

28/07/2031

Permission received for 12-day trial including implantation in artificial uterus. New trials start tomorrow with second planned seven days later. If first 12-day trial is successful, we'll have a week to get authorisation for extension on second trial before they need to be destroyed.

Chapter 25

'WE'LL ONLY MAKE it to the end of this journey if we plan it all out properly and make all the necessary preparations.'

Joe didn't object. He trusted Cain one hundred per cent, and each day they could put off leaving was one more day on this little windswept sanctuary that was becoming home...and one more cheerful meal with Nats.

The basic plan was that Joe and Cain would set out in the boat one evening as if they were going fishing. But instead of going out a little way and dropping their net, they would keep going. Once on the mainland, they hoped they could get most of the way by train, although without any proper money, they couldn't just buy themselves a through ticket to Dover. They'd have to sneak on and off trains, not staying on any one train long enough to be caught without a ticket. Their journey to Dover could easily take up to a week rather than hours.

Of course, it would be no good trying to pass as neuts dressed as they were here, in the mix of antique coats, jackets, and jumpers left behind by the previous inhabitants and the inexpertly stitched garments made from old curtains and bed sheets. Whatever had become of the sea-soaked clothes they'd arrived in, they really needed to get them back.

'Perhaps we shouldn't have buried those thirteen with all their decent clothes still on them,' mused Cain.

Thankfully, he stopped short of suggesting any form of grave robbery.

Then there was food. How would they carry even a week's worth of food between them, let alone the two weeks' worth they'd agreed on as a precaution? It was hard to predict how long it would take them to commandeer a suitable boat and make the sea crossing to France, even if they did make it to Dover in a week. You weren't supposed to help yourself to more than a couple of days' food at a time. They would just have to take a little bit extra each time they went to the food store and take turns to buy the high-energy luxury items. It all had to be bought or acquired in the right order too. It was no good spending tops on something that would be mouldy or rotten before they even set off for the mainland.

To avoid carrying huge bundles of food down to the boat in front of curious eyes on the day of departure, they'd found a little cave with a low, narrow entrance in a secluded bay. As well as being a secure hiding place, it served as a pretty good cold store.

Even once they'd got everything ready, they wouldn't necessarily be able to leave the very next night. They wanted to be well on their way before anyone noticed they were missing. Not that anyone would be able to come rowing out after them or stop them once they were out on the water, but it felt better that way and they'd be more likely to go through with it if people weren't hollering at them from the clifftop to come back. So that meant going when the moon was just a thin sliver in the sky and preferably with some cloud cover as well, and they wouldn't set out in a gale. Yes, they could handle the boat in pretty high winds if they needed to, but it would be no good drowning or losing all their provisions in a storm before they reached the mainland.

Joe rubbed his eyes. He'd spend most of the afternoon map copying. Nats was all for tearing the relevant pages out of atlases, but Cain wouldn't countenance tearing any page out of any book. Joe enjoyed making his careful pencil copies, but it was eye-blurringly challenging when he was worn out from hours of fishing.

'Joe, have you been listening to anything we've said in the last five minutes?' goaded Nats from behind a pile of books on Cain's table.

Joe hadn't a clue where the conversation had gone in the last few minutes. When he'd tuned out, they'd been talking about clothes, specifically Nats having found some decent clothes that looked about right, tucked away in a drawer at Sandra and Eva's. She'd managed to have a poke around when she'd taken Charlie and the kids back to their house yesterday.

'Well, how many have you got left?' persisted Nats.

'What, clothes?'

Nats sighed. 'You're still not listening, are you? How many tops have you got? You must have a fair few left from that starter bag Sandra gave you.'

Oh, she meant the plastic tops, not the T-shirt variety. Did the clothes need paying for? 'Yeah, I think so. At least seven or eight I'd say. Shall I go back and get them so we can be sure?'

'No, don't worry about that. We were just saying that I've run out and Cain's only got one left, so if we need some more honey for a new batch of biscuits, it might be best if you bought it. Also, Cain bought the last one, so it will look better...'

The incident with the biscuits had been a bit of a disaster. They'd come out all right. In fact, Joe was very proud of them, remembering and adapting a recipe that Georgy had taught him. But then he'd left them out on the side when Charlie and the kids had come round. Not yesterday, but the time before. So of course, they had to let them each have one. Then when Nats had gone back to her house for a few minutes and Joe and Cain were engrossed in trying to teach Charlie to read some simple words from one of Cain's books, Katie and Peter had somehow managed to snaffle an extra four biscuits each! Suddenly, two weeks' supply of biscuits for two people had become little more than a week's worth.

Joe wouldn't miss those two kids when they left, but he'd miss Charlie. The little boy had formed quite an attachment to him, like he was a younger sibling, not that Joe really knew what it was like having a sibling, younger or older. He'd miss Nats too, of course. He was trying not to think too hard about that. She'd carry on bouncing along with life. She'd look out for Charlie, but she did have a habit of treating him like he was just one of the kids, even though she had herself once been the talked-down-to youngest.

'I think we've lost him again,' Nats said to Cain in exasperated tones. 'I hope he's more use to you out on the boat tonight.'

'Hmm, I would say we'd take the night off,' Cain mused, 'but having entertained the kids yesterday and not gone out cos of the weather for the two nights before that, people'll be complaining they've run out of fish if we don't go out tonight.'

Joe was jolted back to the present by his heavy coat landing on top of him.

'Go on then, go catch some fish,' commanded Nats. 'Don't worry. I'll tidy away all our secret stuff here. Make sure it's not out for all to see – or eat!'

Cain was already heading out. Joe yawned, pushed up onto his feet, and allowed himself to be shooed towards the door by his bossy third parent.

Chapter 26

BECOMING JOH'S TEACHER put meaning back into life.

When he started school, I'd not even considered trying to find a job because my old job was hundreds of miles away, both geographically and psychologically.

Thinking further back, when we first talked about having a child, we'd sort of assumed that Cris would be the one to go for reduced hours to look after our baby when it wasn't in nursery. My job was the better-paid one and, as an actuary, I'd assessed all the different factors in play and worked out the relative probabilities of my future career success versus Cris's. It was a no-brainer, particularly for someone who spends their life assessing and being cautious about risk.

What I hadn't factored in was the small probability that our baby might not be 'normal' because all babies were 'normal'. If abnormalities were detected, a conspiracy between the government, the fertility units, and my own insurance industry ensured that they were quietly eliminated. Abnormalities were inconvenient and too expensive to deal with, involving either corrective surgery, lifelong special care, or both. In fact, the uniformity of society made my job almost boring and not worth doing, except that for historical reasons, you needed to be mathematically brilliant to get into the profession in the first place and, once qualified, the pay made it completely illogical to switch to something more exciting.

Of course, the logical thing to do would have been to go for the single-parent option, with just one of us donating our genetic material, then allowing the fertility unit's carefully controlled gene randomisation system to modify the genome of our future child to ensure that it wasn't just a clone of its parent. The system could even scan the DNA of the non-donating parent, if there was one, and use this to program in some compatible genetics to give the appearance of inherited features and traits.

So perhaps it was the lack of excitement in my work, which was supposed to be all about evaluating and mitigating against risk, that led me to persuade Cris that it was worth the risk of abnormalities if we could have a child that was truly a bit of each of us.

What were the chances, though, really, that not only did we end up producing a male foetus but also that we were with a fertility unit where someone from DiG worked, and that they looked at the two of us and decided it was worth the risk to tell us the truth about our baby?

Some people say there's such a thing as fate. I'm not sure, but I can say, somehow, from that first time when I sat in the back of the car and took hold of the tiny hand of our newborn baby boy, I knew that my fate, whether I wanted it or not, was to protect this little abnormal miracle.

So you see, there was no question of me looking for work when Joh started school. I needed to be the one who walked him to school in the morning and was back at the school gate in time to see him come out at the end of the day. Some would say that in between those hours, there would have been time to get some small, part-time job. But even when he was at school, I needed to be available for him, just in case. Besides that, what sort of job would I have realistically had a chance of getting? I lived in a still unfamiliar city. I'd been out of the profession for five years, and trying to get a reference from my old firm would have opened us up to unquantifiable risk.

But I won't pretend that my life felt fulfilled in those nine months between Joh starting school and the decision to home educate. I dared not stray too far from the school, in case I needed to go rescue him from some calamitous incident, though I knew with certainty that the chance would be slim of changing any outcome if what he was had been uncovered. But the further I was from the school, the lower the probability would be of getting there in time. So, when I wasn't wandering the streets near the school, I confined myself to the flat, just seven minutes' walk from the school gate.

After nearly a fortnight cooped up in the flat pretending that Joh was ill, I was desperate to get out somewhere with him as soon as the deception was dispensed with, so for our first proper lesson, we took the bus out to the ruins of Kirkstall Abbey to see what the stones might tell us about the people who built it, what they built it for, and why at some later point in history it was reduced to a ruin.

Thanks to the absence of official history from pre-neutral times, we could only speculate, and I had to be careful with my speculations in case our innocent young child said the wrong thing when the inspectors came to visit. I longed to make up stories about male and female humans who perhaps once worked together to construct this amazing building and celebrated diversity rather than uniformity, but we limited our imaginings to how they cut the stones and built them up so high to form the enormous arches with technology that must surely have been far less advanced than our own.

I did feel very self-conscious during those first few weeks, certain that everyone was looking at us and wondering why that child wasn't in school. But apart from the frown I got from the bus driver when I insisted Joh was old enough to need a ticket, I suspect nobody really gave us a second glance. Joh wasn't big for his age so could easily pass as a preschooler, which perhaps explains the astounded looks we did get when people were close enough to listen in on our scholarly contemplations – another reason to keep our lessons strictly within the boundaries of the approved curriculum.

Within a few weeks, the schools had broken up for the summer, which gave us a greater sense of freedom to continue with our nomadic lessons. By the time autumn arrived and the daytime was emptied once more of children, we were past caring how others might interpret our educational excursions.

We took up Jay's suggestion of Joh learning a musical instrument and the offer of help to find a teacher. Yani seemed to enjoy teaching Joh to play the clarinet even more than Joh loved and looked forward to his clarinet lessons. I often suspected that Yani was in on our little secret, the way they enthused about Joh's powerful lungs – 'so much stronger than us mere mortals.'

It wasn't long before Yani suggested Joh was good enough to join a little junior wind band, from which he graduated, in less than a year, to the intermediate wind band and then to the senior orchestra a couple of years later – much to the disgust of some older clarinet players who had to stay in the intermediate group. He attended dutifully every week but for my benefit or his, I was never quite sure. I think he enjoyed playing his small part in the harmony of the whole, particularly when he got into the senior group, but he never showed much interest in mixing with other kids during the breaks. On the few occasions I suggested we could invite one or two of the others round for tea, he shrugged and mumbled, 'If you like,' so we never did.

There was, of course, one part of the teaching curriculum where I did feel that I ought to diverge from the official version. In that area, I also felt woefully ill informed, but neither could I find a specialist tutor. Jay had given us so little information about how Joh's body might develop, in part because they were only just beginning to uncover these things for themselves. Yet I needed to prepare Joh, as best I could, for those inevitable changes and equip him for the day when he would have little choice but to leave us to join his own kind. So I began by showing him how, in another world, his name might have been spelt 'Joe', because he was a boy.

Each week past his twelfth birthday felt like a gift, and when we got past his thirteenth and were well on the way to his fourteenth with no sign of any changes, I began to wonder if DiG had been wrong and we'd been stressing over nothing, or maybe Joh was different from the other boys.

In the end, though, the changes did come, and awkward as it was, I am glad that we had talked about it when he was young because Joh wasn't frightened to tell us. When the first hairs started tickling around the base of his penis, with some embarrassment he let us know. And when the soft, dark shadow became more noticeable across his top lip, we didn't worry. Well, he didn't worry. I, on the other hand, knew it would soon be time to get back in touch with Jay.

WE'D FOUND THE professionally printed flyer for a holiday home in our letterbox a week after Jay had visited to find out why Joh was off school. I recognised the picture of the farmhouse with its neat rows of vegetables in front of what I assumed was the kitchen window. It was almost identical to one of the pictures Jay had insisted I scroll through, trying to warm me to the idea of sending Joh there. Except that the cheerful-looking children had been cropped out.

Find a home from home on our cosy working farm, the flyer enthused, directing its reader to a familiar holiday cottages hubsite for more details. Handwritten on the back were just ten explanatory words: *Follow the link and send an enquiry when you're ready.*

Nine years later, almost to the day, heart in my throat, Cris standing behind me with hands on my shoulders, I typed in the hub address from the unevenly faded flyer that had been pinned on our kitchen noticeboard under a heap of takeaway menus.

Without bothering to study the facilities on offer or details of local tourist attractions, I clicked straight through to the enquiry form and filled in our contact details. What dates to select for this fictional holiday? Would they interpret whatever date we suggested as *the* date that Joh would go? If so, how do you choose when to say goodbye to your child? I picked a random date at the end of June, before the school holidays started, since we weren't tied to school holidays.

Cris noticed that my finger was hovering with faltering resolve over the submit button. Feeling the gentle squeeze on my right shoulder, I took a deep breath and clicked the button.

Wide awake at one o'clock in the morning, I tapped refresh on my hubmails for the twelfth time in the past hour, not really expecting to see the reply pop up. Heart pounding at double speed, I opened the message.

> *Dear Georgy,*
>
> *Thank you for your enquiry. We regret that this cottage is no longer available. We will contact you in due course to offer alternative accommodation.*
>
> *Best wishes,*
> *Best Cottage Holidays.*

Chapter 27

03/09/2031

Three potential surrogates identified. All three have undergone surrogate pregnancies before for male couples. Appointments arranged tomorrow for examinations and possible start of hormone treatment.

DHSC want me to select just best candidate for first trial λY pregnancy to start as soon as possible. Mix of urgency and caution over this revolutionary step.

Started fertilisation on new batch of λ-ova ready for possible transfer to live uterus next week.

04/09/2031

Blood tests, hormone tests, and hysteroscopy examinations carried out on three candidates (S1, S2 & S3).

All three ANFV-positive. I didn't expect otherwise.

S3 has minor scarring on uterus wall. Also oldest candidate at 35.

S1 & S2 both healthy with no signs of scarring. Both report continuing to have apparently normal menstrual cycles.

S2 estimated she was on day 25 or 26 of 30-day cycle. Thickness of uterine lining appeared to substantiate this, as did low levels of oestradiol. Progesterone also low and no corpus luteum suggesting anovulatory cycle.

S1 estimated she was on day 17 of 28-day cycle. Matched thickness of uterine lining oestradiol still relatively high. Again, no sign of ovulation and progesterone very low.

S1 selected as best candidate: youngest at 27 but already undergone two surrogate pregnancies for two different male couples. No partner or children of her own.

Also at day 17, possible to start hormone treatment with progesterone immediately to prepare for embryo transfer early next week.

S1 consented to participate in trial. Lots of paperwork to sign. Also consented to implantation of newly developed wireless utero-nanocam, so far only used in animal trials.

Sent S1 away with progesterone pessaries. Returning tomorrow for nanocam implant.

05/09/2031

All went smoothly with nanocam implant first thing. Insisted S1 stayed in until after lunch in case of rejection and haemorrhaging. No sign of any problems so allowed her to go at 14:00. She'll move into disused maternity unit on Monday ready for embryo transfer Tuesday.

08/09/2031

S1 settled in maternity unit with round-the-clock one-to-one midwifery care. Visited this afternoon to check hormone levels. Both progesterone and oestradiol good for tomorrow.

Quick hysteroscopy showed nanocam still in place and no signs of irritation. Activated power and checked links with external monitor. Crystal clear picture. Will help with transfer process tomorrow.

09/09/2031

Transferred one healthy six-day embryo into S1's uterus.

Post-transfer hysteroscopy and feed from nanocam both indicated minimal disturbance of uterine wall from catheter and healthy-looking blastocyst ready to embed itself.

11/09/2031

Visited S1 to check on progress. Patient comfortable. Nanocam showed embryo starting to implant in uterine wall. All good.

Now we watch and wait to see how embryo develops.

Chapter 28

CAIN BURST THROUGH the door with uncharacteristic haste, just off his watch duty. 'We go tonight!'

For a moment, Joe was about to ask the stupid question, 'Go where?' but then the coin went clunk in the vending machine that was his brain and allowed the right response to drop down the chute.

'Do you think we're ready?' Had they got enough food? Had they packed the right clothes? Was everything they needed down at the cave? Were their maps detailed enough for them to work out where they were going? Could they really pull this off?

'Don't know,' came the honest reply, 'but if we don't go tonight, we could be waiting nearly another month. The moon's still pretty thin, and it's cloudy but calm. Reckon the wind's going to pick up in the next few days. Even better,' continued Cain, 'Anthony's on watch tonight, and he's got Gemma up there with him.'

Joe frowned, perplexed by this latest bit of bonus news. 'Won't that make it harder? Two pairs of eyes watching us instead of just one?'

'Don't you see anything?' Nats chipped in with a grin. 'If Anthony's got Gemma up there with him, chances are, there won't be any eyes looking out to sea tonight.'

Joe didn't know Gemma that well. She was one of the girls with a baby. No idea what the baby was called. Although they were growing up and starting to gain characters of their own, they still all looked pretty much the same to him. He wasn't even sure which were boys and which were girls half the time. He'd genuinely had no idea there was anything special going on between this Gemma and his housemate.

Cain wandered over to stir the pot of stew bubbling on the stove. 'Anything we can add to this to bulk it out a bit? I know we don't want to carry too much extra weight, but it's probably best if we feed ourselves up before we go.'

'Sorry,' said Nats, 'Used up all the vegetables Joe had left. I've got almost a whole loaf of bread back at mine. I could go fetch that.' Before they'd had a chance to answer, she was out of the door and back again with what looked more like three-fifths of a loaf than 'almost whole'.

They wolfed down the stew as quickly as the heat of it and their constricting throats would allow and then jumped into action. Cain and Joe pulled on their big coats, grabbed their buckets, and marched down to the boat as if they were just off out for a normal evening's fishing.

By the time they'd rounded the promontory into the secluded bay, Nats was already well on with lugging the bags out of the cave and piling them up on the beach. It was hard to be certain from the boat, but surely, that mound of stuff was already far too much to load into their little rowing boat or, for that matter, for the two of them to carry once they got to the other side.

The three of them worked in silence to load everything into the boat. Joe and Nats carrying the luggage from the pile to the boat and passing it to Cain to tessellate into the available space.

'Hang on, what's in this bag?' Cain called back as they retreated back up the beach for the final few items.

'Oh, that's my things,' replied Nats.

'What do you mean, *your* things?'

'The things I need for the journey, of course. Clothes, towel, hairbrush –'

'Since when have you used a hairbrush?' joked Joe with a grin, admiring once again her wild hairstyle and reflecting on all that he'd miss about Nats over the coming weeks. He desperately hoped this worked out, if only to see Nats again at the end of it all.

Cain was asking another question. 'What are we loading it into the boat for then? You're not coming with us.'

'Who said I wasn't coming with you?' Nats fumed, flinging the heavy backpack that Cain had just passed back crashing down on the shingle.

Joe frowned. He thought they'd agreed all along that it would be him and Cain going, but had that ever being vocalised? Had Nats assumed all this time that it would be her as well or even instead of one of them?

'What do you mean? The plan's been clear from the start. Joe and I set out as if we're going fishing but then row across to the other side instead.'

'Yeah, so you've done that. You've set out as if you're going fishing and come round to the cave for us to load the boat up and set off on our journey to find the world beyond. Anthony always said that there should be at least one girl, to show them we're just like them.'

Joe had forgotten that, but Nats had a point.

'Just keep your voice down, will you?' Cain hissed. 'Or we'll have the whole island wanting to join us! Since when has this been Anthony's mission? And since when have you come fishing with us? If we're spotted, it'll be obvious we're up to something, particularly with all this other stuff.'

'Then I'll hide under the nets until we're too far away to see,' Nats hissed back, glaring with dagger eyes at Cain.

'But we're not taking the nets with us. Can't you see? We've left them in the cave to make room for all this other stuff.'

'Ha!' Nats scoffed. 'You think you'll convince watchers that you're just going out fishing if you haven't even got your nets with you? That's ridiculous! And they'll see all this other stuff in the boat from a mile off.'

Cain thought for a moment. 'OK, so perhaps we were planning to fling the nets over this lot to hide it, but we never agreed to hide *you* in the boat as well.'

'Well, it seems to me there's only one way to resolve this.'

'That's right. You need to accept that you're not coming.'

'No, we put it to a vote. All those in favour of me coming too,' said Nats, hand already in the air.

'Hang on a moment,' Cain objected. 'If we are having a vote, it should only be a vote of those who are actually supposed to be going, which doesn't include you. All those in favour of Nats staying here.' Cain raised his hand as Nats snapped hers down. Both turned to look at Joe.

Joe had been spectating in stunned silence, thankful that the other two had been too busy arguing to notice him, until now. Like Cain, he had assumed Nats wasn't coming, but now it was clear that she thought she was, he could only feel excited by the idea of the three of them continuing as travel companions. Despite the odd abrasions between them, Cain and Nats got on surprisingly well, most of the time. There was also some sense in having a girl with them, if they were setting off to find the world beyond where both male and female humans were the norm.

'So which way are you voting then, Joe? Do you want me or not?' Nats folded her arms and waited. Cain sat down on the edge of the boat, stabilised by its heavy load. He looked up at Joe, confident he would make the right decision but also urging him with his eyes to follow through with it.

Joe took a slow breath in as they waited. 'I think I'd like it if Nats could come with us.'

Nats seized on his words and whooped with delight. 'Yes, that settles it. Let's get this boat on the water.'

'Hold your horses!' hissed Cain, blocking the trajectory of Nats' bag toward the boat. 'If you'd listened carefully, you'd have noticed that Joe said he'd like it if you could come, not that he thought you should.' He dropped his arms. 'Of course it would be nice if you could come. I think I'd have probably liked that too, but it's not practical. You'd make the boat too heavy for a start, with all this stuff we've got.'

'Well, actually, it is quite a calm night,' Joe mused, almost only to himself, 'and we managed to carry a lot more weight in much worse conditions on the night of the wreck. So maybe, if she promised to lie very still and not get in the way...' He tailed off and looked at Cain, trying to see whether he might be persuadable.

For a good few seconds, Cain just stood there shaking his head. Nats crouched by her bag, fiddling with a strap, holding her tongue with unusual restraint.

'All right, you can come, but on one condition.'

'Why should there be...what's that then?'

'You'll need a haircut.'

'What? Why?' Joe and Nats laughed together.

'Have you ever seen a neut with so much hair? You'll stick out like a sore thumb. I'm sorry, but if you want to come with us, the hair stays here.'

Joe expected Nats to object, but instead she grinned and pointed at the two of them. 'Well, if I need a haircut, I reckon you two do too. Have you seen yourselves lately?'

Joe ran a hand over his own shaggy mop. Cain was doing the same. Joe laughed. 'I think she might be right, you know.'

Nats started rummaging in her bag. 'Good job I packed these then,' she said triumphantly, brandishing a vicious-looking pair of scissors.

In the rapidly failing light, Joe sheared first Nats and then Cain. He tried to argue that he was sure he was the least qualified to do it, but neither would let the other one near them with the scissors. Finally, Nats attacked his hair. A shiver passed between them as they pulled up their hoods, the chill night air tickling their naked-feeling scalps.

Chapter 29

WHEN THE BUZZER went that Saturday morning, I knew straight away it would be Jay, so I didn't even bother talking to them over the intercom before pushing the button to let them up. Four minutes later, I was beginning to wonder whether they were still waiting outside when there was a knock on the door to the flat.

Flinging it open, I was about to give Jay a roasting over the worrying and cryptic message from *Best Cottage Holidays*, but the round face smiling up at me definitely wasn't skinny Jay.

'Oh, it's you,' was all I could manage to say at first. The face was definitely familiar, but my brain's facial recognition software was struggling more than usual. Admittedly, it had been over fourteen years since the last and only time we'd met this person, just before we got Joh. But if anything, they looked like they'd lost the years that the rest of us had gained – like they'd had a new lease of life.

'Er, sorry,' I said, 'that was a bit of a rude welcome. I was expecting Jay. Do come in. It's Leslee, isn't it?'

'My, you've got a good memory, yes,' Leslee replied, finally moving clear of the door far enough for me to shove it closed behind them. 'Although actually I prefer to go by the name Lily these days, if that's OK with you.'

'Oh? What's that all about then?' questioned Cris rather bluntly, standing up from their seat at the table and scanning Leslee from top to bottom and then back again. Cris's candidness did have its uses, but it could also be damned embarrassing. I wasn't sure who was blushing more, me or Leslee.

'I'm sorry, Leslee, I mean Lily,' I said apologetically. 'Cris has never been backward in coming forward. Would you like a coffee?'

'No, it's fine,' they began. 'Well, actually, yes, a coffee would be nice, please. What I meant is there's no need to apologise, either of you.' For a moment, their eyes flitted from me to Cris as undoubtedly well-practised words were dredged up. 'The thing is, although biologically I'm neutral like you, I've actually always felt different. Then when I started working with the children we'd rescued, I realised what it was. I'm actually um... female.'

They stopped speaking and looked at us both expectantly. Expecting what, I wasn't entirely sure.

'So how do you know?' I asked hesitantly.

'It's difficult to explain, but –'

'I'm sorry. I can't believe this,' Cris butted in. 'Surely, it's very simple. You're a neutral, I'm a neutral, Georgy's a neutral. Joh, on the other hand, is a boy. You know how we know he's a boy? Because he's got these weird bits that none of the rest of us have dangling down between his legs. Now, I've not seen what bits girls have exactly, but it doesn't look to me like, under those clothes, you're really any different to the rest of us.'

Hurt swelled in Lily's averted eyes, spoiling the smile she was still fighting to hold. I tried to stop Cris, but it was like trying to stop a high-speed train by standing on the tracks and waving your arms at the driver.

'This isn't just a game, you know. You can't just choose what you want to be. What choice did Joh have? What choice *does* he have? He has to hide who he really is. We had to take him out of school because he couldn't hide at school anymore. You've set up a bloody commune of these different kids to keep them hidden when the differences have become too noticeable. I'm assuming that's what you're really here to talk to us about, not this self-centred twaddle.'

'Cris, stop!' I shouted at the top of my voice. 'Can't you see she's hurt.' Poor Lily tried to smile back at me.

'What do you mean, *she*?' Cris retorted. 'Don't tell me you accept this? It's an insult to all we've been through.'

At that moment, I realised that as soon as Cris had started railing about how ridiculous and insulting it was and I'd seen the look on Lily's face, I saw how genuine it was. Being 'she' so obviously made her happier and healthier. What's more, it somehow felt natural to think of her as 'she'. I'd had nearly fifteen years to get used to Joh being 'he', so it didn't feel all that strange to suddenly be referring to someone as 'she'. Or perhaps my mathematical and actuarial training had long ago subconsciously awakened in me the understanding that however much we attempt to iron out or eliminate any probability of difference and the unexpected, nature remained beautifully entropic. Who was to say we didn't all have a bit of 'he' or a bit of 'she' inside us?

I reached out a reassuring hand. 'I'm sorry, Lily. I can't imagine how it must have felt all your life to –'

'Can't imagine? What about them imagining what it's felt like for us?'

I glared at Cris. 'What about getting that kettle boiling and brewing us up some coffee?' I turned back to Lily. 'Milk and sugar?'

'Just milk thanks, love,' she said, smile growing back. 'And thanks for your understanding too. I'm always a bit nervous about seeing people for the first time as Lily. To most, I still have to be Leslee, of course. But even those who know, there aren't many who get it like you have.'

Cris dumped a mug of coffee in front of each of us and then pulled a chair round so that I was obscuring their view of Lily. 'Can we just get down to business now?' Cris asked, apparently trying to be conciliatory. 'What's the story on this farmhouse, and what's that hubmail message all about – cottage no longer available, alternative accommodation?'

JOH CAME IN as Lily finished explaining things to us. A muddy shoe kicked at the door to keep it open as he manoeuvred his equally muddy bike into the kitchen I'd finished cleaning only an hour and a half before. As usual, a pedal scuffed the doorframe on its way in.

'Oi, watch that paintwork!' Cris complained, frowning up at Joh, then, with a little more parental love, 'How about you leave that muddy bike out on the landing for now?'

'He can't do that, Cris. There's no space for it out there and we'll get complaints again.' According to some of our neighbours, it was an accident waiting to happen. We'd also had moans about mud on the stairs, despite all the other muck and grime that was nothing to do with us.

'Oh, it'll be all right out there for a few minutes, and then Joh and I can take it back outside to give it a good wash down.' I loved it when Cris actually offered to do stuff with Joh, and to be fair, they were doing more and more together, at the times when Cris wasn't working. 'You don't need to be here that much longer, do you?' Cris asked, turning towards Lily but refusing to look at her. 'I think you've put us in the picture, so we won't keep you.'

'Well, yes, of course, although I had hoped you would introduce me to this impressive young man here before I go.'

'Oh? You mean you haven't met him before?' Cris retorted with unnecessary brusqueness. 'I'd sort of assumed that your lot must have all taken their turn at getting to know our son without telling us about it.'

'Cris, all that was years ago now and I'm sure it was only Jay that visited Joh at school.' I turned towards Joh, still holding his bike half in and half out of the front door, staring open-mouthed at the smiling stranger smiling back at him from her place at the kitchen table. We never had visitors.

'Joh, this is Lily. It was Lily here who came to see us a couple of weeks before you were born. She helped us to get ready for you.' My tongue felt enormous in my mouth as I formed the word 'she' to actually introduce a real person to Joh. I'd tried to get Joh used to the idea of being he/him and had also explained that a girl would be she/her, but this was no longer hypothetical, even if Lily wasn't biologically female.

'Ah, well, perhaps another time,' conceded Lily, recognising that Cris might explode if she wasn't gone soon and that Joh wasn't sure what to do with himself.

Decision made, she stood up. Cris stayed resolutely at the table, leaving me to usher Joh and his bike back out onto the landing so that Lily could get out of the door.

'Thanks for coming, Lily. It was good to meet you, again. We'll be in touch as soon as we've decided.'

Joh gave me a quizzical look as Lily set off down the stairs. 'Decided what?'

I looked to Cris for help. Sooner or later, we'd have to talk with Joh about all this.

'Oh, nothing important.' Cris planted their hands on the table to push themselves up. 'Come on, let's go get that bike cleaned up.'

THE DOOR SLAMMED shut harder than was necessary to make sure the latch engaged. Working with Joh to clean the mud off his bike clearly hadn't been as cathartic for Cris as I'd hoped. They'd had some fun out there, though, judging by the purposeful mud smears across both their faces.

'You need to go get yourself in the bath, son,' I commanded, handing Cris a freshly brewed cup of coffee at the same time. As soon as we heard the bathroom door being pulled shut, Cris and I both opened our mouths and started talking at the same time.

'There's no way we're sending our child off into the unknown with that lot.'

'Cris, I get how you feel about Lily, but you could have been a bit kinder to her.'

'I mean, can we really trust people who left a group of kids on their own to nearly burn to death?'

'I know her decision feels a bit weird, but I genuinely believe she's sincere about what she's doing.'

'And now they don't even have any contact with the kids as such anymore.'

'And what it showed me was that maybe we all struggle a bit to really be who we are and to feel we fit in somewhere in this world.'

'I mean, did you notice how evasive they were when I was asking about how they actually get the kids to the island?'

'But Joh's struggle is going to be ten times greater than even what she's been through if we make him stay here with us.'

'Will you stop calling them 'she'? It doesn't matter how they choose to think of themselves, they're still a them, not a she!'

I was so taken aback by the fact that Cris had actually heard some of what I'd been saying whilst we were talking over each other that I stopped and lost track of what I was going to say next. We both paused and looked at one another.

'OK, so maybe at some point, it might be best for him to go and live on this island with others that are like him, but does that need to be soon? He doesn't really look any different from other kids yet, not with his clothes on, and he's still far too young to be expected to look after himself, even if some of the kids there are nearly grown-ups.'

I'd never expected that, when it came to it, our argument would be this way around. Much as I saw that Cris loved our son, they'd been the one who'd hinted from time to time that it might be better for all of us if Joh went to live at the farmhouse.

I can't explain how, but despite what logic told me about the risks of sending Joh off to live on a windswept little island in the middle of the sea without any real adult care, I felt strangely at peace with the whole idea. Maybe it was seeing how Leslee had become Lily and wanting that for Joh – that he could really live as Joe. Maybe it was because I'd felt quite excited that against all the odds, that little community of kids had got themselves to a place of safety where all the evidence suggested they were thriving.

Admittedly, no-one from DiG had actually been across to the island. Lily had explained how Hani, the houseparent from the farmhouse, had watched with binoculars from a nearby coastal hill as the first two boat loads of kids had been ferried out in the direction of the distant little island. Over the next few weeks and months, Hani and Jay had taken regular boat trips out near to the island, but Jay had insisted that the kids had shown they could look after themselves, and it was safest if DiG observed only from a distance. The last thing they wanted to do was alert either the authorities or vigilantes to the existence of this fledgling community of male and female humans.

It was time to let him go. But how would I now convince Cris?

Chapter 30

IT WAS PROPERLY dark by the time they were finally ready to go. So dark, in fact, that they spent several minutes searching the beach with their hands to make sure they had packed everything back into the boat. Cain had insisted on reorganising his packing to make a space for Nats to lie in, under the nets. In this darkness, Joe felt there wasn't really any need for Nats to hide as they paddled away from the island, but was it really worth pointing this out? Besides, how did he know that the clouds wouldn't suddenly part and cause the sliver of moon to shine a spotlight on them just as Anthony and Gemma tore themselves away from whatever they were up to and decided to look out across the sea?

Having felt around one last time and found only large clumps of hair, they agreed that it really was time to go.

'Should we scatter this hair a bit more so it's not too noticeable?' Joe questioned. Someone was bound to discover it at some point in the next few days.

'Nah,' said Cain. 'We'll be long gone before anyone finds it and when they do, it'll give 'em something to puzzle over.'

That lightened the mood, imagining Victoria suggesting they'd somehow dematerialised, leaving only a few strands of hair, or Anthony spinning a spooky yarn that they'd been gobbled up by a ravenous sea monster, spitting out their indigestible hair before sinking back down into the depths. Sandra would instantly suss out what they were up to, of course, and would manage the situation to discourage any other silly ideas about leaving. Not that anyone else could leave very easily without the island's one boat.

That got Joe wondering whether it was fair of them to run off with the only means of getting safely off the island. What if there was some sort of emergency? Another boat load of kids and another wreck? They'd have no hope of rescuing them without Joe's little rowing boat. He didn't voice any of these thoughts, though, because...well, they'd come this far and had probably better go through with it now. Besides, how would they explain to everyone else what they'd done to their hair?

A pebble tumbled somewhere up at the top of the beach.

'Did you hear that?'

It was too dark to see Cain now, and Nats was buried in the boat. For what must have been a couple of minutes, none of them moved or made a sound. Was Cain even still there? Perhaps the disturbed pebble had been him sneaking off, leaving Joe and Nats to attempt the journey without him. Was Joe waiting for a signal from Cain that would never come?

'Are we actually going to set off sometime tonight then?' Nats' muffled whisper pierced the stillness. 'If we don't go soon, I might just drop off to sleep under here.'

'Huh, might be a more peaceful journey if you did,' Cain muttered. 'You ready to push, Joe?'

'Ready when you are,' Joe whispered with relief.

'OK, one, two three...push.'

Joe pushed on the back of the boat as hard as he could. Was Cain really still there? If he was, he couldn't have been pushing or he must have got disorientated and was trying to push the boat up the beach rather than out onto the water. Joe's feet slipped and scraped up the shingle.

'Are you pushing, Joe?' Cain's straining voice hissed towards him.

''Course I am!' Joe puffed. Again, his feet slid over the shingle, and at the same time he heard a splash and a curse from Cain.

'Told you she'd be too heavy.'

'Oi, I heard that,' came Nats' whispered outrage.

'I wasn't talking about you – or to you, for that matter. It's the boat I was calling *she*. Didn't you know that boats are always *she*?'

'Would be easier if Nats got out and gave us a hand, though, wouldn't it?' Joe suggested. 'It's not like anyone'll see her, even if they *are* watching.' Joe felt the boat lean as Nats, without awaiting further instruction, clambered out of her hiding place. In the next instant, he could feel her warmth beside him at the back and sensed her hands beside his on the stern. 'Ready for another push, Cain?'

This time, the boat did move, scraping and crunching its way toward the water.

'Why did we have to drag it so far out of the water?' rasped Nats.

'Something called the tide,' Cain called back sarcastically, no longer bothering to keep his voice down. 'When we first thought we were ready to go, the boat was half in the water.'

Another heave and the buoyancy of the sea began to take charge.

'Right, you jump in now,' Joe instructed Nats. 'That way, you won't get wet feet.'

For once, Nats obeyed. Joe braced himself to give one last push, but hesitated. Someone was crunching their way at speed down the beach towards them.

'Hey, you three! Wait!'

Chapter 31

I DIDN'T WANT TO let go of his no longer squeezing hand as his head lolled towards the car window. I'd never been one for sleeping in the car, but Joh had always been a car sleeper, from that first journey, when we'd strapped him, screaming, into his car seat, to the hurried relocations to Manchester and then to Leeds, and since then whenever we'd had enough money set aside and Cris could take the time off the various jobs to go off for a few days camping. I certainly couldn't have slept on this journey, winding our way across and up the country. It had been Cris's idea to follow the more direct but slower, scenic route rather than racing to our destination along the motorways.

Stroking the limp hand, I couldn't stop another tear bleeding out of the corner of my left eye. I squeezed my eyes tight, trying to once more dam the flow. Fourteen years and seven months ago, as a brand-new, inexperienced, frightened parent, I'd instinctively reached out to hold and stroke the tiny hand sticking out from the tight embrace of the enormous car seat.

This time it was the other way around. It was I who felt imprisoned by a seat belt, unable to control the wailing inside me or the sobs that escaped my attempts at calm resolve. Meanwhile, it was our confident, self-assured son who had reached out to squeeze and stroke my hand as we set off. I could see the fear and uncertainty in his eyes. Not fear and uncertainty of what lay ahead for him, but of what this would do to me.

Cris's gaze met mine in the rear-view mirror. I tried my best to blink away the wetness around my eyelids.

'I still don't get why we're only taking him as far as Carlisle,' Cris said. 'I really wouldn't have minded taking him all the way to where he needs to get his boat. We could have taken the tent and had a few days' camping. We could still have a few days away after, if you want. Find a little cottage or B and B to stay in.'

'No, Cris, let's just get this done and get back home.' I couldn't face maintaining a calm, polite façade in front of any effusive B and B owner for the next few mornings.

We had tried to persuade DiG to let us get Joh closer to the island ourselves, but there was no budging them from the deal they had proposed. Bring him to Carlisle with a minimum of one thousand five hundred in cash. They promised that they wouldn't be taking any of this for themselves. I was shocked to hear it, but from Carlisle, he would be on his own. They were unwilling to do anything that might endanger their delicate operation of smuggling children to the island or, worse still, risk the island community itself being discovered.

When he bought his ticket at the train station in Carlisle, it wouldn't be a straight-through ticket to wherever it was he'd be getting a boat. The folk we were meeting in Carlisle only knew the destination for the first leg of the journey. From there, we were relying on the integrity of a chain of 'trusted friends' who had been put on standby to look out for him and give him his next destination. We were assured than none of them would demand any of his money, except for the boat operator at the end.

I wondered again how it was that we'd ever consented to do this. But then I'd remembered that it hadn't in the end been our decision.

I'm ashamed to say that Cris and I had argued almost daily for a solid two months after Lily's visit. As we did, I became less and less confident of my own arguments but more and more stubborn about defending my corner. Then one evening, as I bent down to kiss him good night, Joh propped himself up on his elbow, looked at me with exquisite calm and said in a quiet voice, 'Can you go and get Cris?'

'But Cris has already said goodnight to you, my love, and is eating tea now.'

'I know, but I need to talk to both of you,' he insisted. 'At the same time.'

So I dragged Cris out of the kitchen and into Joh's bedroom, and we sat either side of his pillow and waited to hear what was so important that he needed to say it to us both at the same time.

'I want to go to the island.'

We sat there and, for a moment, stared over his head at one another. My face must've displayed my shock because I was flabbergasted that Cris might have talked to Joh about the island. I'd assumed they would have done everything possible to keep Joh ignorant of its existence. Cris, meanwhile, looked at me with accusatory contempt. I could see their thoughts. *How dare you tell him about it without my consent and then use him to manipulate me into agreeing to it!* The truth of it was that we'd neither of us told him, yet we both had.

'You think you've only been arguing about it when I've been asleep. But it's hard to sleep when you're shouting at each other, and I couldn't help overhearing what you were talking about. I'm sorry.' With that, his chin dropped down onto his chest, and I noticed the almost imperceptible quivering of his shoulders as he tried to hold in his emotions.

'Oh, Joh, don't worry. You don't need to go anywhere. We'll stop shouting at each other, I promise.' I looked up at Cris, who nodded and agreed in comforting murmurs, resting a hand of affirmation on our son's shoulder.

'But I want to go. It's the right place for me.' He sat up straighter with that characteristic self-confidence that I'd nurtured and had come to treasure. 'I want to be Joe with an "e", like you've told me I might have been, in a different world.'

'You don't know anything about the island, though, love. *We* don't even know anything about it. Not really.' It was finally time to surrender my stubborn corner.

'I've heard enough,' he said. 'You've told me all the good things about how I'll be with other people like me, Georgy. And Cris, you've told me it might be dangerous for me to get there and how there'll be no adults to look after me if I do.' Was this really our boy speaking, who, though he'd be fifteen in less than six months, still felt so far from adulthood?

'OK, we'll talk about it tomorrow. But we're not making any promises, OK? Except that Cris and I will stop arguing about it.'

He didn't need to hear anything else. He snuggled down back into bed, and together we pulled the crumpled covers up over his shoulders and kissed his head.

'HAVE YOU HEARD back from them yet?' I was asked every day, at least twice a day, for two long weeks of putting it off, hoping that he'd change his mind or miraculously forget about it.

'You have actually contacted them, haven't you?' was the new question on day fifteen, and my moment of hesitation was both his answer and the end of putting it off, as Joh sat at the keyboard and we worked together on the wording of the message I finally consented to send.

So IT WAS that however slow and scenic the route Cris had taken us on, we both knew it was also impossible to put off forever our arrival into the little city of Carlisle.

A few minutes later, we were pulling up in the station car park and walking towards the agreed meeting point below the bell tower and clock. Joh insisted on carrying his own small backpack. We'd been instructed not to pack much – a spare set of clothes, a few snacks, the money, and one or two special personal items if we wanted. For Joh, it was his clarinet, a sketchpad, and box of drawing pencils.

They were both already there. Not Jay and Lily but two strangers who we knew from their looks and nods were the people we were meeting. They could have been the same two we'd met in that layby fourteen years and seven months in the past. I couldn't be sure, and neither gave us a name, then or now.

One stayed back with us by the clock whilst the other led Joh into the station to help him buy his ticket. 'You can see him off on his train, but you can't know where he's getting off,' our minder explained.

The train was due in twenty minutes – twenty minutes that I begged to pass quickly and never pass at all as we sat in a grubby station café hugging our coffees and hot chocolates, stealing glances at the two strangers discreetly guarding us from a few tables away, one irritatingly tapping Joh's ticket on the table.

And then it was time. The café darkened as the train squealed to a halt outside. As one, half of the café stood up and shuffled towards the doors. There was time for one final, short, three-person hug.

'Go and be Joe with an "e",' I whispered in his ear before the ticket tapper moved alongside us and, without touching, tore us apart.

For a painful second, Joe was hidden from our sight on the platform edge as the stranger slipped the ticket into his hand. The stranger stepped aside as Joe looked over his shoulder. A little smile, a little wave, a little step up, and the doors thunked shut with our son trapped behind them.

The two strangers were gone when we finally turned towards the exit. Hand in hand, we walked silently to the car and took the motorway back to Leeds.

Chapter 32

A DAZZLING ELECTRIC BEAM blinked on, and Joe immediately regretted turning around to face the shouting voice. He lifted a hand up to shield his eyes and almost toppled backwards into the boat, stumbling to find his balance. Turning his head to stare back into the darkness, spots danced before his eyes. As the cavorting blobs settled and faded, he was confused to see the silhouette of a short-haired stranger standing beside him, just centimetres away. The head of the stranger turned towards him, revealing the wide-eyed face of Nats without its normal frame of curly dark locks.

'Sorry,' said the voice. 'Didn't mean to blind you.' The beam of light dropped, and their faces were shrouded once more in darkness. Their headless shadows bounced up and down on the rippling waves. Joe dared to look back towards the light and, as he suspected he would, picked out the tall bulk of Tom behind it.

'Aw, Tom,' said Nats. 'Couldn't you have left it just a minute or two more? Then we'd have been sea bound and out of reach before you stopped us.'

'You knew he was coming? Did you tip him off?' Cain called out, unable to disguise his disgust at the betrayal.

'Of course I didn't! I was just saying he'd come too soon. Oh, never mind.'

'S'pose that's it then, is it?' Joe mumbled dejectedly. 'All those careful preparations and we've been foiled at the last moment.'

'Well, we could have been away a whole hour ago if it hadn't been for *her* announcing at the last minute that she wanted to come with us.'

'And if you two hadn't stopped pushing as soon as Tom called out, we could have been out of even his depth before he'd reached the water.'

'Oi, put a sock in it, all of you, for a moment,' Tom shouted above the bickering. 'How are you going to make it all the way across neut Britain if you can't even get yourselves off this island without tearing each other to pieces?'

If there had been socks to hand, it wouldn't have been difficult at that moment to post at least a pair into each of their wide open, unspeaking mouths.

'Who told you about our plans?' Nats demanded.

Joe felt his ears burning. Not that he'd said anything to anyone that might have even hinted at what they'd been planning, but if it hadn't been Nats and it certainly wasn't Cain, they'd both assume he'd let the cat out of the bag.

'Nobody told me, and don't worry. I haven't mentioned it to anyone else,' Tom reassured them. 'One of the benefits of keeping myself to myself is that other people don't pay me much attention, including you three, it would seem. I've been watching you, though. You've been spending a lot of time together and making a lot of trips to and from this little cave here. I couldn't resist having a peek at what you were hiding in there.'

'Was it that obvious what we were planning?' asked Joe.

'Nah. I must admit, it didn't make much sense until I overheard you arguing tonight. I mean, I'd worked out you were planning to leave the island for some reason, but I couldn't work out why. You all seem so happy here.'

'Oh, we are all happy here, Tom,' said Nats. 'Well, Joe and I are. I'm not so sure about Cain sometimes, but even he's been less grumpy recently.' Even in the dim, torchlit darkness, Joe could sense Cain's disgruntled glare at Nats. 'Guess he'll be back to his old grumpy self now we'll have to stay.'

'Who said anything about you staying?'

'You mean you're not going to try to stop us?' Joe asked in disbelief.

Tom chuckled. 'If I'd wanted to do that, I'd have saved you the trouble of loading up the boat, twice. And I'd have saved your dignity by stopping you from giving each other those ridiculous haircuts.' He shone the torch briefly in each of their faces, making them all squint once more. 'I suggest you have a good look at each other and do a bit of tidying up before you set off anywhere in daylight.'

'So I suppose you want to come too,' said Cain.

'Ha, not likely! No, much as I might be able to beat you in any grumpiness competition on this island, I quite like my life here, and I certainly wouldn't let any of you near me with those scissors.' The torch beam wobbled as he rubbed his chin. 'Even if you could shave off this beard, I'm not sure I'd manage to pass myself off as a neut. You three, though, are young enough to still be in with a chance.'

Cain waded back into the water. 'In that case, give us a push, Tom, and we'll be off. If we're not gone soon, we'll not be across before the sun comes up. Thanks for coming to see us off.'

Nats and Joe followed Cain's lead, echoing their own gratitude to Tom and then turning back to the job of getting their little overladen tub afloat.

'Hang on a moment. I didn't just come down to scare you half witless before waving you off. I've got something for you.'

Tom held out an old leather wallet. 'It might not get you all the way, but there's just over eight hundred in there. It's no use to me here.'

Cain's attention was now fully back on the shore and on Tom. Having cash meant they could pay for train tickets, and that must at least double their chances of making it to Dover. 'Where did you get that from?'

'Most of it I rescued from the farmhouse as we were leaving. The rest, I've managed to salvage off people who've arrived here with some left over. Sandra knows I've got it. At least, the bit I got from the farmhouse. She's never been that bothered for proper money because we haven't got any use for it here. It's far easier to run our island economy on favours and tops. People somehow don't get as greedy or selfish over those as they do these strange bits of paper with faces on.'

Tom stepped forwards and planted the bulging leather wallet in Joe's hand. Joe muttered a thank-you, but before he could step back towards the boat, Tom clamped his shoulders in a vice-like grip.

'Don't let those two boss you about. Either of them,' he said in a quiet, low voice. 'You're the level-headed one, and they wouldn't have got even half this far without you.'

Tom let go of Joe and looked over towards the other two. 'Aren't you going to come and say goodbye too?'

Nats bounded over and buried herself in Tom's chest. He ruffled her short hair. Cain sidled over to join them and held out his hand to shake Tom's. 'Keep an eye on Charlie for us, won't you?'

'Consider it done,' Tom replied with a salute.

'Oh and,' Cain started, 'don't suppose we could borrow your torch? We'll buy you some new batteries.'

Tom chuckled once more. 'It's yours,' he said, handing it to Cain. 'I was on my last set of batteries anyway, and they're probably nearly used up after tonight.'

Over the next few moments, the four of them pushed the boat out onto the water. Tom stepped back as they floated off and gave them a final wave.

'You going to keep that torch on so Anthony and Gemma can spot us?' Joe chided Cain.

The light clicked out, plunging them into utter darkness, the island just a blacker blackness bobbing up and down as Cain and Joe fumbled around for the oars.

Chapter 33

27/11/2031

Eleven weeks since implantation, ~14 weeks into pregnancy by standard measures.

Still no sign of phallus development but urogenital groove is beginning to fuse. Had expected this λY foetus to develop as male, given its Y chromosome.

Hormone tests indicate low levels of DHT and androsterone. Placenta appears functional but underdeveloped.

Apart from sex organs, foetus appears to be developing normally:

- Crown-rump 91 mm, a little above average.
- Head circumference 95 mm, a little below average.
- Heart rate 150 bpm – normal.
- Arms, legs, hands, and feet all developing normally and active.
- Regular facial movement now detectable.

Mother doing well. Blood pressure normal. Maintaining good weight.

Psychological analysis of mother also very positive, raising no concerns.

28/11/2031

Meeting in London with SAGE all day today.

Further work from O'Leary & Carmichael has failed to come up with any more stable pseudo-ova than the first iteration of λ-ova, as used in our developing foetus.

Mixed opinions on whether to proceed with further surrogate trials. Consensus is to wait until start of third trimester for S1.

Virologists are no closer to eradicating virus from water supplies. It appears indestructible. Only known impact of virus is destruction of X chromosome gametes and deformation of Y chromosome gametes. Given this damage is irreversible, work on development of any retroviral treatments is currently futile, particularly following UN statement published on Wednesday (see below).

UNITED NATIONS GENERAL ASSEMBLY

STATEMENT FROM THE SECRETARY-GENERAL ON BEHALF OF THE GENERAL ASSEMBLY ON UN RESPONSE TO UK/IRELAND BIOLOGICAL ATTACK AND ONGOING QUARANTINE AND INTERNATIONAL SUPPORT

NEW YORK

WEDNESDAY 26TH NOVEMBER 2031

The delegates to the United Nations General Assembly today voted unanimously to stand shoulder to shoulder with the United Kingdom and Republic of Ireland in condemnation of the devastating biological attack which took place earlier this year on 25th March 2031. We commit to doing all in our power to apprehend any persons in any of our territories suspected of involvement in the UK attack or any attempt to proliferate the virus further.

We praise the fast response and full cooperation of the UK and Irish governments and citizens, which has enabled us to contain the virus and prevent its spread into mainland Europe and beyond. Without this action, we would undoubtedly be facing the mass extinction of the human race.

As an assembly, we have committed ourselves to the continued support of our friends in the UK and Ireland in whatever way we can, through scientific research and ongoing unmanned delivery of food and medicines until such time as the quarantine can be lifted, or the governments of the UK and Ireland advise us that our aid is no longer required.

All member states of the United Nations have also committed to grant unconditional permanent residency to any UK or Irish citizen currently living within their borders and to make provision for supporting and maintaining the British and Irish ways of life in these dispersed communities.

Isabella Santos Pereira

Secretary-General of the United Nations

Part 3

Chapter 34

THE BLACKNESS OF that night had been so all consuming that at times they could have been rowing themselves around in circles and wouldn't have known it. Perhaps as the sun rose, they'd find themselves back where they'd started or, worse, far out in the endless ocean with a horizon of salty water in all directions.

After what felt like an eternal night, however, the grey light of a cloudy morning began to draw edges around what had been shapeless darkness. The boat rocked as all three scoured the horizon for evidence of land, and there was a collective sigh of relief as they saw first the distant pimples of familiar islands and then, much closer, the endless stretch of mainland peaks and troughs. The oars that had, for at least the last hour, bobbed up and down aimlessly under the guidance of weary hands plunged with new energy into shallower and shallower water.

Working with surprising synchronicity, the three children leapt out of the boat, gasped as they sank to their waists in icy water, and dragged their now-refloated vessel away from the sea's grasp.

Their cargo safely beached, the companions finally took the time to look at one another. Within seconds, their purposeful seriousness was displaced by uncontrollable giggles.

'Tom was right, Joe. You need to do a bit of a better job on Cain's haircut before we take him anywhere in public.' Nats paused to get her laughter under control. 'Perhaps I'd better have a go instead.'

Cain's laughter ceased as he glared with incredulity at Nats. 'You think I'm letting you get anywhere near me with those scissors? I'm sorry, Joe, but if you could see what she's done on your head, you'd be weeping instead of laughing.'

'What do you mean? I think I did a pretty good job, considering I could barely see when I finally got hold of the scissors. At least it's symmetrical.'

'Ha, only if you're meaning symmetrical front to back.'

'Hey, that's not fair! What gives you the right to criticise anyway? You didn't even do any of the hair cutting.'

'Only cos you grabbed the scissors first when it came to Joe's hair. I reckon if we'd given him the chance to choose who cut his hair, Joe would have asked me to. I'm much more careful and could have done a much better job.'

'Hey! Stop it, will you?' Joe had to shout to get either of them to even acknowledge he was still there. 'Tom was also right when he said we'd never make it if we kept on with all this arguing.'

'Well, to be fair, those weren't Tom's exact words. What he actually said was –'

Joe surprised himself when he managed to silence Nats with the sternest glare he could muster.

'We *do* need to sort out our hair, and to be honest, I don't really mind who does mine. I trust both of you, believe it or not. But what I want to do before anything else is have something to eat. I'm famished.'

Joe got a grunt of agreement from Cain. 'I don't think there's any hurry to move on from here either. It doesn't look like we've landed anywhere near any sort of civilisation. I could do with a couple of hours' kip before we start walking anywhere.'

They had agreed to avoid landing anywhere near Mallaig, the busy fishing port from which Joe and Cain had each departed when they first travelled to the island. Apart from anything, it would have been a lot further to row. Instead, they'd headed for the nearest bit of mainland they could see from the island. By Joe's reckoning, they'd actually hit land a bit further south, which wasn't a bad thing. Surely, the further south they were, the closer they were to their final destination.

Once they had eaten, rested, and reorganised their packs, the plan was to set off in an easterly direction and to keep walking until they met the railway line that sliced down the country from north to south. They'd then turn south along the track until they came across the first station. From there, they hoped to travel by train all the way to Dover, particularly now they had the cash from Tom.

JOE ESTIMATED IT couldn't have been too many hours away from midday when they finally left the beach and their boat behind.

There had been no more arguments about haircutting. It was clear Joe was the only one who was going to cut Cain's and Nats' hair, which was much easier and quicker in daylight. When he finished, he was confident they both looked respectably neut. None of them had thought to pack anything like a mirror, so he couldn't be certain about his own new hairstyle, but it felt evenly cut as Nats wielded the scissors again with Cain making the odd grudgingly accepted observation from the sidelines. But there were no arguments, which was good.

They moved the boat to a spot where it was tucked away out of sight, in case they ever needed it again, though none of them spoke of why that might be. Their redundant nets were folded and stowed neatly underneath it. Everything else was bundled up, packed, and strapped onto their backs or around their waists. They assured themselves and one another that their loads would only get lighter as they worked their way through the food.

Making use of the compass Joe had salvaged from the junk room back on the island, they faced due east and strode with confidence over the sand dunes and off the beach. They were barely off the beach before they had their first disagreement over which way to go.

Just the other side of the sand dunes was an old, tarmacked track, overgrown but still in better condition than the one that meandered most of the way across their island. The problem was that the track went north to south while their plan had been to start by travelling east. Cain was all for marching straight on up into the rocky hills that rose up on the other side of the track, but Joe reasoned than any human-made road would surely lead them inland and towards villages or towns with railway stations. So they headed south along the track, given it was their ultimate direction of travel.

Nobody was happy when the track abruptly ended with the sea to their right and even rockier, steeper hills to their left and in front. Again, Joe reasoned that if this was where the road ended, then if they followed it back the other way, it would lead them inland. Sure enough, just a few paces from where they'd first come off the beach, they met a fork in the road with one direction continuing north and west and the other almost due east, inland.

The road east was mostly flat and they ate up the miles quickly, certain they'd soon reach some sort of civilisation, about which they were all clearly nervous. Every now and then, they passed small clusters of old buildings, all long derelict, with no signs of recent human attention. As they trudged on, the road wound its way around the hills, making for slow and steady but wearisome climbs. In the middle of the afternoon, the road brought them back towards a bit of coast before turning again inland. It was in the dim light of evening that they arrived back near the coast once more to find a small, deserted village where Cain announced they could stop and spend the night in one of the houses that still had a roof.

'How long did you say we'd need to walk for to get to the railway line?' enquired Nats moments after they'd got themselves moving after their lunch break on the second day.

'We didn't,' replied Cain, striding on ahead.

Starting with food that would go stale, mouldy, or squishy soonest, they'd eaten some bread, a spoonful of cheese, and a pear each for breakfast, followed by more bread and some hard-boiled eggs for lunch.

The road kept them within sight of a sea channel, which narrowed and widened and narrowed again as it worked its way further from what Joe thought of as the *real* sea. But like the road, the channel appeared that it might go on forever until it widened its mouth again to merge with the eastern sea.

'So we might be walking for another week yet?' Nats probed the unresponsive boys.

'It's possible,' Cain replied with no hint of a joke.

‘But I thought we were supposed to be taking the train,’ Nats persisted. ‘That’s how you and Joe got to the island in the first place, wasn’t it, except for doing the last little bit by boat?’

‘Yes, but if you’d been listening at the times when we’d been planning the route, you’ll know that we were never intending to go back via Mallaig. It would have been too risky with people who might recognise us from before or be looking out for any of us island kids. So we always knew we’d have to start by walking for a bit. Except that you might not have, cos you were never supposed to be coming.’

‘Hey, let’s not get into all that again,’ Joe interceded. ‘I think it’s better that there’s three of us.’

‘It would be if she wasn’t so moany.’

‘You’re calling me moany? You’re the grumpy one out of the three of us. Anyway, I was only asking. I mean, be honest, you weren’t really imagining we’d be on this forced march for a whole two days without even a glimpse of a train track, were you?’

The fact that Cain didn’t answer told Joe that he couldn’t disagree with Nats. They were all fed up with this endless road.

Joe tried to mediate as well as he could. ‘You’re right, Nats, but the plan should work. We will meet the railway line eventually, particularly if we stick on this road. At least we’ve not had any real hills to climb yet.’ He glanced with a sense of trepidation at the mountainous peaks across the water. What if they were still walking when they reached somewhere like that?

Day two ended, much like its predecessor, camping out in a derelict cottage in a deserted village.

'Why doesn't anybody live around here anymore?' wondered Nats as they explored the dank rooms for the one that looked the driest. 'It's all a bit spooky.'

'Did your parents never tell you about the wildlands?' said Cain.

'I don't remember.'

Joe rubbed his eyes as they threatened to well up with memories of stories his parents had told him, and in sympathy for Nats, who'd been too young to really remember any from her parents. 'Didn't Tom's ghost stories mentioned the wildlands, sometimes? You even lived out here somewhere in that farmhouse, didn't you?'

'Yeah, but I didn't think the spooky wildlands were actually real.'

Cain grunted. 'Reckon people just all moved to the cities once they needed the fertility units to have babies.' It made sense, as Cain's logic usually did.

ON THEIR THIRD day of walking, the sea channel petered out into a shallow, stony river, which they might have considered crossing were it not for the grey, forbidding hills on the other side. Besides that, the road continued to lead them steadily eastward along the river valley, so the walking was tedious and their feet ached, but it could have been worse. The tarmac of the road had also widened, which gave them hope that they might soon reach the yearned-for railway.

In the late afternoon, they almost considered taking a narrower road that turned off to the south, but they were by now resolved to stick to their plan of east until they hit the tracks. What they didn't expect to meet first was more water. An enormous lake loomed into view on their right, forcing their road to turn annoyingly northwards.

'Now what?' moaned Nats.

Chapter 35

UNABLE TO CONTINUE east and reluctant to turn north, they all agreed that exploring the implications of this new expanse of water was a job for a fresh morning. Looking back from where they'd come, they were relieved to spot the white buildings that had been camouflaged behind the thick greenery of trees as they had passed them. They retraced their steps and followed a track through the trees to a lonely old farmhouse nestled amongst tumbledown barns and outbuildings.

AWAKE WELL BEFORE dawn, Joe left a note for the other two and ambled the short distance down to the lakeside. It felt strangely weightless to walk out along the road without his heavy pack. A pink tinge gave definition to the layered eastern peaks across the water. He breathed in the now-familiar smell of fresh morning sea air as he sat and watched the colour in the sky grow and brighten from pink to peach to orange. As the sun's bright rays began to appear in a dip between two hills, something else was also rising: the lake, which had been tickling pebbles a few metres away, threatened to nibble at Joe's feet.

'WE'VE GOT TO follow the road north,' Joe announced as he burst in to find the other two frying eggs and dried fish in a pan they'd found wrapped in cobwebs in the back of a cupboard the previous night.

'Morning, Joe,' chirped Nats, cheery from an apparently good night's sleep. 'We had begun to wonder whether you'd decided to set off along that road without us.'

'Didn't you see my note?'

''Course we did, she's only joking,' chipped in Cain, almost as cheerfully as Nats. 'Besides, we deduced you wouldn't have left without your pack.'

'True, although I could be tempted. It was so nice going out for a walk without that heavy thing on my back.'

'So you say we have to go north. What makes you so certain?' asked Cain.

'It's simple, really. That lake out there, standing in our way, isn't a lake at all. It's more sea. It took a while for it to dawn on me. Well, it took dawn for it to dawn on me, to be honest.' Joe chuckled quietly at his own joke, which the others didn't seem to get. 'Thing is, I could already smell the salt and seaweed on the air, but it wasn't until I noticed the tide coming in that I realised what it meant. And I think I've worked out where we are.'

Joe thrust his arm deep into his pack, felt around for a while as if searching for the most exciting-feeling parcel in a lucky dip, and pulled out the folded, hand-drawn map that, until now, they'd forgotten to even look at. To be fair, it was never going to be a map from which they could have usefully worked out a walking route. For that, they'd have needed one of those massive, detailed maps like Georgy had bought to teach him about map reading and to allow them to explore the countryside north of Leeds. Sadly, the former inhabitants of their island hadn't been kind enough to leave one of those sorts of maps behind for them.

Joe smoothed out his inadequate little map on the old farmhouse table and grabbed the pencil to use as a pointer. 'I think we landed about here.' He pointed at a little nobble of mainland, surrounded by islands. 'And we've walked along here.' He lightly traced an easterly route. 'And now we're about here.' He tapped the pencil at a point that he remembered well from when he'd been copying the map out of the book. He'd had to rub it out several times, determined to make it just right. A narrow channel seemed to cut its way an unbelievable distance towards the centre of Scotland in a northeasterly direction – a narrow channel which wasn't narrow at all in real life.

'But why does that tell you we have to go north?' Nats asked, accompanied by one of her endearing frowns.

'Because if we follow the lake, or whatever it is, south, it will just get wider as it gets closer to the sea,' Cain explained as much to himself as to anyone else.

'That's right,' Joe confirmed. 'We need to find a way around it or across it, and the only way we're going to do that is if we follow it as it heads north.'

'Guess we'd better eat up and get going then,' Nats concluded. 'Want some egg and fish, Joe?'

Over an hour later, they set off at a comfortable pace and in a more relaxed mood than on previous mornings. The sky was almost cloudless, and the sea sparkled and shimmered in the light of the sun, which had already risen high above them. It felt good to know where they were, even though it meant heading somewhat away from their final destination.

The road mostly traced its way along the coastline, only once passing a little tree-covered peninsula, which temporarily obscured their view of the water. As they caught sight of it once more, the opposite shore grew rapidly closer and the road suddenly widened, briefly becoming three times its normal width. A few paces further on by what looked like an old inn, a concrete ramp sank from the road into the water. Across on the not-so-far-away other side, they spied its twin rising up again onto dry land.

'Reckon there was a ferry here once,' observed Cain.

But there was no boat available to carry them across the water now. Beyond this point, the waveless sea channel quickly widened again, and if it did eventually narrow to a river, that point was lost in the hazy distance.

'Could try swimming it,' Cain muttered.

Is he being serious, Joe wondered, *or just turning over the options in his own mind?*

Seconds ticked by, marked by the water lapping the edge of the concrete ramp.

'Are you serious?' ventured Nats eventually. As she continued, the wobble in her voice betrayed her suspicion that Cain really was considering it. 'I'm sorry, but I can't. I know I've spent half my life living on a tiny island, but, well, I've never actually tried swimming.'

Cain didn't answer but squinted in the direction of the ramp on the other side. 'I might be seeing things, but I'm pretty sure there are one or two boats over there.'

Joe followed the direction of Cain's gaze, and yes, there appeared to be boat-shaped objects bobbing gently on the water just a short distance from the ramp.

Cain started untying the straps that held his pack secure. 'You might not be able to swim it, but I could.' He lowered his pack to the ground. 'If you two stay here with the stuff, I'll swim over and bring back one of those boats.'

Joe was about to protest that it was a crazy idea, but then this whole venture was crazy. What other option was there? If Cain could swim out and retrieve bodies in a storm, he'd make it across this calm, narrow channel to retrieve a boat, wouldn't he?

'OK,' Joe conceded. 'But let's have something to eat first. You need some energy in you to swim across there.'

Chapter 36

THERE HADN'T BEEN many occasions when Joe had missed his old watch, which he'd left in his room on the island just a few days into his new life there. A few months later, when he'd started to plan what to pack, he'd momentarily picked it up, but noticing the blankness of the digital screen, he placed it back in its outline of dust on the bedside table.

At a guess, it must have been about two or three in the afternoon when Cain bravely stripped off his heavier layers of clothing and dived into the water, which Joe and Nats had both dipped their toes in earlier to confirm that it was freezing.

They watched in silence as the ripples around Cain's splashing form spread and then washed against the shoreline. For a moment, Joe looked away as a dark cloud moved ominously in front of the sun. When he looked back toward Cain, it took a while to locate him, and even then, he wasn't confident it wasn't just a rock with water splashing over it. If it *was* Cain, it was harder now to plot his progress towards the other side.

Large, heavy droplets of rain began to plummet to the ground around them, and Nats leapt into action, stuffing Cain's discarded clothes into the top of the bag and heaving it onto her shoulders.

'Come on, Joe, let's get this stuff inside before everything gets drenched.'

Joe hesitated for a moment, torn between getting somewhere dry and maintaining a vigil as Cain ploughed his way across the increasingly churned-up channel. Keeping their things dry quickly won the argument, and he grabbed both his and Nats' packs and bounded after her, towards the old inn.

The inn was dark, damp, and musty...or was that the smell of their own clothes? They found a window from which they might look out for Cain, but with the mix of ancient dirt on the inside and rain hammering the outside, it was impossible to see anything meaningful.

Joe didn't realise he was shivering until Nats put a hand on his shoulder and thrust an old brown, square-shaped bottle in front of his nose.

'Have a little taste of this. It's a bit odd, but it warms your insides up.'

Joe sniffed it suspiciously and looked uncertainly towards Nats.

'Go on. It's obviously meant to be a drink. I found it behind that long table-type thing over there.'

It smelt not unlike some of the drinks that Georgy and Cris would sometimes share on the rare evenings they had in together.

'But how old must it be?' Joe wondered out loud.

'Don't think it matters with these types of drink,' Nats commented with her characteristic knowledgeability. 'I think Tom and Anthony had a go at making something like this during our first winter on the island, but Sandra found it before it was ready to drink and poured it all away.'

Joe put his lips to the bottle and tipped it up, allowing the tiniest trickle to run down his throat. Although the bottle was cold, the liquid instantly warmed his insides. As Nats had said, it tasted odd, but the warming effect was nice. He took another, more confident swig and promptly coughed and spluttered as the pungent gas hit his lungs. Nats rescued the bottle from him before he tipped it over and took another large gulp for herself.

HE COULDN'T REMEMBER closing his eyes, but when he woke, the rain had stopped. He stood up and then dropped quickly back down onto his seat as the sudden movement made his head go all fuzzy. He turned, carefully and slowly, towards the window and peered out into the gloom. He wiped away a little more of the dirt and remembered Cain diving into the water, disappearing off towards the opposite shore. He remembered the rain, the inn, the bottle. The bottle still stood lidless on the table. Opposite him, Nats was slumped over the table, mouth open, snoring and dribbling.

Joe stood up carefully and slowly and reached over to give Nats a gentle shake. No response. He shook a little harder. Still no response. He turned, head pounding, and forced his heavy body to take him back outside. His ears were assaulted by the incessant grating of stones as the water lapped against the shore. The rainclouds had cleared, and the low, waxing moon danced its silver light over the gently rippling sea. But there was no boat moored up or dragged onto the little bit of beach. Nor was anything bigger than placid waves moving across the channel.

'Cain?' Joe called out, first hesitantly then three more times with increasing vigour. Only his own pathetic shout bounced back at him off the hills.

Trembling with cold, guilt, and fear, he hurried back inside. Nats was still well out of it. He opened Cain's pack and pulled out his big coat, tugging it on over the top of his own. He moved back towards the door but then returned to Cain's things and, finding his thick trousers, put those on as well. For now, they'd keep him warm and then they'd also be warm for Cain to put on as soon as he arrived.

Pulling both hoods up, he waddled out of the door and across the road. 'Cain?' he shouted once more without any hope of reply. He sat at the top of the concrete ramp that dropped down into the blackening water, pulled his knees tight up to his chest, and fixed his eyes firmly and unblinkingly on the quiet sea.

'Come back safely, please, Cain,' he whispered. 'We need you.'

Chapter 37

I TURNED THE KEY, nudged open the door to our flat. Strange. Cris had company. It wasn't the radio or TV I could hear but the low murmuring of serious conversation.

'Are you sure those are the only ones you recognise?' an unknown voice asked.

'Yes,' replied Cris's voice without any hesitation. 'But like I said, we've had very little contact with any of them throughout the whole ordeal.'

It was sixty-four days since we'd waved goodbye to Joh. The two strangers sitting with Cris at the kitchen table turned and looked towards the door as I let myself in. Cris didn't turn around, even when the latch clicked into the doorframe.

One of the strangers stood up and moved towards me, hand outstretched. 'Hello, my name's Finch Stephenson, and this is my colleague, Drew Williams. You must be Georgy. Cris has been assisting with some investigation work that we're doing.'

I cautiously shook the hand offered to me. Cris was still trying to avoid even acknowledging my presence. Spread out on the table were twelve photos. I spotted the one of Jay first and then Lily, although it was an old one from when she looked more like Leslee. It didn't take long for me to also find the two faces from Carlisle station amongst the remaining ten.

'What's going on? What sort of investigation work? Are you the police?' My heart pounded my ribs. What had Cris done? What had they said to them?

'I'm sorry, yes, I suppose we are the police, although we belong to a division that is...somewhat off the grid, shall we say. And don't panic, we've not come to arrest either you or Cris.' Finch Stephenson paused to smile, I guess as a gesture of reassurance. 'For some years now, we've been gathering information about this group of people.' Their hand waved towards the table. 'I understand that you are acquainted with one or two of them?'

I tried to look as blank as possible, although I knew Cris had already told them all they needed to know.

'Some of these people have been abusing positions of trust and responsibility in our fertility services. I know I don't need to explain it all in detail to you. You yourselves have been victims of their deception and dangerous experimentation.'

'I always said they were running some sort of experiment,' muttered Cris.

'Yes, and thanks to your help today, Cris, we're a lot closer to shutting those experiments down. To ensure that nobody else needs to go through what you've been through.'

'But what about the children? What will you do to them?' I blurted out.

'Ah, yes, yours is called Joh, aren't they?'

I wanted to correct them. Tell them to say 'he', not 'they', but I checked myself. How much did they really know about the true nature of these children? Did I want to say anything that might suggest I was a DiG sympathiser when it looked like they had failed in their cause?

'Don't worry,' Stephenson continued, 'the best interests of all children is our primary concern. We don't yet know where Joh and the other children stolen by these people are.'

My heart leapt with relief at that news.

'But if we were to locate them, you can be assured that they would be given the best possible care and medical attention. Joh could come and live with you again, if that was your preference. Cris told us you hadn't heard anything from Joh since they were taken from you. That is the case, isn't it?'

Now Cris turned to face me. Did they really think I'd keep something like that to myself? While I was glad not to have to lie, I had hoped we might have heard something from Joe over the last two months, even just a message to reassure us that he had safely arrived on the island, though in truth, we didn't know what had become of him. All we had was the hope that no news was good news.

'Well, do please contact us if you do ever hear from Joh. It would be in their best interests and yours.'

I WATCHED OUT of the window until I saw Stephenson and Williams walking down the path in front of the flat towards a nondescript black car. Then I turned my attention on Cris, who'd got busy with making some soup for tea almost before the two police officers left the flat.

'What the hell have you done?' I seethed.

'Only what you'd have done if it'd been you here instead of me when they turned up.'

Was that true? Would I have cooperated as it appeared that Cris had done? I hadn't exactly put up any resistance in the few questions they'd asked me before they left. But still, by the time I arrived, the damage had been done. It was Cris who had identified Jay, Lily, and the other two from the photos.

'OK, I'm sorry, perhaps you would have handled it differently,' Cris conceded, 'but what difference does it make, really? Joh's been gone two months. We need to get on with life and do what's best for us. Don't you think we've been through enough? In fact, if what I've done this afternoon means that nobody else has to go through what we went through, I reckon I've done good.'

'You mean you wish we'd never had Joe?' Cris had voiced regrets in the past, but I thought things had changed in those last few months, that Cris and Joe had grown so much closer and that in the end, they had found it as hard as I had to let him go.

'No, of course not,' Cris replied without the conviction I'd hoped for. 'But maybe it would have been better if he'd had the surgery. If he hadn't needed to hide anything. If they find Joh, Stephenson has promised they'll help him to have a life back with us. That's got to be better than hiding away on a little island, hasn't it?'

Could we trust Stephenson? Could we trust the government to let Joh live as Joe, or would they even now insist that he went through 'corrective surgery'? And what about Lily? Could she ever live openly as a female?

'And I'll tell you something else that's better,' Cris went on. 'Stephenson says they've pulled some strings with my old firm.' A grin spread across Cris's face. 'They're offering me a job almost identical to what I used to do but with twenty per cent more pay. We can go home, Georgy.'

I looked around at the kitchen of this little flat that we'd raised Joe in for most of the fourteen and a half years we'd had him. The scuff marks on the chair we'd strapped his booster seat to. The scratches on the worktop from when we'd used a craft knife to construct a cardboard castle. The orangey-red stains up the wall next to the fridge where he'd insisted on standing to squirt ketchup on his chips rather than bringing both chips and ketchup to the table.

'What do you mean, *home*? Cris, *this* is our home.'

Chapter 38

JOE ALMOST DIDN'T spot the bedraggled figure stumbling down the road. It was only the rasping cough that diverted his attention from the still, moonlit water he'd not dared take his eyes off since coming back out here.

He leapt up, also stumbling, as pins and needles jabbed at his numb feet. 'Cain!' he tried to call out, managing only a croak. The figure stumbled on, seemingly unaware that he had reached his destination. Joe cleared his throat and tried again. 'Cain!' he called. This time, the figure stopped and turned around.

'Cain, what happened to you? Did you find a boat?' Joe pulled Cain's coat off himself as quickly as he could and wrapped it around Cain's quaking shoulders.

'Y-yes, got boat,' Cain rasped through chattering teeth. 'B-b-back there.' He pointed with his thumb over his shoulder, almost knocking his coat to the ground. Joe caught it and pulled it back tightly around him.

'S-s-s-stupid,' Cain stuttered. 'S-s-set off when t-tide was going out.'

'Don't worry about explaining it all now. Let's just get you inside.' Joe guided Cain towards the inn.

'N-n-no proper oars,' Cain persisted. 'G-g-g-got dragged w-way too far down the c-c-coast.'

Inside the inn, Joe pulled over an old armchair for Cain to drop into and then hurried to fetch Cain's clothes. He came back to find Cain bent double, tugging at wet muddy socks that stretched and refused to budge. 'Here, let me help with those.' Joe knelt at Cain's feet and eased up his equally sodden trouser legs to find the top of each sock.

Meanwhile, Cain fumbled in vain with trembling, uncoordinated hands to undo the button at the top of his trousers.

'I can do that for you too if you like.'

Cain's hands flopped to his sides in resignation, which Joe took as consent to continue helping to undress him. As he pulled at the trousers, Cain's wet underwear came away too.

'Oops, sorry.' Joe's face flushed.

'S-s-s OK,' Cain managed to reply. 'Th-th-thank you.'

Throwing Cain's moth-eaten towel over his lower half and leaving him to pat himself down a bit, Joe concentrated on finding underwear and the two warmest-looking pairs of socks to replace those they'd taken off. In as dignified a way as possible, he helped to pull them up over Cain's legs and ice-block feet and then transferred the hopefully warmed second pair of trousers from his own legs onto Cain's. He worked for a minute or two at rubbing warmth back into those feet before realising his poor, shivering friend was still wearing a soaked T-shirt, the water from which would be seeping through into his dry coat and dripping down onto the dry trousers.

Lifting Cain's limp, heavy arms to remove his T-shirt was easier said than done, as was dressing him in four successively thicker and tighter layers of dry clothing. Finally, Joe rubbed Cain's thick but thankfully short hair as dry as he could before adding the final touches of Cain's special woolly hat that no-one else was allowed to wear and then pulling the hood of his coat over the top for good measure.

Even so, Joe's friend continued to shudder and shiver.

With more than a few reservations, Joe crept back over to the table by the window. Nats was still slumped over it, snoring unremittingly. He gave the bottle a little shake and was glad to discover that a few drops of the fiery liquid remained.

'Here, have a sip of this,' he urged, holding the bottle to Cain's lips. Cain allowed him to tip the bottle up and then coughed, spluttered, and dribbled its remaining contents down his front.

Within a few minutes, Cain was sound asleep. Joe lifted the blanket back over him and pulled up a seat for himself, halfway between his two sleeping friends.

'WHERE'VE YOU HIDDEN the boat then?'

A cold draught and bright morning light gushed in as Nats strode towards the still-sleeping Cain, who had at some point slipped off his chair and onto the hard floor. Joe jumped to his feet.

'Leave him be, Nats, and keep your voice down!' he pleaded in something between a whisper and a growl.

'Oops, sorry!' Nats chuckled with little evidence of remorse. 'Think the effects of that drink might still be wearing off. So what time did he get back anyway? You were both away with the fairies when I came round about half an hour ago. Can't see where he's left the boat, though.'

It didn't look like Cain was about to be disturbed by Nats' loud and boisterous morning voice, but keen for fresh air, Joe took her arm and guided her back towards the door.

'Don't you think we should wake him up so we can get going?' protested Nats, looking back over her shoulder at Cain. 'Reckon we've lost half the morning already.'

'I'll explain outside.'

'So HOW FAR down the coast is it then?'

'I've no idea. He wasn't in any fit state to give me details.' Joe's mind flashed back to the bedraggled figure stumbling out of the darkness. 'He needed all the energy he had left just to help me get him inside and into some dry clothes.' Joe wandered down to the shore and scanned the visible bit of coastline on this side of the channel. There was no sign of any sort of boat for as far as he could see. What if Cain hadn't managed to tie it up or pull it up out of the water well enough? What if it was even now drifting out to sea or back over to the other side? 'I suppose we should get on with trying to find it,' he muttered, mostly to himself.

'OK, let's go.' Nats looked back towards the door of the inn. 'Do you think we should wake him up to tell him where we're going?'

'Er, no. We need to let him rest.' Joe thought for a moment. 'I'm not sure we should be leaving him on his own, though. I can walk up on my own to look for the boat if you don't mind staying here with him.'

'You mean you're trusting me to be left alone with my weakened and defenceless arch-enemy?' Nats rubbed her hands and cackled, an impish grin dancing across her face.

'Ha, I didn't say I trusted you, but I probably won't be gone more than a few minutes.'

IT WAS WELL past noon by the time Joe turned the final corner in the road that brought the inn back in sight. He'd found the boat, but a lot further on than he'd expected. Not because it had drifted further out to sea. Cain had done a good job of dragging it up out of the water and above the high-tide mark, which must have been no mean feat given the weight of the thing. It was some sort of old sailing dinghy but missing its sails and at least half its mast.

How Cain had managed to propel the thing across the water, Joe couldn't even guess. Cain had said there were no proper oars. Joe hadn't even been able to identify anything that might have made an improvised oar. All Joe could imagine was that Cain had paddled it with his hands.

After all that, Cain must have stumbled and shivered along the road for as much as two hours to get back to the inn. It had taken Joe at least a good hour before he'd found the boat, and he hadn't been hanging about. In fact, he'd walked so far that he'd reluctantly concluded that the boat was gone but had kept on pushing himself a little further, just to be sure.

Joe knew it would be foolish to try on his own to refloat the dinghy and somehow paddle it up the coast without any oars. As he retraced his steps back to the inn, his mind worked hard, designing a means to construct sturdy and effective oars out of inn furniture.

'Thank goodness you're back!' exclaimed Nats as soon as he pushed the door open. 'It's Cain. He's burning up, like that girl Hope did before she died!'

Chapter 39

CAIN CAN'T DIE! Cain's the strong one. He's the one who always knows what to do. He can't possibly die.

Joe pushed past Nats. Cain was still lying on the floor, in the same spot as this morning. Nats had done a good job of making it more comfortable for him, and he was wrapped in every blanket and towel that they had, but still he shivered as if he was lying naked in snow. At the same time, beads of perspiration ran down his face and around his neck.

'What have you done to him?' Joe demanded in accusatory tones.

'What do you mean? I haven't done anything. Well, except give him some more blankets because he looked so cold and shivery.'

'But he was fine when I left earlier. Just sleeping peacefully.' Joe knew he couldn't blame Nats. He could see she'd done the best she could.

'Well, maybe he was, maybe he wasn't. Not long after you left, he starting moaning and calling out. I thought he was calling after you at first, but when I went to him, he kept on just asking, "Where's Therry?" Who's Therry? Is that one of his parents? I don't think he ever told us what his parents were called. But whoever it was he was asking for, he wasn't himself. He was shaking all over, so that's when I gave him the extra blankets. I had to put them back over him several times. They kept slipping off he was shaking so bad. He's calmed down a lot.' Poor Nats seemed to be sweating almost as much as Cain.

'But he must be too hot now. He's sweating all over.' Joe removed his hand from Cain's forehead and wiped it down his trousers. 'We need to take some of these blankets off him.'

'I've tried that. He just starts shaking really badly again, and then he calms down when I put the blankets back over him.'

Running a temperature were the words Georgy always used when Joe was all hot and cold at the same time. Then Georgy had always made him drink loads.

'When did he last have something to drink? We need to make sure he's drinking. How are we for water?'

'Yeah, well, that's the thing. I've been gasping for a drink of water all morning, but our bottles are all empty. I thought about going out to look for more, but I couldn't leave Cain on his own. You've been gone ages. What took you so long?'

'Well, we need to get him some water then,' insisted Joe, ignoring Nats' question for now. 'You could go out and look for some now that I'm back.' Nats had proven herself to be an expert at locating sources of fresh water on their journey so far, and making sure that they kept their bottles topped up whenever they found some. They'd just be walking along, and she'd suddenly stop and listen and then announce that she could hear running water over the other side of a rambling hedgerow or behind a rocky outcrop, and sure enough, it was always there. In this way, up until now, they'd never been short of water.

As Nats pulled the door shut behind her, Joe gathered up Cain's sea-soaked clothes that still lay in a heap on the floor. That was something else Georgy would do when he was ill. He picked up the soggy T-shirt and dashed outside to dangle it in the sea.

Moments later, he was back at Cain's side, dabbing his forehead with the cool, damp cloth. Was it OK to cool a fever with salty sea water? It was surely better than nothing.

Nats was soon back with bottles of fresh water, and between them, they managed to raise Cain up a bit so they could carefully pour some into his mouth. They nearly choked him, but once they'd worked out how to avoid flooding his face, he eagerly swallowed little sips. He closed his eyes and his breathing settled into a regular rhythm. Joe and Nats sat back on their haunches and looked at each other, relief seeping into both of their faces.

A loud rumbling broke the momentary peace. Nats laughed as Joe put his hand to his stomach.

'We've not had anything to eat today, have we?' She leapt up and started walking off towards a door in the back corner. 'I did find the kitchen earlier. The only cooker it's got is a gas one, and that must have run out decades ago. There are some old pans, though.'

Joe lost whatever it was she said after that until she re-emerged with a large, heavy-looking pan – the sort with a handle on both sides.

'I thought we could make some sort of soup with some of the veg we've got left. That'll be good for Cain, won't it? Do you want to chop veg or get wood for the fire?'

'Don't mind,' Joe said. Nats liked lighting fires. She liked to be in charge of the cooking too, but she could take charge of that if she wanted once she'd got the fire going. 'I'll do the veg if you like,' he offered.

'Great. See you in a bit.' Nats didn't need any persuading and was out of the door to look for firewood almost before he'd finished his sentence.

It took a while for Nats to get the fire going with the wood dampened by last night's heavy rain. In the end, Joe agreed that they could break up one of the wooden chairs to get things going with something dry but insisted that they dismantle it as carefully as they could. Before Nats set to work, Joe rescued the wide piece of wood that formed the seat and one of the long legs that extended all the way up the chair's back. They'd be a good starting point for his oar-making project.

It was easier said than done getting the soup into Cain. Nats did her best to pulverise it into a mush, but more ended up down his front than inside him. And still he shivered and sweated and called out for Therry – all through the night. What if he was worse in the morning? What else could they do? Joe told Nats to shut up when she reminded him about the girl Hope, who'd been found dead one morning when she'd shivered and sweated for two days after jumping off a boat into the sea. That wasn't going to happen to Cain. He'd swum in the cold sea plenty of times. Even so, Joe's dreams were filled with the grassy mounds of the island graveyard.

During the day in between two restless nights, with a tired head, Joe puzzled over the construction of his oars, dismantling another couple of chairs in the process, the spare bits of which fed the fire. He yearned for Cain's practical mind and strong arms to help.

'Could this be any use?' asked Nats, holding up something big and cylindrical that she'd found somewhere in the kitchen, trying her best to be helpful.

'Does that look like string to you?' Joe snapped back. 'Why hasn't this place got anything useful like string?'

'I reckon we can make something like string out of this. Look, just hold this a moment.'

What was she on about? How could a large plastic cylinder be turned into string?

'Oh! I see!'

Nats handed Joe the cylinder but kept hold of the ends of the thin clear plastic that was wrapped around it – no, in fact, the cylinder was itself a massive role of thin, clear plastic. Metres and metres of the stuff.

'I'll hold this end still and you twist that round. That's it, like that.'

Sure enough, as Joe turned the roll over and over, the plastic film twisted into what looked like some pretty strong cord, and there was plenty of it.

'Not bad, Nats. Cain will be impressed.'

But what if Cain just got worse? Would they carry on with their journey if he died? No, Cain couldn't die. But what was the point in making these oars if this was the end of the road for them? How long could any of them survive with the food they had left? Maybe Joe should leave Nats with Cain and turn back, go and get help from the island. But on the island, they hadn't been able to save Hope, and what if Cain died in the days that he was away?

'I'M SURE HE's not as hot this morning.' Nats was bending over a still Cain.

Joe sat up. 'Are you sure he's still breathing?'

'Yes, of course he is.'

They needed to make some sort of decision today. If Cain was getting better, perhaps they didn't need to go back to the island. Joe crawled over to check on Cain himself. He did look and feel a bit better. So if Joe wasn't heading back, maybe he could...

He pulled on some extra layers of clothing, wolfed down a breakfast of honey cake, and picked up his oars. 'I'm going to see if I can bring that boat down here.'

It was a risky strategy, trying to move it on his own, but gazing up at the ceiling that morning, trying hard to dispel the graveyard images of his dreams, he'd worked it all out. If he got moving and walked quickly, he'd reach the boat about an hour before high tide. That should mean the water would be close to the boat, and once he got it floated, the tide would carry him up towards the inn and not back out to sea as it had Cain.

It still proved a challenge to get the heavy boat back out onto the water, first tugging at its stern, then moving around to the bow to give it a shove and a joggle, hoping to loosen it a little more from the sand's concrete grip, then back to heave once more at the stern. How on earth had Cain got it this far onto the little beach, weary from his swim and frozen half to death? *Don't think about death!* Gradually, the hull began to edge its way down the sand as the tide rose in sympathy to meet it.

As soon as it was afloat, the draw of the tide started tugging the boat on up the channel. Only one oar was needed. In fact, they were that heavy and unwieldy that Joe needed both hands to operate just one. Slowly but surely, he and the boat drifted on in the right direction and out towards the centre. Ideally, he'd have hugged the shoreline all the way, but there was a little peninsula to navigate around before the channel narrowed towards the old crossing point. If he was going to beat the turn of the tide, he had to get past it in as straight a line as possible.

It worked! Once in the centre of the channel, the rush of water carried him on faster and faster, past the peninsula, until suddenly the elements began to fight back. Was this the tide turning? Or the churning of currents as the channel split in two? Or was it simply the wind he could now feel gusting towards him down the valley?

Grunting and panting, he ploughed his cumbersome paddle through the water. He had to beat the tide before it beat him. He should have waited till Cain was well enough for Nats to come and help. It would have been even better with a fit Cain on the other paddle. But what if they were wrong and Cain wasn't getting better at all? This was a stupid plan. The whole trip was stupid. He should have headed back up that road toward the island first thing this morning, even if Cain was getting better.

Finally, the concrete ramp on the opposite side came into view and then the ramp on their side. Joe thrust his oar through the water, again and again. Just as he felt like he'd reached terminal velocity, the power and weight in his hand vanished. He stopped and lifted the oar clear of the water. The chair seat paddle dangled like a pendulum off its handle, the plastic string loosening and unravelling before his eyes. He grabbed the chair seat just in time as it threatened to break free and plunge into the depths. Thank goodness he had a spare.

By the time he'd manoeuvred his unused oar into position, he was facing the wrong direction, and the tide was now surely against him. He *had* to drive onwards on full power, trusting that his second oar would last for as long as the first.

Nats splashed out to meet him, the water soon engulfing her chest. 'Why aren't you with Cain?' Joe shouted.

'You need my help!' she hollered back.

As soon as she had a firm hold on the edge of the boat, Joe jumped out of the other side, and together they hauled it in.

'Good job, not bad boat work, Joe,' a familiar voice praised as he dragged his bedraggled oars across the road to the front of the inn.

'Cain! What are you doing outside?' he rebuked before he could stop himself or appreciate the weak smile that played across Cain's pale but fresher-looking face.

'Ha, that's a nice greeting for our recovering friend.' Nats squelched over to join them. 'How about "Good to see you looking so well, Cain," or "Well done, Nats, for nursing him back to health while I was out having fun on the water"?'

'Hey, that's not fair! I've worked hard bringing that boat up the channel. It's not been much fun, I can tell you.' Although to himself, Joe had to admit that the challenge had been exhilarating, and his well-thought-out strategy had worked. 'But yes, it is good to see you looking so well Cain,' he said, echoing Nats' words. 'And well done for looking after him so well in my absence,' he added for Nats' benefit.

Chapter 40

CAIN WAS DETERMINED that they should get on and cross the channel that same afternoon before the sun went down. He wouldn't countenance aborting the mission and returning to the island.

'But Nats has told me how much food you've used over the last few days, and we can't afford to hang about,' he argued when Joe raised doubts about whether Cain was fit enough to carry on. 'I'm not sure I'll be up for going far once we get to the other side, but if we don't have to start in the morning with a boat crossing, we'll get further tomorrow. Might even get to a shop.'

'What about the tide, though? It's on its way out now, and we don't want to be dragged back out to sea.'

'We'll be OK if we just point ourselves a bit north as we go,' reasoned Cain with his usual rational confidence. 'And it'll be easier done in the light. If you want to wait till the tide's coming back in daytime, it'll be nearly this time tomorrow.'

Nats seemed willing to take Cain's side for once, and Joe couldn't argue with his logic. 'Well, we're not going anywhere until I've done something to repair this oar.'

'All right,' said Nats. 'I'll get the bags packed up while you sort that out.'

'What can I do to help?' Cain asked.

'You can stay there and keep out of our way,' Nats commanded before Joe could issue his own rebuke at him for even considering trying to help.

As it was, Cain did help. He held the roll of plastic wrap whilst Joe twisted it into some fresh string to repair the oars. He was also helpful with his ideas too.

'Why not wrap a load of it round flat as well?' he suggested, holding up the rest of the roll, on which there were still metres of the clear plastic wrap. They became a machine as Cain let it spool out whilst Joe flipped his oar over and over in its path. The finished product could have rowed them twice around Britain.

'Let's do the same with the other one,' said Joe. There was plenty of the stuff left.

With Joe and Nats rowing and Cain shouting instructions for who needed to paddle when, having been flatly denied the chance to take an oar himself, it took no time for them to make the crossing, maintaining a persistent northeasterly course and landing with perfection just north of the concrete ramp on the eastern shore.

The ramp turned into a little road, which soon brought them out onto another road, wider than any other they'd met and might well have been one cars still sometimes raced along, though the weeds invading from the verges and the grass sprouting along the middle testified that it was no longer a frequently used highway.

Cain was all for powering on south down this easy-looking route, but Joe would go no further.

'You're all right, you've just been sitting around all day!' he teased. 'I need a good night's sleep before I walk another step.' There was a good choice too of solid-looking old houses on either side of the road. 'If we leave this little place, who knows how soon we'll find somewhere else to stop for the night?'

Over each of the next three days, Joe reckoned they walked little more than half the distance they'd managed per day in the time before reaching the ferry crossing point. The terrain wasn't really any harder than before, though when the road climbed steadily along a valley, it did so with a little more persistence. Although neither of them spoke of it, Nats and Joe both saw that Cain was no longer setting the pace, and he never argued against stopping for rests.

Morning one, they were almost mown down by their first sight of other human life. Walking side-by-side along middle of the road, Nats was nattering away about something or other until she was drowned out by metallic clatter, echoing off the hills. They looked up just in time to see a growing shape charging towards them.

Crouching amongst nettles, they panted with shock as the small truck thundered past, its canvas sides bulging with a full cargo. If the driver had seen them, which surely they must have done, they showed no interest in stopping to investigate what three kids were doing ambling along the road in the middle of nowhere.

Once the truck had hurtled into the distance, they untangled themselves and crossed the rusty but solid-looking metal girder bridge whose elderly rattle had sounded the alarm. It spanned yet another narrow channel of the sea water that seemed to keep on following them even though they had to be tens of miles from the actual sea.

As evening closed in around them, they hurried past a cluster of occupied houses. Clean cars stood ready for duty outside homes glowing with electric lighting. Soon, they would have to brave that first encounter with neut life. For now, they kept to the shadows and passed as quickly and quietly as possible. They'd used up all their vegetables in soups at the inn. But if they were careful, the fruit, honey cakes, fish, and bits of stale bread would last a few more days. It would be better to make that first contact in a busier place where their presence might draw less attention.

Could they now rely on finding a convenient derelict house to bed down in? Joe was determined, for Cain's sake, that they would not spend the night out in the open. Thankfully, past the clusters of houses that hugged the road, a few buildings were set further back, nestled amongst wilder vegetation and emitting no warm electric glows. Warily approaching the most isolated, it was a relief to discover the familiarity of shattered windows and a holey roof.

Morning two, the road returned them to comfortable isolation and wilderness as they finally left the familiar company of tidal waters. Imposing, rugged peaks watched over them, the road cutting its path between ever-steepening sides. They couldn't miss the sound of the heavy van, straining to keep its momentum up the endless slow incline, and were out of its path and out of sight well before it reached them.

Night two found them a large house, nestled in the mountains, just after the road reached its summit and started rolling them down the other side.

Morning three. Their knees ached as each step landed them a little lower than the last. Steep ridges on either side gave way to large expanses of open rolling moorland. The wind gusted back and forth across their path, wheedling its way under their lifted collars.

Evening three. The sun refused to disclose any roof to shelter under before it sank behind the hills. They trudged on until they could no longer see the road ahead, then huddled together on the driest bit of ground they could pick out amongst the bogs in the feeble light of Tom's torch.

The following morning, under a leaden sky, three stiff bodies twisted into sitting positions and shivered as their blankets fell away. Wordlessly, they passed around cold food and water, stamping the blood back into their feet. Before he'd finished chewing, Cain had bundled his blanket and bottle back into his bag and started off down the road. Exchanging weak smiles, Joe and Nats stumbled after him, glad that he seemed ready to take the lead once more but uncertain how much further they could go on.

'WHAT HAVE WE stopped for?' Nats asked, almost colliding with Cain.

'Shh, listen.'

They stood stock still.

'I can't hear...' began Nats, but then her face lit up at the unmistakable hoot of a train.

Jogging on down the road, the invisible engine accelerated first towards them and then along in front of them. To their right, the ground sloped down from the road to the shores of a lake. To their left, it rose up in the start of a grassy hillside.

'This way,' called Cain from the top of the slope.

And there they were. The railway tracks, still buzzing with latent energy. The train was gone, but that didn't matter. They could follow the tracks to the next station and wait for another. Before this day ended, they would be racing south on dozens of pairs of wheels.

Nats strode with ease along the middle of the track, insisting that she'd hear the train way before she needed to move out of its path. Cain was almost as bad, crunching along the raised gravel edge as if walking a tightrope. Joe wanted to head back to the road that so obviously ran parallel to the train line and would surely lead them to whatever town or village hosted the nearest station. He did his best to keep up with the other two whilst leaping and tripping through the undergrowth, as far away from the tracks as he could manage.

The tracks remained empty for the hour or so it took them to reach the old station – a concrete island around which the single track split into two.

Cracked and crumbling, the platform had collapsed altogether in several places as saplings had pushed their way through fissures and then forced them wider, year after year. Half a rusting sign hung off one of its two supporting posts, telling the friends they had now arrived at *Bridge of...*

The remains of a long, low building stood in the centre of the platform, in oddly better condition than its crumbling foundations.

'That's strange. There are beds in here,' Nats called out from inside the derelict building. 'Who puts beds in a station?'

Whatever vocations this station and building had fulfilled through its history, it was plain to see that it served no purpose now. The only attention it got, if any, was that of the occasional maintenance team clearing the detritus it cast onto the tracks.

'Don't think we'll be catching our train from here,' muttered Joe as the three reassembled on the desolate platform.

Chapter 41

12/03/2032

Twenty-six weeks since implantation, ~29 weeks into pregnancy by standard measures. Also only two weeks from first anniversary of virus attack.

- Crown-heel 389 mm, a little above average.
- Head circumference 254 mm, small for 29 weeks but developing normally.
- Heart rate 139 bpm – normal.

Baby was sleeping and relatively inactive during my visit today but mother continues to report regular vigorous movement and is in good spirits. Video recording from nanocam also shows an active foetus.

The existence of S1 and her baby has so far remained a strict official secret, but this is about to change. With first anniversary fast approaching, Prime Minister wants to do media interview at maternity unit and release videos of foetus. S1 and exact location to remain anonymous. Not going public on foetal abnormalities for now.

Interview to also coincide with roll out of programme to 100 more potential mothers. Screening of candidates starts Monday.

Chapter 42

THEY ALL KNEW that the best thing to do would have been to get moving again, but they stayed at the crumbling station for the rest of that day. At first, despite Joe's undoubtedly correct postulation that the station was no longer in service, none of them was really willing to give up hope that perhaps the next train to pass through might take pity on them and stop to allow them aboard.

It was Cain, again, who first heard the train approaching, levering himself off the ground where they'd all been sitting for at least an hour, backs against the lonely old building. He took a few steps forward until his toes peeked over the platform edge.

'What is it, Cain?' Nats asked, breaking what felt like the longest silence she'd ever held.

'Train coming,' was all he replied.

Nats leapt up and then groaned as she straightened her aching back. Joe remained where he was. There was little point in moving for a train that wasn't going to stop.

The high-pitched metallic whistle of the wheels bounced off the concrete. 'Come on, Joe, get yourself ready,' encouraged Nats and swung her pack onto her shoulders.

Cain too stepped back a little from the platform edge, looking towards their heap of belongings, ready to follow Nats' hopeful example. Joe pushed against the wall and into a squat, ready to spring into action if the need arose but unwilling to muster the faith necessary to actually reach for his bag.

Sure enough, the train and its driver took no notice of Nats' frantic waving, although Joe thought he caught sight of a couple of younger passengers pointing and waving at the three strange, bedraggled travellers standing on the platform of a long-disused station.

Joe slumped back against the wall. Cain dropped his pack and ambled back to join his friend. Nats stood over them, looking every part the disappointed teacher of an apathetic class. 'You could have at least tried to help flag it down.'

'There was no way that one was going to stop,' said Cain bluntly. 'Even if it had seen us, it would never have got its brakes on in time. Sorry, Nats, but I think we all know Joe's right.'

'Well, I, er...' began Joe, not quite sure what he was going to say or why he was trying to protest against Cain's concurrence, wishing it was possible to prove himself wrong.

'OK, so that one didn't stop. But the next one might.' Nats' teacher admonishment had changed to the stubborn whine of a child half her age.

So they didn't move on that day. Obstinate Nats stayed close to the tracks, waiting and listening for the next train, frustrated by the boys' decision to move inside the building as the temperature dropped and the light failed. Another train did pass through just before the sun's residual light dimmed beyond detection, but again its speed betrayed the truth that it hadn't the least intention of stopping to let them on.

The one redeeming feature this station had was the beds. After their sleep-deprived night on the open hillside and the adrenalin rush of hope and relief draining to disappointment and despair, none of them needed any persuasion to each claim one of the least nibbled of the disintegrating mattresses and settle down into exhausted sleep.

THE NEW MORNING brought new resolve. No-one questioned the unuttered decision to continue their walk. Whilst they gnawed at their breakfast of stale bread and iffy-tasting fish, not even Nats gave the train that whistled past more than a disdainful glance out of the scratched and clouded window of the station building.

A few minutes later, they were following the train down the tracks. Joe argued again that they'd make better progress heading south on the road, but a united Cain and Nats were adamant that now they'd found the train tracks, it was nonsense to risk losing them. At least following the railway through this increasingly mountainous landscape meant fewer ups and downs; following the contours rather than scaling them.

In the isolated quietness, trains always betrayed their approach through the tinnitus-like singing of the rails long before the metal caterpillar came into sight and certainly giving enough time for the three to get well clear before it clattered past. There'd been one in each direction at what Joe estimated must have been about an hour apart.

In hindsight, it was foolish and reckless to have started out across the viaduct when they did. Although between them, they had no means of telling the time, it had been more than long enough since the last train for the next one to be about due. The sensible choice would have been to drop down into the valley and then climb back up to re-join the railway on the opposite side, even with a river crossing thrown in. But the level railway line reaching out on its stilts across the wide valley tempted them with a far quicker and easier route.

They very nearly made it too. They must have been at least three-quarters of the way across when the ironwork began to hum. At first, the lower-pitched resonance caught them off guard, hypnotising them for a few seconds longer than was prudent. When the veracity of their situation dawned, time galloped on as they assessed their narrow, elevated surroundings for somewhere to leap that wouldn't entail throwing themselves over the edge.

The blunt face of the unforgiving locomotive was already framed by the squat, castellated tower at the northern end of the bridge. Joe and Cain darted in unison for the same insubstantial-looking railing post to the left of the oncoming train. They collided, wobbled, and steadied each other. Joe's heart hammered, and his brain prickled with neural energy. How close they'd come to knocking each other down to the valley floor.

But what about Nats? Nats was still straddling the far side rail, rooted to the spot, eyes darting this way and that. Why wasn't she moving?

'Nats!' Joe screamed, stepping towards her as the train cast its midday shadow across the river below. Cain's strong grip clamped around Joe's upper arm, forcing him back into a restraining embrace.

The hurricane that followed as the carriages hurtled past threatened to lift them up and over the railings. Joe was certain that would have been his fate were it not Cain's added weight holding him down.

The train took an eternity to pass. But then, within seconds, it was a distant rattle, leaving behind an empty space where they had last seen Nats.

The more Joe blinked his grit-filled eyes, the more his vision blurred with stinging tears. Cain's grip loosened as he slumped to his knees behind him. Insecure in his own stability and unable to see clearly, Joe eased himself down gingerly beside Cain and pushed the heel of his hand hard against his pounding heart to stop it breaking free from its bony cage but only succeeded in constricting further his shallow, gasping breaths.

Cain curled up into a tighter and tighter ball beside him. Memories crossed Joe's visual cortex of that first time he'd seen Cain, rocking on a chair in his doorway, wrapped up in his own strange thoughts.

There was a crunch of ballast and the headache-inducing sun was eclipsed by a person standing over them both.

'Phew, that was close!' exclaimed the familiar, blithe voice.

'Nats, how did you...?' Joe left his question hanging in the air as he jumped up and then dropped back down to a safer position for his swimming head.

Nats squatted in front of him, concern creeping into her voice. 'Joe? Are you OK?' She paused, taking in Cain's situation as well. 'What's up with you two all of a sudden? We survived, didn't we?'

'Well, I can't say I'm sure how you did,' Cain bellowed back at her after a few moments. 'You were right in its path the last we saw of you. Joe here would have been too if I hadn't had the good sense to hold him back.'

'Is that right, Joe? What would we do without Cain's good sense, eh?' Nats asked sarcastically.

Vexed by Nats' apparent complete lack of alarm, Joe pushed back up onto his feet and lunged for Nats. His plan had been grab her and shake some sense into her.

Instead, he threw his arms around her and pulled her into a relieved, breath-stealing hug.

Cain *humph*ed behind them, but it was a relatively contented and stable-headed *humph*. 'Are we getting off this bridge before the next train comes then?'

With legs of jelly, they walked side by side off the viaduct. Joe was glad when nobody objected to the idea of stopping for a rest and a few bites from some of their last remaining honey cakes before resuming their journey.

No more than an hour after they'd set off again, they met another derelict station, this one crumbling even more than the last with no remaining evidence of what it had once been called. For a moment, as they paused for a few gulps of water, they thought they could hear another train approaching with its familiar rhythmic drumbeat, but no train appeared and its sound soon faded into the distance.

'Sounds like another line,' Nats observed. 'Shall we go look for it? Might find a train that actually stops.'

'Let's stick with what we know,' said Cain, leaving no margin for possible argument or compromise. 'Chances are we'll find they join up at some point anyway.'

They trudged all afternoon without stopping, and as dusk arrived, the alien glow of electric lights beckoned them like moths to a flame.

'Look.' Nats pointed along the track to where lights clustered around it, silhouetting squared-off platform edges. 'Surely, the trains must stop there.'

They hung back at the entrance to Crianlarich station, nervous of their first contact since leaving the island. Two other prospective passengers occupied the platform. Neither showed any sign of noticing each other, let alone any interest in the arrival of three raggedy children. But still, it felt as though those penetrating eyes studied them whenever their backs were turned. There was no staffed ticket office, just a ticket machine halfway down the platform.

'We'll have to hope they'll take our cash without any questions once we're on board,' Cain concluded after they'd searched the machine with both hands and eyes and found no means of feeding it with real money.

The other two had turned back towards the track when Joe caught sight of a small, faded but sternly worded notice next to the ticket machine.

ALL CHILDREN MUST CARRY A VALID TRAVEL PERMIT.

Following recent cases of child trafficking, all children, whether accompanied by parents or not, must carry a valid travel permit.

CHILDREN WITHOUT A PERMIT WILL BE TAKEN INTO IMMEDIATE EMERGENCY GOVERNMENT CARE.

Chapter 43

'WAIT! WE CAN'T get on that train!' Joe called out as the other two approached what looked like it would become their nearest door once the carriages had squealed to a halt.

Nats' finger stopped inches from the flashing button that would initiate their speedy transition back into the world of neuts. The two neuts from the platform had already boarded at another door, and the train guard hopped from one foot to another as the children hesitated.

'You kids getting on or not?' came the holler.

'Well, I'm not waiting for the next one.' Nats' finger travelled the remaining distance to hit the button. There was a clunk and a hiss and the warm air rushed out of the door to welcome them.

Cain reached out a restraining hand towards Nats. 'No, wait. We need to listen to Joe, and there will be another train.'

Was that guard about to head towards them?

'Come on, kids, stop your messing, we haven't got all day!'

Cain took a step back, pulling a reluctant Nats with him.

Nats huffed and shook herself away from Cain's grip. 'There'd better be a good explanation for this,' she said with a scowl as the door sealed itself shut in front of them.

'So WHAT DO we do now?' whined Nats. 'We can't just walk all the way to Dover. That'd take months, wouldn't it?'

The two boys stood there thinking.

'Could we call your parents, Joe, or yours, Cain? See if they can get us one of these permit things? I've no idea where either of my parents even live, but yours are in Leeds, aren't they, Joe?'

'OK, hand over your phone then, and I'll give mine a call,' Cain muttered sarcastically. 'I think I can remember their number.'

'Don't be stupid, I haven't got a phone. But maybe we could find one. We've got money. Maybe we could pay a neut to borrow their phone.'

'Yeah, right. "Excuse me, we're trying to get to Dover so we can sail across to France to see if we can find other people like us. Here's a tenner. Can we use your phone to call our long-lost parents?"' Scornful Cain then shrivelled into an abandoned child. 'Besides, I think my parents were glad to see the back of me by the time I left. I bet they've even made sure to change their numbers.'

Joe felt sad for Cain. True, his own parents had gone through a lot of trouble because of him and there'd been a lot of arguing towards the end, but he knew they loved him, and neither had really wanted to send him away. Hopefully, now they'd stopped arguing and were happy with each other again. He didn't want to cause them any more problems.

'I think we just have to keep on walking for now. Maybe we'll work something out along the way,' Joe cut in thoughtfully. 'It'll be different, now there are neuts around and we can buy some food.'

'Good thinking, Joe,' replied Cain, perking up a little. 'That's the first thing we need to do – buy more food. We can't keep going without food, whatever way we travel.'

They found a small general store in the middle of the little village and nominated Joe to go in and do the shopping. Nats hadn't been in a shop since she'd been handed over to DiG, aged four, and Cain didn't like talking to people he didn't know. Joe was, after all, the one who'd used a shop most recently. From when he was younger than most thought appropriate, Georgy had encouraged him to go out to the shops on his own as much as possible, to get used to doing things for himself.

Even so, a lump rose in Joe's throat as he pushed at the door, and he let it slam back in his face at first when a loud, electronic honk sounded as soon as it opened a crack.

'What shall I get?' he asked the other two.

'Things we can cook easily and that taste nice,' instructed Nats.

'Light stuff, nothing too heavy,' Cain chipped in.

Faced with shelves stacked with packets and tins, Joe was shocked to realise how alien all this now felt. How different it was from the dirty and misshapen fresh produce and heavy, nutritious oat bread he'd grown to love. He meandered up and down the claustrophobic aisles, pausing to stare at random items without taking in what they were or whether they would meet Nats' and Cain's criteria.

'You planning on buying anything, kid, or have you forgotten what you were sent out for?'

Up until now, Joe had tried to forget that there would be someone in here, looking after the shop. Jolted into a sharper consciousness of his surroundings, he spotted stacks of baked bean tins. *'You can't get a much more balanced meal than what you get in a tin of beans,'* Georgy had said when they were learning about healthy eating. He grabbed a bundle of four tins wrapped together and then decided they could carry one of those in each of their packs so helped himself to another two of the same.

Weighed down by twelve tins of beans, he moved on to look for some vegetables but could only find a measly selection, well past their best: a couple of soft, shrivelled peppers; a tiny, lonely onion, not even enough for a meal for one, rolling around in an otherwise empty crate; a few bendy carrots; and a floppy bit of cauliflower.

Watched and self-conscious, Joe searched around for a basket to put the tins of beans in so he could pick out a handful or two of the best carrots. He grabbed a bag of plasticky-looking apples as well and then moved on to the bread section. Six packets of wholemeal rolls were thrown in on top of the beans.

His basket already heavy and full, he balanced a few stodgy-looking slabs of fruit cake on top. That would have to do. Perhaps he should swap some of the beans for something else, but he just wanted to pay and get out now. At least they could eat the beans hot or cold.

Joe avoided eye contact with the neut behind the counter as his peculiar selection of purchases was scanned through the till. He fumbled with the wallet to pull out the right notes without disclosing how many more were folded up inside. Shoving the change in a pocket, it dawned on him that he hadn't come in with anything to put his shopping in. 'Can I have some bags please?' he asked with a squeak, finally looking up at the stranger's face.

'I've only got these and they're a pound each,' came the blunt reply, 'but doesn't look like that'll be a problem for you,' they concluded with a slight nod towards the wallet. Joe dug the change back out of his pocket and dropped the right coins onto the counter to pay the ransom for two bags.

'How come you've got so many of these?' Nats asked, holding up one tin of beans, having untangled it from its three siblings. 'In fact, are these all you've got?'

Joe had tried to explain how practical and nutritious baked beans were, but Nats just complained that she'd have preferred it if he'd got more vegetables.

'All you got was carrots! In fact, everything in here's orange!'

'Look, there wasn't really much choice. Not fresh stuff anyway. And I was being watched all the time, so I couldn't think straight.'

'It'll feed us for the next few days,' said Cain, 'and there are bound to be more shops we can go to.' The important thing now was to find somewhere safe to stop for the night, and that probably meant walking a little way out of this occupied village. There was no guarantee they'd find derelict homes to sleep in anymore.

So it proved to be that first night out of Crianlarich. Having left the village behind, there was nothing but empty road surrounded by scrubland, with pine forests a little further off. It was in one of these dark, dense forests that they made camp for the night. Failing to light a fire with the damp wood, they sat in sullen silence, each with a tin of cold beans and a bland bread roll.

After spending the night with the nocturnal creatures of the forest, none of them felt like moving, except that nobody wanted another night like that. At regular intervals, another train shuttled past not far from the road they were crawling down, taunting them with its speed. When they saw a derelict old cottage a few metres from the road not many hours after lunch, nobody argued when Joe suggested taking this chance of a night under a roof. They even managed to light a fire on which to heat up their beans, along with the last few bits of fish.

The going should have been easy the next day, as the road traced the western shore of another long lake, but Nats kept dropping further and further back. Every now and then, they'd stop and wait for her to catch up, but no sooner had they set off again than she became a little dot shrinking into the distance behind them. Each time they were together, she would insist that she was fine. Cain remained mute but his eyes betrayed his thoughts: *I told you we shouldn't have let her come with us.*

'Reckon it'll be all those beans we're forcing her to eat,' he grunted when she owned up to having tummy pains next time they were all in the same place on their third morning after Crianlarich.

'More likely that last bit of fish,' Nats groaned. 'I said it smelled off.' Even so, she stayed off the beans that night, chewing on a little bit of bread instead.

'GIVE US THE money, Joe,' demanded Cain holding out his left hand without any further explanation. They'd just caught up with him properly for the first time since their fourth breakfast of fluffy brown rolls. Why did Cain want the money all of a sudden? Joe had been custodian of the wallet ever since Tom had handed it to him.

'On second thoughts, just give me a few notes. Fifty pounds should do it,' decided Cain, still giving no more clues as to his plans for the money.

'Are you leaving us?' Joe asked. This was it; Cain was fed up with the slow pace and had decided to go it alone.

'What? No, of course not. I've just come back from a run down that road over there, and it leads to a bit of a town with shops. Thought I could go do some shopping while you two have a bit more of a rest. But I probably shouldn't take all the money, just in case we do get separated.'

Joe dug into his bag for the wallet. Cain was right. It had been foolish of him to hold on to all the money. He peeled off roughly one-third of the notes and held them out to Cain. He'd split the rest between himself and Nats when Cain had gone.

'I wasn't planning on buying that much!'

'No, but, you know, just in case,' Joe muttered, reluctant to tempt fate as Cain busied himself with emptying the contents of his bag into a neat pile to make room for the shopping.

JOE JOGGLED NATS awake as Cain repacked their bags with his admittedly much better selection of food. 'Can't we just stay here?' She groaned, curling herself up even tighter.

'I don't think she's in a fit state to go much further.'

'But it's not even midday yet. We've got to up the pace somehow.'

'Maybe if we let her rest properly today, she'll be better tomorrow.'

Cain looked doubtful. 'She's been like this ever since we let that train go. I can't see her snapping out of it.'

'She's getting worse, though. She wasn't as bad as this when we first left Crianlarich. Then she was just grumpy, like we were, but now she's in pain.'

'Then we have another go at getting the train,' announced Cain.

'What? But we can't, we'd need a permit, remember?'

'Well, we might, or we might not,' said Cain, thinking it through as he spoke. 'There's another station in the town, and there were loads of kids hanging around it without any parents. Do you really think the train staff check them all for permits every time they hop on a train to the next stop down the line?'

At the mention of getting on a train, Nats perked up so much that Joe began to wonder whether her stomach pains were psychological after all. She didn't have half the reservations Joe had expressed about Cain's new plan, and soon they were ambling along the busy streets of Balloch.

Chapter 44

How many times over the last nearly fifteen years have I fantasised about having a few days to myself with nobody else to worry about? I'm not sure I want to answer that; it would make me sound like a terrible parent...and partner. Now I was on my own, though, I wasn't sure I liked it. Of course, it might have felt different if I'd been in a cosy little holiday cottage with a wood-burning stove, or being pampered in a luxury hotel and spa, instead of coming home in the evenings to a cold, empty flat in Leeds, filled with memories of Joe and Cris.

I barely noticed Cris's absence during the week, now I had a job – a simple, low-paid accounting job that a computer could have done, but it filled the time I'd previously spent educating Joh and gave me regular contact with other humans. I was so used to Cris working evenings, nights, or early mornings that going to bed on my own or finding the bed empty in the morning was all perfectly normal.

The one reminder that Cris wasn't just out at work was when the phone rang each evening at eight-thirty and we chatted about how our day had been and skirted around any talk of how long we'd keep this up, or what 'this' even was – living apart or maintaining a relationship – but Friday evening was different. The weekend stretched out ahead of me with nothing and no-one to fill it. Cris had often ended up doing shifts for one or other employer over the weekend, but we always had some time to spend together as a family or, latterly, as a couple.

It hardly seemed possible that only a week had passed since I'd been down there helping with the move into that massive, new house – far too big for just one person.

'You'll come down again next weekend, won't you?' Cris had insisted. 'Don't worry about the cost, I'll pay for your ticket.'

I'd resisted because although we weren't separating, me staying here in Leeds was about more than the job I'd worked hard to get. I was staying because it was our home. Joe's home. What if he came back for some reason? If he turned up at his old home and found it empty and deserted or, more likely, found strangers living here. Even so, it wasn't logical, passing up spending the weekend with my partner of twenty years in the event our son, happily living with others like him on some remote island somewhere in Scotland, decided to pop back home for a visit.

I looked down at my phone for the thirteenth time that evening. Cris hadn't missed a night so far. Eight-thirty on the dot, the phone would ring. Was this the beginning of the end for us? How was I already wondering whether our relationship would last? It had only been a week! I grabbed another handful of crisps to help swallow the knot in my stomach. I really should get properly into bed, switch off the droning TV, work out what I wanted to do with my weekend.

The next thing I knew, I awoke to a grey light and with a crick in my neck. My phone was ringing.

'Hello?' I said, desperate to hear Cris tell me they were OK.

'Hello,' the voice croaked. Sounded like a hangover, but Cris didn't get hangovers. Sure, we enjoyed the odd glass of wine at home but never enough to get drunk, and Cris was the sort of partner who had never taken the liberty of going out for drinks with mates on evenings off. Time off was time together; that's just how we are...*were*. I supposed I couldn't really expect my other half to stay in alone on a Friday night, two hundred miles away, just because I had.

'Are you OK? I missed you last night.' The words tumbled out before I had the chance to check them.

'Yeah, yeah. We went for a few drinks after work. Didn't think you'd want me to call by the time I got in.'

'You could have...no, that's OK, don't worry.' For a few moments, I'd been ready to confess how much I missed us being together. How perhaps I could hand in my notice, and then maybe look at moving down permanently in a month or so. But I didn't belong down there anymore. Did I even belong with Cris anymore?

'...glorious day down here. Thought I might reacquaint myself with the town centre. It was always nice there on a sunny day, do you remember? What about you? Bet you've got loads lined up for the weekend.'

Those carefree Saturdays spent shopping, before Joh. Then shopping for all the baby paraphernalia. When had we last gone shopping together? I suddenly craved the carefree company of others, but right now...not Cris. Problem was, I didn't know anyone else. Well, I'd got to know some of the others at work, but not to the point of exchanging numbers. Besides, they'd all be busy with their normal weekend activities.

'Oh, one or two things, yes,' I lied.

If there was one positive from our conversation, it was my renewed determination not to spend all weekend languishing in the flat. I grabbed my coat and left, pulling the door firmly shut behind me. Must nag the owner again about that dodgy latch.

Catching the first bus that passed, I took myself to the ruins of Kirkstall Abbey, to see what the stones might tell me today about the people who built it, what they built it for, and why at some later point in history, they let it fall into ruin.

Chapter 45

THERE WAS A ticket office, but it would be a bigger gamble to try buying a ticket without one of those permits than to risk travelling without a ticket. On his journey to the island, with its frequent changes and meet-ups with the next contact on the route, only once had Joe's ticket been checked by anyone on the train.

Clusters of other kids hung around for the next train to arrive at the southbound platform. Why weren't they in school? Of course, it must be a school holiday. Georgy used to tell him to take no notice of the looks people gave them when they were out on one of their trips whilst other kids were in school. Even if it did mean more questioning stares, Joe much preferred those days to the ones when the world was flooded with kids on their school holidays. Now, though, the presence of other kids made Joe and his companions feel more conspicuous, not less. None of the other kids wore big, tatty coats or carried large bags bulging with stocks of food, spare clothes, and blankets.

As soon as the train pulled into the station, Nats surged forward and climbed aboard before Joe or Cain could announce any change of mind. They stood aside to allow the disgruntled neuts she'd pushed past to disembark and then followed her lead.

It was hard to decide which sensation felt more odd – sitting on a soft padded seat, being in a big metal box sealed off from the outside air, or racing through the countryside at what must have been at least twenty times the travelling speed to which they'd become accustomed. Cain didn't let them get too familiar with any of these, though, deciding just three stops and eight minutes down the line that it was time to get off.

'But we've only just got on! Why do we need to get off again?' whined Nats.

'Let's just do as he says,' Joe whispered in her ear. Others in the carriage had already turned their heads and frowned at the three of them.

Cain waited until they'd tumbled off onto the waiting platform before he explained. 'Firstly, we always said that we'd not stay on any train for more than a few stops. Makes it less likely the ticket inspectors will get to us before we've got off.'

'But surely, more trains mean more ticket inspectors, so more chance that one of them will want to check for the tickets we haven't got,' interjected Nats.

'Secondly,' Cain continued, undeterred, 'the ticket inspector on the train we just got off started at the front of the train in Balloch and was heading towards us. You couldn't see because you were facing the wrong way, but I could see them coming down the next carriage up from ours.'

'All right then.' Nats crossed her arms and huffed. 'How long are we going to have to wait now for the next train to turn up?'

'Only twenty-five minutes,' answered Joe, who had been studying the electronic signs while the other two argued.

This time, they paid closer attention to where they got on. The ticket inspector was right at the back of the train, so Cain led them to the very front of the front carriage. Unfortunately, this train was less busy, so the inspector was already entering their carriage as the train drew to a halt at the next station – a somewhat larger station called Dumbarton Central.

'This isn't going to work,' complained Nats. 'Sooner or later, we're going to be midway between stations when the ticket inspector gets to us, and then we're done for.'

'No, I think we can do this,' Joe said with quiet confidence. 'Look, from this station there are loads of trains going south. They're every few minutes. All we have to do is choose the one that looks busiest. If a train's not so busy, we wait for the next one.'

It worked too. Half an hour later, they were on a train so packed with passengers that there was no room to sit. There was no way the inspector was going to make it through even one of the sardine tins that passed for carriages on this train.

'Fwarr, it smells in here,' exclaimed Nats as they jostled against each other in the only space they could find to stand.

'Think you'll find that's us,' grunted Cain, embarrassed by his travel companion.

Once in Edinburgh, they had intended to leave the station. To do what, they weren't sure, but having reached Scotland's capital city, it felt appropriate to stop and re-evaluate their plans for the rest of their journey. Perhaps they could even find somewhere to buy some more detailed maps. They hadn't counted on being imprisoned in the station. Every exit was blockaded with automatic ticket barriers. It felt like the station boundaries were constricting around them.

'Don't panic,' Joe urged as Nats started wittering about different outlandish options for getting out of the station and Cain seemed to sink into himself, overwhelmed by the crowds. 'All we need to do is find another train to catch and only get off at smaller stations.'

As long as they were heading generally southeast, it didn't much matter which destination they picked other than one where the train would be busy. Joe guided Cain and Nats to an empty bench and left them with all their luggage whilst he went to study the departure boards and platforms. There was a bewildering plethora of possible destinations. Which ones took them in the right direction? He pulled the crumpled, hand-drawn map out of his pocket in a vain attempt at matching up place names on the boards with the few major towns and cities he'd marked on his map. Then the announcement blared out across the station and the conundrum was solved.

'Come on, we need to move,' he called as he raced back towards them. 'There's a late-running train to London, and the platform's heaving.'

'You mean we're going all the way to London?' Nats called back. 'Awesome!'

'I don't know about that,' Joe panted, 'but I think it's the train we need to get on.'

They got to the platform just as the train was grinding to a halt. Nats pushed forward with the crowds of impatient passengers, towards the opening doors. Joe grabbed her arm to hold her back.

'What? I thought you said we were getting this train.'

'We will do, but we need to look for where the guard is first, remember?'

Sure enough, as the crowd surged forward, they spotted the guard standing a couple of carriages up from where they were. To be safe, they dashed three more carriages down the platform, but they didn't need to rush; every door still frothed with people jostling to get onto the already creaking, bulging train. By the time Joe, Nats, and Cain got themselves aboard, the door could barely pull itself shut behind them. In under a minute, the growling engine was hauling the overweight train slowly out of Edinburgh station.

It wasn't the most relaxing of journeys, sitting perched in silence on their stuffed packs in the tiny lobby at the end of one carriage. Their tummies rumbled in sympathy with the train, but now wasn't the time or place to make a start on the goodies Cain had bought earlier, surround as they were by smartly dressed businesspeople. They were already polluting the stuffy space with their unwashed bodies.

More got off than on when they arrived, forty minutes later, in Berwick-upon-Tweed. It was still standing room only though, and there were no worries about being suddenly pounced upon by the ticket inspector. The further south they could get on this train, the better. Maybe they *could* even get as far as London tonight.

About half an hour later, as the low sun strobed through the windows, Nats got to her feet and glanced up and down the train, looking agitated. 'Need to go to the toilet,' she whispered into Joe's ear and then pointed down the crammed carriage as she started excusing and pushing her way through towards the other end, where the nearest toilet was situated.

The first thing Joe noticed was a dark, damp stain on top of Nats' pack. Then the same on the back of Nats' retreating trousers. As Joe put two and two together, halfway down the carriage, somebody shrieked.

'Hey, kid, you're bleeding!'

Chapter 46

A COMMOTION BUILT IN the carriage over the bleeding child. A melee of concerned and disgusted exclamations rippled up the length of the narrow, congested space.

'Somebody fetch the guard!' was the shout that rang in Joe's ears.

Already on his feet, he shouldered his bag and turned to Cain. 'I need to go after Nats, and I think we'll need to get off. Can you manage both your stuff and hers?'

Cain nodded and started securing his own pack on his back as Joe pushed his way down the carriage in pursuit of Nats.

People were only too keen to give Joe a wide berth as he shuttled down the carriage, though a few shouted complaints after him as his bag, wider than he was, thumped against heads that were leaning out into the aisle to see what was going on.

About three-quarters of the way down, a tall figure stood in his path.

'Excuse me, I need to get to my friend,' he pleaded, his voice cracking as he spoke. Had they heard him? He pushed on, squeezing his way through the narrow gap between the stranger and the seat.

'All right, pal, don't worry. I only want to help. You go and wait with your friend. I'll go find the guard.'

'It's OK, I don't think you need to do that!' Joe called after them as they strode off in the direction he had come from. Further up, Cain struggled along, lugging Nats bloodstained bag as well as his own through the narrow space. Hopefully, he would hold up the helpful stranger a little bit.

'Hey, this kid's bleeding too!' someone shouted.

'No, no, it's not my blood. I'm not bleeding,' Cain protested.

The helpful stranger took hold of Cain by the shoulders and drove him back towards the far end of the carriage. 'Don't worry, your other friend's already gone to be with the kid who's bleeding. Best if you stay put. It's already pretty crowded up there.'

Joe reached the locked toilet door. 'Nats, you've got to come out. The guard's coming!' he shouted, hammering on the door at the same time.

'OK, people, if you can just let me past, I'm sure we can sort out whatever this is.' The officious voice rang out down the length of the carriage.

Quick-thinking Cain pushed himself and his bags in front of the guard. The helpful stranger tried to reason with Cain and explain things to the guard at the same time, helpfully holding things up a little more.

They needed to get off this train. The green handle beckoned from behind its glass panel, its green emergency instructions alongside. Without a second thought, Joe smashed the glass and pulled with all his might on the handle.

For what felt like an age, nothing changed except for a piercing and persistent beep. It wasn't working!

'Hey! What do you think you're doing? There's no need for that!' shouted the guard, still struggling to get past Cain.

The train slowed and squealed to a halt.

A sheepish Nats emerged from behind the toilet door. 'Sorry, Joe, I couldn't help it.'

'It's OK, but we need to get off now,' he wheezed as, turning back to the doors, he strained to pull them open. Nats came alongside to add her weight and the sliding doors agreed to part.

'Now jump!' Joe gave Nats a firm push to prevent hesitation.

As Nats half jumped, half fell out of the carriage and rolled down the grassy bank, Joe turned back to look for Cain, but Cain had been wrestled to the floor by two passengers and even as Joe hesitated, the guard advanced on him.

'Just go!' Cain bellowed.

He glanced out towards Nats, now kneeling on the ground a frightening distance below, then back towards Cain and the guard one more time. He made his decision and leapt.

Chapter 47

02/05/2032

S1 went into labour early hours of this morning, approx. three weeks before due date. All happened very quickly. Baby delivered without intervention by spontaneous vaginal delivery with no complications at 07:10.

Postnatal examinations indicated normal heart and lung function. Infant is alert when awake, responded well to visual, aural, and tactile stimuli. Feeding well from bottle.

Head circumference: 303 mm (on 3rd centile) – could account for easy birth.

Crown-heel: 46 cm (around 10th centile)

Weight: 2.20 kg (around 5th centile)

As predicted from antenatal scans and photographs, visible genitalia approximately fit somewhere between stage II and stage III on Prader scale. Small, underdeveloped penis or enlarged clitoris sits inside outer labia with urinary opening just behind. No inner labia as such and no vaginal opening. Also no palpable gonads.

Initial results from pelvic ultrasonography, carried out four hours after birth, show no evidence of ovaries or uterus. Further scans to be scheduled in the coming days.

We have successfully engineered a form of apparently healthy human that can gestate in ANFV-infected environment. However, this new human appears unlikely to be capable of any form of natural or even assisted semi-natural reproduction itself.

03/05/2032

Infant fed well through the night and remains healthy. Also successfully passed urine and faecal material. Tests on samples normal. No further scans or checks carried out.

Five weeks since first implantations in 100-surrogate trial: 83/100 successfully proceeding to date. Remarkable uniformity in embryonic development across all subjects.

Chapter 48

BACK ON HIS feet, Joe grabbed Nats by the arm and dragged her into a stumbling run away from the embankment, across an open field. He had managed a fairly graceful landing; the heavy pack on his back had tilted him backwards as he leapt, so that he landed half on the pack and half on his bottom and then bounced and slid down the bank towards Nats.

Nats, on the other hand, had rolled and tumbled her way down the bank and was already in a fragile state before being launched off the side of a railway carriage, but although she was hobbling, she doggedly matched his pace.

They didn't dare look back, sure that at least the guard and probably half the passengers from the train were chasing them down. But no thundering feet churned up the ground behind them, and the commotion of shouts soon drifted away in the breeze. In fact, the air around them soon became eerily silent, aside from the muted thuds of their own feet as they bounded through the grass and the ever-accelerating throb of Joe's pulse reverberating around his skull.

The growl of the train's engines behind them threw them to an abrupt halt. The growling settled into a mechanised purr, accompanied by the familiar metallic squeal of wheels gaining traction on rails. They turned and sank to their knees panting. Their hearts pummelled away as if they too were being driven by the locomotive's powerful pistons. Unsure whether to be dismayed or relieved, they watched the window-lined carriages disappear behind a screen of trees and buildings, then, in exhausted silence, listened until the rattles and screeches of the train sank below even the hearing of their imaginations.

'Where's my bag?' Nats asked, looking down in anguish at her bloodstained crotch and then at Joe. 'In fact, where's Cain?' She hunted in all directions for their crotchety but cherished companion.

Joe squeezed his eyes shut, wishing that the stinging tears now rising behind the leaky dam that was his eyelids could wash away the truth flashing across them. Nats poked a fingertip into his tightly clenched fist and eased his fingers apart to squeeze hers in between. It took minutes and many blinks before the blurred watery lenses subsided to give him a clear view of his surroundings once more.

Nats smiled at him as his gaze came to rest on her face, but her eyes betrayed the same mixture of stomach-churning fear, worry, and guilt that would have threatened to deposit his last meal on the grass in front of him, had his tummy not already felt so hollow.

'I'm sorry, I didn't manage to get your bag off the train,' quaked Joe's voice eventually. 'I left it for Cain to bring. I should have grabbed it myself. I could have done. If I had, maybe he'd have...' Bile rose in his throat and stifled his confession, replacing it with retching and a renewal of uncontrollable sobs. Nats leaned in, resting her head on his shoulder, and her grief joined his, buzzing through his bones.

They heard but didn't really register the approaching sirens. Nor at first did they recognise the warnings conveyed in the militaristic instructions shouted by a commanding officer to their troops. It was only with the excited barks of the dogs that Joe's mind pieced together the jigsaw of sounds. He jolted away from Nats.

'What is it?' she asked anxiously. Then hearing the dogs for herself, she sprang to her feet. 'Come on, Joe! We've got to run!'

Joe used her outstretched hand to pull Nats back down to join him in a crouch. 'We can't just run. We need to decide which way.'

'That way!' declared Nats milliseconds before Joe reached the same conclusion.

They leapt to their feet and together launched themselves towards a dense cluster of trees. Nats was soon racing ahead, unencumbered by the weight of a heavy bag on her back. Joe's mind somehow found space in his working memory to revisit the image of chasing after the same girl on that first carefree day on the island.

He almost knocked her over as he caught up at the edge of the copse. She hopped from one leg to the other, tugging at her trousers.

'What on earth are you doing?' he panted.

'Taking my trousers off. Don't worry, they haven't even set off across the field yet. We've got a few seconds.'

'But why are you taking your trousers off?'

'Because they stink.'

'Is now really a time to be worrying about that?'

'Yes, now is precisely the time. Those dogs'll smell me already.'

Nats pulled off her underpants as well and then ran along the edge of the field to deposit her discarded clothing a hundred metres or so to their right. 'Right, let's go,' she commanded as she returned.

Joe looked down at her bare legs. 'Don't you want to put on something else?'

'No time for that, they're coming now, but my underwear should hold them up for a minute at least.' And with that, she bounded off into the woods.

LATER, JOE WOULDN'T be able account for how they evaded the army of searchers and their dogs. Perhaps it was the failing daylight that rescued them or maybe the intuitive way that Nats seemed to lead them from one bit of woodland to another, always a few paces ahead of Joe and frequently changing direction. At times, Joe felt certain that the dogs would soon be nipping at his heels and then pouncing and tearing him to shreds, but he had to admit that he never actually saw a dog that evening, or any of their handlers.

Eventually, Nats stopped running and Joe saw her standing there just in time to stumble to a stop beside her in the dusky gloom.

'They've gone,' she announced, and sure enough, there was no longer any sound of barking dogs or shouting searchers, nor any noise that might suggest an ongoing pursuit.

Agreeing it was safe to stop for a while, Joe dug out his spare trousers and underpants for Nats to put on. Meanwhile, Nats conjured a large wad of toilet paper, salvaged from the train toilet, which she stuffed down into the underpants.

'Does it hurt, the bleeding?'

'Not much really – well, actually, now you mention it, yes, but it's not a bleeding sort of hurt. It's like having a tummy ache. It was really bad earlier, but now I'm not sure what's hurting, or why, anymore. I was a bit sore down here when I still had my trousers on, but running without them helped with that.' She paused and thought for a moment. 'Sorry, this is all my fault. We'd still be on the train, or off the train somewhere sensible with Cain, if my bleeding hadn't started.'

'But you couldn't help when it started, could you?' Joe said with uncertainty and a growing feeling of ignorance about everything.

'No, I don't think so, but I should've realised what was happening before we even got on the stupid train.'

Joe thrust the spare trousers towards her. 'Here, put these on and let's work out what we do next.' It would do no good to dwell on what they could have done differently.

The trousers turned out to be quite a lot too wide in the waist, which surprised Joe because he'd always thought of Nats as being roughly the same size as him, unlike Cain, who was quite a few centimetres bigger in all dimensions. Nats said they were fine, but she had to hold them up as she walked; there was no way they'd make it to Dover like that. Is that what they had to do now? Walk all the way to Dover? Could they even consider it without Cain?

They had no clear plan even which direction to walk in. The compass was in Cain's bag, on the train, and neither could remember where the sun had been before it fell out of the sky. The one certainty was that the further they could get from where the search party had called off their search, the less chance there was of being caught if the search resumed in the morning.

Rain filtered through the trees in bigger and bigger drops. This was no passing shower. Nats shuddered beside Joe as rivulets trickled off her short hair and down her face. If they stayed out in these woods, they might catch their death like Cain nearly had. But this place they'd landed in now, which can't have been far north of Newcastle, was quite different from what they'd left behind in Scotland. Gone was the wild, uninhabited country of lakes and mountains. This was not the sort of place to offer up empty derelict buildings to let yourself into. So, contrary to what their instincts screamed at them, they headed towards the urban landscape, rationalising that more buildings meant more chance of finding somewhere dry and unoccupied.

Emerging from the woods, they squelched across a lumpy field towards distant streetlights blurred by sheets of water falling from the sky, beckoning them closer but doing nothing to illuminate the way for them.

'Ouch!' Heads down, they didn't notice the forbidding metal sentries in their path. An elderly floodlight blinked itself awake, bouncing its light off the raindrops and casting menacing shadows across a haphazard jumble of crunched and dismantled cars that littered the muddy, potholed ground on the other side of the long, high fence.

They had no choice but to paddle along the outside edge of the fence, not intending to stop there but to find their way around it. In the end, they traced three sides of the perimeter before meeting a cul-de-sac that ended at the tall, chained gates.

They were about to head down the murky, unlit road away from the scrapyard when they both nearly jumped out of their soaked skins at the rattling of the gates. A cat yowled. Scraggy, black fur bolted right between the two of them, hotly pursued by a bigger but equally scrawny-looking tabby. Joe and Nats were still staring after the cats as, behind them, the gate clunked itself shut.

'Hang on a moment.' Nats turned towards the gate at the same time as Joe took a step towards the road. 'Do you think we could squeeze between those like the cats did?'

'What would we do that for?'

'Shelter?'

Whoever looked after this yard obviously wasn't too concerned about nighttime security. It was barely a squeeze at all to duck under the chain that held the two gates lazily shut, and it took no time at all to find a car with all its windows intact and all its doors unlocked. They tumbled onto the back seat and pulled the door shut behind them. Joe chuckled to himself as Cris's voice echoed around his head. *Get those muddy shoes off before you spread it all over my seats!* Rain hammered down on the metal roof.

Others might have advised against hiding out in a fenced-off yard, which would presumably be staffed in the morning, with only one way in or out. But the two drenched kids assured each other they'd extract themselves before anyone arrived to unlock the gates.

Chapter 49

JOE'S HEAD SURFACED into consciousness to the sound of unmelodious singing, which randomly crescendoed and diminished in a way that bore no correlation to the much more tuneful rendition that sometimes filtered through. Even that was not of the best quality, being played at a volume far louder than the unfortunate speakers had been built to sustain.

He wriggled his toes in his still-sodden socks; the sharp stabs of subsiding numbness zigzagged across his soles. He groaned as the knots in his neck refused to unravel then stifled a yelp as his skull met an unforgiving steering wheel. His head dropped down to its original, uncomfortable position in the lowest point of the sagging car seat.

Opening one eye, he immediately regretted it, as the low morning sun shot an arrow, which bounced off a wing mirror and embedded itself into the inner surface of his cranium.

He'd let Nats have the much more inviting back seat with the one blanket they now had wrapped around her otherwise bare bottom half. She'd been the one to reason that a stained blanket could be hidden in their bag when they resumed their journey, whereas the pale-green trousers needed to remain unstained, at least as far as blood was concerned. Joe had tried to settle across the two front seats with his bag wedged in between them over the handbrake. He'd felt sure he wouldn't sleep a wink as the burning, icy numbness crept up his legs. How had dawn managed to sneak past him?

Bracing, he shuffled onto his tummy and then pushed up on his elbows. The song on the radio had come to an end, but the tone-deaf voice was still replaying the catchy chorus on a repeated, ever-shortening loop.

... LOVE IS...SHOW ME...WANNA KNOW...SHOW ME... YEAH-YEAH-YEAH...

The cheery-sounding banter from the radio, of which Joe had caught short snippets in between the monotonous echoes, was replaced by the less ambiguous articulations of a newsreader. Joe's ears pricked up at the second item.

Northumbria police are searching for...LOVE IS... who jumped off a train just outside...SHOW ME...one is thought to be...WANNA KNOW...and is in need of urgent medical attention...YEAH-YEAH-YEAH-YEAH-yeahhh.

As another catchy tune struck up on the radio and the live backing vocals faded to the other side of the yard, Joe manipulated the passenger door handle with his foot and slithered his way out of the car into the narrow gap between it and its crumpled neighbour.

Nudging the door to clunk it shut as quietly as he could, he crawled on hands and knees until he could peer out from the back of the car. He sprang back and held his breath. Stomping right towards him, between two rows of wrecked cars, was a bare-armed neut with tattoos and muscles to rival those of the skipper who'd almost stopped Joe from getting to the island. With one hand, the neut swung the entirety of a car's exhaust system ripped off some unfortunate vehicle. With the other, they clutched a phone to their ear.

'Yup, I've just found one for you. Might need a bit of straightening out, but there's not a speck of rust on it.'

Joe crouched with his back against the rear bumper, forcing himself to take long, slow breaths. He turned and eased slowly upwards until he could peer through the mucky rear windscreen to get a view of the world beyond. The neut had turned a corner and was now stomping back towards the wide-open gates, still swinging the exhaust parts as if they had no weight at all. The car wobbled, and Nats' silhouette popped up above the line of the back seat. 'Joe?' came the muffled, anxious enquiry from inside.

Joe galloped back around to the passenger side rear door and cracked it open. 'Nats, get down!' he hissed.

Nats swivelled around in confusion, making the car wobble some more as she tried to work out where his voice was coming from, and then the door was pushed a little further open and her questioning face appeared in the gap.

'What is it?' she whispered.

'It's morning, and we've got company. Move back, but keep low, and I'll get in alongside you.'

'SORRY, IT'S MY fault, I thought I could stay awake,' Joe said for the third or fourth time as they crouched on the cramped bit of floor between the front and rear seats.

'Couldn't we make a run for it?' Nats suggested. 'Just wait until they're well away from the gate and then run?'

'Yeah, but if they see us, they'll just call the police, and now we've been on the news, the whole world'll be on the lookout for us.'

Nats banged her head repeatedly against the back of the front seat. 'It's all my fault really, isn't it?'

Joe didn't know what to say. Of course it wasn't Nats' fault. They'd gone over all that yesterday. She wasn't to know that the tummy ache meant her bleeding was about to start, and even if she could have guessed, there was no point dwelling on it now. 'Are you feeling any better? Are you still bleeding? Does your tummy still hurt?'

'A bit,' was all Nats said. Joe wasn't sure which question she was answering. Perhaps all three. But it wasn't something to probe further.

SITTING OR CROUCHING or kneeling for eight hours on the floor in the rear footwell of a car, holding your breath for an eternity whenever the singing stomper came closer – it was murder. Their toes and bottoms throbbed with pins and needles. Each time one of them changed position, the car oscillated like the pendulum of a metronome. Neither had eaten or drunk all that much in the last twenty-four hours, so at least the calls of nature were not too urgent.

The stomper had almost no customers. Once in the morning and once in the afternoon, they heard the rumble of an engine and the crunching of wheels over the muddy gravel by the gate. There'd be some unintelligible conversation, and in the afternoon visit, the sound of Stomper and customer prowling the yard was followed by metallic banging and scraping as some old wreck was relieved of a still-useful body part. Fortunately, their own place of sanctuary must have been of the wrong make or model to be able to donate any organs to new owners.

When they were sure Stomper wasn't nearby, they managed to extract some of the food from Joe's bag and nibbled on it as if each bite and chew would reverberate out across the yard. Eventually, as they both slumped in a dehydrated daze against their respective car doors, the radio went off and they heard the creak of the gates being swung shut, the clang of the chain being draped around the inner bars, and then the revving and sputtering of a truck engine as it carried its weighty driver away to wherever they spent the night.

They pulled themselves up onto the back seat and both groaned at their achy stiffness. Nats re-tucked the top of the blanket around her waist. 'Pass us those trousers then,' she instructed, indicating the bit of floor between them where the trousers lay in the damp, crumpled heap she'd left them in last night.

'Is it safe?' Joe began, nodding towards Nats' lower half. 'Don't you need to get cleaned up somehow, before you put the trousers back on?' He knew she'd used up all the toilet paper from the train.

'With what exactly?' she asked. 'I'll just go and have a quick bath, shall I?'

'I didn't mean...I mean, how can we make sure these trousers don't get stained? As you said last night, they're the only ones we've got left, apart from the ones I'm wearing.'

Joe didn't think she'd heard his questions until she said, eventually, 'I don't know, but I'm going to have to put them back on at some point, unless you're planning for us to just stay here until...'

Pulling open his bag, Joe fished out his one spare T-shirt and, before he could change his mind, tore it down the seam. Ripping off about half of the back, he handed it to Nats. 'OK, but can you use this like you did the toilet paper, for now?'

THEY DIDN'T LOOK at the heavy chain until they'd both had a go at pushing and rattling the gates. For some reason, the neut had gone to the trouble of wrapping the chain around twice tonight, rather than draping it loosely around once, as it had been the previous night.

'What do you think they've done that for? What are we going to do now? How are we going to get out now, Joe? Do you reckon we could climb over?' Nats persisted with rattling the gates as she fired out her volley of questions.

Did Stomper know they were in here? Had they been trapped here on purpose? What if Stomper was already on the way back here with a convoy of police cars? But why wait all day? Why not call the police straightaway and pull the gates shut to keep them in until the police arrived? There was no other way out. Vicious-looking razor wire adorned the top of the three-metre-high fence and the single set of gates. Whether intentionally or accidentally, they were imprisoned.

'There must be some other way out,' Nats insisted as she dragged Joe once more around the perimeter. Could there be a weak section of fence that they could bend out of the way? Or a little pedestrian gate they'd somehow overlooked? Or perhaps a discarded ladder, just waiting to be deployed?

'Maybe there's a spare key in the cabin,' Nats suggested, but the cabin was locked as securely as the gate.

What they did find was a tap, stuck on the top of a bit of pipe protruding out of the ground a metre or two from the fence. The pipe looked like it had seen more than a few collisions, but as soon as they turned the tap, fresh, clear water gushed out. They drank from it thirstily, and later, Nats returned to it for a shivery wash whilst Joe stood at a distance keeping watch over the gates.

They maintained their watch throughout that night, taking turns to rest in the back of the car whilst the other stood or paced up and down out in the open. The plan was simple. As soon as the world started to wake up, whoever was on watch would wake the other. They would then take up position, concealed from view but right next to the gates. Stomper would have to open the gates and then get back into the truck to drive it into the yard. When the truck came through the gates, that would be their cue to move. With any luck, they could sneak out unnoticed whilst Stomper was busy parking the truck.

Only, Stomper didn't show up, either that morning or the following morning when they repeated the process.

During the hours of daylight in between, they grew in boldness with their explorations of their prison yard. Having stumbled across a spare blanket in the boot of one of the cars, they conducted a thorough search of all the vehicles and turned up a number of other treasures: a working torch whose batteries appeared to have a lot more life in them than Tom's old one had, which in any case had lived in Cain's bag so was now lost to them; nearly sixty pounds, mostly in loose change; seven empty bottles, from which they chose the least skanky three and rinsed them twenty times over before filling them and adding them to their pack alongside their one remaining original bottle; and most treasured of all, as far as Joe was concerned, a dog-eared but detailed book of maps showing the vast network of roads that crisscrossed the whole of Britain.

As Nats continued the forensic search for more treasures, Joe spent hours poring over the pages of the map book, first untangling the route they had most likely taken from their landfall on the west coast of mainland Scotland across and down to Crianlarich and then on to Balloch. Not knowing their precise starting point meant he couldn't be certain about those first lengths of road they had walked, but he'd be willing to stake all of the nearly sixty pounds and more on that channel crossing, where Cain had nearly perished, being from Ardgour to Corran, and that first crumbling station could only have been Bridge of Orchy. If they'd turned north at Corran, they'd have been in Fort William the next day, a bustling little hub that Joe remembered as one of the stopping points on his train journey to the island, still indelibly etched in his brain tissue, despite it being from a completely other lifetime.

At Fort William, they'd have bought fresh food and maybe other provisions for their journey. Perhaps even a map like this one. They might also have dared to get on a train, over a week earlier than they eventually did. But then they'd have probably reached the same conclusion they had in Crianlarich, that the train wasn't safe.

If only they'd never boarded a train. Nats would have had her bleeding without anyone else seeing it. They could even have stopped for a day or two if she'd needed it before continuing their steady progress southwards. The three of them all together. Where would they be now?

Of course, the real question was where *were* they now? The train had been less than fifteen minutes outside Newcastle when Joe had arrested its progress by pulling that green handle. But how far in miles was fifteen minutes by train? They could have been on the outskirts of any one of the 'tons' that clamoured for attention around the railway line to the north of Newcastle: Ashington, Bedlington, Cramlington, or even Longbenton. They could even be as far north as Widdrington, West Chevington, or even Acklington. The truth was that until they got out of this yard, postulations were pretty pointless, but that didn't stop Joe from burying his nose in the book, plotting out possible routes from here, wherever here was, on to their final destination of Dover. It was a very long way, especially if they were walking.

A spray of rain hit his cheek as the car door was flung open. Joe snapped the book shut to stop the pages from getting any wetter.

'Shift across, will you.'

Joe obeyed, shuffling on his bottom to the other side of the back seat. Nats tumbled in and pulled the door shut.

'Why couldn't you get in on this side?'

'Your side was closer, and it's raining, in case you hadn't noticed.'

Joe hadn't noticed but wondered now how he had been able to block out the constant hammering on the metal roof. He leaned forward to drop the map book onto the passenger seat in front of him, away from the wet layers that Nats was peeling off.

'I guess it's my turn now then,' he said without much conviction.

'I wouldn't bother,' Nats replied. 'There's no point in us taking turns to keep watch through the night. We'll only get cold and wet and even more miserable.' She looked up at the ceiling. 'I can't see either of us getting much sleep anyway with that racket.'

Nats was right. What was the point in them taking turns to try to stay awake through the night? Even if they did both sleep, one of them would probably be awake before dawn came.

'Well, if we're both trying to sleep in here at the same time, do you think we can work out how to lower this seat so we can both lie down properly?' Joe tested the plastic button in the top of the seat back, and although it cracked a little at his first touch, the spring underneath complied, and the seat back released with a click.

JOE WRIGGLED HIS frozen toes and opened his eyes. Somehow, in the night, Nats had ended up with two-thirds of both blankets. It had seemed a good idea to lie as close as possible to each other, sharing bodily warmth, spreading their two blankets over both of them, and it must have worked, given how well he'd slept.

The chain clanged as it was pulled through the bars of the gates. The ironwork creaked as one gate and then the other swung open. Nats groaned and turned over, pulling the remaining bits of blanket off Joe's body. Joe groaned too. Stomper was back, the gate was open again, and they should have been there ready to make their escape. There was no way he could wake Nats and get them there in time to sneak out as the truck drove in. Even so, he ought to wake her so they'd be ready to run if they were discovered.

Once he'd woken Nats and broken the bad news to her, they agreed that they might as well eat something from the remains of Cain's provisions before attempting any escape. They didn't want their grumbling tummies to betray them as they tiptoed around to the gates, although that was just an excuse, given that the radio was once again blaring its medley of classic hits, drowning out even the loudest growl that a digestive system might produce.

Each time they did set out across the yard, another vehicle would come thundering in through the gates, which might have been a good time to make their escape, whilst Stomper was otherwise engaged, but it was another pair of eyes to which they might expose their movements. So, whenever Stomper got a customer, they'd stop and skulk behind the nearest car to watch and wait for a good time to move. Then, at the instant they decided it was safe to make a run for it, the customer and Stomper would emerge and stand alongside the customer's vehicle for ten minutes or more with one of them, if not both, gawking out at the gate as they chewed the cud.

That evening, Joe and Nats ate the last of their food supplies, aside from one stale bread roll each, which they were saving for the morning. They'd wasted their day with dithering and silent bickering over when to make their move and whose fault it was the last time they'd missed their chance. The gates held them in once more. The slovenly way in which they'd been secured on their arrival now appeared to be a careless mistake on what must have been an off day for their proprietor.

Next morning, Nats was shaking Joe awake well before dawn and insisted that they take up their position behind the gate-side van before even thinking of tucking into their unappetising breakfast, which Joe struggled to swallow down anyway through his nerve-constricted oesophagus.

As he gulped down his last mouthful, a pair of headlights swept across the still-murky yard and an engine idled outside the gates. There was no clatter and clang of chain being pulled free. After a few minutes, the engine spluttered to a stop and the headlights dimmed but continued to stripe the yard with the long shadows of the gates and fence.

Whoever it was now guarding the gates, it wasn't Stomper. What if they'd been spotted by Stomper or one of their customers the previous day? What if it was the police, staking out the joint until Stomper arrived?

A second vehicle pulled up outside the gate. Doors were flung open and slammed shut, and they heard the now-familiar holler of Stomper, closer than ever, just the other side of the fence.

'You're early.'

'Yeah, hope that's OK. I decided to come up and stop over last night.'

'S'all right. How long d'it take you then? Yesterday, I mean.'

'Oh, less than three hours, but I wanted to come up as soon as I heard you'd got them. You've held on to them for me, I assume?'

'Yeah, yeah, don't worry. Both are still here. I said I'd keep them safe for you, din't I?'

They were done for. By the sound of it, Stomper already knew they were there, and now someone had come to collect them. There were a few more exchanges between the two outside the gate, but these were mostly lost under the noise of the chain being untangled combined with the throbbing of Joe's pulse in his ears. It was tempting to make a run for it as soon as the gates were cracked open, but then they'd no doubt run straight into the arms of the stranger waiting to take them away.

Joe was surprised that Stomper was opening both gates fully. If it had been him, he'd have opened them just wide enough to let the police officer in and then secured the gates behind them whilst they hunted down the children. Instead, both figures, Stomper and the officer, were returning to their trucks to drive them into the yard. The large truck seemed a strange choice of vehicle for the police, and even though he'd heard only one voice, other than Stomper's, Joe had fully expected there to be a sidekick waiting, incognito, in the vehicle. But as far as he could see, the second truck to enter the yard carried no passengers. Perhaps this wasn't the police. Maybe it was some sort of private bounty hunter.

They would have made a run for it even as the trucks drove in, but the bounty hunter was making such a hash of reversing through the gates that, on the first attempt, they clipped the rear light on the gate hinge and, on the second, left no more than five centimetres between the long flat bed of the truck and the side nearest to where Joe and Nats were hidden. Their only means of escape would have been straight across the flatbed as it jerked its way into the yard. Neither of them was that stupid!

'OK, that'll do,' hollered Stomper before the truck's cab had even fully cleared the gateway. 'We can load you up no problem if you stop there. No point makin' it harder for you to get out again after.'

'Sorry. It's usually my partner who drives this thing,' the gangly driver shouted before cutting the engine and jumping down. They had to walk all the way around the front of the cab to get into the yard. To get out now, Joe and Nats would also have to go around or maybe under that truck first.

The two neuts disappeared off into Stomper's cabin. The door had barely closed behind them before Nats dashed out from behind the van. She dived under the truck as the cabin door reopened. Joe ducked back behind the van as the pair walked around the truck and stood beside two ancient-looking cars beyond the gateway.

'Wow, what a pair of beauties,' said the bounty hunter, gazing at the two old cars. 'I mean, they both need a bit of work, but you can see they've been well looked after in their former lives.'

Keeping low, Joe scuttled across to join Nats under the truck, pulling the pack in behind him.

'All right, well, I just need to take down a few details and then we'll get them loaded up and you can be on your way. What name are we transferring ownership too?'

'Ah, yes, that'll be Kirkstall Vintage Motors, in Leeds.'

Joe's ears pricked up as soon as he heard the name 'Kirkstall'. Could it really be true that this truck and its driver lived just a few miles from his old home? Just a short bus ride from Georgy and Cris? They had definitely said Leeds, so it had to be the same Kirkstall.

The two neuts worked together to manoeuvre the first of the two cars around to the back of the truck. It seemed that neither was capable of propelling itself into position. Nats kept nudging Joe and whispering, 'Come on, let's go while their busy.'

Joe shook his head. 'It's still too risky,' he lied. They could have made their move several times, and it was now self-evident that the only bounty being hunted here was two vintage wrecks. But Joe had to procrastinate while his brain cogs turned. What if they could somehow get inside one of those two old cars? They could be ringing the buzzer on his old flat in time for lunch with Georgy at their old kitchen table. The more he thought about it, the more he could think of nothing better than going home and spending a few days with Georgy and Cris before working out the best way to complete their journey.

A deafening, whining roar interrupted his fantasy. The ceiling above their heads started tilting towards them. They scrambled forwards, barely getting clear of the crushing metalwork in time. Joe winced as their bag was squashed into the muddy ground behind them. At the same time, the front end threatened to expose them more and more as the space between the truck and the ground gaped open right where they cowered.

They could go now, whilst Stomper operated the machinery needed to haul the first of the two cars up onto the truck and their customer shouted unnecessary instructions, but they'd be leaving with nothing. If they waited, they might lose their chance, or they could gain a ride out of here. If it hadn't been for the trapped bag, Joe knew he wouldn't have been able to hold Nats back.

As soon as the ceiling returned to the horizontal and their bag was released from its jaws, Nats did have to be held back.

'I think there's another way,' Joe urged in a whisper as she crawled towards the bag. 'If we can get into one of those cars,' he pointed upwards, 'we can get to my parents' home. This truck is from Leeds.'

Even in the shadows under the dirty truck, Joe could see Nats' eyes sparkling for the first time since they'd boarded the train in Balloch. 'Do you think they'll help us get to Dover?'

Joe wasn't sure what Georgy and Cris would make of their plans, but right now, all he could think of was getting home.

'Don't suppose I could use your toilet before I get back on the road?' they heard the customer ask. This was their chance. The two neuts walked once more towards the cabin.

They hesitated for no more than a second before rolling out on the far side of the truck and pulling themselves up onto its flatbed. There was no time to get into either of the cars before the cabin door was swinging open. All they could do was squeeze themselves under the low undercarriage of the front car. Within seconds, the floor shuddered below them, and the truck pulled them out of the yard and onto the road to Leeds.

Chapter 50

WHENEVER THE PHONE rang at around half past seven on a Friday morning, just as I gulped down my last few mouthfuls of scalding coffee before dashing out the door, I knew it would be Cris. More often than not, I would let it go straight to voicemail, saving the inevitable message until I'd got my breath back on the bus.

You'd have thought, given I only had myself to get up and out of the flat in the morning, I'd have time to enjoy a leisurely stroll down to the bus stop, perhaps even taking the scenic route through the park. I'd always been the one to regulate time in our family. But time does strange things when it's all your own.

There were only ever three permutations of Cris's message anyway, either:

> *Hi love, sorry, won't be coming up this weekend. They want me in work tomorrow morning. Big deadline. I'll definitely make it up to you next weekend though. Love you lots, have a great one. Kiss, kiss.*

or:

> *Hi love, sorry, gotta work late tonight so probably best if I get the first train up in the morning. Can't wait to see you. Love you lots, have a great day. Kiss, kiss.*

or:

Hi love, sorry, might be best if you don't come down this weekend. I mean, you can if you want, but I'm gonna have to work all day tomorrow and, well, I don't want to put you to all the trouble of coming down here if we're barely going to see each other. Really sorry, hope you've not bought your ticket yet. I'll pay you back, or just come down anyway. I'll still come to you next weekend. Love you lots, hope you find plenty to do this weekend. Kiss, kiss.

Our weekend visits to each other were getting less and less frequent. Although I don't think Cris realised this, I'd only actually been down to visit once since that first weekend when I'd helped with the move. That had been an awful weekend, making polite small talk with a gaggle of new work colleagues that Cris seemed desperate for me to fall in love with. I'm sorry to say that, despite the added disruption to my Friday morning dash, the ringing phone and subsequent voicemail was becoming a welcome relief rather than a disappointment. I'd grown to value my weekends of solitary exploration. Even before the call came, I'd be planning what I'd do, where I'd go if I was given the weekend back to spend doing my own thing.

So why did I answer the call this time? Perhaps it was because it came a couple of minutes earlier than usual, when I was still kidding myself that I had plenty of time and wouldn't need to rush today.

'Hi, Georgy, Finch Stephenson here. Don't know whether you remember me.'

The voice was familiar, but even with the accompanying name, it took the utterance of quite a few more syllables before I joined the dots to make the picture of the person whose voice now echoed in my right ear.

'I'm wondering if you might be able to help us with a little problem we're having?'

The caller paused. I'd still not quite resolved their identity and was trying to formulate some sort of neutral reply when they decided to continue, despite my silence.

'Er, one of my colleagues in the northeast is currently looking after a child. A child a bit like your Joh, that is.'

The buffering came to an end and the picture resolved itself. This was Finch Stephenson, the police officer who'd sat in our kitchen while Cris picked out pictures of DiG members from a photo line-up. This was Finch Stephenson who had set Cris up with their new-old job and swanky new house. This was Finch Stephenson who knew about Joe and was now telling me they had a child like him in custody.

'The child was unaccompanied on a train from Scotland. Well, I say unaccompanied. They didn't have any adults with them and nor did they have a permit to travel.'

'And you think it's Joh?' I said, jumping in – and jumping several clauses ahead in the narrative.

'Well, we can't be sure. If you remember, you were quite adamant when we visited that you didn't have any pictures of Joh for us to borrow, and the child we have is being quite...how shall I put this? Uncooperative? Won't give us a name, nor where they or their companions thought they were heading.'

'Companions?' I tried to keep the anxious excitement out of my voice. If it wasn't Joe, maybe he was one of the companions. Stephenson obviously thought they were somehow mixed up with Joe, otherwise why would we be having this conversation.

'Look, I can't really give you any more details over the phone. But, er, we were wondering whether you might be free to come and see this child later today, after you've finished work. See if they're willing to have a little chat with you.'

I looked at my watch – 7:33. Shit. Clamping the phone between my shoulder and my ear, I pulled my work bag off the back of its usual chair and headed for the door, then swerved back towards my bedroom and the bathroom.

'If it is Joh, I'm sure we could make the necessary arrangements for them to be released into your care.'

'Have you spoken to Cris about this?' The question suddenly surfaced in my thoughts as I grabbed my toothbrush and toothpaste off the shelf above the washbasin.

'We thought it might be better for you to be the one to come and talk to the child. Correct me if I'm wrong, but Joh was closer to you than to Cris, yes?'

'OK, so where am I meeting him, I mean *them*? Where do I need to come to?' I folded my pyjamas, picked out some clean underwear from my top drawer and stuffed them into my now-bulging bag.

'We'll send a car to pick you up. You finish work at four-thirty on a Friday, don't you? We can pick you up from work and stop off at your flat on the way if you like.'

I paused outside Joe's old room and then pushed open the door and gathered together a clean set of clothes from his drawers, hoping they'd still fit him.

'No, it's OK. If you pick me up from work, I'll be ready to go straight to wherever you're taking me.' I swung the front door shut behind me and clattered down the stairs. 'Sorry, gotta go now,' I puffed. 'I'll be outside work at four-thirty.'

As I sat on the bus, a million thoughts and questions stabbed at my brain. *What if it is Joe? Will they really let me take him home? Why is he not on the island anymore? Maybe he is. Maybe it's not Joe. What about these companions? Have all the kids had to leave the island? If so, where are the rest of them now? What will Stephenson want me to find out from Joe or whatever poor child they've picked up? How does Stephenson know so much about me? Where I work. What time I finish.* It was spooky. *Do I trust Stephenson? Do I speak to Cris? How will Cris take the news that Joe might not be on the island anymore? Probably best to wait until I know whether it is Joe before involving Cris.*

Why did my brain tell me to pack overnight things? I didn't even know where they're holding this kid.

Chapter 51

I FELT INSTANTLY GUILTY about the relief that flooded through me when I saw that it was somebody else's son occupying the hard, bare Newcastle police cell. I'd expected to be escorted into an interview room where I'd sit across a table from him, perhaps with a solicitor alongside him and all our words being recorded. Instead, I was shown into a cell, which at first appeared empty, giving me quite a fright as the door slammed shut behind me. Was this all a trap to capture me as an accomplice to DiG? Or maybe a veiled threat that this is what things would be like for my own child if he was also captured? The discreet cameras mounted in every corner of the ceiling watched my every move.

Then, as my eyes drifted down to the floor, I saw him. The shaggy, grubby little boy sitting as far away as he could manage in the back left-hand corner of the cold concrete floor. I say little boy; he was bigger than Joe, or at least bigger than the image of Joe in my memory, and he definitely wasn't Joe. I knew that as soon as I saw him, although there was precious little to go on, the way he hid himself with his knees pulled right up to his chest, his scruffy head face down on his knees. Joe could be this big now, if he'd had a growth spurt in the last few months, and the hair was a similar colour to Joe's, but it definitely wasn't him. How did I even know that he was a boy, not a girl or a neutral like me? I can't say. I just did.

'Hello, I'm Georgy.' I moved over to sit on the floor nearby, but not so close as to spook him. Even so, his already-fidgeting hands betrayed increased agitation.

'I think you might know my son, Joe?' I continued, inflecting my voice to make my statement a question and making an effort to come across as calm and compassionate despite the torrent of emotions assaulting me, not to mention the overripe smell of sweat, dirt, and urine that made me want to gag.

At the mention of Joe's name, I'm sure I saw the slightest hint of a reaction, though he didn't show his face and no sound emanated from his mouth, other than his slow, heavy breathing.

I tried again. 'Joe's my son. Was he one of the others with you on that train that you stopped?'

Stephenson had filled me in on what had been discovered from their interviews with the train guard and passengers. There was no indication as to whether the other two were also boys, or if either or both were girls. They wouldn't know.

'It sounds like one of your friends was hurt, and we'd like to find them so we can take them to a doctor. Have you any idea where they might be now?'

I got no further reaction of any sort out of the poor, traumatised boy. I whispered to him for over half an hour, recounting some of the many treasured moments I'd had with Joe over the years, explaining how in the end it had been his decision to go and live on the island and how I hadn't wanted him to go and still thought about him every day.

'I expect your parents wonder about you every day too,' I prompted, 'and that other child's parents too. They'd want to know about it and do something to help if their child was injured.

'Where were you heading to on that train?' I persisted, 'and why did you leave the island? I promise no harm will come to any of you.' Of course, I could do nothing of the sort.

The clam shell remained tightly shut, no matter how carefully or hard I prised. I pushed myself up the wall and stepped towards the door.

'If you talk to me now, you could come and live with me in Leeds – you and Joe both when we've found him. That'd be better than this horrid, cold cell, wouldn't it?'

Again, I was promising what I probably couldn't deliver. Stephenson had suggested I could take my own child back home, but they'd surely draw the line at me taking in somebody else's stray, abnormal child.

Should I go out there and tell them that yes, it was my Joh they had in their cell, then insist that they release him to me immediately? It probably wouldn't work. I bet they already knew it wasn't my boy in there. They'd just used the idea that it could be as bait to get me here. Should I be flattered that I was their best hope?

I turned and knocked twice on the heavy steel door, which opened at my command and allowed me back out into the fresher air of the dank corridor.

I DIDN'T NEED to stay up in Newcastle for the night. Stephenson was all set to commission a junior officer to drive me home straight away. I'd packed my overnight things for some reason, though, and Cris had left a message whilst my phone was in a police safe box. *Not coming up tonight. Will be on first or second train in the morning though.* It was always the second train. Cris still had a key to the flat, so I didn't even need to be back first.

So that settled it. I'd catch the train back to Leeds in the morning too. Tonight, I'd explore a new city, enjoy a nice meal out somewhere and a carefree night in a hotel.

The streets of Newcastle were filled with rowdy revellers in very few clothes considering the ambient temperature outside. I'd never understood why so many people seemed content to wander around outside without a coat in any month except July or August and came to the conclusion that I must be a different species to the majority of the human race. Although, if that were the case, Joe belonged to their species, not mine; the way he'd sit around in our draughty flat in shorts and a T-shirt and no socks, even in January, and if I made him take all the layers I thought he needed when we went on one of our trips, I'd end up carrying most of them.

What if Joe was even now also in this city? According to Stephenson, it had been five days since the boy in the cell had been handed over to police at Newcastle station. His two companions had jumped off the train about fifteen miles north of here. What did they do after that? The police had searched for them, but apart from some discarded, bloodstained clothing a few hundred metres from the train track, they'd disappeared without trace. What would Joe have done then? Where would he have gone? He'd always struck me as a resourceful child, inheriting both Cris's get up and go and my careful, systematic thoughtfulness. Even so, I struggled to imagine my little boy out there fending for himself, finding his own way in the world with just one, similar-aged travel companion. Wherever it was they were travelling to.

As I walked the streets, I scoured the faces of anyone the right sort of height, sometimes swerving to take a closer look, tapping at random on my phone as I did so to create a cover story for my erratic path.

Of course, the probability of actually finding him was stupidly small. For a start, I had no evidence that he was even one of the two companions. I got the impression there were about fifty kids in that island community, so perhaps a one in twenty-five chance that Joe was one of the two that jumped from the train. Then multiply that by the probability of them travelling the fifteen miles between there and here over the last four days. Who knows? Average walking pace of three miles per hour, that's only five hours of walking. If they had a definite destination in mind with Newcastle on their route, they'd have passed through here days ago. Unless the one with the injury had slowed them down. What if it was Joe who was injured? Overall probability of that, all things being equal, was about one in fifty. That sounded quite high to me.

The statistician in me argued that it was illogical to waste time searching for the boy whose life I'd given up being a part of over six months ago. But the parent in me wanted to travel the length and breadth of Britain night and day until he was found.

Chapter 52

JOE'S HEART FLUTTERED as he stood outside the block of flats, finger poised over the button that would trigger the sound of the buzzer in his old home. The faded label next to the button still read *C, G & J Turner* in Georgy's neat and precise block capitals.

'Are you going to press it then, or do you want me to do it for you?' came Nats' impatient voice from just behind him. He'd detected an increasing nervous excitement in Nats as they'd ridden the old familiar bus from Kirkstall.

They'd clung to whatever they could under the cars as they plummeted down the motorway. Even more impatient vehicles threw up spray and grit at them. Joe waved and smiled at the surprised-looking driver of the car behind as they slipped off the side of the truck at the traffic lights, doing his best to act as if riding on the back of a mini car transporter was, for him, the most natural pastime in the world, whilst every cell in his body tremored.

'That was awesome!' shrieked Nats as soon as Joe had ushered her into a quiet side street where they could brush each other down. Did nothing scare her?

The buzzer buzzed. They waited. But no inquisitive greeting came crackling through the hardy little speaker.

'Try again,' Nats urged a few seconds later. 'Maybe they were on the toilet or something, or maybe it didn't work properly.'

Joe pressed again, longer and harder this time. Again, their entry request received no acknowledgement or welcome. Joe swallowed hard. Over the last few hours, as he'd played over and over in his mind the exchange that would take place and done multiple rewrites of the script. He'd stupidly not considered the possibility that there might simply not be anybody in.

'Never mind. We'll just wait until they get home then.' Nats gave his shoulder a tender squeeze after he'd pressed the button to no avail for a third time. And so they fell back and took up residence on the neglected old bench, evidently more often a perch for pigeons than it was for humans, though an archaeological dig under the guano would have uncovered a plethora of letters scratched into the wood, revealing a rich history of human liaisons taking place at this very spot. Joe couldn't recall any occasion when this bench had been occupied before so felt very conspicuous, looking rougher than the homeless beggars that he and Georgy had sometimes offered hot drinks and sandwiches to around the city centre streets. Nats huddled in close, resting her head on his shoulder. That bit felt nice.

It had been just after two in the afternoon, according to the digital display on the bus when they'd disembarked at the stop opposite the end of their street. They had no way of knowing, of course, how quickly or slowly the minutes had ticked by since then, but the evening closed in around them as they huddled on the bench, pulling their coat collars up around their cheeks to keep out the growingly persistent drizzle. They wandered back to the button now and then in the intervening interminable time, testing the buzzer in case someone was in but hadn't heard it the first time. It wasn't inconceivable, if Georgy was out and Cris had been asleep before a nightshift.

Then, just as Joe began to rack his brains for where else they might go locally to find shelter for the night, a familiar *tap, tap, tap* came up the pavement, followed by the stooped silhouette of ancient Adey from flat three. Walking stick in one hand and heavy bag of shopping in the other, ancient Adey began their usual agonising struggle of gaining entry to the building.

'Good evening, Adey,' Joe sang out as if it was only yesterday that they'd last greeted one another.

Adey studied him for a few moments, searching cobwebbed memory banks for a name to put with this oddly familiar child. 'Ah, yes, young Joh isn't it?' the kindly geriatric eventually croaked. 'You been away, have you?'

'No,' Joe blurted without thinking. 'Just not been playing out as much recently,' he added hastily, hoping he sounded convincing. 'Can I help you with that door?'

With Adey's gratefully grunted consent, Joe took possession of the keys from the wrinkly arthritic hand, effortlessly disengaged the lock, returned the keys, and held the door open for the elderly neighbour to shuffle through.

'Thank you, you always were a helpful one,' the reedy voice called back as the walking stick sought out the first of the many stairs. 'Give my regards to your parents. Tell them to bring you round for a cup of cocoa sometime.'

'Will do!' Joe called after them, keeping hold of the open door.

'Can we get up to your flat now?' Nats asked as she bounced across, shaking the water out of her hair.

'We'll have to wait down here a few minutes first,' whispered Joe, allowing the door to click shut behind them. 'Old Adey takes an age to get up those stairs.

Good job they only live on the first floor, but I suppose we could go up to our floor. Can't get into the flat without a key though.'

'Oh, OK,' Nats said, deflating a little. 'Well, at least it's not raining in here.'

Despite all the walking they'd done, Joe realised how out of practice he was on stairs as they puffed their way up the five flights to the small landing outside his old home.

'This your door?' Nats asked with energy, pointing at the right-hand door of the two as Joe stood catching his breath. He nodded, and without hesitation, Nats planted three assertive knocks on the centre of the door.

Joe was about to protest that there was no point – they already knew there was nobody in – when the door responded to the last of the knocks by swinging open, just a little. Joe frowned. That was impossible. He'd had it drilled into him to always listen for the click when pulling the door shut. Who'd left it open like this?

'Can we go in then?' Nats was asking, already pushing the door open wider and stepping across the threshold.

'Hang on,' Joe whispered with uneasy apprehension, still trying to make sense of the circumstances. Maybe Georgy or Cris were in. Maybe the buzzer wasn't working or they'd not heard it for some reason. But even so, the door should have been firmly shut. 'OK, but I'll go in first.'

Nats stood aside for Joe to squeeze past.

'Hello?' he called out. 'It's Joh, and, er...I've brought a friend with me.'

The empty flat offered no reply.

As soon as they crept into the vacant kitchen, Joe could tell that something had changed. It wasn't the same home that he'd left behind late last summer. It wasn't just the echoes of his absence. In fact, his own childhood was still very much present with the curly, faded pictures clamped to the fridge with brightly coloured magnetic letters and the graffitied height chart in its same old position with the rubber sole scuff marks on the skirting board below. The kitchen wasn't tidier or cleaner than Joe remembered. They hadn't redecorated. The same old kitchen table hogged the centre of the cramped room with its four wobbly chairs. Nothing obvious had changed, and yet something undefinable was different.

'What's up, Joe?' Nats' voice reflected the unease she sensed in him. 'I'm sure they'll be back soon, and everything will be just fine again.'

NOBODY ELSE DID come home that night. Joe showed Nats his old room, which looked frozen in time, identical to how it had been on the day he left. They rifled through the neatly folded clothes in his drawers, finding clean, new-looking items to replace the old rags they were currently modelling and some spares for the bag. Nats enjoyed a luxuriously long shower as Joe sat morosely in the kitchen, nervously hoping to hear the scrape of the key in the lock of the now securely shut door and rehearsing again his words of explanation, preluded now with how they'd found their way into the flat.

Joe showered as quickly as he felt he could get away with, desperate to rid himself of the weeks of encrusted dirt and smells but unwilling to leave Nats loose in the rest of the flat and paranoid that his parents would return during those few inopportune minutes.

He emerged, dressed in his clean, tight-feeling clothes. His tummy rumbled as the soapy smells of the bathroom were displaced by the welcome aroma of frying eggs and bacon.

'What are you doing?' he asked, indignant that Nats had invaded his parents' fridge and cupboards without permission.

'What? Aren't you hungry?'

'Well, yes, but...' He let his unjustifiable objections founder as Nats put two plates of eggs, bacon, and beans on toast onto the pre-laid table.

'I've even cooked up a tin of those baked beans you like so much.' She smiled.

'Thanks, and sorry. I shouldn't have snapped. I just don't understand what's happened here,' Joe offered in explanation as he sat in Cris's seat whilst Nats sat in Joe's usual place.

THE CLOCK ON the cooker ticked over into the new day. Nats had done a sterling job of keeping Joe's mind occupied with questions about his life here with Georgy and Cris before he came to the island. Joe couldn't help but allow the tears to roll at times as he recalled the occasions that went with some of the pictures on the fridge, and he gratefully accepted the tenderness Nats managed to conjure out of her cheery soul.

'I know you'd sit here all night if you could, but we should get some rest,' she said, looking at the clock. 'Do you think it would be OK for me to take your parents' room if you sleep in yours?'

It wouldn't do for Nats to sleep in Cris and Georgy's room. One of them might still come home before morning. Although he wouldn't admit it, he also couldn't countenance the possibility of spending the night alone in his old room. 'I think we should both be in my room tonight, just in case,' he suggested. 'You can have the bed, though.'

They made the most of their situation, opting for the luxury of sleeping in pyjamas rather than their cleanly put-on day clothes.

JOE JOLTED AWAKE. How had even been asleep? The hard floor hadn't bothered him, but as he'd settled beside his old bed, his heart hadn't felt like it would ever find a resting rhythm. Now it raced faster than ever as he replayed that once-familiar dream of standing naked in front of his class at school, only this time, some of the faces had morphed into young versions of Nats, Cain, the singing stomper from the scrapyard, and even ancient Adey.

'Joe, are you OK?' whispered Nats in the darkness.

'Yeah, I'm fine.' Joe slowed his breathing, trying to bring to heel his runaway heart.

'You were making some very strange noises just now.'

'Sorry, just a dream.'

'Will you get in with me for a bit? I'm cold.'

Joe couldn't imagine how Nats could be cold in this stuffy, airless flat after the days they'd spent sleeping out in the open or in draughty, derelict buildings and chilly wrecked cars. But they had become used to sharing each other's warmth over the last couple nights at the scrapyard, and it had felt good. Joe pushed up off the floor and slipped under the covers alongside her.

'Ooh, what's this?' Nats said as her hand brushed against the stiff tonker that he'd accidentally poked her with as he clambered in.

Joe flinched, thrown back suddenly to his previous experience of having a strange girl in his bed, but Nats was far from being a stranger, and she wasn't naked either.

'I'm sorry, Joe. I didn't mean to...I shouldn't have... Shall I get out and sleep on the floor?'

'No, it's OK.' Joe's heart thumped harder. 'Actually, I don't mind if you want to...' Joe found her hand and guided it towards him. Let her feel. Gave up on catching his now-galloping heart.

'Will you touch me too?' whispered Nats.

Joe reached towards her, though they'd never been closer, and began his own explorations of the strange yet familiar body that was drawing him in.

Chapter 53

'SO...IS THAT WHAT you have to do to make a baby?' Joe asked, soon after Nats' eyes had opened and blinked a few times. The sunshine streamed through the gap in the curtains, where Joe had peeked out onto the empty street below. Ever since he'd woken up, as he'd scouted round the still empty flat, he'd been trying to make sense of what had happened with him and Nats. Did he really wanted to know the answer to his question? Would Sandra have said that they shouldn't have done it because they were both still too young and not ready?

Nats rolled over and gazed at him, drawing a fresh hot blush up his neck and out through his face. 'I think so, yes. It made sense from what I've heard the other girls whispering about.'

'So will you be having a baby now?'

'Oh, no, I don't think so. I think it takes a few goes normally to make a baby.' Her thoughtful frown turned to a mischievous grin. 'Shall we have another go?'

Cold sweat seeped out of his forehead and trickled around his ears. He couldn't imagine doing again what they'd done in the dark of the night, but now in broad daylight – in his old bedroom, in his and Cris and Georgy's flat. And was he really up to being a parent? Not that such thoughts ever seemed to bother Anthony.

The sound of the front door slamming shut, followed by a distant, 'Hello! Are you in? I got the early train.

Are you impressed?' saved Joe from articulating any response to Nats' offer.

'Who's that?' she whispered, pulling the bedcovers right up over her so only her face peeped out.

'Sounds like Cris,' Joe replied as he pulled some clothes over his pyjamas. 'Stay here. I'll go out and speak to them first.'

Dizziness threatened to overcome him as he reached for the door handle. How would Cris react to his sudden appearance in their flat? Although he loved both his parents, he'd have preferred to face Georgy with his return before seeing Cris.

As silently as he could manage, Joe lowered the handle and eased open the bedroom door. He crept along to the kitchen, passing Cris and Georgy's empty room and the open-doored bathroom on the way. He hovered at the threshold. Cris stood with their head in a kitchen cupboard, searching for a mug. Strange. Cris's mug was always at the front, no matter how many mugs were put away after it. The kettle rocked violently as it reached boiling point and steam billowed out under the open cupboard.

Selecting a random mug, Cris turned and caught sight of Joe. Their jaw dropped in a floor-ward direction as their hand fumbled to lower the mug onto the worktop and missed. The random mug fell to the floor, the shattered pieces skating off in all directions. The handle collided with a small black holdall, abandoned by the front door. That hadn't been there last night.

'Sorry,' Joe began, and then, 'Where's Georgy? Why was no-one home last night?' There were all sorts of more important questions he should be asking, and at the same time, shouldn't Cris be questioning him? This wasn't happening the way he'd rehearsed it.

Cris, for the moment, was lost for words, so Joe attempted to fill in some of the gaps. 'We found the door open but the flat empty when we got here. What's happened? I don't understand why the door was open, and the flat looks different. Where's your mug?'

At the mention of a mug, Cris looked down at the shattered pieces on the floor and began to process Joe's questions, which had reached a temporary hiatus. 'Joh, hi. Wow, you've grown. And your voice, it's...'

'It's what?'

The second hand on the kitchen clock ticked its way around as they stood, staring at each other.

'Oh, no matter. It's good to see you, Joh, but what are you doing here? Why have you left the island? Has something gone wrong?'

'We're going to Dover,' interrupted a chirpy voice from Joe's right shoulder. 'We were hoping you might be able to help us get there.'

Nats pushed her way into the kitchen, sporting the old pyjamas of his she'd put on last night. He'd intended not to divulge any details of their plans to Cris yet. Not until he knew where Georgy was and had worked out what had changed in the flat. What had changed between Cris and Georgy. Too late now, though. Nats had done her usual thing of speaking first and thinking after.

'Cris, this is Nats, a friend from the island.' When had his voice changed to sound like this?

'Oh, yes, and it's just the two of you, is it? Travelling by yourselves to Dover? What's in Dover then? Somewhere down south, isn't it?'

'Well, we also set off with – ouch!' Nats' pulled her bare toes out from under Joe's heel.

'Where's Georgy, Cris?' asked Joe, steering things away from Dover and their journey whilst trying to make his voice sound normal. 'Why wasn't Georgy here last night? Have you both got nightshift jobs now?' Joe thought back for a moment and remembered the greeting he'd heard Cris call out on arrival at the flat. 'Are you and Georgy still together?'

'Of course we are!' Cris replied with too much haste. 'Georgy was expecting me this morning, though, so I'm sure they'll be here soon.'

They all stood in silence in the kitchen, not sure what to say to one another. Joe pondered the new information gleaned from what Cris had said. *Georgy was expecting me this morning*. Cris wasn't living here anymore. That explained the holdall by the door, but it didn't explain where Georgy was.

'Have you still got your pyjamas on under those clothes, Joh Turner?' A playful frown passed across Cris's face.

Joe rummaged through his mind for a good excuse, once more the child caught not doing what he should have done.

'How about I make us all some breakfast while you two go and get yourselves up properly. What do you say to pancakes?' Cris had always insisted on them being washed and dressed before breakfast. Joe preferred the days when Cris was at work and Georgy let him eat cereal in his pyjamas.

'Ooh, can I help? I'm good at making pancakes.' Nats advanced into the kitchen, all ready to take on the batter making.

'Not in your pyjamas, you don't!' decreed Cris. They weren't very good at letting others help with the cooking at the best of times, but more than that, Joe could also tell Cris wasn't sure how to handle an unfamiliar young person in their kitchen. 'Er, that's a very kind offer, but I think I can manage on my own, thanks. Why don't you go and have a shower? There'd be time to, if you're quick.'

'But I had a shower last night. Although...your shower is amazing. Perhaps I will have another one now. If that's OK?'

Cris raised an eyebrow at Nats. Joe knew exactly why. The pathetic dribble of unpredictably heated water that called itself their shower was a long-running saga. The owner of the flat had promised countless times to install a better one, but it had never materialised. But then the dribble had felt heavenly compared to the icy tap water in the scrapyard or the quick, wakening splash over the face of sea or lake water.

'Well, go on then,' urged Cris, eggs, flour, and milk already assembled on the worktop, 'or it'll be pancakes for lunch, not breakfast!'

'I LIKE CRIS,' declared Nats, as soon as they were out of the kitchen, door pulled shut behind them. 'I reckon we can persuade them to help us get to Dover. After we've stayed here for a few days, of course.'

It would be nice to spend some time with Cris and Georgy before moving on, and Georgy would love Nats as soon as they met. But where *was* Georgy? And why did it look like Cris didn't really live here anymore?

'You go have your shower,' said Joe, not yet ready to share these confusing thoughts with Nats.

He waited for the bathroom door to shut and then crept into Cris and Georgy's bedroom. Or was it just Georgy's bedroom now? Only Georgy's bedside table carried its usual clutter, although Cris had always kept theirs tidier. Joe popped the catch on the wardrobe and peered inside. It was half empty, though Georgy's clothes were still all pushed to one end.

Cris was now talking in the kitchen. Georgy must be back! Leaving the wardrobe doors hanging open, Joe bounded back towards the kitchen, ready to burst in and throw himself into Georgy's arms. But why hadn't Georgy come straight through to find him as soon as Cris had announced that he was here? He hesitated at the still shut door.

'Yes, just two of them. Joh and one other. About the same age, I reckon. Maybe a bit younger... Yes, I'll keep them here...and you promise that afterwards, Joh can come back and live with me? With us, I mean... Yes, I'm sure I'll be able to persuade Georgy to move down to mine if it's with Joh as well... OK, so someone'll be here in fifteen, you say... Yes, no problem...'

Who was Cris talking to on the phone? It wasn't Georgy. Whoever it was, there was someone coming to the flat in fifteen minutes. Why would Cris call someone else to tell them he was here? What had they meant by *afterwards*. After what?

The shower was running at full dribble. Nats was cheerfully humming one of the tunes that had played incessantly on the scrapyard radio. Joe knocked quietly on the door.

'Nats!' he urgently whispered at the locked door. 'Nats!' he hissed again as loud as he dared. The water stopped. 'Nats!' he tried a third time.

'What is it? Just a moment.'

The bolt was pulled back, and Nats emerged, a towel wrapped tightly around her body. Her shoulders glistened with droplets of water. Freshly used soap mingled with that familiar Nats smell. Rivulets trickled down her sparkly face. Joe blushed and cleared his throat.

'What is it? Are the pancakes done already?'

'Go get some clothes on. We need to go.'

'Go where? Why? What about the pancakes?'

NATS TOOK AN age to dry herself and pull on some clothes. Joe hovered outside the bedroom door, at her insistence. Finally, she emerged, still rubbing water out of her hair with the towel.

'Is the bag packed?' Joe asked, irritated by Nats' apparent untroubled demeanour.

'Not yet. Aren't you going to get those pyjamas off and put some proper underwear on?'

'No time.' He bustled past her and bundled the rest of their belongings into the top of the bag.

Pushing the door open, he edged into the kitchen, holding out a warning hand to Nats to stay in the hallway with the bag until he could check that the coast was clear.

'Pancakes won't be long now. Can you set the table for me? Oh, Joh, you've still got those pyjamas on!'

Cris turned back to the frying pan with a resigned shake of the head. Without a word, Joe sidled over to the front door, unlatched it, eased it open, and beckoned to Nats.

They were already two floors down before they heard Cris's disheartened voice above them. 'Hey, Joh, wait up! Where are you going? Don't you want to see Georgy? What about the pancakes?' Cris's footsteps started rushing down the stairs but then stopped, hesitating at the remote but unmistakable sound of the door buzzer.

Down two more flights, and Joe knew Cris had turned back. There was another buzz, but this time, it was the harsher tone that accompanied the unlocking of the outside door.

'This way!' ordered Joe, pulling Nats back towards ancient Adey's door, which stood ajar, pumping out heat, beckoning them in.

'Oh, hello. Have you come for that cocoa?' came Adey's reedy voice as they entered without an invitation and stood panting behind the now-shut door. They listened as at least three sets of feet pounded up the stairs from the entrance.

'Thanks, but I'm afraid we can't stop this time,' Joe managed to get out between pants, whilst Adey shuffled with surprising speed towards a fully laden mug tree. Taking another deep breath in, Joe reopened the door a crack and peeked out. The stairwell was empty, though fatiguing feet still climbed the stairs above them. 'OK, time to go again,' he hissed.

They cleared the final flight and Nats headed for the main door. 'Hold on, we'll go this way!' Joe managed to direct before she burst her way out past the uniformed figure standing guard outside, thankfully with their back to the door. Joe had never used the rear fire exit, but he knew exactly where to find it. Georgy had, on a number of occasions, made the worried little boy show the way to this alternative exit just in case he ever needed to use it.

Mercifully, whoever had posted a guard on the main door hadn't thought of, or maybe hadn't considered it necessary, to also secure the fire exit. No obstructions awaited them as they thrust their way out through the door, threw themselves over the retaining wall, and down onto the side street below.

Chapter 54

THE POLICE WERE regularly battering someone's door down on our estate. It was that sort of neighbourhood. But at the sight of the pack of hurriedly parked cars at the front of our block of flats, together with the uniformed officer guarding the door, my stomach rose into my chest. Had Joe been found?

As I climbed the stairs, the guard having stepped aside as soon as I approached the door with my key, I convinced myself that whatever was going on must be nothing to do with us.

Reaching my wide-open front door, however, and sensing the crowd of strangers assembled in the kitchen, my thumping chest drew my hands into fists, ready to thump whoever might be first to announce the news that Joe also now cowered in a cold, concrete cell.

'What's going on?' I demanded with as much indignation as I could muster through my quaking larynx.

The anonymous uniforms and suits stepped aside to expose Cris, hands tightly cuffed. 'Georgy, thank goodness you're back. Did you see Joh? Please, tell these crazy people that I had no idea that Joh was here.'

My mind scrambled over and around the panoply of information that my eyes and ears were receiving and found a handhold in the most important phrase. 'Joh was here? What, here at the flat? When?'

'It would appear that your child and a companion arrived here yesterday and spent the night in this flat,' said one of the suits. 'Your partner here claims to have arrived this morning, expecting to find you here but not your child or their companion.'

I thought back to my hurried exit from the flat the previous morning. Was it possible that in my haste to both get out to the bus and get off the phone to Stephenson, I hadn't shut the door properly? Had Joe come back hoping to find me here, only to find an empty flat? I silently cursed myself for my aimless meanderings in Newcastle when I could have been racing back here to look after my son and his friend.

'Where were you last night? Were you here with the two children?' continued the suit.

'No, no, I wasn't here. I was up in Newcastle last night.'

'What on earth were you doing in Newcastle, Georgy?' Cris inserted into the confused exchanges.

'So if you weren't here, perhaps you can enlighten us as to how the children gained entry to this flat? Cris here says that you are always very particular about leaving it locked. Were you expecting the children? Did you leave the door unlocked for them?'

'No, I'm sorry, I don't know. Perhaps I didn't shut the door properly. The latch is dodgy. I've been on to the owner about it for ages. It's been getting even worse recently. I was on the phone to one of your colleagues, Sergeant Stephenson, when I left the flat and was in a bit of a hurry. That's why I wasn't here last night. I was meeting Stephenson in Newcastle. But where's Joh now? What have you done with the children?'

'You were meeting Stephenson? What about?' asked Cris in disbelief.

'Sergeant Stephenson is on their way here now. I'm sure they can clear a few things up,' the suit said, addressing Cris, then turning to me. 'I'm afraid your partner allowed the children to abscond before we got here.'

'But how did you know they were here?' I pressed, looking around at the company of people gathered in my kitchen. As my glare reached Cris, eye contact was not returned, and I rapidly fitted the last few pieces into the ugly jigsaw. 'How could you?' I seethed.

'Citizen Turner,' interrupted the suit with calm and well-worn officiousness, 'aiding and abetting fugitives is an arrestable offence. I am therefore arresting you under suspicion of collaborating with your partner, Cris Turner, in the harbouring of and subsequent escape of the child Joh Turner and their companion. I have been advised this morning that these two are currently wanted for questioning by the police in connection with a serious incident on the railways.'

'But I've told you, I wasn't here!' I insisted as cuffs were clamped around my wrists. 'Speak to Sergeant Stephenson. I've been collaborating with your people, not Joh, though if I'd known they were here in the flat, I would have –'

Cris coughed loudly, and then started to speak over me, arresting my own self-condemning sentence. 'Look, this is crazy. Like Georgy says, we're doing everything we can to assist you so that we can be reunited with Joh and you can lock away their kidnappers forever. I've already told you the children were planning to go to Dover for some reason. It was you people who somehow let them get away as you arrived. You should be out there now looking for them, not arresting us.'

I gave Cris a long, cold, hard glare for all the betrayal contained in that impassioned speech. Thinking back to our first encounter with Stephenson, rightly or wrongly, I also now held Cris responsible for whatever might have compelled Joe and his friends to leave the safety of their island.

Chapter 55

THEY DARTED FROM the cover of one building to the shadows of another, peering around each corner for any signs of uniforms before sprinting on.

'What's going on?' Nats asked the first time they stopped. 'Why were the police at your flat?' The next time, and the time after that, 'How did you know we needed to leave?'

Each time, Joe simply replied with, 'I'll tell you in a bit.'

A large bus thundered past as they hovered behind some big bins, waiting for a quieter moment to dash across the busy road. A couple of cars and a van brought up the rear of an endless stream of traffic behind the bus. Another bus in the distance crept along from stop to stop on the other side of the road.

'We'll get on that bus, and then I'll explain everything I can,' Joe said, but then, as were about to dash, across he grabbed Nats' arm. 'No, on second thoughts, we should wait for another one on this side.'

'But we've just missed one going that way. We might have to wait ages for one coming this way again.'

'Loads come down this way. I'll explain the rest when we're on the bus, I promise.'

Sure enough, another bus was soon trundling down the road, and as it pulled to a stop a short distance away, they left their bin-side hiding place and casually joined the back of the small queue of travellers already accumulated at the stop. Joe had the cash ready and paid the fare required with as little communication as possible. Apart from their pack, which looked like it belonged on the side of a mountain, they both looked more like regular city kids now.

Joe was barely given the chance to plop down on the seat beside Nats before she demanded answers to her barrage of questions, thankfully muttered quietly under her breath.

'The reason we're going this way is because it'll take us away from Leeds, not towards it.' For reasons he couldn't explain, Joe felt uneasy about taking a bus into the city.

'But I thought we were in Leeds already?'

'Well, it's a big city. This is just one of many suburbs, so when I say 'towards Leeds', I mean the city centre, where all the big shops and the big bus station and train station are. And the police station.'

Mention of the police station got them back on to what had happened in the flat.

'While you were in the shower, I overheard Cris telling someone about us on the phone,' Joe began. 'It wasn't Georgy, and whoever it was, they were coming to the flat.' He left out the bit about Cris asking for assurance that he could go and live with them and Georgy again. 'I'd also worked out that, for some reason, Cris is no longer living with Georgy.'

'*How* did you work that out?'

'There was a holdall on the kitchen floor, and when Cris arrived, they called out something about having caught the first train.' Although that hadn't been the first clue. Cris wasn't using their favourite mug – the one they always used, even when it hasn't been washed for days. That was because it was no longer in the flat.

Joe realised later that neither was the mirror from the kitchen wall, which Georgy had always said was ugly. Cris's things were missing from their bedroom too. So Cris was just visiting for the weekend.

'So where was Georgy then? Do they live somewhere else too?'

'No.' Joe didn't think so, but that was what he could make no sense of. Maybe now he wasn't around, Georgy had got a job with nightshifts, but then Cris should have known Georgy wouldn't be home when they arrived. Unless it was a new job that Cris didn't know about. Maybe they didn't talk to each other anymore, but then why would Cris be coming to spend the weekend with Georgy?

'But you're saying that it was Cris who called the police? Why would your parent give us up to the police?'

A lump rose in Joe's throat. He couldn't really answer that one either. Cris had always been suspicious of DiG and reluctant to hand him over to their care, but that was always because Cris wanted to protect him. If they'd stayed at the flat, would the police really have let him go and live with Cris and Georgy again but living openly as a boy? Was Cain already reunited with his parents? What would have happened to Nats?

'I don't know,' he admitted.

'When we were in the farmhouse, Hani told us the police were dangerous and that the doctors wanted to do operations on us. That's why none of us could go out to the town with Hani.'

Joe didn't know what to think anymore. He had always trusted Cris and Georgy's judgement. It was only really to stop them arguing with each other that he'd decided to go to the island in the first place. But now it seemed they might have carried on arguing so much that they couldn't live with each other anymore. The one thing he did know now was that he couldn't ask Cris and Georgy to help them get to Dover. They'd have to do it on their own. And if they couldn't trust Cris and the police, they needed to get as far away from Leeds as they could, as quickly as possible. Joe could think of no other way to do that than to get back on a train, and he told Nats as much.

'So if we need to get another train, don't we need to get to Leeds train station?' Nat said.

'Remember the ticket barriers in Edinburgh? It's the same at Leeds, only this time, we'd need to have tickets to get in,' he explained. 'There are lots of smaller stations around Leeds where there aren't any ticket barriers, though. That's where we're going.'

With Nats' out of questions for now, Joe could finally ask the one he'd been holding on to since Nats had gone for her shower. 'Why haven't you said anything about my voice?' he whispered, suddenly self-conscious again about the octave he was using.

'What about it?'

'Well, it's gone all strange, lower sometimes, hasn't it?'

'Oh, that? Yeah, didn't you notice Cain and I grinning at each other when it first started happening? Cain's just gradually got lower, but yours has been all over the place.'

How had he not noticed his voice box had developed a dodgy reed?

'Don't worry, it's settling down now, and I think you've got a nice new voice.' Nats winked at him. Was that a teasing wink or a flirty one?

'But how can I speak to anyone now? Neuts I mean?'

Before Nats' could answer, Joe jumped to his feet and dragged her down the bus. He'd meant to get off two stops back. He led them from the bus stop, back to the train station in Bramley. From there, they boarded a train destined for Halifax, but, as Cain had taught them, they hopped on and off trains as often as necessary, to evade the ticket inspectors that prowled up and down the trains and avoided altogether any trains that looked too empty. Cain would have been impressed. Had Cain's parents welcomed him home now?

When on the trains, Nats kept her eyes open for the approach of a ticket inspector whilst Joe studied his treasured book of maps. When they waited on station platforms, Nats scoured the departure boards and ran back to Joe with possible destinations whilst Joe plotted out the perfect route to Dover. Not that he really expected to get all the way to Dover this way.

The railway line was like a long taper fuse, the train being the flame racing along it. The challenge was to get as far along the taper as they could but to jump out of the fire before the explosion happened and without leaving a trail that anyone could follow. If only they knew how much fuse was left before they got to the firework. But the firework didn't have a fixed location. It could be a ticket inspector reaching their seat before they reached the next station. It could be a police officer getting onto the train or noticing them on the platform, having received instructions to look out for two kids travelling south from Leeds. It could even be a member of the public accosting them, recognising them from some description of the two young felons, which was surely now buzzing around the news and chat channels. And if he had to speak to anyone, well, they were done for.

On the last two trains, Joe insisted that they sat apart. 'If people are on the lookout for two kids travelling together, they'll take less notice of us if we don't look like we're together,' he whispered to a doubtful Nats.

As Nats pointed out, it meant that one of them had to sit nearer to the ticket inspector's approach and also wouldn't be able to see them coming, unless they both faced the same direction. But if they did that, they'd not be able to communicate with one another. Even so, she conceded to try out Joe's plan and even insisted on being the one to sit in the more vulnerable position, as long as she could look after the map book so there was nothing to divert his eyes from the job of keeping watch.

'See? I was right,' said Nats as they stood in the shadows just outside March station. Perhaps she was. Joe had discreetly watched the gradual progress of the ticket inspector down their carriage, avoiding looking too often so that Nats didn't get too worried. He'd been convinced they'd get to March before the official got to her. It was a busy train. But then their speed abruptly slackened to little more than a moderate jog. Meanwhile, the momentum seemed to carry the inspector at twice their previous pace towards Nats.

Nats twisted herself around in her seat just as the ticket inspector decided to loudly remind the nearby passengers of the need for 'tickets please!' She leapt out of her seat so sharply that for a split second, Joe felt sure her fellow passengers would wrestle her to the floor. Nats strode purposefully towards the toilet. What if her bleeding started again, right now? Visions of Cain pinned to the floor invaded Joe's head. He could barely breathe as he counted to two hundred before following Nats to the back end of the train as it accelerated for a few moments and then slowed on its approach to the station.

The ticket inspector raced towards him. This was it; the firework was about to blow up right in their faces. Nats emerged from the toilet, the train came to a halt, and the guard stepped into their path.

A heavy set of keys jangled as the ticket inspector opened a little hatch in the train wall. Was this where the handcuffs were stored? A quarter turn of the biggest key, the press of a button, and the door cranked open.

'Thank you,' called Nats cheerfully as she jumped off the train.

'Hope you've got a ticket and travel permit somewhere in that bag o' yours, kid,' the guard called after Joe as he followed Nats, only daring to offer a mute nod in reply.

'How are you suggesting we get ourselves to Dover now then?' questioned Nats when Joe concluded that they shouldn't risk getting anymore trains.

'Well, I haven't measured it exactly, but I reckon we're no further from Dover now than the distance we walked to get to that first train in Balloch.'

'You mean you want us to walk again?' exclaimed Nats.

'We managed it before, didn't we?' Joe calmly declared. 'And it'll be easier this time. This time, we know exactly where we are, and we've got these maps to show us the way.' What they didn't have this time was Cain. Cain who had so often set the pace, spurred them on, and instinctively known which direction to follow without needing to consult any map. Could they do this without him?

Chapter 56

25/03/2033
07:45

On train to London for big press conference, two years to the day since virus attack.

Prime Minister making a speech surrounded by all surviving babies and their mothers from our 100-surrogate trial.

New fertility services to open on Monday, open to all. Would have liked to run more trials first but government is determined to 'restore normality'.

19:20

Not sure how useful it was being there today. Might have been better use helping to get clinic ready for next week. All media attention was on the eighty babies and their mothers, and on the politicians.

Copy of Prime Minister's speech below.

Clarification: There are actually 82 surviving babies from the trials, but two were not present today. The one with microcephaly and the one with Down syndrome. Made enquiries, but nobody could tell me why they weren't there. So I'm left wondering how sincere the PM was when she said, 'In our nation, no human will be an aberration.'

Two years ago today, life for our nation was changed forever by a small group of intolerant individuals who thought that they could dictate to the rest of us what a 'natural family' should look like. Their attack was aimed at people whose lifestyles they considered an aberration. But in attacking them, they attacked us all. In threatening those whose family choices they considered unnatural, they unleashed a threat on the very nature of family.

Today, thanks to the tireless efforts of our world-class geneticists and fertility experts, I stand here surrounded by eighty new, miracle babies and their mothers. What was stolen from us by judgemental bigots has been restored by these scientists, who have dedicated their lives to helping others without passing judgement.

Today, I can announce a new hope for all those whose dreams of raising a family were so cruelly destroyed two years ago. Our fertility clinics are reopening, and all who wish to now start a family, whatever their family looks like, will have access to these services.

Sadly, I have no doubt that some in our communities will try to claim that these new families are unnatural and that the babies themselves are an aberration. It is true that these babies are different in nature from us. But these children are our future. Let us raise them well and protect them from ever having to endure anything like the pain we have endured these past two years.

How do we do this? How do we learn from the past and protect the future? I shall tell you.

We will build a society in which all children, all people, are recognised, accepted and loved as fellow humans; whether male, female, or intersex; cisgender, transgender, or nonbinary; heterosexual, homosexual, bisexual, or pansexual. In our nation, no human will be an aberration. All families will be deemed to be natural.

Chapter 57

ALTHOUGH THE DISTANCE was indeed similar, the walk from March to Dover would be quite unlike their long walk across the wilderness of the deserted Scottish Highlands. Here, for a start, there were people, and although Joe and Nats had seen quite a lot of people in their more recent travels, they still felt as conspicuous as a pair of tubas in a flute choir. Well, OK, maybe Nats was a squeaky cornet, but Joe felt more and more like a tuba or a trombone whenever he said anything near any neuts. Even if news of the two young fugitives had not reached this part of the country, if they travelled during school hours, curious eyes would ask why these two saw fit to truant from whatever educational establishment they should be attending.

They had to reach Dover without drawing any more attention to themselves. That meant keeping hidden through the middle of the day. If they ever found a good hideout at a time when they could have gone on a little bit further, they would stop and not take any chances. When they needed more food, just one of them would visit the shops, and they would only buy enough for two days at a time.

In this way, they progressed from March to Chatteris, from Chatteris to Somersham, from Somersham to Willingham, from Willingham to Girton, from Girton to Cambridge.

In the drizzly half-light of a new day, they trudged down a long street of huge houses on the outskirts of Cambridge. It was obviously bin day, as every few metres, they had to go one in front of the other to skirt around a bin that had been wheeled out onto the pavement.

'Hang on, Nats,' Joe called out in as quiet a voice as he thought would work but not wake any local residents.

Nats turned and walked back the few paces to join him by the latest bin. 'What is it?'

Joe glanced around. 'You can't see anyone about, can you?'

Nats looked worried. 'I don't think so. Why? Do you think we're being followed?'

'No, I just want to look in this bin a moment.' He glanced around one more time and then raised the lid of the overfilled bin. He was right about the strap he'd seen dangling over the edge. 'Here, we could use this.' He shook the debris off the discarded empty backpack and handed it to Nats.

'Why would anyone throw this out? It looks brand new.'

'Some folk have more money than they know what to do with,' replied Joe, parroting one of Cris's favourite phrases. 'Here, there's another one, and...' He tugged at a heavier item further down the bin. 'I think this might be a little tent. Someone's obviously been having a clear out.'

'It'll be broken, though, won't it, if it's in the bin?'

'Not necessarily. The bags look all right, don't they? Even if it is a bit broken, we can probably fix it. We'll try putting it up later.'

They crouched beside the bin and shared out the contents of Joe's tatty old antique backpack into the two new ones. There was so much room that even the tent fitted inside one of them.

'What do we do with this now?' Nats asked, having double checked they'd left nothing in any part of the old bag that still bore the scars of being squashed under the car transporter.

'Well, there are plenty of bins around to put it in.'

They walked on with it past a few more houses until they found a bin with plenty of space in the top. As Joe lowered the lid, Nats reached for his hand and tugged him on, leaving behind them the last piece of the island.

THE TENT WAS perfect. For the past forty-eight hours, they'd failed to find anywhere dry to shelter in the miserably damp weather. Now, in secluded enough spots, they could at least avoid getting wetter while they rested or slept in the countryside around Duxford and Saffron Walden.

'I still can't believe someone would just throw this away,' Nats mused as they lay on their backs watching the rivulets of rainwater trickle down the outside of the flapping roof.

'Hmm,' Joe agreed, but his mind was on deeper things. It didn't feel like only a week since they'd found their way into the empty flat. What if they had stayed? Would Joe now be enjoying one of Cris's cooked breakfasts as Georgy hugged a cup of coffee? Or would he be recovering in hospital from some horrific operation? He couldn't discuss these questions with Nats because then they'd have to face the question of where she'd have ended up; the girl who'd never even met one parent and was given up by the other at the age of four. So he talked it through in his head with Cain instead.

Do you like being back with your parents then, Cain? I'm sure they were pleased to see you. Are you helping them with their fishing business or do they need to keep you hidden? Do you think you'll go back to the island sometime? Do you still think we need to find France?

'*Just go!*' his internal Cain urged, as he had on the train.

The memory of Cain pinned to the train floor always brought their conversations to an abrupt end.

THE ARRIVAL OF the new weekend granted them the freedom to travel throughout the day without looking like kids who were skipping school. Joe could barely conceal his delight at how quickly they were eating up the miles.

'This is brilliant,' he announced as they reached the strangely named Chipping Ongar just before dusk on Sunday evening. 'We've only been going a week and a day, and look, we're halfway there.' He pointed at a spot in the middle of one of the many pages he'd been leafing through in his beloved map book.

Nats nodded but wasn't really looking. She never could follow his rapid flipping between the pages when he tried to show her where they'd been, where they were, and their route from there to Dover. If only Cain were here to double check the plan.

Back into their weekday patterns of travelling only in the early mornings and evenings, it took them three more days to reach West Thurrock and the north bank of the wide, forbidding Thames. It had looked simple on the map to cross the river on that little green line. But the river, with its vast mudflats, was more like the sea, and that little green line was a wide, fast road bridge that soared into the sky.

'There's no way we're crossing that on foot,' Joe groaned as they stood, open-mouthed, gazing at the towering serpent. This road bridge dwarfed the viaduct they'd nearly killed Nats on and was definitely not designed to be shared by pedestrians.

'Well, I can't see any other way across,' replied Nats belligerently. It had been a difficult evening with numerous wrong turns to get to the shoreline, their sense of foreboding growing all the time as the large, multi-lane highway climbed higher and higher on its stilts, racing them to the river. Cain would have even now been pulling off his coat and shoes, ready to swim in search of a boat. Could Joe do that? *Don't be stupid, it almost killed Cain, and you're not Cain.*

Once more, he buried his nose in his map, searching for the more convenient walkers' bridge that he already knew didn't exist. All the other bridges that crossed the Thames inconsiderately clustered together in the very heart of London where the river appeared so narrow that one could surely just step across without the need for a bridge. Walking to London would take them miles off route and into urban danger.

Whilst Joe still urged the map to unveil another route, Nats started bouncing up and down on the balls of her feet. 'Got it! We *can* use this bridge.'

'I don't like the sound of this,' muttered Joe, looking up from his map, his mind painting scenes of the two of them clinging to the underside of the towering monstrosity. His arms quivered and ached at the thought of it.

'Don't look so worried,' said Nats with a chuckle. 'While you've been trying to draw extra bridges on that map with your eyes, I've seen about three buses go across this one. We got the bus no problem back in Leeds. All we need to do now is find the nearest bus stop, hop on a bus, and we'll be over the bridge.'

Nats made it sound so simple. Perhaps that was Joe's fault, the way he'd been so confident guiding them on and off the buses in Leeds. He knew Leeds and its buses well from all his trips out with Georgy, but this was different. How would they even find the right bus stop and then the right bus down here?

'Come on,' encouraged Nats, losing patience with Joe's lack of response or vision for her new plan. 'We can start by following this centipede of a road back to where it meets the ground.'

By the time they found the bus stop, which was actually a bus station on the edge of a large shopping centre, the last buses had long since departed. The bus station was deserted, aside from a couple of rowdy drunks, best ignored. There was nowhere to pitch a tent in this concrete jungle, so they resigned themselves to a draughty and sleepless night in a bus shelter. The drunks eventually took themselves home, or wherever their inebriated minds led them, leaving behind a spooky silence.

NATS WAS RIGHT; once they got on the bus, it was easy. Having studied the different timetables in the bus shelters, they'd deduced that a bus to another shopping centre, called Bluewater, would get them over the river. It seemed incongruous that anyone would actually want to get a bus from one shopping centre to another shopping centre. Surely, most people travelled from their homes out to shopping centres and back again. Be that as it may, the driver appeared not to share their curiosity and didn't bat an eyelid when they boarded and requested tickets all the way to Bluewater. Joe had made sure Nats did the talking.

Soon the bus was climbing the back of the enormous centipede, which carried them over the vast, tidal river. Not wanting to arouse the driver's suspicion, they remained on the bus, past several other stops, until it reached its terminus and the destination on their tickets.

THEIR ROUTE FROM Bluewater to Dover was an almost perfect straight line of what Joe measured out to be fifty-five more miles through Gravesend, Rochester, Sittingbourne, and Canterbury. With the benefit of another weekend coming up, they could be there by early next week!

SATURDAY MORNING. THE sun glowed green through the fabric of the tent. A gentle breeze flapped the loosely pegged guys. Perfect weather for a stride through the weekend that could put them less than ten miles outside Dover by tomorrow night. Nats smiled through her sleepiness and snuggled in closer to Joe.

SATURDAY MORNING, THE dawn chorus no longer mid-symphony, the sun now a blurry orb, well on its way up the tent's domed inner surface. A shout in the distance.

'Oi, you can't camp on this golf course!'

Joe sat bolt upright. 'Nats, we've got to move!' he hissed, shaking her awake.

'Who d'you think you are? This is private property. You've got no right!' The angry voice was much closer now, no longer needing to shout, but shouting, nonetheless.

They stumbled out of the tent, their stuffed bags twanging on the guy ropes, and bolted for the nearby trees, not daring to look back.

'Hey, come back! You can't just leave that there!'

'Ow!' *Thud!* Nats writhed around on her back, knee to her chest, hands clasping her ankle.

'Nats! What have you done?' Joe leapt and skipped back over the jumble of tree roots and offered his hand. 'Can you get up? Come on, we've got to keep going.'

'I don't know. It's my ankle.'

'Oi, you two, come out of there and clear up this mess. Bloody kids!'

They stumbled on through the woods, holding each other up, Nats wincing whenever her left foot hit the ground.

'I've seen your faces. I'll be talking to the schools. I'll find out who you are!' the distant voice threatened.

'IT'S PROBABLY JUST a sprain,' Joe diagnosed with groundless confidence as he prodded at Nats' ballooning left ankle, once they were sure the neut hadn't chased after them. 'We'll take it slowly today, and I'll bet it'll be all back to normal in the morning.' So much for racing on this weekend, eating up the remaining miles.

'But what if it's not? And what about our tent? I liked our tent. It was cosy.'

Hmm, too cosy, it seemed. Why had he let himself fall back to sleep this morning? Why had they even pitched it on a golf course? His internal Cain berated him for his carelessness, then dragged him out of the water before he drowned. As long as Nats was OK to keep moving, the tent didn't matter. They'd only have got a few more days' use out of it anyway before their crossing to France. It would be OK, as long as they could keep moving.

'What if that neut from the golf course has called the police about us?' Nats continued.

'I think it was just hot air. They thought we were just school kids messing around. But maybe we should find somewhere to hide today. Give your ankle a chance to go down.'

'But it's Saturday, isn't it? And we were going to walk all through the day today. I think we should still try to do that. If you think it's safe.'

Despite their slow pace throughout the day, nobody caught up with them to arrest them. But perhaps they should have found somewhere to hide instead, and Joe should have forced Nats to rest her ankle for a day, or even two.

'I'M SURE IT'S a bit less swollen today,' said Nats the next morning, stroking the purple lump attaching her foot to her leg.

Joe was doubtful, but still. It was Nats' ankle, and if she thought it was getting better and was all right to walk on it, why contradict her? It would be frustrating not to get any further today. Even if they didn't move on, they'd need to find somewhere else to sleep tonight. It wouldn't do to be caught camping out under this school bike shelter on a Monday morning.

He shouldn't have made her walk that far, but it would have been a waste of a Sunday to go no further after lunch, and whenever he asked her if she was OK, she assured him she was fine. It was obvious that she wasn't. But then, on Monday morning, she was barely hobbling, except when she decided she wanted a rest. The enforced rest throughout the middle of the day probably helped. She was much chattier again too as they walked, even if it was all critical of the things around her.

'Don't like this southern countryside. It's too flat.' Even though any hills would have put a lot more strain on her ankle.

'Those are ugly houses. Why can't they build houses like the nice old ones up in Scotland?' The ugly houses were just like the modern eco houses that Joe knew Georgy had always dreamed of being able to move to, if they'd ever been able to afford it. Maybe Cris lived in a house like that now.

So maybe it hadn't lost them all that much time after all because by Thursday, they were nearly there and Nats wasn't hobbling at all.

Joe was the first to hear the car for once. Nats was whinging that the crop in the fields on either side of the road was making her sneeze. That was why she was walking down the middle of the road, to keep as far away from both fields as possible. Perhaps the pollen was also affecting her hearing because any other time, she'd have been the first to hear the revving engine as it careened around the bends in the road.

'Nats! Car!'

With no Cain to hold him back, he lunged at her. Together, they tumbled onto the hard tarmac. Wrapping himself around her, he rolled them both into the verge. A squeal of brakes. The car swerved. Braked some more. Hesitated. Raced away.

'Ow! Get off my ankle!' was all the thanks he got.

The bags had to be left right there on the verge as Joe all but carried Nats down the farm track to a nearby barn. From the look of the cobwebs that had shrouded the door and still adorned the rafters, nobody had taken any notice of this barn for a long time. They could probably risk stopping here for a few days without being noticed.

When he returned to fetch the bags, he paused, gazing down the road. They couldn't have had more than five miles left to go.

Chapter 58

IT TOOK A while, but as soon as Stephenson arrived at the flat, our cuffs were off and we were treated as witnesses and allies rather than suspects and enemy collaborators. Not that I really wanted to be considered an ally of theirs, or of Cris's for that matter, but at least it was more comfortable and less humiliating.

'Sincere apologies for my colleagues, Georgy, Cris,' Stephenson droned, pausing to look with mock compassion at each of us in turn, 'but I hope you understand they were just taking precautions and following standard procedure, if a little too enthusiastically.'

'Has Joh been found?' I asked apprehensively, half hoping he had and half that he had not.

'Regretfully not, as yet, but I'm sure it's only a matter of time before you can all be reunited. Did we get any sense of where the two of them were headed?'

Cris was about to speak but registered the almost imperceptible shake of my head and wisely chose to step back from the precipice.

'Er, Sergeant,' butted in the suit. 'Our primary witness, who was with the children before they escaped –'

'Please, let's keep this informal and use the names people were given by their parents,' interrupted Stephenson with mildly veiled contempt for their colleague.

'Sorry, Sergeant, er, Cris here told us that the children had it in their heads they were going somewhere called Dover.'

Stephenson frowned.

'We looked it up, Sergeant. It's a little fishing town down south somewhere. I wondered whether that's where the other kid comes from.'

'Hmm, perhaps.'

I could tell Stephenson was doubtful but was keener to extricate the suited colleague from the investigation than encourage speculation of Joe and his friend's motives.

Eventually, the various species of law enforcement officer who had congregated in my kitchen decided that there was nothing more to be gained from remaining and, having conducted a cursory final sweep of the flat, they took their leave. Apart from some rather dirty washing, which the officers decided was not worthy of taking to analyse as forensic evidence, Joe and his friend had left nothing behind. It seemed they'd even done their dishes from the meal they'd helped themselves to last night. I'd trained him well.

Cris took a little more persuasion to disappear back off to the new pad. 'But I don't understand! I've actually made it up here for once and now you're sending me away?'

'After all you've done to put harm into Joe's path, I'm surprised you have the gall to even question me,' I raged. 'You didn't see the poor boy they're holding in that inhumane cell up in Newcastle. It's nothing short of child abuse. The poor mite is obviously petrified. Is that what you want for Joe?'

'But that won't be what happens to Joh when they find him. If we cooperate, Stephenson's promised he'll be able to come and live with us.'

'Us? There is no *us*!' I pulled on my discarded coat and carried myself resolutely out of the flat.

As soon as I got out onto the street, I suspected it. When I returned, over three hours later, I knew for certain. The flat was being watched. The same car, hosting the same bored-looking nobody was parked in exactly the same position, front-left tyre twisted at the same slight angle and squashed against the kerb.

When I got into the flat, it was a relief to find that Cris hadn't been so patient or determined. The holdall was gone, mugs washed up and inverted on the drainer, and in the middle of the table, a note exhorting me to call soon, signed off with the requisite three kisses.

Quite what the police hoped to gain from staking out the flat was anyone's guess. Perhaps they thought Joe might try to return. I knew him better. Maybe they thought that some yet-to-be-captured dissident member of DiG would suddenly show their face. Or did they think that my flat had become a staging post in a new exodus of these abnormal children from their Scottish island to whichever place they'd decided to relocate?

If they were watching the flat, there was a fair chance they were tracking my movements too. So I didn't leave the flat on Sunday, not really in case Joe came back, because I was certain he wouldn't. Then, from Monday through to Wednesday, I dutifully went into work. By the time my alarm persuaded me out of bed on Thursday, the clandestine car had finally dislodged its tyre from the kerb. I called in sick, packed a suitcase, and took myself to Dover.

Chapter 59

'I'VE SEEN FRANCE!' Joe exclaimed as soon as he'd eased the barn door shut with its most silent creak yet.

ON THEIR FIRST day in the barn, Joe had stayed by Nats' side throughout the day. After a couple of hours of flicking through the map book, he put it to one side. He'd begun sense that it was getting on Nats' nerves, and besides, he'd long ago memorised the simple route from here to Dover. So he put the map down and turned his attention to Nats.

'Anything I can do for you?' he enquired in a gentle voice.

'No, you've asked me that three times already,' Nats grumped. 'And like you've already told me, all I need is rest.'

The rest of the day crawled by in sullen silence.

On the second day, Joe felt it was safe enough to venture out in search of food. It would give them both the bit of space they needed and give Joe's fidgety limbs the exercise they'd been craving, Besides, if he didn't go for food today, he'd definitely need to go tomorrow.

He was most of the way to Dover before he found a shop. He could just keep on going. Just to take a look. But then he'd already been gone an hour. *She'll be fine,* said the Cain in his head. He hefted the shopping back onto his shoulders, turned, and headed back the way he'd come.

It was a relief to return and find everything unchanged. Nats opened her eyes and smiled as he dropped the bag beside her.

'Would you mind if I took a stroll into Dover tomorrow?' he began. 'I mean, I'd rather wait till we could go together, but we can't risk that yet, in case we need to run.' The wince as she'd shifted to check out what he'd bought had already shown that she wouldn't be going anywhere tomorrow. 'But I could go down there and scope things out. It's not really that far, and I shouldn't think I'll be gone for any longer than I was today.'

Her smile gone, Nats shrugged and muttered that he should do whatever he thought best. It pained and frustrated him in equal measure to see such weary resignation. They were so nearly there!

DOVER HAD EVIDENTLY once been a significant gateway out to the world beyond. It was a wonder that its handful of inhabitants didn't seem to puzzle over what the enormous crumbling concrete quays and harbour had once been for and what land it was that they could see on a clear day across that narrow stretch of sea. Joe had seen it as clearly as he'd seen the opposite bank of the Thames, or the mountains on far side of that sea channel Cain had managed to swim across, even if it had nearly killed him. Surely, others could see what he saw; and if so, how was the existence of the world beyond kept a secret?

But nobody else lifted their heads to gaze out to sea as Joe did. Were they paid not to notice? Or perhaps they had inherited the knowledge that if they did, things would not go well for them.

'I THINK I'VE found us a boat,' he declared when he returned late in the evening from his third foray into Dover. 'There's a fisher with a little motorboat, and for the last two evenings, they've done exactly the same thing at almost exactly the same time.'

'What's that then?' asked Nats, trying to match his enthusiasm.

'They've moved the boat from its mooring, in amongst a load of other old boats, to an open bit of the harbour, and then they've got off the boat, leaving the motor running, to go and buy chips from a little shop just round the corner.'

'Chips sound good.' For a moment, Nats was her old bright self.

'So I reckon we could kidnap that boat while they're at the chip shop.'

'Do you know how to drive a motorboat?'

Good question. *Could* he drive a motorboat? It didn't look like it could be too hard, but he'd only have one shot at it. *Can I do it, Cain?* Of course, Cain would have known how. 'I'm sure we can work it out.'

'BUT YOU GO again,' she insisted when they'd resolved that yet another day of rest was needed. 'It'll give you a chance to make certain about this fisher's routine.'

This was a fair point. Two occasions didn't make a habit, and it wouldn't do to drag Nats all the way into Dover if they weren't sure they'd be getting on that boat.

HE HOVERED IN the shadows behind an old rusty container that looked like it may once have travelled around the world on the high seas. He edged forward, peering through the dusk to look out for the little boat that, with any luck, would soon be sputtering into the harbour. A figure on his right took a step towards him. Had he been seen? He withdrew further into the shadows. A very familiar voice uttered his name.

'Joh, is that you?'

Chapter 60

As soon as I reached the harbour and looked out to sea on my first morning in Dover, I knew why this was Joe and his companion's destination. Except that this wasn't really their destination. Their true destination was, without a doubt, that hazy but distinct streak of something else that lay along the horizon, separating the sea from the sky. This was no little alternative island to go and hide away from the world on. This was another world itself. How had I never known about this? How had those kids discovered it from their remote little island, such a long way away from here?

I'd booked myself into a rundown little bed and breakfast, paying for a whole two weeks upfront in return for a doubtful promise that they would deny my existence if anyone, official-looking or otherwise, came asking after someone matching my description. I intended to keep a low profile whilst spending as much time as I could scouring the town for any sign of my son. That night, I attempted to quiz the sole proprietor of the establishment about the land across the sea and was surprised when all my questions were met with apparent ignorance of the plain to see, and evasive vaguery about the history of this once obvious portal to another world.

After three miserable, fruitless days, I was convinced I'd arrived too late. I should have jumped on a train to Dover as soon as I'd seen off the police and Cris last Saturday. If Joe and friend had continued to travel by train, as they had before, they'd have surely got here days ago, and now I knew that this wretched place was never intended to be the end of their journey, what was the point in searching for them here?

But I couldn't leave. Sergeant Stephenson would have put the local police here on high alert the moment they'd learnt from Cris that this was where the children planned to come. For some reason, they seemed pretty damned determined to capture them. If Joe had got here before me, he was surely already festering in one of those cold, unfriendly cells. They would have called me to let me know, wouldn't they? I didn't dare call them, though.

The days passed and my hope fortified. As I grew familiar with the geography of this shrivelled town and brooded over the boats in the harbour, I came to recognise the strangers on street corners who quite clearly didn't belong here any more than I did.

Just one more week, I promised myself as I handed over my card to be debited the requisite amount for a further seven nights' board and lodging. After that, I would have to accept that Joe and I had said our final goodbyes, as I'd thought we had, months ago in Carlisle, and I would have to trust that somehow, somewhere, perhaps out there beyond the sea, he had found a world where he could truly be himself.

Resigned to this reality, I weaned myself off my addiction to the harbour and instead took long walks out onto the clifftops where the views of the land on the horizon were even more compelling. I stood waving and hollering into the wind, convinced that, though he wouldn't be able to see me, I was waving and shouting to Joe, and that he was waving and smiling back.

On what I promised would be my final night in Dover, I went for one last sneaky look at the harbour, whilst treating myself to a large portion of battered fish and chunky chips – the best thing this whole wearisome place had to offer.

Stepping out of the chip shop, I ambled the short distance down to the huge concrete harbour that now hosted only a couple of tiny boats. This place must have been so busy in its heyday, whenever that was. A few relics of those old days still littered the space between town and water, like that rusty old container, which looked like it may once have travelled around the world on the high seas.

A teenager stepped out from behind the container, hesitated, then sank back into the shadows. I stopped and blinked, convinced I must be mistaken but yearning for it to be true. I edged a fraction closer. The package in my hand starting to burn as I dug my nails through the paper to its hot, greasy contents. I opened my mouth, but no sound would come out. I closed it, inhaled salt and vinegar air through my nose and tried again.

'Joe, is that you?'

Chapter 61

HE HESITATED JUST long enough for me to doubt and begin to back away. But then he stepped out from the shadows of the old shipping container and into the lamplight so I could see his face.

'Georgy?' he quaked. His familiar, strange voice covered about two octaves in just the two syllables of my name. I dropped my bundle of food to the ground as his arms were thrown around me and hot tears dribbled down my neck.

Reluctantly, I pushed him away and held him at arm's length. 'You need to leave, don't you? Over the sea.'

'Yes,' he replied, 'but how do you know?'

'Anyone with eyes could work it out, but I think the folk round here have lost the use of theirs.'

A smile spread across his damp face. 'Thank you,' he said with a maturity I'd forgotten he had, or perhaps had never seen so fully. 'I'd begun to wonder whether I was just imagining the world beyond. I've been longing to show it to Nats. But if you can see it too, it must be there.'

'Is Nats the friend you've been travelling with?'

'Yes, but she's hurt her ankle. We've been staying in a barn a few miles inland. She's not made it here yet. We couldn't risk it until she's better.' I saw the uncertain child emerging again as his inner eyes explored the challenges of the journey that I could only begin to imagine. 'When we started out, there were three of us, but Cain didn't manage to get away from the people on the train, after Nats started her bleeding. And we nearly lost him before that, to a fever when he swam across the sea channel to find a boat on the other side.'

Cain. So that was the poor boy's name. I would keep to myself that Cain and I had met. Joe didn't need to be burdened with anything else if he and Nats were to finish the journey they'd all set out to complete.

'How are you planning to get across,' I asked, nodding towards the darkening sea.

'On that boat that's just coming now, but not tonight. I'm coming back tomorrow, or the next night, with Nats and we're taking it then. The fisher it belongs to gets chips just round the corner.' He pointed in the direction I'd come from myself minutes before. 'They leave the engine running, see.'

I watched as a figure stepped off the boat, looped a rope over a bollard, and ambled towards and right past us, no more than a metre to our right. Then, further to my right, the corner of my eye caught the flash of approaching torches.

'You need to get that boat Joe.'

'That's right. We'll do it tomorrow.'

'No, you need to get that boat now.' I said nothing more but took his head between my hands and turned it towards the advancing lights. 'Tell me where I can find Nats, and I will bring her across the water myself as soon as I can.'

Even as I made that rash promise, and as I recited back Joe's directions to the barn, I knew I would not be able to keep it. Not because his instructions were unclear or because I wouldn't remember them, but because my job now was to waylay Joe's pursuers, whatever it cost me.

I released my grip, gave him a shove towards the harbour edge, and tried my best to be a firm parent. 'Go now.'

'But I can't leave without Nats.'

'You've got no choice. Nats will understand.' Would she? I had no idea.

He hesitated for a moment and then turned, stumbled towards the rope, unhooked it, and leapt down into the fragile little boat, which now rocked violently on the water.

The torches accelerated towards us, accompanied by authoritative shouts. As the engine revved, churning the water below it, I bent to pick up my food and then turned to face the two infuriated officers.

I ran towards the nearest, thrusting my still burning fish and chips right at their face. They faltered. Grabbed my wrist to swipe it out of the way. Fragmented food splattered the ground. The second skidded up behind their colleague, losing their footing in the fat and grease that lubricated their path. All three of us tumbled to the ground, my wrist still locked in another's grasp.

I yanked at my wrist and twisted around in time to see Joe figure out the controls and pull the boat away from the harbour edge, far enough that no-one would risk a jump. One other boat bobbed against the harbour wall.

'Go, Joe!' I shouted as the cold steel of cuffs clamped around my resistant but willing wrists. I grinned as the other officer blustered down their radio that they'd apprehended me, but Child B had got away.

'Negative. No sightings of Child C, Sarge. Permission requested to pursue Child B. There's another boat we could requisition. Over.'

'Negative. No way. Do not go after them. Can't go outside our jurisdiction,' came Stephenson's crackly reply. 'The other side will pick it up from here – if the child makes it that far. Over.'

'Go, Joe!' I urged, under my breath. 'You can make it.'

Chapter 62

THE CONSTANT THRUM of the engine dropped to a *put-put-put* as Joe pushed the throttle down into the horizontal position and allowed the tide to carry him closer to the foreign shore that he could just make out through the darkness. The familiar sound of the waves polishing a sandy beach echoed around him.

The bow ground to a halt. Joe didn't move, except to finally release his tight grip on the wheel and rub his salt-encrusted eyes. Why was he here, on his own, and not back with Nats in the barn? He should have waited with her until her ankle was better. But then he might not have seen Georgy again. And what would happen to Georgy now? What would the police do to them? This was all such a mess. Why had any of them even thought this was a good idea? *But you've made it,* a chorus of voices said in his head – Georgy? Nats? Cain? *Go and find the help you've come here for.*

Joe jumped down into the shallow water and splashed his way the final few metres to France.

A powerful light blinked on and advanced towards him over the dunes.

'*Arrêtez là*!', came a strange, barking shout. '*Se mettre à genoux*!'

Joe stumbled forwards, waving towards the light. 'Hello, can you help me?'

A loud crack echoed through the darkness. Joe's thigh erupted in pain, throwing him to the ground.

Two pairs of heavy-booted feet thudded across the sand towards him.

'*Que fais-tu ici*?' the voice barked again, now from right over his head.

'I'm Joe,' he rasped. 'Joe with an "e", cos I'm a boy.'

Epilogue

NATS GRABBED THE sandwich from the child's hands and wolfed it down. The timid neut child watched in silence. How long could she trust them to keep their secret? She shuffled back into the shadows and under the extra borrowed blankets in the barn that had become her home. The twinge in her ankle had stopped robbing her of breaths several days ago. One day soon, she would have to venture out – see if she could find her way to Dover. Or somewhere. Why had she persuaded Joe to go again that day? He'd already worked out a plan. If she'd asked him not to go, to wait, he would have. He couldn't have taken that boat without her. He wouldn't have. Which left only one conclusion. Like Cain, he'd been captured.

SERGEANT FINCH STEVENSON crouched down, pushed the tray of food through the hatch in the bottom of the cell door. Straightening up, they slid back the shutter and peered in through the window. The strange child hadn't moved and remained in their usual position in the back left-hand corner of the cell. Knees up to their chest, rocking backwards and forwards, head down, fidgeting hands. The food would be eaten, though. It always was.

Others feared this strange, unnatural aberration of a child, but Finch could feel only sympathy for the poor lost soul who hadn't chosen to be different. It was probably a good thing that the other one had got away – had hopefully made it to the other side.

A WALL OF excited murmuring hit Stokes' ears as the doors swished open. It was a rare sight to see the one-hundred-and-fifty-seat chamber so nearly full. Just her own seat and three others remained vacant. An almost indecipherable mix of French and English swirled around her head as she made her way to the place reserved for her in front of the old Union Flag. The official language of the British Assembly remained English, but most were more fluent in the language of the country where they and five or more generations before them had been raised.

Premier Stokes docked her *tablette* on the desk in front of her, cleared her throat and raised her hand. It was almost a minute before the silence took hold, but Stokes stood there with characteristic patience. Even when the last echoes of sound had been banished, she counted another ten seconds in her head before opening her mouth.

'*Merci*, thank you all for making the time to come to the assembly in person today. The information I am about to share with you will, for the moment, need to remain secure within these walls. This is the reason why you were all asked to hand in your *appareils* at the gate today.' She and several of her neighbours glanced at her own tablette, its little blue light blinking for attention. 'I hope you will forgive the exception that was made for me.' She put on her most disarming smile as a hum of assent rippled around most of the chamber.

Stokes waited again for stillness before continuing. 'Yesterday, I received a call from President Arnaud.' Some disgruntled mutterings washed over her about the French president, who tolerated their little council for ethnic Brits but rarely graced them with any attention. 'Two nights ago, border police apprehended a child single-handedly piloting a small, ancient-looking oil powered boat in *La Manche*. The boat was not a French boat and the child was not a French child.'

The room erupted with whispers, which soon crescendoed to a noisy din as the assembly members tried to pre-empt the implications of what had already been said.

A short, red-faced, stocky man got to his feet, from a seat diametrically opposite to her own. 'Well, I hope you told Arnaud straight out that if it was one of our own, he needs to hand 'em over to our custody.'

The Premier did her best to maintain eye contact with the leader of the opposition as she raised her voice to speak over the still-noisy undirected exchanges bouncing around the chamber. 'Thank you for your question, Mr Jones. I can assure you that this child was not from our own community. Well, not as such.'

All other conversation halted as she uttered these final few words.

'The French are convinced that the boat was sailed all the way across the channel, from British shores.'

Much as she wished to share the rest of her information uninterrupted, Stokes knew that this time, the multitude of questions, shouted over one another, would not be so easily quenched. As far as she knew, there had been no contact of any sort for decades from the island that their ancestors had called home. Planes and ships all steered well clear of what had become known to the French as *les îles maudites*.

The *mêlée* of questions continued to echo around the chamber in a loop.

'They can't be serious! There can't be anyone left in Britain or we'd know about it.' This was the publicly acceptable line, though Stokes had the privilege of knowing what others did not.

'Is it one of the mutant freaks?'

'Is it alive?'

'If you will allow me to continue, I think I can answer at least most of your questions.' Mercifully for her strained vocal cords, the room fell silent once again. 'Firstly, the child is alive, but injured, and currently being kept under sedation for his own safety. He was shot in the leg by a border guard when he didn't obey the guard's instructions to halt and get on his knees. The poor boy was no doubt ignorant of the French language.'

Stokes sighed as voices started raising questions again, but they relented as she ignored them and persisted with her narrative.

'You will notice that I have indicated that the child was a boy. The home of our ancestors is still populated, but we should not call them mutants.' She paused, but thankfully, the attentive silence did not. 'Until today, we thought that male and female humans in Britain had all died out long ago because of the virus that afflicted them in the 2030s.'

Her mind replayed the images in those classified files, handed on by her predecessor. Images of bodies washed up on French shores over the decades. No male or female bodies for over a century.

'It had been thought that the population of New Britain was now exclusively sex-neutral, though still human – not so different from some in our own community who are born intersex.' She made sure not to look at Assembly Member Wright as she met the eyes of various others.

'But I repeat, the child, currently being kept in quarantine and under sedation, in an undisclosed French hospital, is a normal, apparently healthy British boy.'

She paused to sip some much-needed water from her glass, and surprisingly, the assembly held its stunned silence.

'The French authorities are almost certain that he is British because the guard who shot him claims that he spoke a few words in a form of English before he was shot, and also because of this.' She tapped her tablette a couple of times to wake it up. The picture she had been sent reformed itself in front of her and instantaneously duplicated itself on the large screen behind her.

There was a unanimous intake of breath as everyone took in the clear image of a crumpled but detailed hand-drawn map of *les îles maudites* with the coast of France accurately positioned in the bottom right-hand corner. A fine dotted line could be seen snaking its way from a point on the French coast somewhere around Sangatte, across the channel and then north and west to a part of the island that some remembered was once called Scotland. The same people also recognised the names of various British place names marked along the route. Dover, Cambridge, Peterborough, Leeds, Berwick, Edinburgh. The dotted line appeared to end at the fragmented northwest coast.

'I have had a little more time than you to ponder this incredible news.' Stokes no longer needed to wait for her audience to listen. 'I cannot believe that a child would plan such a journey for any reason other than to reach out for help. I also presume, or at least hope, that before he set out, he was not alone. And therefore, we must assume that there are others like him, by whom he was perhaps sent.'

Jones got to his feet again and broke the silence. 'So are you suggesting that we launch some sort of rescue mission? The French would never allow it!'

There were muted mutterings of agreement from all around him.

Stokes gave a nod of understanding, and uncharacteristically, Jones meekly returned to his seat, causing his compatriots to cease their annoying, anachronistic bleating.

'At present, the French are asking us to permit them to handle this alone, but they have promised to keep me fully informed. Satellite images show small pockets of habitation around that northwest coast – the area from which it appears the boy began his journey – including one on a small island. As we speak, eight microdrones are being deployed to gather more intelligence.'

Stokes tapped her tablette again to remove the picture from the large screen and then pulled it off its docking port. 'I must remind you that all of the information I have shared with you this morning must remain strictly confidential until you are advised otherwise. Any hint of a leak will be dealt with severely both through our own systems and by the French authorities. Thank you again for your attendance.'

A barrage of unanswered questions from the floor of the chamber hounded Stokes as she left her seat. She waited for a moment, just beyond the threshold, as the sliding doors sealed off the clamouring noise she'd left behind.

THE END

Joe is safe, but what about Nats, Georgy and Cain? Will help be sent to the island? Will that help be accepted?

The story continues in *Them and Us*, the sequel to *Joe with an E*, out in December 2024.

To be emailed a sneak peak of what's coming next, please scan the QR code below, or visit paulrandwriter.co.uk/them-and-us.

Acknowledgements

When the idea for *Joe with an E* came into my head, I knew it was a novel but wasn't sure whether I could write one of those. But I sat down and started to write. I've learnt a lot about writing along the way, and I'm grateful to all the people – family, friends, and others who have agreed to read the various drafts and been brave enough to give me their honest feedback.

Thank you to Rachel and Sam – colleagues at school – who read early drafts and told me it was as good as some of the published novels they'd read. It probably wasn't, at that stage. Thanks to my dad, whose suggestions I have usually ignored, but who has made me think about why certain aspects of the story were important to me. Thank you to wider family members Terry and Emma, who, at different times in its development, both said they wanted to see more emotion in the story. I hope I've done enough of that now. Thanks to Paul, who's known me since I was little and gave me some sage advice, particularly about the ending, which I'm afraid I didn't change much as a result, but I have written what I think is a cracking sequel.

Of course, the best beta readers are people whom you don't know, but it's hard to find strangers who are prepared to read and give helpful feedback on your 100,000-word novel, for free. Thankfully, there are lots of online writers' forums out there and it made a real difference to my writing when I discovered Jericho Writers, WriteMentor and Litopia, had the chance to get feedback from other writers on short extracts of *Joe with an E*, and learnt the mantra *show don't tell*. You also learn a lot from reading and critiquing other people's work-in-progress.

There were some from those online communities who offered or agreed to read the whole thing, or a substantial chunk. Thanks to Rebecca, who was the first stranger to read *Joe with an E*. Thanks to Jess, who offered to read it and give feedback, even though I'd not been selected to be part of the WriteMentor summer mentoring programme, and was full of great advice and encouragement. Thanks to Kate Salisbury (*The Face That Pins You*) who was very positive about my opening 700 words when they featured on Litopia's *Pop-Up Submissions* and later agreed to read the other approximately 99,300 words and write a review for me. You can see Kate's review in the front of this book.

I was excited and nervous in equal measure when fellow Greenbelt Festival goer and award-winning, Usborne-published author, Sarah Hagger-Holt (*Nothing Ever Happens Here, The Fights That Make us,* and several others), replied to my email to say that she was happy to read and review my novel. Thank you, Sarah. I was bowled over by what you said about it when you'd read it, and it was a huge encouragement, particularly given your experience of writing LGBTQ+ themed books.

In spring 2023, I was determined that at some point in the next year or so, I was going to find a way to publish *Joe with an E*, but having tried and failed to find an agent, I wasn't sure how. Then Jennifer Burkinshaw (*Igloo* and *Happiness Seeker*) approached Jo, my wife, looking for a local perspective on her book set in Grange-over-Sands. Jo introduced Jennifer to me, and we became each other's beta readers. Not only did Jennifer help me to refine my story, but she also introduced me to her, and now my, publisher and has been an inspiration as I've started to think about the marketing side of being a writer.

Debbie, thank you for saying yes to my story, so quickly, and for your insightful comments, which give me confidence that *Joe with an E* is in the best of publishing hands. I'm in awe of your careful and precise editing skills and attention to detail. I hope we can sell lots of copies between us.

As a cisgender writer, I knew I was treading a fine line, writing a book centred on questions of gender identity, particularly when my antagonists are intersex and (possibly) nonbinary 'neuts' and my heroes are (apparently) cisgender boys and girls. I've been told more than once that perhaps I'm not the right person to try to write a story with these themes. So if it was going to be published, it was essential to find someone who could do what's called a sensitivity read. The last thing I wanted to do was publish something that would be offensive or hurtful to transgender, nonbinary or intersex folk. When I went to a talk on transgender issues at Greenbelt 2023, I was impressed by the speaker's easy-going eloquence and wisdom. When I found his website after the weekend and discovered that he was also a talented illustrator, I knew what I needed to do, but almost didn't dare hope that he'd say yes.

Andy, not only have you created a beautiful cover design, which I absolutely love – looking at it several times every day for at least the first week after you sent it to me – but your enthusiasm for, and affirmations of, my story gave me the confidence I needed to go ahead with publication. You also pointed out some sloppy bits that needed to change, and you told me about nuances you loved, which I hadn't even realised were there. Thank you, Andy with a 'y'.

Last but not least, thank you to Jo (without an 'e'), Martha, and Amos, who have put up with me talking about all this, and reading versions of *Joe with an E* and *Them and Us*, for the last five years. The three of you have also been instrumental in leading the way to being more open-minded and inclusive than I was in my youth and becoming a staunch LGBTQ+ ally.

Content Warnings

This novel includes scenes and themes which may be upsetting to some readers, including:

- Sexual assault of a teenager by another teenager.
- References to 'corrective surgery' to make male and female children into 'neuts'.
- A character refusing to accept the gender identity of another character.
- Infertility, IVF, and miscarriage.
- Young people drowning in a storm.

About the Author

Paul Rand grew up in Hampshire, UK but has now lived well over half his life in the North of England - in Yorkshire and Cumbria. After thirteen years working as an engineer, he completed teacher training and has since been working as a secondary school teacher, teaching a mixture of maths, business, and computing. Paul currently teaches part-time, and when he's not teaching or writing, he's probably doing something for the Methodist church of which his wife is the minister.

Paul and his family like to holiday on small islands, both at home and abroad, preferring islands that are a little off the beaten track. They have enjoyed several holidays on the Isle of Muck, which is the inspiration for the island in *Joe with an E*.

Follow Paul online at:

paulrandwriter.co.uk
facebook.com/paulrandwriter
instagram.com/paulrandwriter

Beaten Track Publishing

For more titles from Beaten Track Publishing,
please visit our website:

https://www.beatentrackpublishing.com

Thanks for reading!

Milton Keynes UK
Ingram Content Group UK Ltd.
UKHW021504120524
442505UK00004B/93

9 781786 456427